GEORGIA ON MY MIND

MARIE FORCE

Marie Force
Copyright 2011 by HTJB, Inc.
Published by HTJB, Inc.
Cover by Courtney Lopes

ISBN: 978-1-942295-31-0

marieforce.com

For my mom,
Barbara J. Sullivan
1937–2004

Author's Note

Writing this book was a labor of love in so many ways. I had the opportunity to feature my hometown of Newport, Rhode Island, and I got to write about a young woman grappling with the aftermath of her mother's death, something I understood all too well. After my mother died in 2004, I experienced some of the same things Georgie does in this book. Like her, I still have my mother's robe.

When creating the cast of characters at the senior center, I needed to look no further than my dad and his band of pals to find true characters. Thank you to George, Bob, Good Gordon, Bad Gordon, Harry, Arlene, Diane, Agnes, and Mary for letting me "borrow" your personalities, and to the late Tom Dawson, whose one-liners were unforgettable.

To my husband Dan, who inspired my treehugging, running hero, thank you for all the fodder. Will you ever forget the dental floss? Emily and Jake, you guys are the best kids ever. Thanks for letting me do what I love to do while loving you, too!

Thanks, as always, to my friends Christina Camara, Julie Cupp, Paula DelBonis-Platt, and Lisa Ridder, who read, edited, and critiqued. To my readers, Mary Grzesik, Aly Hackett, Ronlyn Howe and Kara Conrad, you all have become such a great friends! Thanks for the beta reads.

To all my readers and friends who have made my writing journey so extraordinary, thank you for your unwavering support. I hope you enjoy *Georgia on My Mind*.

CHAPTER 1

Her heart thumping, Georgie grabbed a cup of coffee and followed her other roommate, Tess, to the spacious front porch, where Cat made an effort to appear nonchalant. Georgie took her usual place on the wicker sofa for an unobstructed view of the show.

The steady cadence of footsteps on pavement announced his arrival, right on schedule.

Georgie would have taken a sip of her coffee if she could've gotten it past the lump of anticipation growing in her throat. *How very sad that these thirty seconds will be the highlight of my day. Oh, there he is!*

The top of his golden head appeared at the crest of the hill. And . . . *oh* today he was bare-chested, his shirt tucked into the front of tight running shorts. Sweat ran down between spectacular, tanned pectorals and taut abs, making his light dusting of blond chest hair sparkle in the morning sun. *Just the right amount of chest hair.* During the final grueling weeks of her mother's illness, "jogger stalking" with her sister Ali as well as Cat and Tess had given Georgie something to look forward to each morning.

He brushed a hand over his forehead, pushing the dampness into his close-cropped hair.

Georgie swallowed. Hard.

"Mmm," Tess said, licking her lips.

"You said it," Cat whispered, perching on the railing for a better view.

The footsteps grew closer, and he jogged past with a smile and a wave. "Morning, ladies."

"Morning!" Cat and Tess sang in girlish stereo.

Georgie said nothing, mesmerized by his glistening back and the sweat pooling at his waist. The overwhelming desire to lick him clean both horrified and titillated at the same time.

"Utter perfection," Tess declared when he was out of sight.

"Better than coffee," Cat said as she did every day. She hopped down from the railing. Wearing fatigues, black flip-flops, and a tank top that showcased her spectacular breasts, she said, "Off I go."

"You're going in early today," Tess said.

"And staying late. I've got a new band starting at the club tonight, so I'll stay for their first set." Scowling, she added, "Today, we're cleaning, and I have a ton of paperwork I've been putting off forever." Cat wore her bright red hair in short spikes that on anyone else would have been harsh. On her, the effect just added to her over-the-top sex appeal. Her pale complexion, big brown eyes, pierced eyebrow, mermaid tattoo and that amazing body combined to make her the most fearless and fabulous female Georgie had ever met.

"I'll be late, too," Tess said. "I'm working a double at the hospital."

"I don't know how you keep up that pace," Cat said, shaking her head.

"I need the money. My ex got everything in the divorce, so I'm starting from scratch."

"How in the world you let that happen, I'll never understand," Cat said with her typical bluntness.

Tess shrugged. "I just wanted to be rid of him."

"I'm available to kick his ass if need be," Cat said with a smile. "In fact, nothing would please me more." Cat and Georgie suspected that Tess's ex had knocked her around, but they hadn't yet reached the point in their burgeoning friendship where they felt they could ask her, and Tess wasn't talking.

As she scooped her long, dark hair into a high ponytail, Tess's delicate laugh lit up gray-blue eyes that were usually far too drawn and somber for such a young woman. "Where were you when I needed you a year ago?"

"Offer's on the table," Cat called as she bounded down the stairs to her Jeep. "See you chicks later."

After Cat left some rubber at the curb, Tess turned to Georgie. "Earth to Georgie."

Locked in her sweat-licking fantasy about the mysterious jogger, Georgie looked up to find Tess watching her with amusement. "Yeah?"

"Still nursing that thirty-seconds-a-day crush?"

"I have these insane thoughts about what I'd like to do to him," Georgie confided in her new friend. The women had been roommates for three months—since just after Georgie's mother got sick and had to stop working—and had bonded over their shared lust for their jogging neighbor. "I've never had such fantasies about a complete stranger."

"Nothing wrong with that. I think it's safe to say he's figuring prominently in all our fantasies these days. I thought Cat was a lesbian until I saw her drooling over him. Saved me the trouble of asking her."

"I would've liked to have been around for that conversation," Georgie said, smiling as she got up from the wicker sofa and took a sip of her coffee.

"How are you, Georgie? Really."

"Fine. Busy."

"Any word from your dad?" Tess asked.

"Nothing. I'm starting to wonder if he's dead, too. I mean why else would he suddenly stop paying the alimony to my mother?"

"If something had happened to him, surely you or your sister would've heard by now."

Georgie shrugged. "Who knows? It's not like we've been close to him since he left our mother for another woman."

Tess rested a hand on Georgie's arm. "I'm sorry you're having such a crappy time of it."

"Thanks. I sure hope I can get things cleaned up here pretty soon. I can't extend the leave of absence from my job indefinitely. At some point, I have to get back to Atlanta and back to work. I'm sure I'll feel better once I return to some semblance of normalcy."

"Well, if I'm being selfish," Tess said, "I hope it's not *too* soon. I love living here with you girls. This is just what I needed after the hell of my divorce."

"I'm glad it's working out for you. You guys saved me by moving in. There was no way I could swing all the bills for this place *and* my apartment in Atlanta on what I'm making at the senior center."

"Still no movement on getting a replacement for your mom?"

"Nope," Georgie said with a sigh. "Ironically, no one seems to want the headaches that come with the place for the pitiful salary the city is offering. We actually had a live one last week, but once the dirty old men got a hold of her, she ran for her life."

Tess laughed.

"Yesterday I heard them talking about 'annual' sex," Georgie said with a cringe and a shudder.

Groaning, Tess said, "Please tell me they were talking about once a year and not—"

Georgie held up her hand. "Don't even say it. The visual is enough to give me nightmares."

Tess laughed until there were tears in her eyes. "Your mother was a saint."

"She spoiled those people rotten, that's for sure. Unfortunately, they're expecting me to pick right up where she left off. Georgie, can you call Blue Cross for me? Georgie, will you drive me to my doctor's appointment? Georgie, play Euchre with us. Georgie, what's for lunch? Georgie, did you book the entertainment for the monthly social? Your mother would have done this, your mother would have done that. It's no wonder she was diagnosed with advanced breast cancer. She was so busy taking care of them, she had no time to take care of herself."

"I so admire that you refuse to let all her hard work and sacrifice be abandoned now that she's gone."

"I know it's the right thing to do, but sometimes I get so scared when I think about how long I've been away from my real job."

"It'll still be there when you're ready to go back."

"I sure hope so. Thanks for the pep talk, Tess. I don't know what we would've done without you and Cat around to help keep us sane the last few months." The two women answered the ad for temporary roommates Georgie and her mother placed in *The Newport Daily News* after her father's alimony payments dried up and the bills for her mother's large Victorian home began to roll in. Thank God she owned the place free and clear, but the taxes and upkeep were substantial.

Tess folded Georgie into a spontaneous hug that took her by surprise. Tess's loving support was such a gift in the midst of the chaos Georgie's life had descended into the last few months.

"Thank you," Georgie said softly.

"You're going to get through this. I know you are."

Georgie nodded. "Since you're working a double, I guess I'll see you for jogger stalking tomorrow morning."

"Wouldn't miss it for the world," Tess said as she went down the stairs to her car.

Georgie plucked the dead blooms off her mother's geraniums in the boxes attached to the porch railing and watered the four planters that sat on each of the stairs that led to the street. The three-story white house had black shutters and a bright red front door that matched the geraniums.

As she refilled the watering can and imagined her mother tending to these very plants, Georgie's eyes flooded once again. She had cried more in the last three months than in the previous thirty years combined. Even more than a week later, it was still a shock to wake up each day and realize once again that her mother was really gone.

With the daily watering done, Georgie went upstairs to shower and get dressed for "work." Not in one of the sharp suits she wore to Davidson's, the swank Atlanta department store where she worked in marketing and fashion merchandising. No, here she wore shorts and a T-shirt that would be dirty by noon. She tugged a brush through her shoulder-length dark blonde hair and applied the three-hundred-dollar-a-jar moisturizer she had bought with her store discount. In another week or two, she would have to call someone in Atlanta to send her more. Some things a girl just shouldn't have to do without.

Georgie studied her face in the mirror. Her hazel eyes were shot through with specs of gold. Her nose was upturned and reportedly cute, a word Georgie hated. Her cheeks were fuller than she preferred, dimpled, and also reportedly cute. She vowed to kill the next person who called her cute. She'd show them cute.

Her cell phone rang, and she dashed across the hall to grab it. "Hello," she said breathlessly.

"Georgia, when are you coming home?" asked Doug, her boyfriend of two years, for the hundredth time since she had been in Newport.

"Hello to you, too, Doug."

"Honestly, your mother's affairs can't be this complicated, can they? Tell me you'll be back for the charity ball at the country club on Saturday. I need you with me."

Sighing, Georgie sat on the bed. "Not looking good, I'm afraid."

"Can you come for the weekend?"

"I can't leave the center for that long."

"Oh *come on,* Georgia! I *need* you. I'm getting an award. You know how important this is to me!"

"I know. I'm sorry."

He was silent for a long moment, which meant he was brooding. "I hate to say this, especially after all you've been through recently."

"Just say it, Doug."

"This isn't working. I think we need to see other people."

It wasn't like she hadn't seen it coming. He had been making noise about breaking up for weeks now. "Whatever you want."

"That's it? That's all you have to say?"

"What do you want me to say?"

"I want you to come home." A sports agent who represented three of the PGA's top stars, Doug was used to getting what he wanted when he wanted it.

"I can't. I've told you that. If you want to see other people, go right ahead. I can't stop you."

"You don't care at all, do you, Georgia?"

"Not enough," she said truthfully.

"And that's always been our problem, hasn't it?" She pictured him blowing the dust off his little black book even as they spoke. "Take care of yourself. Call me if you ever get back to Atlanta."

"I will."

"Good-bye, Georgia."

"Bye."

CHAPTER 2

By nine thirty, she was in line for the two dozen donuts and coffee she had learned the hard way to have ready when the old men started arriving at ten. The treats went a long way toward ensuring a good day.

Still smarting from the conversation with Doug, she drove to the senior center on Spring Street and parked her silver Volkswagen Passat in the executive director's space. With a wistful glance at the Georgia license plate, she felt a sudden urge to kick something—or someone. She should have broken up with Doug months ago, long before he'd had the chance to do the dumping.

She almost died herself—of shock—when he arranged to have her car delivered to Rhode Island when it became clear she would be staying awhile, and then he came to her mother's funeral. The selfless acts were so far out of character that they had backfired on him by illustrating what was lacking in their relationship the rest of the time.

Life with Doug was all about him—his work, his clients, his life. Georgie had grown weary of meals interrupted by urgent calls from prima donna golfers, weekends spent watching golf on TV, shooting balls at the driving range, or worse yet, attending golf events during which she hardly laid eyes on him.

As she unlocked the center and flipped on the lights, she reasoned that it should have been *her* decision to end it with him, but that too had been taken away from her by the events of the past few months.

A whiff of stale air greeted her at the center. From her first day there, she had marveled at how the place smelled like old people. How she longed for the perfumed gentrification of Davidson's. *Anyway, where was I? Oh yes, Doug.*

As he liked to remind her, he could have any girl he wanted, so she was certain he wouldn't be on the market for long. She hadn't planned to marry him—no way. In fact, long after she decided their relationship wasn't going anywhere, she'd stayed with him because so much of her social life in Atlanta was tied up in him. She had to admit, though, she'd liked the attention he had showered her with—fancy dates, flowers at the office (no doubt arranged by his secretary), spontaneous weekends away with him, his cell phone, and his BlackBerry. But she hated the way he called her *Georgia* in that snooty upper class accent he had worked so hard to perfect.

Leaving the donuts and coffee on a table in the large common area, she went into the kitchen to fetch cream and sugar, closing the old refrigerator with a harder-than-necessary kick.

"God, it's hot in here," she muttered, turning the air conditioning down to sixty-eight. They complained if it went any lower, but after living in the South for twelve years, Georgie had grown used to frigid air. This place was stifling in more ways than one.

She took a good look at the big, open room full of beat-up round tables and orange folding chairs to make sure everything was where it belonged before the daily invasion began. In one corner, her mother had arranged sofas around a big-screen TV where the women enjoyed morning talk shows and the men watched afternoon Red Sox games. Off the far end of the main room, a hallway led to the office.

Georgie remembered her mother battling the city council for the money to buy the TV. Somehow Nancy always managed to find what she needed to keep the center going—like the hideous orange chairs that had been donated by the Elks Lodge after they bought new ones. The only decorations were the scenic Newport posters on the wall. So while the place wasn't pretty, it got the job done. And where Georgie was used to stylish, here she was stuck with serviceable.

The front door swung open, and Georgie suppressed a groan. *Five more minutes of peace. Please.* But it was not to be. In walked Gus Souza, or Good Gus, as they called him to distinguish him from the other Gus at the center. Of all the old men, Good Gus was Georgie's favorite. He always had a warm smile and a friendly greeting for her, and unlike the others, he didn't hit on her or make inappropriate comments about her body, her hair, her smile, her dimples, her clothes, or anything else they could think of. Nothing was off limits.

"Morning, Gus."

"Hi there, Georgie. How are you today?"

"Same as yesterday." Since they had the exact conversation every day, she could have written the script.

His snow-white hair was combed back off his cherubic face. Even at seventy-six, his blue eyes were still bright and animated. Once he had told her about his proud military service during "the war," which meant Korea or Vietnam with this crowd, and his long career as a car dealer and entrepreneur.

"Georgie, I wondered . . ."

Satisfied with the display of coffee and donuts, she turned to him.

"I hate to ask because I know you're inundated with requests."

"What's up, Gus?"

"Do you think you could call Blue Cross for me today? I can't hear them on the phone, and I got this notice that says they denied my claim."

He was so cute and so sweet, how could she say no? "Of course," she said with a sigh she knew he couldn't hear. "I'd be happy to."

His face lifted into a relieved smile. He had children somewhere, but from what the others told her, he didn't see much of them, which was their loss. She heard he played Santa the previous Christmas when the seniors invited their grandchildren to the center. Georgie could picture him pulling it off with his easy charm. She took the denial of payment notice from him, wrote down his date of birth and the social security number she'd learned she would need to gain access to his account, and promised to get back to him before the end of the day.

"Thank you, honey." He reached out to squeeze her arm. "Your mother was so proud of you for stepping up for us the way you have."

Mortified by her emotional response to the compliment, Georgie mumbled, "Thank you," and escaped to her office at the end of the hallway before she could embarrass herself by bawling all over poor Gus.

The morning flew by as she attended to a number of crises, broke up an argument over who was prettier—Angelina Jolie or Farrah Fawcett in her prime—waited on hold for twenty minutes with Blue Cross to find out that Gus had failed to notify his primary care provider that he was seeing an "out of network" doctor for his prostate cancer follow-up—info she could have lived without knowing—and helped the kitchen staff dole out more than one hundred servings of breaded flounder with baby red potatoes and asparagus.

The smell of fish permeated the center, and Georgie fought off a gag as she went around the common room collecting the used Styrofoam lunch trays into a big garbage bag. On her way past their table, she heard Bad Gus, Gus Richards, telling a filthy joke about a woman, a goat, a bucket, and something else Georgie chose not to stick around to hear. The other old men gathered around him at the table—Walter Brown, Henry Stevens, Bill Bradley, Good Gus, and the oldest of the regulars, Donald Davis—hung on his every word. Their guffaws at the raunchy punch line followed Georgie out the back door to the Dumpster.

Stinking of flounder and vinegar that had somehow splashed onto her shirt, she wrestled with the top of the big Dumpster but couldn't get it open. Sweat ran down her face as she gave one last heroic but unsuccessful attempt to get the lid open. Defeated, she slid open the side door and took a step back when the stench of yesterday's Salisbury steak smacked her in the face.

Since the garbage bag wouldn't fit through the smaller opening, she gritted her teeth, reached into it, and, dreaming of Lancôme and Clinique and Donna Karan and Jones New York, she grabbed a handful of smelly Styrofoam and jammed it into the Dumpster. She was on her third handful when the slam of a car door startled her.

"Hey! What're you doing? That stuff is recyclable!"

Georgie whirled around and almost passed out from the shock. *Him! Jogger Guy!* He wore a crisp dress shirt with pressed khakis and a glare in his deep blue eyes.

Taking the garbage bag from her, he peered inside and winced. "Are you aware that Styrofoam *never* breaks down? It'll still be sitting in the landfill when your great grandchildren become grandparents."

Georgie stared at him, unable to breathe, let alone form a coherent word. Apparently, he had the same effect on her when he was outraged as he did when he ran by the house dripping with sweat.

"Where's your recycling Dumpster?"

"We, um, don't have one," she sputtered.

"Are you *kidding me?*" His face got very red. "You jam all this Styrofoam into a *regular* Dumpster *every day?* Oh my God!"

Wiping away a piece of flounder that had somehow gotten stuck to her cheek, she felt the surge coming and couldn't stop it. It was only two o'clock, but she'd already had more than enough of this day. She burst into tears.

He stared at her, seeming shocked by her emotional reaction.

"What's going on here?" Bad Gus demanded from the doorway. The other old men followed him as he pushed Jogger Guy out of the way and put his arm around Georgie.

"What did you do to her?" Walter asked, invading Jogger Guy's personal space.

"Nothing," he insisted. "I asked her why she wasn't recycling all this Styrofoam."

Georgie's tears descended into deep, gulping sobs that had little to do with garbage and everything to do with months of unbearable stress.

Good Gus took over from Bad Gus, leading Georgie into her office while whispering gentle words of comfort. The others made a barricade at the door to keep out Jogger Guy, who had followed them.

"There, there, now Georgie, honey." Good Gus squatted next to her, offered his monogrammed handkerchief, and gripped her hand. "Someone get her a glass of water."

"I've got it." Pushing past Jogger Guy, Bill stopped all of a sudden and eyed the younger man with suspicion. "Where do I know you from?"

"I work with your daughter."

"You're a cop?"

"Detective Nathan Caldwell, Newport Police Department." He extended his hand. "I've seen you around the station with Roxy."

Because he was too polite not to, Bill shook Nathan's hand while continuing to give him the once-over. "You made Georgie cry. We don't care for that."

"I'm sorry. I didn't mean to. I was just driving by, and I saw her—"

"It's not me you need to apologize to, young feller." Bill nodded toward Georgie, who was still mopping up the torrent of tears.

The men parted to let Nathan through.

Good Gus stood up but didn't leave his post at Georgie's side.

They waited expectantly.

"I'm sorry I yelled at you," Nathan said.

If he'd had a hat, it would have been twisting in his hands. The old men could be intimidating when they wanted to be, a discovery Georgie found intriguing—and endearing.

"It's okay," she said, mortified by the entire episode.

"I was just wondering why you don't recycle," he mumbled.

"My mother requested a recycling Dumpster from the city a year ago." Georgie gestured to the stack of paper on the cluttered desk. "There's a copy of the form here somewhere. Apparently, she didn't get anywhere."

"That's ridiculous," Nathan said.

"So go arrest someone at City Hall," Bad Gus growled. "And stop picking on Georgie."

"I wasn't picking on her—"

"You can move along now, son." Walter tugged on Nathan's arm to lead him from the office. "We'll take care of her."

"I really am sorry," Nathan said. "I didn't mean to upset you." On his way out, he brushed past Walter and Bill, who was returning with the glass of water.

"I'm okay, you guys," Georgie insisted. "I'm sorry to make such a scene."

"You have nothing to be sorry about," Good Gus said.

Georgie took a long sip of water. "Thanks. Go on back to your game. I'm fine. Really."

They began to filter back into the common room for their afternoon round of Euchre, a card game Bill had imported to Rhode Island from Minnesota. Good Gus lingered. "Are you sure you're all right? It's not like you to break down like that."

"I miss my mom," she said, knowing she could confide in him and it wouldn't be all over the center in ten minutes.

His face softened. "Of course you do, honey."

"And to add insult to injury, my boyfriend in Atlanta dumped me this morning."

"*What?* Is he *crazy?* I'll tell you what," Gus huffed, "if I was thirty years younger, why I'd court you myself. He's a fool."

Amused by his righteous indignation, Georgie smiled. "I'd be honored to be courted by such a lovely gentleman."

"Don't you worry. You'll meet a nice young man in no time. Once the word gets out that you're on the market, we'll have to beat them off with a stick. Heck, Walter is ready to run away with you the minute you say the word."

Smiling, she got up to hug him. "Do me a favor and don't put out the word, okay?"

"Sure thing," he said, returning her embrace and kissing her forehead. "Your secret is safe with me. I'll let you get back to work, but we're right out there if you need us." He headed for the door.

"Gus?"

Turning back, he raised a white eyebrow.

"Thank you. Tell the others, too."

"Our pleasure, honey."

When she was alone, Georgie dropped her head onto her folded arms and took a deep, rattling breath. So embarrassing. Flipping out over trash of all things. What he must think of her. Nathan Caldwell. It was a nice name that suited him. Too bad he'd gone and ruined all her fantasies by being a jerk. Now what would she have to look forward to every day?

A cloud of depression hung over her as she slugged through the rest of the day. Closing the center at the stroke of six, she felt bad—as she did every day—ushering the last few stragglers to the door, knowing many of them wouldn't see or talk to another living soul until they returned the next morning. They were why she kept coming back every day, despite her overwhelming desire to be anywhere else.

After an hour of paperwork, she walked through the heavy humidity to her car.

Parallel parking in front of the house a short time later, Georgie focused on what to have for dinner and the things she needed to get done that night—including laundry and a list of her mother's assets for the probate attorney.

She came to an abrupt halt at the sight of a huge arrangement of fragrant, festive lilies sitting on the porch. With a glance around to see if anyone was watching, she went up the stairs, her heart heavy with dread. How predictable of Doug to do something like this. He'd probably had his secretary order the consolation bouquet. *So sorry to dump you,* she imagined the card would say. *Have a nice life. Love, Doug.* She plucked the envelope from among the flowers.

Inside she found a card describing the eco-friendly environment the flowers had been grown in. *That's odd. What does Doug care about that?* Reading the message, her heart skipped a crazy beat. "Sorry I made you cry. Forgive me? Nate Caldwell."

"Oh," she gasped, turning to find Jogger Guy, still fresh and polished in his work clothes, standing in the street watching her with his hands jammed into his pockets. Tongue-tied, she stared at him.

He made his way toward her. "Do *not* cry," he ordered, softening his tone when he added, "Please don't."

"I won't." The stink of flounder clung to her clothes and hair as he reached the bottom step and looked up at her with startling blue eyes. "How did you know where I live?" He'd seemed so intent during his runs that she was certain he hadn't paid much attention to them drooling over him from the porch.

"I'm a detective," he said with a smug expression.

"Oh, so you just, like, tracked me down?" she asked, not sure how she felt about that.

He grinned, causing his tanned, handsome face to crinkle in all the best ways.

Her heart pounded. God, he was *hot* and not as much of a jerk, apparently, as she had thought earlier.

"Actually, I run by here every morning and recognized you."

"We didn't think you ever looked," she said, quickly adding, "not that we've discussed you or anything." She was babbling. She knew it but was powerless to stop it. Why did this particular guy have this particular effect on her?

"I've taken an occasional peek. Running in this neighborhood has become *much* more interesting since you ladies moved in. Are you new in town?"

"I grew up here. My roommate Cat is also from here. Tess is from Connecticut."

"Which one has the spiky red hair?"

"That'd be Cat."

"Wasn't there another one? I seem to remember four of you."

"Oh, that was my sister, Ali. She's gone home to New York." Georgie wondered if he could smell the flounder from where he stood on the sidewalk. Fortunately, the lilies were putting out a powerful perfume that she hoped was strong enough to do battle with the fish stench.

He glanced at the flowers. "So what do you say?"

"About?"

"Forgive me?"

Why do you care? she wanted to ask but didn't. "Of course. Thank you for the flowers. They're gorgeous."

"You're welcome. Since I'm not in the practice of making pretty girls cry, I needed to make it up to you."

Did he just call me pretty? Looking like a frump and stinking like fish? Georgie ran a self-conscious hand through her rumpled hair and yearned for the shower. "Well, thanks again for the flowers." She reached down to pick them up off the porch. "You didn't have to do that."

"Yes, I did. Are you free for dinner?"

Stunned, she could only stare at him from behind the huge bouquet while wondering if her mouth was actually hanging open with surprise or if it just felt that way.

"Hello?" He waved a hand. "Georgie?"

"Um, I . . ."

"You what?"

"I stink. Like flounder. Today's lunch special."

He tossed his golden head back and laughed. "I can wait while you clean up. But if you don't want to go out with someone who made you cry, I'd understand."

Studying him, she remembered the list of things she had planned to do that night, but suddenly none of it was at all appealing when stacked up against him. *Why the hell not? After all, Doug did say we should see other people, right? And I like what I'm seeing...* "Are you sure you don't mind waiting?"

He gestured for her to go for it, and she turned toward the house, stopping at the front door. "Do you, um, want to come in?"

"I'll wait for you out here." He strolled up the stairs and plopped down on the porch sofa.

Georgie wondered if it was a coincidence that he picked the very spot where she watched for him each morning. "I'll be just a few minutes."

"Take your time." He put his head back and closed his eyes.

She studied him in all his exquisite beauty for a long moment before she went inside, stashed the flowers on a table, and bolted for the stairs, withdrawing her cell phone from her pocket as she went.

"Come on, come on, pick up," she whispered as she waited for Cat to answer her cell phone.

"Hello?"

"Oh, thank God you answered."

"Georgie? What's wrong?"

Georgie could hear loud music and voices in the background at Club Underground where Cat was the manager. "You're not going to *believe* who I'm having dinner with tonight."

"Don't tell me you finally agreed to go out with that old guy, Walter. That's just so *wrong*."

"No, no! The jogger guy."

"No *way!*" Cat said with a loud whistle. "*No freaking way!* How'd you meet him?"

Georgie gave Cat an abbreviated version of the story. "He's waiting for me on the porch."

"Then what the hell are you doing calling me?"

"I was flipping out and needed to tell someone."

"What's he look like in clothes?"

"Amazing," Georgie said with a sigh, remembering the way his pale blue shirt had magnified his already glorious eyes as he looked up at her from the street.

"I'm going to need you to take notes—copious notes—so you don't forget to tell us everything, do you hear? I know I speak for Tess when I say we'll want every, single, salacious detail."

"We're going to dinner, not having sex," Georgie said dryly as she worked around the phone to peel off her clothes.

"If there's ever been a time in your life for first-date sex, this is it. Might be just what you need to take your mind off everything."

"Not happening. I've got to go. I told him I'd be quick."

Cat snorted. "You? Quick in the shower? I hope he's not hungry."

"Bye, Cat."

"Don't do anything I wouldn't do," Cat said, laughing. "I'm *so* jealous!"

"Hanging up now."

"Take condoms! There's a box in my bedside drawer."

"I'm in the shower. Can't hear you!" Georgie cut the connection, tossed her phone onto the vanity, and got busy scrubbing off the eau de flounder.

Twenty-five minutes later, she had dried her hair, done her best with a mascara wand and lip liner, tried on almost everything in her closet, and created a complete disaster in her bedroom. Just so she wouldn't be tempted to take Cat's advice, she purposely wore underwear that didn't match—purple polka dot bikini panties and a yellow bra.

She was beginning to sweat by the time she finally tugged on a sundress that could have used ironing, slid her feet into a pair of flip-flops, grabbed her purse, and headed for the stairs before she could change her mind about her clothes—again.

Everything felt wrong and out of whack, she thought with irritation as she clomped down the stairs. A date like this required significant preparation—including a manicure, pedicure and waxing—not half an hour and no consultation on proper attire with women whose opinions she trusted. Feeling like she was at a significant disadvantage and once again bemoaning the loss of her untroubled, stylish life in Atlanta, she pushed open the screen door to the porch and announced, "Ready," in what she hoped was a breezy, it-was-no-big-deal-to-look-this-good tone.

Sprawled out on the wicker sofa, Nathan was sound asleep.

CHAPTER 3

Slack with sleep, his face was even more handsome than when he was awake. "Nathan," she whispered, not wanting to startle him. "*Nathan.*"

He turned away from her into the back of the sofa.

Georgie reached out to shake his shoulder but pulled her hand back at the last minute. Waking him up meant touching him, and she wasn't sure she was prepared to do that. *Oh, stop being such a nitwit! Just wake him up!* This time when she reached out, her damp palm landed on his shoulder, and she gave a gentle shake.

He startled and looked up at her for a second before his face softened into a grin that made her mouth go dry and her heart beat fast. "Ready?"

She nodded.

Standing up, he stretched and ran his fingers through his hair. "Just what the doctor ordered," he declared, sending his eyes on a lazy journey from her feet to her face. "Very nice."

Flustered, she mumbled, "Thank you."

"Where would you like to go?"

"Wherever you want. I've been away for a long time. I have no idea what's even here anymore."

He gestured for her to lead the way down the stairs. "Away where?"

"Atlanta." His nearness made it hard for her to form a coherent thought, let alone talk. She couldn't believe she was on her way out to dinner with oh-so-hot

Jogger Guy. *Nathan,* she reminded herself. *Stop thinking of him as Jogger Guy before you make the mistake of calling him that!* "I've lived there for twelve years."

"What took you there?" he asked as they strolled down Dean Avenue toward Lower Thames.

"My mother and her family are from there."

"Which is why she named you Georgia."

"Yep."

"I like it. It suits you."

"I used to hate it, but I've gotten used to it."

"How did your family end up here?"

"My dad was in the navy. They were stationed here and stayed when he retired. I spent a lot of time with my grandmother in Georgia growing up and loved it there, so I went to the University of Georgia and stayed after."

"Are you going to make me pull the rest out of you?" he asked with a teasing smile.

She glanced over at him. "The rest of what?"

"Your deal. What kept you in Atlanta? What brought you home again? What're you doing working at the senior center? Come on, give it up."

"I stayed in Atlanta after college because I got a great job at Davidson's, which is a high-end department store company in the South. I majored in fashion merchandising, and I oversee product placement and displays in four of their Georgia stores."

"Wait. I'm confused. Oversee, present tense. If that's the case, what were you doing at the center today?"

"I'm doing a favor for my mother." She decided not to tell him the full story. For one night, she'd like to forget about her mother's death and the mess her well-ordered life had become in the last few months. "It's temporary."

"Oh. That's disappointing."

"Why?"

"Because it sounds like you'll be going back to Atlanta at some point."

"Hopefully soon. My whole life is there."

"Disappointing."

They walked down Dean Avenue in quiet until he stopped at the intersection with Lower Thames. "Is this okay?"

She looked up to see they were standing in front of Scales and Shells. "My mother loves this place," she said, saddened to realize she had once again used the present tense.

"It's one of my favorites. Never been?"

"Not in years."

"It's all seafood. Is that okay?"

"Fine by me."

"Well, then." With a flourish, he opened the door and held it for her.

"Detective!" The exotic, dark-haired hostess greeted Nathan with a saucy smile and a kiss to his cheek that made Georgie wonder if they had a history. "How nice of you to drop by. We thought you'd forgotten about us."

"Never. Patty, this is Georgie." He glanced at Georgie with an odd expression. "This is embarrassing. We haven't gotten around to last names yet."

As Patty chuckled, Georgie felt her cheeks grow warm. "Georgie Quinn," she said, reaching out to shake hands with Patty.

"Nice to meet you. I've got a table right over here."

With Nathan's hand burning a hole in her lower back, Georgie followed Patty to a corner table.

"Georgie hasn't been here in a long time," Nathan said. "Can you refresh her memory on how things work around here?"

"I'd love to. All our seafood was brought in today, and in most cases we can tell you who caught your fish or lobster. Feel free to approach the grill," she said, gesturing to the open kitchen, "with any questions you have for the chef."

"Thanks, Patty," Nathan said.

"Sure thing. Cindy will be your server, and she'll be right over."

"Georgie Quinn," Nathan said when they were alone. "I like that."

She pretended to peruse the menu but was completely aware of him—his nearness, his clean, masculine scent, the rumble of his throat clearing, the play of his long, tanned fingers over the menu. She licked her lips and swallowed as a flush of heat traveled through her. Never before had she had such a strong reaction to a man, especially when he was doing nothing more than studying a menu.

"What looks good to you?" he asked, startling her out of her thoughts.

You. "Everything. What do you recommend?"

"I love the calamari appetizer, and I always get the mussels marinara." With a sheepish grin, he added, "I'm in a rut."

She smiled and closed her menu. "Sounds good to me. Make it two—of the mussels, that is."

"Do that again."

"What?"

"Smile."

Unnerved by the intense gaze he directed her way, Georgie stared back at him.

"Come on," he cajoled. "One quick smile."

Hesitantly, she did her best to comply.

"You have dimples!"

"If you say they're cute, I'll kill you. Do you hear me?"

His deep, rich laugh engaged his entire face. "Duly noted. But they *are* adorable."

"That's perilously close to cute," she said with what she hoped was a menacing scowl. Apparently, she failed, because he only laughed harder. Something inside her shifted as she watched him, and the uneasy realization that this guy could be big, *big* trouble settled in her gut.

Chemistry. Was there any other word for the energy sizzling between them? Georgie thought she'd had it with Doug, but it had only taken an hour with Nathan to show her she had been mistaken. *This* was chemistry, and it took all her willpower not to reach out and touch him.

As he dove into the calamari, he entertained her with stories about growing up as the youngest of the six Caldwell brothers. To hear him tell it, he was the only one with a lick of common sense. The others were all artistic—one was a writer, two were artists, another a musician and single father, and the other an architect.

"And then there's me. The cop who cleans up all their messes."

"Where do they live?"

"Unfortunately, right here in town," he said, but his grin told the real story. Clearly, he adored them. "I'm forever getting sucked into their crap." He speared a loop of calamari and a hot pepper ring, dipped it in the marinara, and offered it to her. "Try this."

"I've never been able to bring myself to eat that," she said, curling up her nose with distaste.

"Come on."

He was so convincing that Georgie leaned forward to let him feed her the bite. Her taste buds exploded in response to the tangy flavor, and she couldn't keep the verdict off her face.

"You gotta love the squid," he said with a chuckle.

Georgie coughed and reached for her glass of chardonnay. "You *had* to say it, didn't you?"

"You liked it. There's plenty. Dig in."

She held up her hand to say no thank you. "So how did the baby of your family end up taking care of everyone?"

"A very good question and one I've never been able to answer. It seems like they've been relying on me since I was old enough to walk." He shrugged. "Just the way it is."

"What about your parents?"

"They told my brothers it was time for them to be independent and moved to Florida about five years ago. Can't say I blame them."

"So now it all falls to you."

He flashed a "what're you gonna do?" grin and shrugged. "They say you can pick your friends but not your relatives."

Thinking of her father's mysterious disappearance at the worst possible time, Georgie smiled in agreement.

"*Mmm,* I sure do *love* those dimples. You really should show them off more often." He made a solemn face. "You're very serious most of the time."

Surprised by his astute assessment, Georgie cleared her throat. "Just lately. I've got a lot on my mind."

"Anything you want to talk about?"

She was both touched that he had asked and tempted, so tempted, to pour out the whole story to this man who was accustomed to fixing messes. "I'm enjoying the break from it all, to be honest."

He raised his wineglass in toast to her. "In that case, here's to you and your night away."

Georgie touched her glass to his. "Thank you."

"My pleasure. Entirely mine."

Oh no, not entirely. Some of it is definitely mine.

Nathan tucked her hand into the crook of his elbow as they left the restaurant.

Georgie was so affected by him she could have melted into him right there on the sidewalk. To take her mind off her rampaging hormones, she forced herself to make conversation. "I'm so full I could burst. Thank you again for dinner."

"Thank *you* for forgiving me and coming with me."

"So what do you do for fun when you're not keeping the streets safe or taking care of your brothers?"

"I buy and sell houses after I renovate them."

"And when exactly do you sleep?"

He laughed. "Fortunately, I don't need much. Want to take a walk and see my latest project?"

Raising a skeptical eyebrow, she asked, "Is that another way of asking me to come see your etchings?"

"Why, Georgie Quinn, you're funny." Stopping, he turned to her and reached for her hand. His hand was calloused but not rough. "Do you think maybe we could just get this out of the way so I can stop thinking about it?"

"What?" she asked, her breath hitching in her throat when she looked up to find his eyes trained on her.

"The good-night kiss." Without giving her time to process what he had said, he cupped her cheek, leaned in, and slid his lips over hers.

Georgie's heart pounded so hard she could hear the roar of it echoing in her ears. Her free hand landed on his chest as he tipped his head and delved deeper, his tongue tracing her bottom lip. His taste was an intoxicating mix of wine and spice, and the moan that escaped from her seemed to infuse him with enthusiasm.

Maneuvering them into a doorway, he pressed her back against the wall and devoured her with just the firm pressure of his open mouth against hers, their world reduced to that quiet, dark alcove off the busy street.

Just for tonight, one night away from it all. She reached up to curl a hand around his neck and leaned into the most carnal kiss of her life. *Oh my God, I'm kissing Jogger Guy, and oh he kisses like a dream—a dirty, sexy, erotic dream.*

Encouraged by her responsiveness, he finally dipped his tongue into her mouth and tightened his arm around her waist.

Georgie clutched his other hand as her tongue dueled with his. *More.* She silently pleaded with him for relief from the aching, burning need that was unlike anything she had ever experienced.

The blast of a car horn startled them. He tore his lips free of hers and kissed a path to her neck. "Why, Georgie Quinn," he whispered. "I like the way you kiss." He dragged his tongue along her jaw. "And the way you taste." With his erection snug against her belly, his hand coasted up over her ribs to cup her breast. "And the way you feel. I *really* like that."

As her nipple tightened under his thumb, Georgie summoned some control. Shouldn't she at least pretend to protest? But all she could seem to say was, "Nathan."

"Yes?"

She tilted her head to give him better access to her neck. "We should stop this."

He nibbled on her earlobe and sent a shudder straight through her. "Why?"

"I don't do this kind of thing." *Kissing in public on a first date, restraining the urge to tear off his clothes to get to the good stuff, again on a first date.*

"You should." Continuing to lavish her ear with attention, he added, "You're good at it."

With a firm hand to his chest, she made one last attempt to rein in a situation that was spiraling into something she wasn't ready for. "Please."

As if she had thrown cold water in his face, he stopped and pulled back from her. "I'm sorry."

"Don't be. I was right there with you the whole way."

He rewarded her with one of those grins that made his eyes crinkle and sparkle with mirth. "Take a walk with me?" Holding out his hand, he used those irresistible eyes to implore her.

She laced her fingers through his. "Since we've gotten the good-night kiss out of the way, there shouldn't be anything else to worry about, right?"

"Absolutely," he said in a light, breezy tone that told her she had everything in the world to be worried about.

"Oh, Nathan, this is beautiful!" she said of the shining hardwood floors, newly restored wood moldings, fresh paint in a dark tan she would have chosen herself, and elegant wall sconces. "You did all this?"

"I've been chipping away at it for the last year or so. It's taking longer than usual because it needed everything."

"This room is gorgeous."

"I have 'before' pictures upstairs. You won't believe the difference. Someone covered this floor with the most hideous carpet I've ever seen.

Tearing it up and discovering this wood underneath it was like finding a million bucks."

His passion for restoration was evident in the way his eyes lit up as he described the work he had done.

"Why anyone would want to cover this is beyond me." Georgie squatted to run her hand over the glossy wood. She looked up to find him staring down at her with fire in his eyes and his jaw set with tension. "What?"

"That's very sexy."

"What is?"

"Watching you caress my wood floor."

"Been a while for you, has it?"

He laughed and held out a hand to help her up. "Come see the rest."

On the way up a steep flight of stairs, she noticed the kitchen had been taken down to studs. To the right of the stairs on the second floor was a large, fully renovated bedroom with a rumpled queen-size bed, a dresser, and bedside tables. "You live here?"

He nodded. "I always live in the houses I'm working on. Saves time and money."

"Don't you get tired of the chaos?"

Shrugging, he said, "I grew up with five brothers. I'm used to chaos."

"I guess you would be. It would drive me nuts to live like this."

"Have a need for order, do you?"

"Some semblance of it, anyway." When the statement reminded her of the current disorder in her life, she quickly pushed the thought aside, determined to enjoy every minute of her brief escape from reality.

He pointed out the new light fixtures in the bathroom. "Energy-efficient lights and hot water heater. I'm kind of into the whole environmental thing."

"*No!*" she said, scandalized. "I hadn't noticed."

"Very funny, Georgie Quinn."

"I hate to tell you, but you tipped your hand with the hissy fit you had at the Dumpster—not to mention the organically grown flowers."

With a sheepish grin, he said, "Everyone has to do their part."

She pointed to a door. "What's in here?"

"My brother Ben has been crashing in there, but he's gone to Block Island for the night with some friends." Nathan's face clouded. "He's going through a bit of a rough patch at the moment."

His distress over his brother made Georgie want to reach out to him, but a sudden bout of shyness stopped her. The passion they'd shared on the street already seemed like a long time ago. She watched him make an effort to shake off his worries and return his focus to her.

"Can I get you a drink or anything? Believe it or not, I do have a fridge in this place."

She shook her head. "I'm good. I should probably be getting home."

"Right."

They stared at each other for an endless moment before both took a step forward in the same instant.

His arms closed around her, lifting her right off her feet into another of those sexually charged kisses that had left her lips tingling and her body burning earlier. *This is insanity! It has to stop!* She would stop it. In just a minute. Surely one more minute won't hurt anything.

His relentless tongue explored, teased, enticed.

Okay, maybe two more minutes.

Georgie clung to him, her fingers gripping his muscular shoulders.

He held her in a vise-like grip.

The next thing she knew, she was falling, and he was coming down on top of her as she landed on his bed.

Alarms! Bells! Whistles! Stop! Now! This is wrong! This isn't you—you don't do this! Oh, but I want to. I really, really want to! I want to let this amazing, sexy man make me forget, just for tonight, all the misery of the last three months. Don't I deserve that much? Yes, but oh how I'll hate myself in the morning. The morning is twelve hours from now, though. Twelve blessed hours of release from the worry, the pain, the uncertainty.

"Georgie," he gasped as he pulled back from her. "I can't seem to resist you." Resting his forehead on hers, he drew in a deep, cleansing breath. "But we should stop. I'll walk you home."

I don't want to go home! I don't want to be in a house full of memories that remind me over and over that I'm never going to see my mother again! Don't make me go back there. Please don't. Telling herself that one night with him—one night of mindless, no-holds-barred, no-commitment sex with the most devastatingly sexy man she had ever met—was just what she needed, she reached up to release a button on his shirt.

He went still on top of her. "Georgie?"

Another button popped free.

Exhaling a long deep breath, he reached for the hand at work on his shirt. "Are you sure?"

She nodded.

"But—"

With a finger to his lips, she told him she was done talking.

CHAPTER 4

Nathan studied her for an endless moment, during which she wondered if he was going to say no, and then he lowered his face to hers for a soft, gentle, mind-altering kiss. All the power he had shown her earlier was gone, replaced by sweet seduction that took their chemistry from simmer straight to boil.

While he went slow, Georgie redoubled her efforts to get rid of his shirt, desperate to get her hands on the chest that had dominated her fantasies for weeks. With her lips still fused with his, she couldn't decide what part of him to touch first.

An opportunity like this was not to be rushed, nor should it compete with the sensations coursing through her from kisses that made her feel cherished as much as desired. That would be something to ponder tomorrow when this sure-to-be-incredible night was just a memory of a one-time lapse in judgment.

With her hands cupping his pectorals, she urged him onto his back.

Tearing his lips free, he resisted for a second. But the urgency he saw on her face must have swayed him because, with a great sigh of frustration, he did as she asked.

"Take this off," she said, tugging at his shirt.

He sat halfway up and slid the shirt off his broad shoulders.

She licked her lips with anticipation.

His eyes narrowed as he watched her tongue move over her lips. "Georgie," he groaned, his voice hoarse with desire.

Leaning forward to nuzzle the golden chest hair that had played such a big part in her fantasies, she said, "Hmm?"

A tremble rippled through him, and a wave of desire shot straight to her core when she realized the effect she was having on him. The light shining into the room from the hallway made it possible for her to see the growing bulge in his pants. Forcing herself to focus on his chest when all she wanted was to get rid of his pants so she could see the rest of him, she grazed her tongue over his nipple.

He sucked in a sharp deep breath and buried his hands in her hair. "Georgie, please. Come up here."

"In a minute." Her inhibitions faded away in a red haze of desire that was all new to her. The overwhelming need made it easy to forget that she had only just met him, that she was having first-date sex, that tomorrow she would be back to reality and most likely horrified by her behavior. None of that mattered now.

With her lips and fingers, she explored every ridge of hard muscle and each patch of soft hair while soaking in his masculine scent—a combination of soap, sporty deodorant, and spicy cologne. When she reached the waistband of his pants, she tugged on the button and unzipped him slowly, going for maximum effect. Where this temptress had come from, she couldn't have said. All she knew was she loved the hissing sound he expelled when she ran her hand over his throbbing length—his *impressive* throbbing length.

"Georgie, sweetheart, come on." He sounded as if he were speaking through gritted teeth.

Georgie was too busy freeing him from his clothes to venture a glance to see if that was the case. She closed her hand around him and stroked him gently, afraid to hurt him because he was so hard. "What do you like?" she asked in her best sex-siren voice, delighted by this new, unexpected side of herself. She had never been so bold or brazen with a man and had to wonder why not. It sure was fun.

"I don't hate that," he said in a choked whisper, his head turned to one side, his eyes closed, his lips parted, his jaw tight with tension.

"How about this?" she asked as she slid her lips and tongue over the head of his penis.

He clutched a handful of her hair. "Yeah," he gasped, his eyes now open and focused on her. "That's good, too."

Georgie dipped her head and went back for more. Using her hand, tongue, and lips, she worked him into a frenzy.

"*Georgie,*" he groaned. "That's enough. Stop."

But she didn't want to. She wanted to do something she had never done before, something she had never *allowed* before. If she was stepping outside herself for one glorious night, why not go all the way? So when he begged her again to stop, when he warned her it was the last chance, she continued on, determined to take him over the edge.

It didn't take long.

Georgie stayed with him for every second of his almost violent release, thrilled to know she had driven him to it.

"God," he whispered as she kissed a path to his stomach and chest. Still breathing hard, he gathered her into his arms and held her tight against him. "What did I do to deserve that?"

She shrugged. "Just felt like it," she said as if it was something she did all the time. He didn't need to know it was one of several firsts for her on a night when anything seemed possible.

"Lucky me. Maybe it was the calamari. I'll have to make sure I feed you that next time, too."

Next time, she thought with a sigh, knowing there wouldn't be one. Like Cinderella at midnight, the morning would transport her back to where she belonged.

"Why the deep sigh?" he asked.

"No reason."

He propped himself up on one elbow and looked down at her. "You're wondering when you're going to get your fair share, aren't you?"

His smile was so sexy and almost cocky that Georgie had to resist the urge to drool. "The thought never crossed my mind."

"Is that so?" He slid a hand under her skirt and, in one swift move, had her dress up and over her head before she had time to determine his intentions.

"Oh," she said, acutely aware of her mismatched underwear and wishing she had taken Cat's advice to plan for this possibility.

"Mmm." He left a trail of hot, openmouthed kisses along the top of her panties. "Purple polka dots. Very sexy."

Saying a silent thank-you to Doug for dragging her to the gym every night after work and insisting on no fewer than two hundred crunches, Georgie took a deep breath as Nathan's lips traveled over her firm belly. "It doesn't match," she managed to say.

He looked up at her. "What doesn't?"

"Underwear."

"And was that intentional?"

"I'd hoped it would be an insurance policy to keep me from doing exactly what I seem to be on the verge of doing right now."

He laughed softly against her belly. "Let me say, for the record, I couldn't care less if your bra matches your panties, because you won't be wearing either of them for much longer."

His words, coupled with the movement of his lips over her fevered skin, had her writhing under him, clinging to him, on the verge of begging him. Through her bra, he closed his lips around a protruding nipple and tore a moan from deep inside her. "*Nathan,*" she pleaded.

"My friends call me Nate, and I'd like to think we're friends." As he spoke, he continued to nip and suck and tease.

"I like Nathan better." Somehow she managed to speak despite what he was doing to her breasts.

"Sweetheart, you can call me anything you want," he said, reaching behind her to unhook her bra, "as long as you call me."

His comment penetrated the aura of fantasy she had surrounded herself with, reminding her that he was a real man with real feelings, not the larger-than-life character she had made him out to be. If he was expecting more than this one night, they had a problem. That she had the potential to hurt him struck her hard. Placing her hands over his on her breasts, she said, "Nathan, wait."

He nudged their hands out of the way so he could get at her nipple with his lips. "What?"

"I don't want you to think . . ."

With a hard tug, he drew her deep into his mouth, rendering her speechless. Swirling his tongue over her nipple, he said, "Think what?"

"That this is more than tonight," she forced herself to say, knowing it had to be said. With her hands on his face, she forced him to look at her. "I'm dealing with a lot of complications right now. I can't handle another one. I don't want to hurt you or lead you on."

His jaw shifted slightly, which was the only indication he gave that he was wrestling with what she had said. "If that's how you want it."

"It is," she said, even though she ached as she said the words.

Shrugging, he returned his attention to her breast. "Then I'll just have to change your mind."

"Nathan—"

"Shh. I've been warned."

Unable to muster another ounce of protest, she fell back against the pillow and gave herself over to him as he used everything in his arsenal to bring her more pleasure than she could have imagined possible.

His broad shoulders forced her legs apart as he pressed his lips to her belly and then tugged at her panties with his teeth.

Georgie moaned and lifted her hips to help him get rid of them. His hands coasted over her legs, pushing them apart again, and coming to rest on her inner thighs. When he leaned in to nibble that sensitive skin, she cried out. He took advantage of her being distracted to sink his tongue into her.

"Oh my God." She sighed. "*God.*" Since he already had her hovering on the brink, it took only a few concentrated strokes of his tongue to send her flying. Clutching his shoulders, she held on for the most intense release she had ever experienced. She'd had no idea it could be like this, and even as she was in the midst of it, she had the presence of mind to wonder if she would really be able to walk away from him in the morning.

Before she could catch her breath, he brought his lips down on hers for a searing, sensual kiss that ensured he still had her full attention. "Let me get a condom," he whispered.

"I'm on the pill."

Shaking his head, he said, "As tempting as that is, condoms are nonnegotiable with me."

She let him up and watched him as he went into the bathroom.

He was back a minute later and pulled the sheet up and over them.

They lay facing each other, caressing, soothing, stirring. He pulled her tight against him and kissed her as if it was their first kiss all over again. "Georgie," he whispered. "I want you so badly. I've wanted you for weeks."

Startled, she said, "You have?"

He hooked her leg over his hip and slid his fingers through her moist center, denying contact to the spot that throbbed for him—again, already. "Did you really think I didn't notice you when I ran by every morning? I never used to go that way until I saw you there the first time."

Swallowing the lump forming in her throat, she said, "You didn't?"

He shook his head, brushed his lips over hers, and slid a finger into her.

Sucking in a harsh deep breath, Georgie arched her back and pushed against his probing finger.

Adding a second one, he kissed her softly. "What a nice surprise to realize who was stuffing Styrofoam into the Dumpster today. You can't imagine how sorry I was that I had upset you."

No! He doesn't mean that! He can't do this to me. He can't make this out to be more than it is. He'll ruin everything if he does that. Desperate to put the focus back where it belonged, she shifted onto her back and reached for him, encouraging him to take what she offered so willingly.

Poised between her legs, he looked down at her, daring her to look away as he entered her.

Georgie gasped and struggled to take in his hard length, which was more than she was used to—much more.

He went slowly until he was fully sheathed in her, holding still for a long moment during which Georgie let go of the worries and the fears and the lingering disgust over what she was doing and gave herself permission to feel.

And then, as if he had no choice, he began to move.

She raised her knees to take him deeper and cried out in shock when a climax slammed into her. Never before had it been so easy to get to that elusive place—never before had she gotten there so quickly. As he tightened his arms around her and let himself go, she had yet another reason to worry that her night of mindless sex wasn't going to unfold quite the way she had planned.

When Georgie awoke the next morning, she knew before she even opened her eyes that she was alone. Sun streamed in through uncovered windows as she lay there trying not to think about the night she had spent with him. But despite her best efforts, flashes and images that would be forever burned in her mind played like a movie—straddling him and riding him with abandon as he held her hands, his face buried between her legs, the intense way he had gazed at her each time he entered her. She had lost track of the number of times and ways and orgasms. There had been a lot of them.

With a groan, she rolled over to bury her face in the pillow and was greeted by a scream of protest from muscles unused to such frenzied activity. A piece of paper crunched under her elbow, and she raised herself up to look at it.

Georgie, thank you for the most amazing night. I'm sorry I had to leave for work so early. Believe me, I'd much rather be in bed with you. There's a coffeemaker in the downstairs bathroom that's all ready if you want a boost before you go, or there's OJ in the fridge. Make yourself at home, use the shower, anything you want. The door will lock behind you when you leave. I know you said this was a one-time thing, but I'd really like to see you again—and not just because of the s-e-x (which was incredible). Call me or come by the house if you change your mind. I'll think of you today. Probably tomorrow, too. And the next day.

Nathan

He had included his cell number at the bottom of the page. She released a pained sigh as she read the sweet note again. Why couldn't she have met him when things were normal? When she had room in her life for all the things he could be to her? Riddled with regret, she sat up, ran a hand through her tousled hair and, ignoring the protest from her sore muscles, darted naked into the bathroom, hoping his brother wouldn't choose this moment to come home. She eyed the shower with longing but decided to get out of there and take one at home.

His damp towel hung from a rack under the window, and she reached out to run her fingers over it. The air was heavy with summer humidity and his cologne, which made her want him like she hadn't had him all night. "Knock it off," she muttered.

Gazing at her reflection in the mirror, she saw puffy bags under her eyes from the all-but-sleepless night, red patches of irritation from where his whiskers had abraded her skin, and, oh *God,* was that a *hickey?* "*No,*" she moaned. Ashamed, she cast her eyes down to find a pile of shiny black condom wrappers in the trashcan. She couldn't resist bending over to count them. One, two, three. *No way.* Four. Her heart pounded, and her stomach surged with nausea as a fifth one appeared under the others.

Mortified by the discovery, she flushed the toilet and dashed back into his bedroom to find her clothes. Her dress was a bundled-up mass of wrinkles, her bra dangled from the end of the bed, and her panties were missing in action. Digging around in the sheets, she finally found them and tugged them on, certain she would never look at purple polka dots in quite the same way again.

Reaching for her earrings on his bedside table, she was swamped with longing. To see him just once more. To feel the way he made her feel, even if just for five more minutes. Was that too much to ask after what she had given him during the night? "You're the one who said it was a one-time thing," she mumbled as she stared at the earrings, which all but dared her to leave them there to give him an excuse to seek her out again.

Before she could change her mind, she slid on her flip-flops and left the room—without the earrings. In the hallway, she heard water running in the bathroom. She went in to find the toilet still flushing. When tinkering with the handle didn't take care of it, she lifted the cover off the back and fiddled with the plunger thingy, but couldn't get it to stay up to stop the flow of water. "He'll flip his lid if I leave it like this all day. I'll bet he's a freak about water conservation, too."

She looked around for something she could use to fix it. Feeling like she was invading his privacy, she opened the medicine cabinet. Mixed in with all the guy stuff, she found a box of dental floss. Her eyes darting from the malfunctioning plunger to the light fixture on the wall above the toilet, she mulled her options and decided there weren't any. It was this or nothing.

With only another moment of hesitation, she grabbed the dental floss, tied it to the plunger and hoisted it up with a knot around the light. Just for good measure, she added a second piece. Satisfied she had done what she could, she returned what was left of the floss to the cabinet, closed the door, dashed down the stairs and out the front door, hoping no one would see her as she left. She didn't take a deep breath until she reached the foot of Extension Street and hung a left onto Lower Thames toward Dean Avenue, back to her mother's house, back to her mother's job, back to the aftermath of her mother's death.

Chapter 5

As Georgie climbed the hill from Lower Thames, she checked her watch. Five minutes until nine. Hopefully, Cat and Tess had already left or were still sleeping and she could get in and out in time to be at the donut shop by nine thirty. She wasn't sure what she wanted more at the moment—a tall cup of coffee or a hot shower to wake her up and work out the knots in her aching muscles.

Rooting around in her purse for her keys, she scooted up the stairs.

"Well, well, well. Look at what the cat dragged in."

Startled, Georgie glanced over to where Cat lounged on the wicker sofa with the newspaper, a cup of coffee, and a smug smile.

"I thought you didn't drink coffee," Georgie said, desperate to talk about anything other than why she was sneaking into the house at nine in the morning.

"I had to do something to get the juices flowing. Jogger Guy was a no-show." Raising an amused, pierced eyebrow, Cat said, "Any idea why?"

"Nope. I took a walk this morning and stopped for coffee at the Handy Lunch."

"You are such a liar." Grinning, Cat put down her cup, stood up, and walked over to Georgie. "Is that a *hickey?*"

"*No!*"

Cat laughed. "Yeah, right. Let's see, we've also got some whisker burn." She took Georgie by the chin to get a closer look. "And judging by the suitcases under your eyes, I'd guess less than two hours' sleep. Am I right?"

Ashamed, Georgie diverted her eyes away from Cat's.

"Oh, you dirty, *dirty* girl!" Cat howled with laughter. "I'm very proud of you."

"*Stop,*" Georgie moaned. "It's awful. I can't believe I did this."

"Why the hell not? Was it good?"

Georgie gave her a withering look.

"The best ever?"

Reluctantly, Georgie replied with the slightest of nods.

"Then I repeat, what the hell is wrong with that?"

"I don't even know him, and there're so many reasons why it wasn't a good idea."

"Because of your boyfriend in Atlanta?"

"He dumped me yesterday."

"He's a putz. I could've told you that just from the way you've described him. He did you a favor—if he hadn't dumped you, you might've missed out on last night." Taking Georgie by the hand, Cat led her to the porch sofa and urged her to sit down. "Tell me everything. Leave nothing out."

Georgie's face heated with embarrassment when she remembered the five condom wrappers in the trash.

"Oh wow, so good your face turns red just *thinking* about it?"

"It was unbelievable," Georgie confessed, dying to tell someone. "I've never done anything even close to what I did with him. It was like I was someone else."

"Must've felt pretty good in light of all the craziness of being you lately."

Impressed by Cat's astute assessment, Georgie nodded. "I wanted to feel good again, you know?"

"I do know, and there's nothing wrong with that, especially after everything you've been through."

Georgie sat back with a sigh. "I just wish I didn't feel like such a total slut. I can't imagine what he must think of me." She shuddered.

"I'm sure he thinks he's one lucky son of a bitch."

"He left me the sweetest note this morning." She tugged it out of her purse and handed it to Cat.

Scanning the note, Cat looked over at Georgie. "Why did you say it's a one-time thing?"

"Because! I've got too much other crap on my plate, and I need to get back to Atlanta—soon."

"Listen, I know you're a couple of years older than me, but I've been around the block a few times, and I'm here to tell you, hot guys who're also sweet don't grow on trees. You'd be foolish to toss aside something that could be great just because the timing isn't ideal."

"It's not just that."

Cat continued on undeterred. "Clearly, you had a connection with him or you wouldn't have done what you did. I know you well enough by now to know that for sure. You should see where it takes you."

Georgie shook her head. "I can't let myself get involved with someone whose whole life is here when my life is somewhere else. I don't need any more pain or aggravation. I've had enough recently to last me a lifetime."

Cat handed her the note and stood up. "I hate to say it, but judging by the I-just-got-the-living-daylights-fucked-out-of-me look on your face, you're already involved."

Cat's words resonated with Georgie as she rushed through a shower and did her best to cover the hickey and stubble rash with makeup. A hickey. *When was the last time I had a hickey?* Ah, never. She'd had her share of boyfriends, but none of them had aroused in her the sheer passion that Nathan had—the kind of passion that led to biting. For all she knew, he had a few reminders of their night together on his neck, too.

Just thinking about it made her want him again as an image of him thrusting into her made her whole body flush with heat and desire. But one night didn't mean she was involved with him. They'd had sex—a lot of sex. So what? People did it, right? They did it and walked away all the time, so why couldn't she? She could. And she would.

Determined to put it behind her, she went into her disaster of a bedroom where the piles of clothes strewn about reminded her of getting ready the night before and of all her vows not to do exactly what she'd ended up doing. She dug through her dresser drawer in search of the oldest, rattiest pair of underwear she could find and slipped on a pair with a hole in the crotch. Perfect. Since she'd made the stupid decision to leave her earrings, she expected to see him at some point that day, at which time she would thank him again for the lovely evening, take a long last look at his handsome face, and send him on his way. With holes in her panties, there was no way she would be tempted to jump him again. No way.

Satisfied that she was as prepared to face the day as she ever would be, Georgie set out to get the donuts and open the center. By noon, she was struggling to stay awake as her sexcapades with Nathan continued to haunt her. While the seniors had their spaghetti-and-meatball lunch, she sat in her office and stared at the wall, remembering one time in particular.

He had turned her over to massage her back, and after he had caressed every inch of her, he'd dragged his tongue over her spine. Georgie had wriggled under him as he urged her to stay still. Grasping her bottom with his big hands, he had opened her to his tongue and had left no part of her untouched or unexplored.

The dark, erotic shock of it had sent her into an orgasm that made all the others pale in comparison. Then he had raised her to her knees and plunged into her from behind, riding the storm of her desire. Clutching her breasts, he had taken her hard and fast, and when he slid his fingers through her dampness, she came again. That never happened. Not to her anyway.

Just thinking about it made her throb with longing. Her mouth went dry, her heart beat fast, and her breath got stuck in her throat. If he walked in there right then, she would push him against the wall and beg him to take her, holes in her panties or not. The realization was both shameful and startling.

"Georgie!"

Bad Gus's booming voice jolted her out of her reverie. Her cheeks burned with embarrassment.

"Sheesh, where were you off to?"

"Nowhere." She cleared the hot ball of shame from her throat. "Right here. What can I do for you, Gus?"

"I brought you and your roommates some corn." He produced a big bag from behind his back. "And tomatoes."

Touched by his thoughtfulness, Georgie stood up to accept the bag from him. For all his bluster and bawdiness, Gus was generous to his friends, which now apparently included her.

"Thanks, Gus. That was really sweet of you."

Flustered, he said, "It's just corn. I used to bring it for your mother." He shrugged, but his eyes were sad.

Knowing her mother's death had hit the seniors hard, Georgie made an effort to change the subject. "Who're you wearing today?"

Gus spun around to show her his back. "Ellsbury. The center fielder."

He had a different Boston Red Sox shirt for every day.

"Oh, he's *cute.*"

Gus scoffed. "Cute. That's real critical to a winning team."

"We think so," she said, speaking for all women.

"Too many years doing the tomahawk chop down there in Hotlanta. It's messed up your head."

Georgie laughed, even though they'd had the conversation a hundred times before.

Walter came to the door. "Are you hitting on my best girl, Gus?"

"Ya snooze, ya lose, buddy," Gus said with a wink for Georgie.

"*Say it isn't so, Georgie,*" Walter moaned. "Tell me you can't be bought off for a couple of ears of wormy corn."

"Ain't no worms in my corn," Gus huffed.

Georgie smiled at their banter. They were as different as two men could be but were the best of friends anyway. Her mother had told her how Gus and his wife Donna had helped Walter through the loss of his wife a few years earlier.

"So what do you say, Georgie my love?" Walter asked with a teasing smile. "When are you going to let me take you out?"

"One of these days," she said as she always did.

"Remember what I told you," Gus said. "If he gets you into his car, it's not a date, it's a kidnapping."

Walter gave him a friendly shove.

"Roxy can get you a restraining order if it comes to that," Bill chimed in as he joined them.

Suddenly, Georgie had a party going on in her office. How her mother had ever gotten anything done here was a mystery to Georgie.

"Or that Caldwell fellow," Gus added. "He could help you get rid of a nuisance like Walter. The way I see it, he owes you one after yesterday."

Georgie tensed at the mention of Nathan.

"Don't bring it up," Bill said as Good Gus came in. "He was so obnoxious yesterday. I asked Roxy about him last night, and she said he's a good guy."

"Could've fooled us," Bad Gus grumbled. "Right, Georgie?"

"Um, yeah," she stammered.

"She doesn't want us teasing her about it," Walter said. "Leave her alone."

Georgie sent him a grateful smile. No, she didn't want to talk about Nathan Caldwell, or think about his fabulous, sculpted chest, or the feel of his rock-hard ass under her hands as he pumped into her. She crossed her arms over protruding nipples. Looking up she discovered the men staring at her.

"What's wrong?" Good Gus asked, his white eyebrows knitted with concern.

"She doesn't look good today," Bad Gus said. "Been saying that all morning."

"Are you sick?" Walter asked. "Your face is all red."

"Um."

"You should go home," Henry added.

Where had he come from?

"Yes, go on home, Georgie," Bad Gus said. "We'll lock up and drop the keys by the house. We did it for your mother when she had bronchitis last winter."

"Dad!" an angry voice yelled from the hallway.

The men exchanged glances.

"That'll be Roger." Good Gus cast his eyes down in embarrassment. "He's driving me to the doctor in Providence."

"Come on!" Roger called.

"Take care of yourself, Georgie," he said softly. To the others, he added, "Please excuse me."

After he was gone, Bad Gus swore under his breath. "That kid's an asshole. Can't even come in and be civil." Glancing at Georgie, he said, "'Scuse my language, honey."

Georgie held up a hand to let him know she'd taken no offense. "What's his story?"

"Been in and out of trouble for years," Bill said. "Drugs mostly."

"Treats his father like crap," Walter said.

"Last guy in the world who deserves it," Henry added.

The others nodded in agreement.

"No kidding," Georgie said. The information made her sad for Gus.

"Go on home," Bad Gus insisted. "We'll take care of things this afternoon."

"What about your bird watching?" she asked. Two weeks after she started, Good Gus had let her in on the secret—their daily walks to downtown Newport had nothing to do with birds and everything to do with girls.

"We can take a day off," Bad Gus said. "The birds aren't expecting us."

Desperate for sleep and an afternoon to herself, Georgie pondered their offer. "You'll have to clean up after lunch."

"We can do that," Henry assured her. He and his equally adorable wife Alice were always so helpful and eager to please.

"Will you do me one favor?"

"Whatever you want," Walter said.

"Put the Styrofoam trays in a separate bag? The Rec Center said we can put them in their recycling Dumpster until we get one of our own."

Her request was greeted with total silence.

"Is that a problem?" she finally asked.

"That Caldwell boy got to you, did he?" Bill asked, his eyes dancing with delight.

You have no idea. "Not at all. He makes a good point, though. You can leave the bags by the back door, and I'll take them to the Rec Center in the morning."

"We'll take care of it," Gus assured her. "Go on now. We'll see you tomorrow."

"Thanks, you guys," Georgie said with genuine appreciation. Taking the bag of corn and tomatoes, she walked out of the center a few minutes later and enjoyed a deep breath of fresh, summer air. On the short ride home, she tried her best to clear her mind and relax. Aching from head to toe, the first thing she planned to do was take a long bubble bath in the tub in her mother's bathroom, and then she would sleep—maybe until tomorrow morning.

Her cell phone rang, and Georgie reached for it while trying to keep her eyes open and on the road. She bit back a groan when she heard the voice of her boss—her real boss, the one in Atlanta. "How are you, Lorraine?"

"Overworked and under appreciated. Nothing new here."

"How's everything in the office?"

"Well, that's why I'm calling."

Georgie's heart began to beat faster. She had been anticipating this call from Atlanta. Lorraine and Doug must have been in conspiracy. Time was running out on both fronts.

"I need to know when you're coming back," Lorraine said without further ado.

"I wish I could say for sure. The city is trying to hire a replacement for my mother, and I have to appear in probate court next week for her estate."

"I admire what you're doing up there. I really do."

"They'll close the center if they can't find anyone," Georgie said, reminding herself as well as Lorraine. "My mother founded the place, gave it everything she had for more than twenty years. I can't let them close it down. I just can't. The people would be lost without it."

"I understand the predicament you're in, but I'm in one myself. We've got the fall lines coming in this week. You know how busy this time of year is. I need you, Georgie. Your staff needs you. They seem aimless without your leadership."

Georgie pulled onto Dean Avenue, which was deserted for once, and grabbed a spot in front of the house. "I need another couple of weeks, at the very least."

"Two," Lorraine said. "That's the best I can do. I'm sorry, Georgie."

Georgie knew it was highly unlikely that she would be free of her obligations in Newport in two weeks' time. "I'll do my best."

"I'd hate to lose you."

Georgie hated being lost. "I'll be in touch." She closed her phone, rested her head on the seat, and closed her eyes. With every passing day, her carefully crafted life in Atlanta slipped further away from her, and there wasn't a damned thing she could do about it.

She sat there for a long time considering her options, none of which was all that appealing. Finally, she decided to take action. Flipping open her phone, she called the city's recreation director.

"Mr. Andrews is in a meeting right now, Ms. Quinn. May I take a message?"

"Yes, tell him this: he can either talk to me now, or I'm going to camp outside his office until he does."

After a long pause, the assistant said, "Please hold."

At least three minutes passed before Richard's smarmy voice came booming through the phone. "Georgie, how lovely to hear from you. I do hope you and your sister are holding up well."

"We're fine, thank you, but I need to know what's being done to find a replacement for my mother at the center."

"We've had the ad running for a month now, with only that one candidate. I never did hear what happened when she visited the center. All I know is she stopped returning my calls."

The dirty old men happened, Georgie thought, as it dawned on her all of a sudden that they'd run the woman off on purpose so Georgie would stay. The realization took her breath away. *Oh my God! They'll never let me go!*

"Georgie?"

"You have to do more," Georgie said in what she hoped was a firm and authoritative tone. "I'm going back to Atlanta in two weeks, with or without a replacement for my mother."

"If you do that, we'll have to close the center," Richard said. He'd said the same thing two months earlier when he convinced her to take the job "temporarily." With her mother terminally ill, Georgie had been unwilling to watch her life's work fade away like it meant nothing.

"Two weeks, Richard. After that, it's not my responsibility anymore." Tomorrow she would tell the old men the same thing. They were *not* going to hold her hostage forever.

CHAPTER 6

Georgie straightened up her bedroom, folded the clothes she had strewn about the night before, and summoned the courage to open the door to her mother's bedroom.

"I can't put this off forever," she said as she stood in the hallway staring at the door for a long time. One of these days, she had to get busy cleaning out her mother's clothes and belongings. Not today, though.

With her hand resting on the doorknob, she finally took a deep breath and turned it. Here, more than anywhere else in the big house, she found her mother. Her scent, her clothes, the framed photos on her dresser, her jewelry box, her bathrobe. The memories and the pain hit Georgie like fists to the stomach, and she had to pause to absorb them before she could step into the room.

On an impulse, she took her mother's burgundy chenille robe with her into the bathroom to turn on the Jacuzzi tub her mother had installed a few years ago when she renovated and updated the bathroom.

Georgie soaked in the tub for close to an hour, and only when she began to doze did she rinse off the bubbles and snuggle into her mother's robe. With her hair wrapped in a towel, Georgie emerged from the bathroom and eyed the big four-poster bed.

So many nights as a child she had taken refuge there after bad dreams or thunderstorms. Before her mother had founded the center when Georgie was in first grade, they had whiled away many an afternoon in that bed reading Nancy Drew and Bobbsey Twins books that had cemented Georgie's life-long love of a good mystery.

Wondering if the bed would provide the same comfort without her mother, Georgie slid under the covers and pressed her face to the pillow where her mother's fragrance still lingered. Georgie could almost feel her mother's strong arms around her.

Despite her best efforts to relax, her mind raced with worries about the center, her job and apartment in Atlanta, what would become of the seniors if she left them, and what to do about the big house that needed constant care. She needed to get in touch with the attorney about the probate hearing next week, needed to pack up her mother's things, needed to do so much she was exhausted just thinking about it.

Not wanting to think about any of that right now, she allowed her thoughts to drift to Nathan. All her worries seemed to disappear as she relived her night with him—his tender touch and gentle kisses, how he had seemed to know just what she needed without being told. As she finally drifted off to sleep, she hoped he would bring those earrings to her soon. Then she would tell him it was over, really over.

Her ringing cell phone interrupted Georgie's nap. The sound seemed to be coming from somewhere far away, and for a moment, Georgie couldn't remember where she was. Then it came back to her in a rush of pain—her mother's death, her mother's room, her mother's bed. In the days since her mother's death, waking up and remembering it all over again had been some of the most painful moments.

Clearing the sleep from her throat, she reached for her phone. "Hello."

"Georgie."

"Al?" At the sound of her sister Alison's voice, Georgie sat up in bed. After what they'd been through together in the last few months, Georgie could tell with one word that something wasn't right with her sister. "What's wrong?"

"Georgie…"

"Are you *crying?* What? What is it? Is it Mom?"

"The blood test."

Georgie's entire body went cold, and she began to tremble. "No... No, I can't hear this."

Ali's sobs echoed through the phone from upstate New York to Newport. "I'm having the surgery. Next week."

"You need a second opinion! Maybe they made a mistake!"

"It's no mistake. Two labs have confirmed it."

"You didn't tell me about the second test—or the results of the first one."

"You've had so much to deal with there with the house and the center. I couldn't add to that." Ali sniffled. "You have to have the test, Georgie. *You have to.*"

"No." She said the word softly even though she wanted to shriek. Since their mother's diagnosis, the sisters had learned their family was cursed with faulty genes that made them much more likely than the general population to contract breast and ovarian cancer. If Georgie never again heard the BRCA acronym, it would be too soon for her.

"Mom had it, I have it," Ali said. "Grandma and Aunty Joan probably had it, too. Wouldn't you rather know, Georgie?"

"No! I would *not* rather know!" The thought of having her perfectly healthy breasts removed was so outrageous that Georgie had refused to even entertain the possibility. "Bonnie didn't have it," she said, referring to a cousin neither of them liked. "You shouldn't rush into anything. Maybe if you wait a year, they'll know more."

"I have two young children to consider. I'm not taking any chances that they'll have to grow up without a mother."

"But you're only thirty-five! Mom was sixty. *Come on,* Al! It doesn't have to happen right now."

"You heard the oncologist say that it's striking decades earlier in every generation of our family. I'm not risking it."

Georgie wiped tears from her cheeks. "What does Joe say?"

"That he'd rather live without my breasts than without me," Ali said, her voice catching on a sob.

"Are we ever going to wake up from this nightmare?" Georgie whispered. Ever since she'd gotten the call about her mother's diagnosis of advanced breast cancer three months ago, Georgie's life had spun out of control. And now this…

"Yes, we are. We're going to wake up and go on with our lives knowing we did everything we could to keep it from happening to us, too."

"It's different for me. You have a husband who worships you. What guy will want me if I have to have my breasts removed?" Georgie finally gave voice to her greatest fear—ending up sick and alone. She refused to allow herself to think about Nathan and what he might have to say about the matter.

"Any man who would value your breasts over your health isn't good enough for my baby sister."

"I'll come there," Georgie said, resigned. "When you have the surgery. I'll come and take care of the kids."

"No, you won't. I have Joe, and his mother will be with the kids. You've got enough to contend with there. I'll be okay."

"Ali…"

"It's all going to be fine," Ali said firmly. Georgie wondered who her sister was trying to convince. "I promise."

Georgie wished with all her heart that she could believe her sister. She had a feeling that things were going to get a whole lot worse before they got better.

"You'll think about having the test?" Ali asked.

"Yes," Georgie said, telling her sister what she needed to hear. She planned to put it out of her mind the minute they hung up.

"I'll have Joe call you after the surgery."

"I'll be waiting," Georgie said. "I love you."

"Love you, too."

Nathan sat at his desk, asleep with his eyes open. The day had been a total disaster, and all he could think about was going home for a quick nap before he went over to Georgie's to let her know this was *not* going to be a one-time thing.

Despite the intimacy they had shared, he barely knew her. But he wanted to. He wanted to know why she had come home to Newport, why she was working at the center, what her life was like in Atlanta, and if there was another man in the picture. *No. If she was seeing someone else, she wouldn't have slept with me. Well, slept is not exactly the operative word here.*

As a detective, he knew he could find the answers to many of his questions by making a few phone calls. After all, he worked for the same city that ran the senior center. But as he reached for the phone, he stopped himself. He wanted her to tell him herself.

He had felt something different for her the first day he ran by the big white house and saw the four women having coffee on the porch. Construction on Lower Thames had forced him to alter his usual route, and the detour led him right to their doorstep. He never had gone back to his old route. Since he was trained to notice everything and file away pieces of information that could be used to make cases later, the four lovelies had caught his attention right away. He liked knowing that they thought he never looked at them. Hell yeah he looked, and hell yeah he liked what he saw.

Thanks to Georgie's descriptions of them over dinner the night before, he could now put names to the other three. On his morning runs, Cat had caught his attention first with her spiky red hair, pierced eyebrow and well, those breasts were quite something. He was only human. He had also caught a hint of a tattoo. Fascinating. Tess had an almost ethereal beauty about her, and Georgie's sister Ali was striking, too. But he hadn't spent much time looking at any of the others after his eyes landed on Georgie. Remembering that first moment of impact—for that's what it had felt like—Nathan tried to recall the last time he'd had that kind of reaction to a woman.

Never, if he was being honest, just like he'd never had sex quite like what he'd had with her. He hadn't known he could be so free and uninhibited—nor had he ever encountered such a generous and willing partner. It was like he had found his perfect match. The thought made him sit up straighter in his desk chair. What if she was his perfect match? What if he discovered she was all that and more? What would he do when she went back to Atlanta?

"This is crazy," he muttered. "She said one night, and you're thinking about chasing her to Atlanta?"

"Talking to yourself, Caldwell?" his partner, Andy Hughes, asked as he plopped a file on Nathan's desk.

"What's up?"

"We've got a possible runaway. Sixteen, history of beating feet, but the parents claim she's turned over a new leaf lately. They don't think she went wherever she is willingly."

Nathan swallowed a yawn as he flipped through the report.

"What's with you today?" Andy asked. "You're like a zombie."

"Didn't sleep well last night." Since the happily married Andy was forever after Nathan to get a love life, he wished he could tell his partner the truth. But if there was one thing Nathan Caldwell didn't do it was kiss and tell.

"Why don't you head out? I'll go talk to the parents. It's on my way home."

Nathan looked up at him. "You're sure you don't mind?" Normally, Nathan would have jumped all over the case, but tonight he didn't have the energy.

"Nah. The uniforms said it sounds like a runaway, so I can handle the parents myself and then pass it to second shift. I'll let you know what comes of it."

"Thanks. I'm about to drop."

"I can see that. Talk to you in the morning, if not before."

Nathan didn't waste any time getting out of there. Unlocking his dark gray hybrid, he decided he was too old, even at just thirty-three, for an all-night sex fest. Without some sleep—and soon—he would probably keel over in the street.

On his way home, he tried to call the cell phone he had gotten his brother Ben so he could keep closer tabs on him, but as usual, Ben didn't answer. Frustrated, Nathan closed his phone and tossed it into the passenger seat.

The phone rang, and thinking it might be Ben calling him back, Nathan lunged for it. "Caldwell."

"Hey," his brother Ian said. "Any word from Ben?"

"No," Nathan said, dejected.

"What time was he due back?"

"I think they were taking the three-thirty ferry."

"I'm sure he'll turn up in the next couple of hours."

"I hope so."

"If he doesn't, give me a call. I'll help you look for him."

"Aren't you playing tonight?" Nathan asked.

"Nope. I'm off the next few nights to give my voice a rest. I'll be around if you need me, Nate."

"Thanks. I'm beat, so I'm gonna crash for a while. If you don't hear from me, he's home."

"Got it."

"Later." Nathan ended the call but kept the phone in his hand. He appreciated Ian checking in. Their whole family was worried about Ben, who had been badly injured in Iraq just over a year ago and was having trouble getting his life back together.

Nathan resisted the urge to drive by Georgie's house on his way home and trudged into his own house, unclipped the badge from his belt, and shrugged off his shoulder holster on the way upstairs. In his bedroom, he stashed the gun and badge in the bedside table drawer and found Georgie's earrings. He picked them up and let the metal slide through his fingers, remembering the way they had dangled from her delicate earlobes.

As he put them back on the table, he wondered if she'd discovered yet that she had left them. He had known women who would leave a souvenir behind to ensure a follow-up call, but Georgie wasn't like that. Besides, she had been adamant that theirs was a one-night stand, so why would she bait him by leaving her earrings?

He reached up to unbutton his shirt, and the memory of her doing it for him the night before stopped him in his tracks as it became clear to him that one night with her wasn't going to be enough. In fact, he feared a month of nights might not be enough to work her out of his system.

Still absorbing the realization, he stripped down to boxers and went into the bathroom, where he once again stopped short. The cover was off the toilet and sitting on the floor. *What the hell? And what the heck is that hanging from the ceiling? Is that . . .* He leaned in for a closer look. *Dental floss?* And then he laughed, a deep belly laugh that made his sides ache and brought tears to his eyes. The damned toilet acted up on a regular basis, but he had forgotten to mention it to her. Suddenly, sleeping wasn't as important as it had been a few minutes earlier. He simply *had* to see her. Right now.

The bedroom door opened slowly, and Tess poked her head in. "Oh, hey, you're awake."

"Hey, what's up?" Georgie had barely moved since the call from her sister. Despite her best efforts to push it from her mind, the dilemma weighed more heavily than ever after getting her sister's grim news.

"I heard you had a big night out," Tess said with a grin that told Georgie she knew the whole story. "I made some dinner and thought you might be hungry."

Georgie realized she was famished. "That sounds good. Thanks. I suppose you're going to want all the gory details in exchange for this dinner you made me."

"Well, *yeah,*" Tess said as she left the room. "Ready in five minutes."

Georgie puffed up the pillow and smiled. She adored Cat and Tess and felt like she had known them for years rather than months. It had been a long time since she'd had girlfriends she enjoyed as much as them. Her high school friends were scattered about the country, and her college friends had either left Atlanta or gotten married and had families. The women she worked with were fun, but she spent most of her work time with subordinates and didn't hang out with them as a rule.

The few women she did socialize with in Atlanta she had met through Doug, and he would no doubt get them in their breakup. Not wanting to think about him, Georgie got up and crossed the hall to her own room. Hanging her mother's robe on the back of her door, she put on shorts and one of the soft cotton camisoles she slept in. She ran a brush through her hair, splashed some cold water on her face, and headed downstairs.

"Oh, wow, something smells really good. What did you make?"

"I grilled some chicken to go with that corn you brought home."

"Bad Gus at the center gave it to me."

Tess chuckled. "What does he think of that name?"

"It's well earned, believe me." Georgie opened a bottle of chardonnay and poured them each a glass as Tess sliced Gus's big tomato.

Georgie fingered the soft petals of a stargazer lily in the bouquet Nathan had given her. "Thanks for doing this. I haven't eaten all day."

The minute they sat down at the table, Tess sent her a pointed look. "Anything you want to tell me?"

"Anything you don't already know?"

"It's always so much better coming from the horse's mouth," Tess said with a wicked grin.

Taking a long sip of her wine, Georgie glanced at her friend over the top of the glass. "The short story is—he chewed me out about not recycling at the center, apologized later with the flowers, asked me to dinner, I went, we had fun, he asked me to come to his house so he could show me the work he's done to it, we had sex—a lot of sex, really, *really* good sex—which I have never, *ever* done before on a first date, and I felt like a total slut all day today. That's it."

Tess's mouth hung open, her eyes agog.

"What?"

"All Cat said was you went out with Jogger Guy."

Georgie groaned. "*Shit.*"

"Well," Tess said, giggling. "This is an interesting development."

"Don't get too excited. It was a one-night thing."

"Why?"

"I'll tell you the same thing I told Cat—in light of everything else that's going on, I don't need the complication."

"Why does it have to be complicated?"

How could she explain that this had complicated written all over it from the moment she first saw him running by and wanted to lick the sweat from his back?

"Why can't you just have some fun with him while you're in town?"

"Come on, Tess. You know it never works out that way. People get their feelings involved, and it gets messy when it ends. I don't need that, and I'm sure he doesn't, either. Besides, I've already done, well, everything there is to do with him. How do we go back to just 'having fun' after that?"

Tess raised an eyebrow. "*Everything?*"

"No stone was left unturned."

"Wow." Tess took a big gulp of her wine. "I need a cigarette."

Georgie cracked up.

The doorbell rang.

"I'll get it," Tess said.

She left the room, and Georgie dove into the spicy barbecue chicken.

Tess returned a minute later. "Georgie, you have a visitor."

With barbecue sauce smeared on her face, she looked up to find Nathan Caldwell watching her, his bright blue eyes dancing with amusement.

"Hello, Georgie."

Looking away from him as her face burned with embarrassment, she grabbed a napkin. "What are . . . I mean . . . why are you here?" She hated the stammer that infected her voice as she tried to spit out the sentence. How did he manage to turn her into a stammering fool just by walking into the room? It was so unfair!

"I was wondering if I could borrow some dental floss."

CHAPTER 7

Tess looked from one of them to the other. "Dental floss? I don't get it."

Georgie burned with mortification.

Nathan turned to Tess. "You must be Tess." He extended his hand. "Nathan Caldwell. Nice to meet you."

Flustered, Tess shook his hand. "Oh, well."

Georgie rolled her eyes. Apparently, he had *that* effect on all women, not just her, which was yet another reason to keep her distance.

"Georgie and I were just having dinner," Tess said. "Why don't you join us?"

"I'd love to."

"But—" Georgie said.

"Georgie, serve the salad." With another pointed look, Tess handed her three bowls.

Flashing Georgie a satisfied grin that told her he knew exactly how uncomfortable he was making her, Nathan plopped down in the chair next to hers. "Oh, is that corn on the cob? I'll really need floss after that."

"Okay," Tess said as she brought another plate and silverware to the table, "what's with the floss? Or do I not want to know?"

"Nothing kinky," Nathan said with a chuckle that earned him a glare from Georgie. "I have this temperamental toilet in my house, and apparently it gave

Georgie some trouble this morning, because when I got home, I discovered she'd used half a box of floss to tie the ball cock to the light."

Georgie, who had been attempting to chew a bite of chicken, choked at the casual way he tossed the word cock out there, like she hadn't spent hours riding his the night before.

Tess laughed. "You get an A for ingenuity, Georgie."

"After the hissy fit he had over Styrofoam yesterday, I figured he'd flip out if I let the water run all day," Georgie mumbled.

"You figured right," Nathan said as he dug into his salad with gusto. "You did a good job. But if that happens again, you can just shut off the water by turning the valve underneath the toilet."

Refusing to even glance at him, she said, "It won't happen again."

"You never know."

Suddenly, they were no longer talking about toilets. "Yes, I do."

"Do you want something to drink?" Tess jumped up. "I can't believe I didn't offer you anything."

It took everything Georgie had not to groan at the way Tess was fawning over him, like he was a celebrity in their midst instead of her one-night stand. *One night. Do you hear that, Nathan Caldwell?*

"Have you got a beer?"

"Sure do." Tess opened one of Cat's Budweisers and brought it to him.

"Thank you," he said with a warm smile that made Tess sigh.

Really, this was the most disgusting display of foolishness Georgie had ever witnessed.

"So, Tess, Georgie tells me you're not from around here."

"That's right," Tess said, getting busy with her food.

"Where are you from?"

"Western Connecticut."

"What brought you to Newport?"

"I was ready for a change of scenery. I'm a nurse, and they had an opening at Newport Hospital in the ER, which is my specialty, so I snapped it up. End of story."

The way she said it told Georgie there was more to the story—much more—and she wasn't a detective. She wondered if Nathan had sensed it, too. *Who cares what he senses? Just get through dinner so you can get rid of him.*

"I'll bet you've seen just about everything as an ER nurse," he said.

"You know it. What do you do?"

"I'm a detective with the NPD."

When Tess's eyes flipped up to gauge whether he was serious, there was no mistaking the flash of panic. "Oh," she said on a long exhale.

After an awkward pause in the conversation, they all got busy finishing their dinner.

"That was the best home-cooked meal I've had in a long time, ladies. Thank you."

"It was all Tess," Georgie said, unnerved by her friend's odd behavior. Was she running from the law? It certainly seemed like she was hiding something. Would Nathan think so, too? "I'll clean up."

"I don't mind," Tess said.

"That's not fair. You cooked. Besides, I'm sure you've got better things to do with a rare night off than cooking and cleaning for me."

"I do have some bills to pay." She got up, rinsed her plate, and put it in the dishwasher. "It was nice to meet you, Nathan," she said on her way out of the room.

"You, too." When they were alone, he glanced at Georgie. "What just happened here?"

"I have no idea."

"How do you know her?"

"She answered an ad I placed for roommates."

"Why were you looking for roommates if you're only here temporarily?"

Cornered, Georgie stood up and started to clear the table.

He came up behind her and rested his hands on her shoulders.

She froze. "Don't."

Turning her around to face him, he said, "Tell me what's going on here, Georgie. Nothing you've told me adds up, and you've got a roommate who's clearly running from the law or something else. I'm a cop, for Christ's sake. How do you expect me to just pretend that didn't happen?"

Rattled by his touch, she shrugged his hands off her shoulders. "That's exactly what I expect you to do. Whatever's going on with her is none of your concern."

"What if she's in some kind of trouble?"

"That's her business. She's been nothing but a good friend to me since the day I met her."

Stymied, he tried a different line of questioning. "Why are you taking in roommates and working at the senior center if your life is in Atlanta?"

"That's my business."

He shook his head. "You're not going to give me a break, are you?"

"I told you." She forced herself to look up at him and tried not to notice the way his soft gray T-shirt fit snugly against his chest or the golden stubble that sprinkled his jaw. The memory of him thrusting into her picked that moment to show up—again. She swallowed and said, "One night."

He stared down at her with intense blue eyes. "We had a connection, Georgie. I know you felt it, too. Aren't you at all curious about that?"

"It was just sex. Don't make it into more than it was."

"I've had 'just sex,' and I'll bet you have, too." He ran his hands up and down her arms as he spoke. "This was more than that, and you know it."

Horrified when her nipples responded to his touch, she pushed him away. "It wasn't more."

A flash of hurt darted across his handsome face.

"Don't do that!"

His eyebrows knitted with confusion. "Do what?"

"Give me that hurt face. That's exactly what I'm trying to avoid. I'm going back to Atlanta in two weeks. I don't have time for this."

"You won't make time, you mean."

"What's the point?" she asked, furious at the hitch in her voice. "It can't go anywhere."

Apparently encouraged by her emotional response, he reached for her and brought her in close to him. "You don't know that. You can't know if you don't take the chance and find out."

Once again she worked herself free of his embrace. "I'm not interested. I'm sorry if that hurts your feelings, because that's not my intention. I had a wonderful time last night, but there's no room in my life right now for this kind of thing. I'm sorry."

He reached into the pocket of his cargo shorts to retrieve her earrings. Taking her hand, he dropped them into her palm and curled her fingers around them. "Thanks for dinner." He held her hand for a long moment before he released it, tipped her chin up, and brushed a light kiss across her lips. "See you around, Georgie Quinn."

Watching him leave, Georgie wanted to chase after him. "Wait!" she would say. "I didn't mean it! Don't go!" But she couldn't seem to make herself move. Engulfed in sadness, she heard the front door close behind him. *It would've been nice.*

Not interested. *Not interested?* Oh, she was interested, all right. He could see it in the way her eyes had widened in the instant before he kissed her. He could see it in the way she'd had trouble swallowing her food with him sitting as close to her as he dared to get without actually touching her. Yes, she was interested. Maybe she just didn't realize it yet.

Nathan made his way down Dean Avenue and hooked a right to head home. On an impulse, he decided to stop for a beer at O'Brien's and was surprised to find Ian sitting at the bar.

"What're you doing here?" he asked his brother. "Where's Rosie?"

"At a sleepover at Caroline's," Ian said, referring to his three-year-old daughter's best friend. He gestured to his cell phone on the bar. "I'm waiting to get the call that she's ready to come home."

Nathan smiled.

"She doesn't get that the *over* part means overnight."

"Soon enough she will, and then you'll never see her."

"I know." Ian's hair was darker than Nathan's and laced with some gray, but he had the same blue eyes the six Caldwell brothers had gotten from their father. "What brings you out tonight? I thought you were bushed."

"I was. I *am*. Just having a quick one." He signaled the bartender, who brought them two draught beers.

"No sign of Ben?" Ian asked.

"Not when I was home earlier. I'm hoping he'll be there when I get back."

Nathan's cell phone rang. With a signal to Ian, he took the call when he saw it was his partner. "Hey, Andy," he said on his way outside to the sidewalk. "What's up?"

"Sorry to wake you."

"Haven't been to bed yet."

"Oh good. So, listen, I talked to the missing girl's parents. I'm leaning toward believing she didn't run away."

"Yeah?"

"She's really made an effort in the last year to clean up her act, like the parents said."

"What do you want to do?"

"The parents said she spends a lot of time online. They let me take her computer, and I've already got our guys working it up."

"I think I know where you're going with this."

"Exactly. McKee and Jones are talking to her friends as we speak, trying to find out if she had mentioned going off with someone she met online or anything like that."

"Amber Alert?"

"I'm going to hold off until we see what the computer yields."

"Probably a smart move." Law enforcement officials saved the missing child notification system for the most dire of circumstances so it wouldn't lose its impact by becoming routine. Since Nathan trusted the two detectives on second shift, he didn't feel the need to rush in. "Keep me posted. I'll come in if you need me to."

"I'm heading home for now. McKee knows to call me if they get anywhere with the friends. If I hear from him, I'll call you."

"Cool. Thanks for the update." Nathan returned his phone to his pocket and went back inside.

"Everything all right?" Ian asked.

Sliding onto the barstool, Nathan reached for his beer. "That was Andy about a case."

"You look like shit, man." Ian took a closer look at his brother. "Did you work last night?"

"Nope."

"Something's up."

Nathan shrugged and trailed his fingers through the condensation on his glass. "If I tell you, do you promise not to be well . . . *you?*"

Hooting with laughter, Ian said, "I'll do my best."

"There's this girl."

Ian let out a low whistle and raised his glass in toast to his brother. "Well, thank you, *Jesus*. It's about freakin' time."

"Is that you doing your best?"

Ian sobered. "My apologies. Please continue."

Despite himself, Nathan smiled. Ian, who was three years older than him, was his favorite brother and the one he felt closest to. There was no one he'd rather discuss this with, and Ian knew it. "There's not much to say. I like her, I know she likes me, we had one great night together, but she doesn't want it to go any further. Frustrating, you know?"

"What's the hang up?"

"She lives in Atlanta, and she's only here for a couple more weeks. But tell me if this sounds weird to you—she says she's here temporarily, but I know for a fact she recently advertised for roommates."

"That is kind of odd. You don't know what her deal is?"

"Nope. She flat out told me it was none of my business."

Ian chuckled. "Sounds like she's got spunk."

"She does, but I know there's something going on. I get all these strange vibes when I'm with her, and you know how I am about my vibes."

Ian rolled his eyes. "You've built an entire career around them."

"Exactly."

"I hate to point out the obvious, but you *are* a detective, bro. Why don't you do some digging around? Won't take long in this town to get her story."

"The thought's occurred to me, but I don't want it that way. I want her to tell me. I want her to *want* to tell me."

"You like this chick, huh?"

"Yeah. There's something about her." Nathan chewed on the inside of his cheek as he thought about Georgie.

"What's she look like?"

"Blonde, kind of petite but not tiny. She has these great, big expressive eyes that are sometimes green and sometimes gold. And dimples. Really, really cute dimples." Nathan smiled when he remembered that Georgie hated to be called cute.

"Hmm," Ian said, sizing up his brother with knowing eyes.

"What?"

"Nothing."

"Knock it off. What were you going to say?"

"I was told I can't be *me,* so I'm refraining from comment."

"*Ian!*"

Laughing, Ian said, "Fine, if you must know, I think you're falling for this girl who wants nothing to do with you."

"No, I'm not. It's not like that."

Ian's raised eyebrow begged the question.

"I just want to get to know her. That's all."

"I've never known you to give up easily."

"She was pretty adamant."

"So?"

Nathan glanced at his brother in time to see a big lazy grin stretch across his face. "Are you suggesting I make a nuisance of myself?"

After taking a chug of his beer, Ian said, "At the very least. That's what we Caldwells do best."

"True." Nathan studied his glass for a long moment before he turned to his brother again. "I really lost it with her the other day. Big time. She was jamming Styrofoam into a Dumpster, and I totally flipped out."

Ian winced. "Uh-oh."

"My reaction was way over the top. Hasn't happened in a while."

"That doesn't mean you need to worry about that being an issue again. Something made you mad, so you reacted. Nothing wrong with that."

"I can't go back there. It took me so long to get to the point where I didn't let my temper rule my life."

Ian put his hand on Nathan's shoulder. "You had a very good reason for letting your anger get the best of you, but that was a long time ago. It's okay to get pissed off once in a while as long as you don't let it go too far."

Nathan nodded in agreement even if he didn't entirely agree. He'd made it his mission in life not to allow himself to get pissed about anything. That was how he kept the demons at bay.

Ian's cell phone rang.

He picked up the phone, checked the caller ID, and smiled. "Right on schedule. Hi, Cheryl, is she ready to come home?" He laughed, paused for a moment, and said, "I'm walking so I'll be there in twenty minutes." Closing the phone, he said to Nathan, "Another aborted sleepover."

"Poor baby. Give her a kiss from Uncle Nate."

"Will do."

"I need to spend some time with her soon. It's been too long."

"She'd love that." Ian finished his beer in one long swallow. "If your vibes are telling you this girl likes you, Nate, don't give up. She'll come around."

Wishing he could be as optimistic, Nathan shook his brother's hand. "Thanks."

"Anytime. Let me know if you hear from Ben."

"You got it."

Nathan arrived home thirty minutes later and was relieved to find Ben slapping together a sandwich at the table they were using while the kitchen was under construction. The tallest of the Caldwell brothers, Ben's dark hair was now shot through with silver, and his once-athletic build had been diminished by his injury. He'd been pulling frequent disappearing acts since being released from the facility where he rehabilitated his shattered leg.

"How was Block Island?" Nathan asked.

"Fine."

"Who'd you go with?"

"Some guys I met at Brick Alley," he said, referring to a pub in town.

"Anyone I know?"

"Jeez! What is this, Nate? An interrogation?"

"No." If anyone tested Nathan's hair-trigger temper these days, it was Ben. "I'm just interested in who you're hanging out with."

"I could say the same thing."

"What's that supposed to mean?"

Ben's face twisted into the hard smile that was new since Iraq. "Who've you been getting it on with?"

"What're you talking about?"

"*Five* condoms? I wouldn't have guessed you had it in you."

Nathan cursed under his breath. He should've emptied the trash before he left. Used to living alone, it hadn't occurred to him.

"So who is she, and what's with the floss spider web in the bathroom?"

"None of your business."

"Must be something," Ben said with a whistle. "*Five times.*"

"Drop it, Ben."

"Stay out of my face, and I'll stay out of yours, *Detective.*"

"Fine." Summoning every ounce of hard-won self-control he possessed, Nathan started up the stairs. He missed the old Bennett, the person his brother had been before he had gone to war and narrowly missed being killed by a roadside bomb that took the life of his friend. Nathan knew Ben was dealing with grief and survivor's guilt and more pain than any of them could imagine, but his nonstop prick routine was getting old.

Nathan gave Ian a quick call to let him know Ben had resurfaced and went into the bathroom to deal with the toilet situation. As he cut the dental floss and fixed the malfunctioning toilet, his thoughts returned to Georgie—the way she tasted, her soft skin, those sizzling kisses. The memory of her clutching him from within as she reached a shattering climax made him instantly hard.

He would be lying if he said he didn't want another night in bed with her. But he had liked talking to her, too. The sharp sense of humor he'd seen fleeting glimpses of, those dimples. He loved those dimples.

Ian was right. He couldn't let her slip through his fingers without a fight. Tomorrow he would get busy trying to convince her that he was worth a shot. *They* were worth a shot.

CHAPTER 8

Georgie finished cleaning up the kitchen, left a light on for Cat, and started up the stairs to the third floor. Before her mother got sick, she had been making plans to rent out the two bedrooms up there, so leasing them to Cat and Tess had been easier than it might have been otherwise. Both rooms were already furnished, and the bathroom they shared had been updated.

Georgie knocked on Tess's door.

"Come in."

She opened the door to find Tess writing checks at her desk.

"Did Nathan leave?"

"Yes."

Tess pushed her glasses up to the top of her head and turned to Georgie. "He's as nice as he is good looking."

"Uh-huh." Georgie picked up a framed photo from Tess's dresser. "Is this your family?"

"My parents and sisters."

Before she could lose her nerve, Georgie turned to her friend. "Are you in some sort of trouble, Tess?"

"Not the kind that Nathan Caldwell needs to worry about."

"Then what kind?" Georgie asked as she returned the photo to the dresser.

Tess's lovely gray-blue eyes glistened. "If I refuse to tell you, will you ask me to leave?"

"Of course not, but I'd like to think we've become friends over the last few months. After all you did for us when my mother was sick, I hope you know I'd do anything I could to help you."

"That means so much to me, Georgie. You and Cat and Ali have just been . . ." She shook her head when she couldn't continue. "A godsend," she finally managed to say.

"For me, too. I don't know what we would've done without you these last few months, Tess. I wish there was something I could do to repay you for that."

After a long pause, Tess looked up at her. "You already know my marriage ended badly."

"Yes."

"I needed a fresh start."

"Do they know where you are?" Georgie asked, gesturing to the photo.

Sadness radiated from Tess as she shook her head.

"Does anyone?"

"No," Tess whispered.

Suddenly, Georgie had a better picture of what Tess's marriage had been like.

"What if he finds you?"

"He won't," she said firmly. "He can't."

"This is why you got nothing in the divorce. You went into hiding."

"There was no divorce," Tess confessed. "I was too . . ."

Georgie crossed the room, urged Tess to her feet, and brought her over to sit with her on the bed. "What, Tess?"

"Afraid." Tess raised her skirt to show Georgie a series of scars on her leg. "He did that to me with a cigar. There're others."

Horrified, Georgie hugged Tess. "Nathan sensed there was more to the story than you were letting on. He'd help you if you asked him to. I know he would."

Tess shook her head. "I'd never take the risk that Kurt would find me. I'm so happy here with you and Cat. I love my job and this town is so beautiful. I just want to start a new life here. I'd never get married again, so it doesn't matter that I didn't divorce him."

"Will you promise me something?"

Wary, Tess said, "Okay."

"Two things actually—will you tell Cat what you've told me so she knows to be vigilant, too, and will you come to either or both of us if you're ever afraid again?"

Tears ran down Tess's pretty face as she nodded.

Georgie held her for a long time before she pulled back and wiped away Tess's tears. "You're not alone anymore."

"Thank you, Georgie." Tess gripped her hand and paused before she said, "Can I ask *you* something?"

"Sure you can."

"Why oh *why* will you not go out with Nathan again?"

"I told you why."

"I don't care what you say, the man is gaga over you, and if I had an adorable, sexy, obviously kind-hearted man looking at me the way he was looking at you during dinner—"

"He was *not* looking at me. He was too busy flirting with you."

Tess laughed. "Are you *jealous?*"

"Oh, *please.*" With a dismissive sweep of her hand, Georgie said, "If you want him, he's all yours." But as she said the words, something twisted in her gut—something that felt an awful lot like jealousy. *I am* not *jealous!*

"As much as I appreciate the offer, it's not me he wants."

"We talked after you left, and I set him straight. He won't be coming around again."

Tess raised a skeptical eyebrow. "You don't think so?"

"I know so. It was a one-night stand and nothing more."

"Got yourself convinced of that, do you?"

"What's more important is I finally have *him* convinced of that."

"We'll see."

"How can I even think about starting something with a guy right now? I can't drag Nathan or anyone else into the insanity that's my life."

"These things don't always happen when it's convenient, Georgie."

"It's not going to happen. Period."

"Do you really think Nathan is the kind of man who would value a woman by her breasts?"

Once again, Georgie went cold from head to toe. "How do you know about that?"

"I have eyes—and ears. Not to mention I'm a nurse. Your mother talked to me about it before she died. She was very concerned about you putting off the test and paying for it later. She asked me to talk to you about it—when I felt the time was right."

"Ali tested positive," Georgie said, still finding it hard to believe. "She's having the surgery next week."

"Oh God." Tess wrapped her arms around Georgie. "I'm so sorry, Georgie."

"I just want to go back in time before any of this happened."

"You need to have that test. You have to know what you're dealing with."

"I just try to imagine a scenario where I end up having the surgery and then having to tell a guy I'm dating that my breasts are fake."

"I ask you again—do you think Nathan, for example, would care about that?"

"How do I know? I just met him."

"I only had dinner with him, and I already know he's made of better stuff than that. Much better stuff."

Overwhelmed by it all, Georgie stood up. "I'm going to bed."

"I'm here if I can help."

"That means a lot to me. It really does."

"Are we still allowed to partake in jogger stalking?" Tess asked with a grin.

"Knock yourselves out, but I doubt you'll be seeing him again."

"Oh, I think we'll see him. In fact, I'd bet my life on it."

Georgie walked away to the sound of Tess's laughter, which didn't bother her at all. If teasing her made Tess feel better, that was fine. After what Tess had told her—and shown her—Georgie felt like punching something. That her own husband could've treated her that way. Sweet, loving Tess.

George lay awake for a long time thinking about Tess and Nathan Caldwell, and how much she had liked having sex with him, how much she wished they could do it again, how she wished she had never heard of the BRCA genes, and how, with every passing day, she was becoming more entrenched in her "temporary" life in Newport.

Georgie took her time in the morning. On the off chance that Nathan did run by, she wasn't going to be out there waiting for him. She waited until well past his usual time before she finally ventured downstairs. Drawn by voices coming from the front porch, she went to the screen door and had to stifle a gasp. He sat in *her* place on the sofa, drinking coffee with *her* roommates, who were laughing like silly fools at everything he said.

Even Cat seemed bewitched by him. Was she batting her eyelashes? *Cat? So disappointing. I expected better from her.*

"Hey, Georgie," Tess said with a smug "I told you so" grin. "Look who stopped by."

"With coffee," Cat added with a grateful smile for Nathan.

Georgie noticed he was dressed for work in a striped cotton shirt and faded jeans with his badge clipped to his belt.

"There's one for you, too," Tess added, pointing to the coffee.

Nathan never looked her way or even acknowledged she was there.

"No, thanks," Georgie said through gritted teeth.

He stood up. "Well, ladies, this has been nice, but I need to get to work. Got a missing teenager who'll no doubt dominate my day."

Despite her efforts to remain detached, Georgie wanted to know more and was grateful when Tess asked.

"We've got a bad feeling she hooked up with someone online and went off to meet him," he said, his expression grim.

"God," Cat said softly.

"Yeah. I've got to run. I'm meeting my partner in ten minutes to talk to the parents again."

"Good luck," Tess said. "Will you let us know how you make out?"

"Sure. Hopefully, I'll be able to run in the morning, and I'll stop by to give you an update."

Oh groovy, Georgie thought.

"See you then," Cat said. "Thanks for the coffee."

"My pleasure. Have a good day."

Georgie watched him bound down the stairs and was furious when a blast of lust went streaking through her at the sight of his perfect ass encased in perfectly faded denim.

"He is *so* nice," Tess said with a dreamy smile.

"For real," Cat added. "I wouldn't mind a shot at him myself."

"Feel free," Georgie snapped as she finally stepped onto the porch.

"She said the same thing to me last night," Tess said to Cat, "but she didn't mean it—either time."

"Yeah, he's totally lusting after you," Cat said to Georgie. "I don't know what kind of sex tricks you pulled on him, but he's got it bad."

"He does not! He never even looked at me! And I didn't pull any 'sex tricks' on him. I don't even know what a sex trick is!"

"For someone who seems so smart most of the time, you can be awfully dense." Cat shook her head with amusement. "You really think that coffee was for *us?*"

"You're the ones who were out here drinking it with him like two simpering fools. I didn't even know he was here."

"From the minute he got here, his eyes were darting back and forth to the door hoping you'd make an appearance," Tess said.

"*You saw that, too?*" Cat squealed.

"Ugh! Enough! I'm going to work. I don't want to hear another word about him." Georgie looked from one of them to the other. "Do you hear me?"

"Sure, boss," Cat said with a teasing smile. "Whatever you want."

"That's what I want." With a defiant glare at Cat, Georgie snatched the lone cup of coffee remaining in the cardboard carrier and marched down the stairs. She had no idea what she would do with the next hour, but she wasn't going to spend it listening to the two of them telling her how crazy she was to be holding Nathan at arm's length. She knew what she was doing—and she knew *why* she was doing it.

Their laughter followed her up the hill to her car.

At eleven o'clock, when most of the seniors had gathered for the day, she called a meeting of the core group, minus Good Gus, who hadn't arrived yet.

"Close the door, please," Georgie said to Walter.

The old men formed a subdued half circle in her office.

"Now I want you to listen to me, all right?"

Perplexed by her stern tone, they nodded.

"I know you loved my mother. She loved you, too. Her work here gave her life meaning and purpose. Long before I ever met you all, I knew you from her stories, her descriptions, her affection for you."

When their emotions got the better of them, several looked down at the floor.

"I, too, have come to care for you very much. You're a fun group, and I enjoy seeing you every day. But this is not my life's work. My life, my work, is in Atlanta, and I need to get back to it before there's nothing left. I've worked very hard to get where I am today, and I can't watch eight years of my life go up in smoke. The city is working to find a new director for this place, someone who'll provide the kind of leadership you need. I'm not cut out for this."

"That's not true, Georgie!" Bad Gus protested.

"You're doing an excellent job," Henry added. "We say all the time that your mother would be so proud of you."

The others nodded in agreement.

Georgie swallowed the lump in her throat. "I appreciate that—more than you know. But it doesn't change anything. I'm leaving in two weeks, whether the city has found a new director or not." Despite their despair, she forced herself to soldier on. "If they haven't, they've said they'll close the center. Since none of us want to see that happen, can you not run off the next candidate they send over? Please? I'm begging you."

They exchanged guilty glances.

Their mumbles included, "I guess so," "If that's what you want," and "We'll try."

"Thank you. That's all I wanted to say." She watched them exchange another round of glances. "What?"

"We're worried about Good Gus," Bill said. "He's not here today, and no one's heard from him. That's not like him."

"Maybe he's just taking a day off," Georgie said. *Who could blame him?*

Walter shook his head. "He'd never not show up without telling one of us."

"Did you call him?"

Bad Gus nodded. "No answer."

"I asked Roxy to swing by his house," Bill said, "but they've got some missing kid sucking up all their time, so she couldn't do it."

"That's Lloyd Turner's granddaughter," Henry said gravely.

"Is it really?" Bill asked. "Oh man."

"So, um, about Gus. " Bad Gus said with a pointed look at the others to get them back on the subject.

All eyes landed on Georgie. "What? You want *me* to go over there? No way." She shook her head. "I'm not disturbing that poor man if he's decided to sleep late or watch TV by himself for a change."

"But Georgie—"

"But nothing. If you want someone to go over there, it needs to be one of you. You're his friends."

"So are you," Walter pointed out.

She couldn't deny that, but still, she wouldn't feel right about going to his house. "I'm not doing it. Sorry, guys, I'm drawing the line. Call his son."

"That asshole won't care," Gus growled.

"I'll go over there after lunch if he still hasn't shown up," Walter offered, and the others seemed satisfied—for now—with that solution.

"Can we ask you something else?" Henry asked tentatively, as if he sensed she was about to lose it.

"Yes," Georgie sighed.

"You, um, you booked the entertainment for the social tonight, right?"

"That's *tonight?* You said the last Friday of the month."

Walter pointed to the large wall calendar.

Where in the hell had July gone? And where in the hell was she going to drum up entertainment on such short notice? "It's all set," she lied. "They're coming at seven."

"You'd better make it six," Henry said. "We start early because no one can stay awake past ten."

"I'll call them to make it earlier."

"Who'd you get?" Bad Gus asked. "That Big Band guy? We liked him."

Swallowing hard, Georgie said, "It's a surprise." She forced a smile for effect.

Satisfied, they filed out of her office. The moment they were gone, Georgie pounced on the phone to call Cat.

"Hey, grumpy," Cat teased. "What's up?"

"Very funny."

"What I don't get is what you've got to be grumpy about after getting a full oil and lube job this week."

"I never should've told you what happened with him."

"Probably not," Cat chuckled. "So what's up?"

"I need a huge favor. Can you find me someone to play at the senior center tonight? Six to ten?"

"Tall order on a Friday in July."

Georgie groaned. "*I'm so screwed.* My mother told me to do it weeks ago, but I totally forgot."

"I'll ask around and see what I can do. No promises, though."

"It's for old people. Don't forget that. No acid rock or anything that'll shock them, okay?"

Laughing, Cat said, "Gotcha. I'll make some calls and get back to you."

"Thanks, Cat. I owe you one."

"No prob."

CHAPTER 9

Cat called back an hour later to tell Georgie she had found someone for the social. "He plays a lot of hokey folk music," Cat said with disdain. "But based on the audience, I figured that was better than some of the other options."

"Sounds perfect. Tell him to be here by five to set up."

"Want his name or anything?"

"Nope. As long as he has a pulse and a guitar, I couldn't care less what his name is."

Cat laughed. "I'll come by later to check him out. If he's as good as I hear he is, maybe I'll book him at the club, even though his kind of music doesn't do it for me."

"Definitely come by. You can take a turn dancing with the dirty old men."

"No way, babe."

"No one is safe around them. They'll go *wild* over you."

"*Great.*"

"Thanks again, Cat."

"Happy to help. So, hey, Georgie, is everything all right with you? I mean, other than the obvious?"

Georgie wanted to tell Cat about the gene test, but since talking about it made it real, she chose evasion. "Nothing other than everything, but thanks for asking."

"I'm sorry you're having such a rough time. If there's anything I can do. . ."

"You already have. I'll see you tonight?"

Cat groaned. "I'll be there."

Georgie ran home at four to shower off the stink of steak tips and onions and to change into a sundress to keep her cool in the stifling center. Tess came in from work as Georgie headed back downstairs. "Oh good! Another warm body."

Tess eyed her warily. "What's that supposed to mean?"

"Big party at the center tonight. Come with me so I don't have to dance with all of them the way I did last time."

"Thanks, but I'll pass."

"Please? *Pretty* please? I'm desperate."

"Friendship only goes so far, Georgia Quinn."

"I'll beg if I have to."

After a long pause, Tess poked a finger at her. "If one seventy-year-old paw wanders south of the border, I'm out of there. You got me?"

"Deal," Georgie said with relief. "Hurry up and get changed."

"Um, Georgie, did you hear the news? About Nathan and the teenaged girl they were looking for?"

Georgie froze. "No," she said, suddenly having trouble getting air to her lungs. "What?"

"They found her in a hotel room on Connell Highway with some guy she met on the Internet."

"How do you know?"

"They brought her—and Nathan—to the ER."

Georgie gripped the banister. "What happened to him?"

"The guy who had her fired at the cops—"

"Nathan was *shot?*"

"Grazed. On the arm. He'll be sore, but he's fine."

"Oh," Georgie said, exhaling a long deep breath. "Good. And the girl?"

Tess shook her head with disgust. "She was adamant that it was consensual, but that's not how it appeared to us. He was rough with her."

Georgie's stomach turned. "God."

"A forty-four-year-old man with a sixteen-year-old girl."

"Horrifying."

"Thank God they found her when they did. Who knows what else he had planned for her."

Georgie bit her thumbnail as nervous energy coursed through her. "Do you think I should . . ."

"What?"

"Nothing. Never mind."

"Do I think you should check on him?" Tess asked. "Yeah, I do. I'm sure he'd appreciate it."

"Too girlfriendy."

"Just because you slept with him doesn't mean you can't show some basic human compassion."

"*Jeez,* Tess. Do you *have* to put it that way?"

Tess shrugged.

"Fine! I'll think about it. I've got to get back to the center before the inmates take over the asylum."

"You're really going to make me go?" Tess whined.

"Basic human compassion, Tess. Show me some, will you?"

Tess laughed and went upstairs to get changed.

They arrived at the center as Cat's guy was setting up a portable amplifier and microphone. Georgie went over to him. "Hi, I'm Georgie, the interim director." Clinging to the word "interim" was critical to her sanity. "Thanks so much for doing this on such short notice."

"Ian." As he took her outstretched hand, he smiled, his blue eyes crinkling at the corners in a way that reminded her of . . . *Stop!*

"No problem. I was off tonight, so it worked out okay. I hope you don't mind that my brother is going to bring my daughter by."

"Of course not. The seniors invite their kids and grandkids to these things, so there'll be other kids here."

"Great, thanks. She doesn't get to see me play out very often because I'm usually in bars."

"Happy to have her. So you do know a song or two they'll recognize, right?"

He laughed, and again she was reminded of Nathan. The man was haunting her!

"I'm sure I've got something they'll like. What time does this go 'til?"

"Ten. I'll get you a check. Is three hundred okay?"

"It's on the house. My grandfather loved this place, and the people here made the last years of his life so special. It's the least I can do to pay it forward."

Touched, Georgie said, "Thank you." Hearing that reminded her of why she was here, fighting to keep the center open and her mother's legacy alive.

Tess walked up to them and handed Georgie her cell phone. "It was ringing."

"Ian, this is my roommate, Tess."

They shook hands and exchanged greetings as Ian's warm blue eyes skirted over Tess with interest.

"Want to help me with the snacks?" Georgie asked Tess.

"Sure."

After they had walked away from Ian, Tess rested her hand on Georgie's arm. "Why does he seem so familiar?"

"That's so weird! I was thinking the same thing!" Georgie didn't add that Ian reminded her of Nathan because she didn't want to get Tess started on that subject again.

"He's cute," Tess said.

"He thought you were, too."

"Shut up," Tess said, giving Georgie a friendly shove.

With the party in full swing, Georgie emerged from the kitchen carrying two huge bags of ice.

"Cold front," one of the seniors, Tommy Dawson, announced. "We've got a cold front coming through." The group he was sitting with cackled as Georgie rolled her eyes at them.

After she had replenished the ice in the coolers, Georgie stopped to say hello to Henry's wife Alice. Beside her sat Bill's wife, Annette—an eighty-year-old redhead who looked and acted thirty years younger. Fond of her gold and diamond jewelry, Annette had a reputation for hiding her romance novels behind decorative covers so no one would know what she was reading.

"Georgie, honey, you've got the world's whitest legs," Marion Sorenson, who had the darkest tan Georgie had ever seen, said as she plopped down with the others. Marion and her husband Don were the youngest-looking "seniors" in the place.

"Do yourself a favor and stay out of the sun, Georgie," Annette said, her porcelain complexion a testament to a life spent practicing what she preached. "She's going to pay for all her sunworshiping."

"Hasn't caught up to me yet," Marion said.

"What are they up to?" Alice asked, gesturing to the old men huddled in the corner. Alice had a trim, athletic build, pretty gray hair, and bright blue eyes.

"Good question," Georgie said. "I'll go see." As Ian sang "Feeling Groovy," she approached the men. "What's up, you guys?" Their expressions grim, they expanded their circle to include her.

"Still no word from Gus," Henry said.

Ashamed to realize she had forgotten all about Good Gus being "missing," Georgie turned to Walter. "Didn't you go over there?"

He nodded. "His car was there, but he didn't answer the door."

"I called Roxy," Bill added. "She promised to go by his house after her shift ends. I guess they had some excitement today. Did you hear?"

All eyes fell on Georgie as she nodded. "Let me know what Roxy says." She turned away from them and gasped when she saw Nathan come through the door with his arm in a sling. An adorable little girl with blond ringlets held his other hand. Behind him, a man on a cane scowled as he followed Nathan into the center.

Nathan looked up to find Georgie staring at him.

His smile stopped her heart.

Leading the child, Nathan crossed the room to where Georgie stood riveted. He never took his eyes off her, as if he were afraid she might get away if he did.

"What . . . What are you doing here?" That damned stammer again! Ugh!

He nodded toward Ian. "My brother."

"Oh," Georgie said as the whole thing clicked into focus. The musician brother, a single dad who looked enough like Nathan that Georgie had all but recognized him.

"This is my niece, Rosie."

Georgie squatted down. "Hi, Rosie. I'm Georgie."

"Nice to meet you," Rosie said, extending her hand.

Charmed by her manners as much as her cherubic cheeks and big blue eyes, Georgie shook hands with the girl.

"That's my daddy," she said, pointing to Ian.

"So I heard. Do you want to go dance with the other kids?"

"Can I, Uncle Nate?"

Georgie's heart contracted at the worshipful gaze Rosie directed at Nathan.

"Sure you can. Just stay where I can see you."

Rosie scampered off to say hello to her father.

Her eyes fixed on Rosie, Georgie stood up. "She's beautiful."

"I think so, too."

"How old is she?"

"Almost four."

She finally ventured a glance at his injured arm. "Are you . . . I mean, I heard what happened."

He watched her but didn't bail her out.

Forced to look up at him, she said, "Are you all right?"

"Just a scratch."

"Looks like more than that to me." His face was paler than usual, his pupils dilated, and it took everything Georgie had not to throw her arms around him. Despite her efforts to stay removed, the relief at seeing him whole and healthy was overwhelming.

He nodded at Tess. "She made me wear the damned sling. Said it would take the pressure off the scratch."

"Did the 'scratch' require stitches?"

"A few."

"How many?"

"I didn't count."

"I'll ask her if you don't tell me."

"Thirty-two inside, twenty-six outside." He flashed her the smile she now recognized as the Caldwell grin. "Satisfied?"

"You call that a *scratch?*"

"Why, Georgie Quinn, you almost sound concerned. That makes getting shot worth it."

She rolled her eyes. "You're insane."

"Dance with me."

She looked up to find his gaze steady and intense. "I can't. I have to get more punch." As she started to walk away from him, his good arm hooked around her waist to bring her back.

"Please?" he said with a childlike pout. "I got shot today. It's the least you can do."

Her hands had landed on his chest. "Are you seriously going to play that card?"

"Whatever it takes."

Ian picked that moment to launch into "And I Love You So."

With inquisitive glances directed at her and Nathan, the old men claimed their wives and headed for the dance floor. Walter tapped Tess on the shoulder, and she followed him with a glare for Georgie.

"Just one dance," Nathan said.

Her traitorous body was already moving with his. "You seem to have trouble understanding the one-time concept. Are you sure one dance will be enough?"

"No," he whispered in her ear, sending a tremble through her. "I'm quite certain it won't be."

"Nathan."

"Shh." With his injured arm between them, he tightened his hold on her. "This is my parents' song. Ian played it for them at their fortieth anniversary party a couple of years ago."

"He's really good."

"Isn't he? He's been playing and singing for as long as I can remember."

Relieved to be back on safer ground, Georgie decided to keep him talking about his family. Maybe then she would be able to ignore the press of his erection against her belly. "Who's that pouting by the door?"

He sighed. "My brother Bennett. I made him come with me in case Rosie needed something I couldn't do for her with the bum arm. I figured that with three good legs and three good arms between us, we could take care of her."

"I take it he wasn't too happy about a dance at the senior center."

"Right you are. I, on the other hand, couldn't get here fast enough when Ian told me where he was playing tonight. Nice how it all worked out, isn't it?"

"Coincidental is a better word," she said dryly.

"Depends on your perspective. From where I'm standing, nice is the operative word."

Georgie couldn't deny that it did feel nice to be held by him, even if it was a one-armed embrace. Then his hand traveled up her back to cup her neck in a gesture so intimate and tender, she almost swooned with desire. This was a huge mistake. Letting him hold her like this would only encourage him. She pressed on his chest in an effort to get free of him.

He just tightened his hold. "The song isn't over yet," he protested.

"I have stuff I need to do."

"One more minute."

With her hands resting on his hips, she tried to think about anything but the spicy, woodsy scent she would always recognize as his. As he moved them to the music, the memory of how his skin had felt against hers came rushing back. Feeling a pull stronger than anything she had ever experienced, she glanced up to find him looking down at her.

"What are you thinking about?"

Because she couldn't very well admit to reliving the thrill of being naked and horizontal with him, she said, "When I heard you got shot today . . ."

"What?" he asked, his tone urgent.

"I . . ." She swallowed and forced herself to meet his gaze. "It scared me."

His smile unfolded slowly across his handsome face. "It's not a declaration of your undying love, but I'll take it. For now."

CHAPTER 10

Nathan watched her stalk across the big room and disappear into the kitchen. He had rattled her, which was quite satisfying. Despite her best efforts to stay aloof, she wasn't immune to him—far from it.

Since Tess was swinging Rosie around on the dance floor, Nathan joined Ben on the sidelines.

"Is Blondie five-condom girl?" Ben asked.

Nathan resisted the powerful urge to deck him. "Shut up, Ben." He took deep cleansing breaths the way the counselor had taught him to do anytime he felt the red haze of rage coming over him.

Ben laughed. "She didn't seem all that into you, if you ask me."

"Did I ask you?"

"Who's the chick with Rosie?"

"Georgie's roommate, Tess."

"I take it Georgie is Blondie?"

Nathan gritted his teeth and nodded. He had no interest in talking to Ben about Georgie.

Ben whistled under his breath. "And who is *that?*"

Nathan followed Ben's glance to find Cat talking to Georgie.

"Their other roommate, Cat."

"Meow."

"Ben, I swear to God."

"Relax, Dad. I'm just looking."

Tess left Rosie dancing with the other kids and walked over to join her room-mates. Nathan couldn't deny that the three of them made a fetching picture. A blast of jealousy caught him off guard as he realized every man in the room—old and young—was focused on Georgie and her friends. He wanted to grab her and get her out of there before someone else did.

"Introduce me," Ben said.

"No way."

"I'll behave. I promise. Come *on*, Nate. Don't be greedy. You can't have them all to yourself."

"One nasty comment or inappropriate word and I'll throw your ass in jail."

"Scout's honor," Ben said gravely, but the glint of the devil in his eyes kept Nathan on edge.

Reluctantly, he led Ben over to where the three women talked with their heads bent together.

"How's the arm?" Tess asked.

"Fine. Good as new."

"It's going to hurt like hell when the painkillers wear off."

He shrugged. "I'm tough. I can take it."

Ben nudged him.

His teeth gritted, Nathan said, "Cat, Tess, and Georgie, this is my brother, Ben."

"Bennett Caldwell." Ben leaned on his cane and shook hands with each of the women. "But please call me Ben."

Nathan wanted to puke at Ben's phony act, but he kept his expression neutral.

Ian took a break and strolled over to join them, holding Rosie in his arms.

Nathan repeated the introductions. As he watched his brothers decide which of the three women they wanted to get to know better, Nathan was desperate to get Georgie out of there and off their radar.

"Thanks for taking the gig on such short notice," Cat said to Ian.

"Any friend of Tony's is a friend of mine," Ian said. "He said you were in a real pinch."

"She was," Cat said, referring to Georgie.

"So how long have you managed the Underground?" Ian asked as he put Rosie down to play with the kids.

With their common interest in the Newport club scene fueling their conversation, Ian and Cat wandered toward the refreshment table.

"Excuse me," Georgie said. "I have some calls to return." She scooted off to her office.

Ben gave Nathan a "get lost" look.

He was reluctant to leave Tess with Ben, especially in light of the vibe he had gotten from her the other night. If she was in some sort of trouble, the last thing she needed was to be stuck with Mr. Trouble himself. Several times during his visit to the ER, Nathan had tried to get a minute alone with her to pursue it further, but she had dodged him—almost as if she had known what would happen if he got her alone. That was enough on its own to confirm his suspicions. Something was definitely up with her.

Keeping half an eye on Ben and another on Rosie, Nathan wandered toward Georgie's office.

"But Lorraine!" he heard her say in a tone that startled him. "You said two weeks! It's only been two *days*."

Nathan leaned against the wall outside her office and eavesdropped.

"He can't just do that. It's not like I *want* to be here." Georgie paused to listen. "I know you did. Yes, I know. I'm sorry, too. You have no idea *how* sorry."

What the hell? Nathan wondered. *Who's Lorraine?*

Georgie slammed the cell phone down on her desk.

Nathan ducked his head around the corner to find her staring off into space, her green eyes big with dismay. "What's wrong?"

She glanced over at him but looked right through him. "I just got fired."

"From the center?"

Shaking her head, she said, "Davidson's."

"Oh." Not sure if he was welcome or wanted, Nathan got a quick fix on Rosie hanging off Ian's leg before he went into Georgie's office and propped himself on her desk. "Is there anything I can do?"

"Not unless you know the regional manager, a jerk named Terry Paulson, who ordered my boss Lorraine to replace me with Nina what's-her-name from Savannah. She's been after my job for years. Well, she finally succeeded in getting rid of me."

"I'm sorry."

"Me, too. Eight years down the drain."

"You'll find something else. With all that experience."

She shrugged, her shoulders stooped in utter defeat.

Nathan hated seeing her that way. "Come on out with us," he said with a cajoling smile. "There's nothing you can do about it tonight, so why don't you try to have some fun?"

"I'm not in the mood."

Not knowing what else to do, he reached for her hand and was relieved when she didn't pull away from him.

"Thank you," she whispered as she released his hand a few minutes later. "I'm okay."

Sensing she wanted to be alone, he stood up. "You know where I am if I can help, right?"

She nodded.

As Nathan headed for the door, Bad Gus burst into the room. "Roxy called Bill." Gus's eyes were wide with shock and disbelief. "It's Good Gus, he's hurt bad. Someone broke into his house and beat the crap out of him."

Georgie leaped to her feet. "No," she gasped. "*No.*"

"They're taking him to Newport Hospital."

She bolted for the door.

Gus's hands on her shoulders stopped her. "It's bad, honey." His rheumy eyes filled. "Roxy said it's bad."

Nathan rested his hand on her back as Gus gathered her into his arms. His eyes met Nathan's over the top of her head.

"I'll drive you," Nathan said.

Georgie stepped back from Gus and turned to Nathan. "But your arm."

"It's fine." He shepherded her out of the office. "Come on."

The news about Gus cleared out the center, leaving Cat, Ian, Rosie, Ben, and Tess in the big room.

"Go on ahead," Tess called to Georgie. "We'll clean up and lock the door."

The others nodded in agreement.

"Thank you," Georgie said, battling hysteria. *How could she have let this happen? They had asked for her help, and she had blown them off. Her mother would have rushed over to Gus's house and broken down the door if she'd had to. She certainly wouldn't have let that sweet man lie there all day hurt and alone.* Unable to stand the pain of it, she finally broke down. Nathan's strong arm encircled her shoulders as he led her to his car.

On the short drive to the hospital, the guilt ate at her. "This is all my fault," she whispered.

"How do you figure?"

"They knew something was wrong, but I didn't do anything. I should've called the police or gone over there myself. That's what my mother would have done. If he dies . . ."

Nathan worked his way out of the sling, tossed it over his shoulder into the back seat and reached for her hand. "If he dies, the only one to blame will be the person or people who broke into his house and beat him up."

Georgie clutched his hand and took comfort in his strong presence. How easy it would be to rely on such a steady and dependable man. "They'll find them, right?" she asked softly.

"We'll get them," he assured her. "And we'll make them pay."

"He's a lovely man. He's my friend."

Nathan squeezed her hand. "Hang in there, sweetheart."

This would have been a great time to remind him that she wasn't his sweetheart, but as he held her hand and offered comfort, she couldn't bring herself to say it. For a little while, she would give herself permission to lean on him.

The emergency room was mobbed with seniors awaiting word of their friend. They were so worried, they failed to make mention of Georgie arriving hand in hand with Nathan. That more than anything told Georgie how grave the situation was.

Nathan led her over to talk to a tall police officer with curly hair and big blue eyes. She stood with Bill and Annette Bradley. "Georgie, this is Sergeant Roxy Bradley," Nathan said.

"Georgie Quinn," she said as she shook hands with Roxy. "I work at the center. Do you know anything about what happened?"

"From what we were able to ascertain at the scene," Roxy said, "he walked in on a robbery in progress. The house was tossed pretty thoroughly. We've got crime scene people working it up now."

"How'd they get in?" Nathan asked.

"Jimmied the back door."

"That's why Walter didn't notice any trouble," Georgie mumbled more to herself than the others.

"How's that?" Roxy asked.

"Walter went over to check on Gus when he didn't show up at the center today. They said it wasn't like him to not come without letting one of them know he wouldn't be there. They were worried, so Walter went over there. He said Gus's car was there, but he didn't answer the door. I guess Walter didn't check the back."

"I'll talk to him," Roxy said. For Nathan's benefit she added, "Walter is one of my dad's best friends."

"Have the doctors said anything about Gus's condition?" Georgie asked.

Roxy shook her head. "They were trying to get him stabilized last I heard."

Georgie's stomach dropped at that news, and Nathan tightened his grip on her hand.

"How you hanging, Nate?" Roxy asked. "I heard you were target practice earlier."

Nathan shrugged. "No biggie."

"Quite a scene you walked in on in that hotel, huh?"

His jaw clenched with tension as he nodded.

"Good thing you got there when you did. Nice work, Detective."

"It was a team effort," he said modestly. "Any word on how she's doing?"

"They're keeping her here overnight. Her parents are with her."

"Good."

"I'm going to go talk to Walter," Roxy said. "Nice to meet you, Georgie."

"You, too."

After Roxy left them, Nathan led her away from the others and wrapped his arms around her. "Relax, Georgie."

"I can't."

He massaged her shoulders. "Try."

"Your arm has to hurt. You shouldn't be using it so much."

"Let me worry about that."

Unable to resist the comfort he offered, Georgie rested her face against his chest. "Why did this have to happen? Who could've done this to such a sweet old man? He wasn't bothering anyone."

"I've been around it for years, and I'm still surprised by what people are capable of."

Georgie raised her head and looked up at him. "What happened today?"

"I'm not really supposed to talk about it."

"What if you *need* to talk about it?"

He framed her face with his hands and ran his thumbs along her jaw. "You make me ache, Georgie Quinn."

His softly spoken words and gentle touch went straight to her heart, and she found she couldn't look away from him even though she knew that standing there staring at him was not doing a damned thing to advance her "don't get involved" campaign. She wondered if he'd still want her so much if he knew about the threat to her health. He'd probably run for his life if he knew the truth. Who could blame him?

Their intense moment was interrupted by a flurry of activity in the hallway. Georgie heard someone mention the ICU as a gurney rolled toward the elevator. She glanced down at the patient, and only a patch of snow-white hair identified him as Gus. His face was black-and-blue and swollen almost beyond recognition.

Georgie released a muffled gasp. "Oh God! Oh *Gus.*" When she was able to move again, she bolted for the door, certain she was going to be sick if she didn't get out of there immediately. Nathan and several of the seniors tried to stop her, but the moment she cleared the door, she took off running.

Georgie walked for hours. She figured if she just kept moving, she could somehow manage to avoid hearing any more bad news. It was laughable, really. Her mother died, her sister was having a double mastectomy, her own life might depend on the results of a blood test, her boyfriend dumped her, her boss fired her, Gus was attacked.

Could it get any worse? *Gus could die. No! He's not going to die. He can't. He can't do that to me.*

She found herself at the top of Dean Avenue and stood there for a long time before she could make herself take the first step down the hill. Exhausted to the bone, she couldn't go on anymore. Besides, she was only postponing the inevitable. "Please, God," she whispered. "Don't let him die. Please."

As she approached the house, she came to a halt at the foot of the stairs when she found Nathan sitting on the top step waiting for her.

They both spoke at once.

"What are you doing here?"

"Where've you been?"

Georgie folded her arms and looked down at the sidewalk. "Did he die?"

"Not that I know of, but I've been looking for you for the past two hours."

"You didn't have to do that."

"Yes, I did. Are you okay, Georgie?"

She shrugged. "I don't even know what that is anymore."

"Why didn't you tell me your mother died?"

Her jaw shifted from side to side as she looked up at him. "The night we spent together . . . I wanted a break from having to think about it."

He reached out to her. "I figured she was away on vacation or something. I'd never even heard she was sick."

Georgie took his hand and let him guide her up the stairs to sit next to him. "It happened fast, and she didn't want people to know how bad it was, so we kept it quiet. She worried about her friends at the center more than she worried about herself."

"I'm sorry for your loss." He cradled her hand between both of his. "And for what it's worth, I think you're doing an admirable thing trying to keep the center open. My grandfather all but lived there the last few years of his life."

"Ian told me." She paused for just a heartbeat, but it was long enough to make the decision to trust him. "For weeks I've been going there every day, doing what needs to be done, trying to get through the days until they could find someone to take my mother's place. And all that time I thought the job was beneath me, like I was too good for the place or something."

"I can see why you'd think that. You worked hard for the career you have in Atlanta."

"*Had,*" Georgie reminded him. "But it wasn't until tonight, at the hospital, that I realized I'm the one who's not good enough for them. My mother would've gone to find Gus. She would have searched for him until she found him, and maybe she would've gotten to him before he spent a day lying on a hard floor fighting for his life."

"Don't do that to yourself, Georgie. You're doing the best you can."

"*But it's not good enough!*" she cried. "Don't you see?" In a whisper, she added, "It's not good enough."

He wrapped his arms around her and held her tight against him as she sobbed.

She cried until her eyes hurt and her chest ached.

He surprised her when he scooped her up and carried her inside.

Georgie glanced up to find his face tight with pain. "You shouldn't be doing this, Nathan."

He forced a smile. "Which way to your room?"

She directed him up the stairs. Embarrassed and touched, she took a stab at levity. "Do I need to be worried about what your brothers have done with my roommates?"

"Nah. They'll take good care of them."

"If they're anything like you, my friends are lucky."

He laid her down on the bed. "Why, Georgie Quinn, was that a compliment?"

She kept her arms looped around his neck. "Stay with me for a while?"

"I can do that." He stretched out next to her and extended his good arm to bring her close to him.

Georgie rested her head on his chest. "Does your arm hurt?"

"Like a bastard. Tess was right."

Alarmed, she lifted her head so she could see his face. "Don't you have pain pills?"

"In the car. I'm okay."

"Want me to go get them for you? There's no need for you to suffer."

"I'll go, but if I do, can I come back?"

She smiled weakly. "Yeah."

He kissed her forehead. "In that case, I'll be right back."

CHAPTER 11

Tess wiped the counter between the kitchen and common room at the senior center while keeping an eye on the rest of the cleanup committee.

Cat sidled up to whisper in her ear, "Ian asked me to go have ice cream with him and the rug rat."

"Don't call her that," Tess scolded. "Her name is Rosie, and she's adorable."

Cat shrugged. "Everything's pretty well cleaned up, so, um, I guess I'll go with them, okay?"

"You can't leave me here with him." Tess frowned as she looked over at Ben hobbling around the center pushing chairs into tables.

"He's harmless."

"How do you know that?" Tess hissed. "You met him an hour ago."

"He's Nathan's brother. That should be good enough to vouch for him."

"Something about him makes me nervous."

"Then why don't you leave at the same time as us? You can drive Georgie's car home."

"Are her keys here?"

"I saw the tennis ball on her desk."

They shared a smile. Georgie was forever losing her keys, so Cat had affixed a tennis ball to the ring to help her keep track of them.

"You're really going out with Ian?" Tess asked with another nervous glance at Ben.

"It's just ice cream. He's got the kid with him, so that's all he can do."

"Rosie," Tess said. "Her *name* is Rosie."

Cat screwed up her face with distaste.

"What've you got against kids?"

"It would be easier to tell you what I *don't* have against them."

"That's terrible!" Tess said. "I've never known anyone who doesn't like kids."

"Now you do."

"If that's how you feel, you shouldn't go out with him at all."

"Why not? We'll get her ice cream and then hopefully she'll leave us alone so I can get to know him better. He's gorgeous, isn't he?" Without waiting for Tess's reply, Cat added, "Seems to be a Caldwell family trait."

"Except for dark and stormy over there." Tess nodded toward Ben, who used his good leg to kick the last of the chairs into place.

"He's not exactly tough on the eyes, either. Don't let his crankiness put you off."

"Too late."

"Hey, Cat," Ian called. "Are you coming?"

Cat glanced at Rosie and then at Ian. "Sure. Count me in."

"Be nice to her," Tess whispered.

"Yeah, yeah."

"I'm leaving, too," Tess said loud enough for Ben to hear.

"Do you mind if I hitch a ride with you?" Ben asked. "Ian's going the other way, and I can't walk home yet."

Tess watched as Cat disappeared out the door with Ian and Rosie. "Um, sure, I guess. Let me get the keys." She went into Georgie's office, grabbed the keys, and turned off the lights. At the end of the long hallway, she locked the back door and flipped the dead bolt. Her heart began to beat faster as she contemplated the long, dark corridor that led to a room where a man she didn't know waited to get into a car with her.

"Walk, Tess," she whispered. "One foot in front of the other. He's Nathan's brother. Nathan's brother. We like Nathan. He's cute and funny. Nathan likes Georgie. Keep walking. Almost there."

She found Ben bent against the wall massaging his thigh.

"Ready?" Tess asked in a bright tone.

He startled, and when he stood upright, the expression of sheer agony on his face stopped her cold.

"Are you all right?"

His lips were white with pain. "Yeah," he said through gritted teeth. "Just a muscle spasm."

She rushed over to him. "I'm a nurse. I might be able to help."

"Don't," he said sharply.

Startled, Tess pulled back her hand and straightened to find his dark blue eyes fixed on her, his complexion waxy with pain and irritation.

"It'll pass."

She gestured for the door. "After you, then."

Grimacing, he hobbled out ahead of her.

Tess shut off the last of the lights, locked the door and pulled it closed behind her. "Do you suppose that's all there is to it?"

"There's a dead bolt above the knob."

Using the overhead nightlight, she scrolled through the fat wad of keys on Georgie's ring until she found one labeled DB.

"What's with the tennis ball?" Ben asked.

"Georgie has issues with keeping track of her keys."

"That's some wad of keys."

Tess turned the dead bolt. "Which is why she can't lose them every day like she did her first few weeks here."

When they got into the car, she tried to ignore his hulking presence while figuring out where everything was in the newfangled car. She had never driven a car this nice or this new. "Where do you suppose the headlights are?" she asked.

He leaned across her to flip them on.

"Oh," she said, shocked by the feel of his body brushing against hers. She cleared her throat. "I was going to run by the hospital before I go home. Do you mind?"

"Are you one of those do-gooder types?"

"If going to check on an old man who was viciously assaulted makes me a do-gooder, then yeah, I guess I am."

"Do you even know him?"

"No, but he's a friend of Georgie's, and I want to check on her, too."

Ben snorted. "You'd make a good pair with Nate, the original do-gooder."

"Nathan seems like a lovely person."

"So why don't you ask him out?"

"Because he likes Georgie."

"So you *would* ask him out if there was no Georgie. I see how it is."

"If there was no Georgie, I wouldn't even *know* him. Besides, I have no interest in dating anyone."

"Why?"

"Are you always this annoying and nosy?" she asked as she drove down Spring Street to Broadway.

"Pretty much. So why don't you date?"

"No desire."

He raised an eyebrow. "None at all? You don't strike me as the frigid type. The exact opposite, in fact."

"I refuse to have this conversation with you. I don't even know you."

"Sheesh, you are one *uptight* chick, you know that?"

Tess glared at him. "You have some nerve saying that. You don't know me, either."

"I know your type."

"And what type is that?"

"Uptight and prissy."

"Don't talk. Do you hear me? Just sit there and be quiet. For someone who needed a ride, you're awfully opinionated."

"Just calling it like I see it."

"You were going to be quiet, remember?"

He chuckled, which annoyed her even more.

"What are you laughing at?"

"I'm not allowed to talk."

"*Ugh!* How can you be related to Nathan? You're nothing like him."

"Thank God for that."

"You could learn a thing or two from him."

"Spare me."

Tess pulled into the parking lot at the emergency room. "Since you're not able to be civil, why don't you wait here?"

"Because my leg gets stiff if I sit too long."

"What happened to your leg, anyway?" she asked, unable to resist.

"Why do you care? I thought you didn't like me."

"I don't, but that doesn't mean I'm not interested as a health care professional."

"As a health care professional," he mimicked.

Tess got out of the car and slammed the door behind her. She took off for the emergency room without so much as a glance over her shoulder to see if he was following her. Inside she found a group of seniors from the center converged in a corner and went over to them. Neither Georgie nor Nathan was anywhere in sight.

"Hi, I'm Tess, Georgie's roommate. I was wondering how Gus is doing."

"They just took him up to the ICU," Walter replied. "We don't know much more than that. They won't tell us because we're not his family."

"I work here, so let me see what I can find out for you."

"That'd be real nice of you, honey," Walter said. "Thank you."

"Is Georgie still around?"

"She got a look at Gus, and I guess it shook her up real good. That Caldwell boy went off after her."

Tess smiled. "Then I'm sure she's in good hands." She patted Walter's arm. "Stay here. I'll be right back."

At the nurse's station, she found Pam and Debby, two of the more senior nurses on the ER staff.

"What are you doing here on your night off?" Pam asked.

"Checking on a friend of a friend. The older man they brought in, assaulted at home? What do you know about him?"

They exchanged glances.

"It's not good," Pam said. "The CT scan showed some bleeding in the brain, but they decided it was too risky to operate."

"He's in a coma," Debby added. "They just took him up to ICU a few minutes ago. The people with him said they weren't leaving until we told them something, but you know how it is with HIPPA and everything." She referred to the federal law that protects patient privacy. "We called his daughter, and she promised to be here late tonight. She can decide what to tell them."

Tess nodded. "I'll tell them he's stable, and they can visit him upstairs tomorrow."

"We'd appreciate that," Debby said. "They're taking up a lot of room out there."

"Who's the tall, dark, and handsome drink of water who came in with you?" Pam asked.

Tess glanced over her shoulder and frowned when she found Ben watching her from the doorway. "Don't be fooled by how he looks. He's a jerk."

"Then what are you doing with him?"

"Giving him a ride. That's it."

"Uh-huh," Debby said with a wink for Pam. "*Sure.*"

"Thanks for the info, you guys."

"No problem."

Tess returned to the waiting room to tell Bill and the others as much as she could, which wasn't enough for them.

"Patient privacy, my ass," one of them growled.

Tess decided he had to be Bad Gus. "I know you're upset about your friend, and I'm sorry to be quoting hospital policy. When his daughter gets here, she'll be able to fill you in more on his condition. In the meantime, why don't you go home and get some sleep? Visiting hours begin at eleven, but you'll only be able to go in one or two at a time in the ICU, so try to stagger your visits."

"Thanks, Tess," Walter said. "We'll do that."

She waited until they had filed out of the emergency room door before she went over to where Ben waited for her. Once again she wished Ian had asked *her* out for ice cream with him and his gorgeous daughter. *Why did I have to get stuck with this one?*

"Ready?" she asked without looking at him.

"That was smooth," he said as he pushed himself off the wall he had been propped against.

"What was?"

"The way you handled those old people. You didn't tell them a damned thing, but somehow you sent them away satisfied."

She shrugged. "It doesn't take much to be human. You might want to try it sometime."

He hooted with laughter. "Ouch."

"If the shoe fits."

At the car, he stopped her with a hand to her shoulder.

Tess did her best not to flinch, reminding herself yet again that not all men are monsters.

"We seem to have gotten off on the wrong foot," he said. "How about we start over?"

Tess eyed him warily.

He extended his hand. "I'm Bennett Caldwell."

With great reluctance, Tess took his hand and looked up at him. "Tess Daniels."

He rendered her speechless when he raised her hand to his lips and kissed the back of it. "Pleased to meet you, Tess Daniels."

They drove to Extension Street in silence. He had unnerved her with the unexpected, romantic gesture. She was so far removed from anything romantic, she had no idea what it meant. Was he just trying to make up for being a jerk earlier? Was he genuinely interested in her? If so, how did she feel about that? It was all so confusing, and it was one of many reasons she had sworn off men forever. Still, she had to wonder if she had witnessed a hint of the man he might be underneath all the obnoxiousness.

"It happened in Iraq," he said.

"Excuse me?"

"You asked about my leg."

"Oh, right. I did."

"I was driving a Jeep when we hit a roadside bomb outside of Fallujah fifteen months ago. The friend who was with me was killed instantly."

Tess had no idea what to say. After a long, awkward pause, she said, "You're lucky to be alive." And then she winced, knowing how stupid she sounded.

"Yeah," he said with an ironic chuckle. "Lucky."

She swallowed and forced herself to continue the conversation. "Were you injured, other than your leg?"

"Shrapnel wounds all up and down my right side. That's how I got the scars on my face. But my leg took the brunt. Totally shattered. Somehow—I have no idea how—I managed to get a tourniquet on it, which is the only reason I didn't bleed to death."

"You don't remember?"

He shook his head. "Not a damned thing. We were just riding along, and then my memory goes dark for about three days."

As Tess drove down Extension Street, Ben pointed to a white house at the bottom of the hill.

"There it is—home sweet home, or at least until Nate sells it and moves on to his next project."

Tess parked in front of the house but left the car running. Her head spun with questions she burned to ask if only she could have found the words.

"Well, thanks for the ride."

"So you live with Nathan?"

He smiled, which softened his gruff features and took him from reasonably good-looking straight to dashing. "I had an apartment in town, but I gave it up when I got called up to active duty with the National Guard. After I came home in pieces, my brothers decided I couldn't live alone until I was getting around better. Nate drew the short straw, but he probably rigged it so he could keep an eye on me."

The bitter edge to his voice led her to ask, "Don't you two get along?"

"We used to before we lived together. Now we mostly get on each other's nerves."

"I'm sure your cranky disposition is a real joy to live with."

"You don't pull any punches, do you, Nurse Tess?"

"What's the point of pulling punches?"

Ben studied her for a long moment. "If that's how you like to play it, what do you say we walk down the hill and have a drink?"

"Oh, um, well, I don't think so. I have to work tomorrow, so I should get home."

"Just one? I promise to behave like a perfect gentleman."

"So you'd be pretending, then?"

He laughed.

"Maybe another time."

"If you decide you don't like me, you can run away. What am I going to do? Chase you? So you see, you're safe with me."

Tess resisted the urge to laugh. When he put forth the effort, he almost achieved human status. In light of the things he had shared with her, the do-gooder in her couldn't help but recognize the wounded soul that rested just beneath his hard exterior. And despite herself, she was intrigued.

"All right." She turned off the car—and her racing mind. "One drink."

CHAPTER 12

While Nathan went to get his pain medication, Georgie didn't allow herself to think about all the reasons it was a bad idea to be in a bed with him. Rather, she thought about how happy she had been to find him waiting for her when she got home, how sweet it had been—with a badly injured arm, no less—for him to carry her to bed and how he had offered just the right amount of support more than once during that long, difficult evening.

He came back with a prescription bottle and a glass of water, which he offered to share with her.

Georgie took a drink and passed the glass back to him.

After he took a pill, he put the bottle and the glass on the bedside table and reached for her. He held her as if she was the most precious thing in his world, his fingers spooling through her hair, his lips pressed to her forehead. "Tell me," he said softly.

"What?"

"Everything."

So she did. From the minute she received the phone call about her mother's grim diagnosis right up to getting fired earlier and the shock of seeing Gus so bruised and battered. The only thing she left out was how her mother's diagnosis had affected her and her sister. When she finished, she was surprised to realize she felt better.

"All that in three months?"

"Uh-huh."

"Well, no wonder."

"No wonder what?"

"No wonder why there was no room in your life for another complication. You weren't kidding."

And he didn't even know the biggest reason she had held him at arm's length. "I'm sorry I hurt you. I didn't mean to."

"We aren't talking about me. We're talking about you, Georgie. You amaze me."

"I do?"

"Yeah, you do. You were beating yourself up for not doing enough for Gus today. What about what you've been doing for all of them for months—while taking care of your mother, too?"

"I don't want to be there, though. I hate every bloody minute I have to spend in that smelly, hot place with old men who don't even *try* to hide that they're lusting after me. Doesn't that make me a bad person?"

"No," he said, laughing softly. "It does not make you a bad person. All your choices were taken away. It's only natural you'd resent that. Anyone would. And I can't blame them for lusting after you. They *are* only human after all."

His words hung heavily in the air for several long, quiet minutes. "Your boyfriend really dumped you over the phone?"

"Yep. In fact, it was the same day I met you. That was one reason why the whole thing with the Dumpster took me right over the edge."

The hand that had been caressing her hair suddenly went still.

"What?" When he didn't answer, she turned so she could see him. "Nathan? What's wrong?"

"So I was like, what, a rebound?"

"No! Not at all."

He tried to sit up, but she wouldn't let him.

"My relationship with Doug was over a long time ago. Months ago. I just hadn't gotten around to officially ending it with him. He beat me to it, and that made me mad more than anything. You were *not* a rebound, Nathan. I swear." She slid her hand up over his chest to caress his face. "What happened between us had nothing to do with anyone but me and you. Do you believe me?"

"I want to."

Against her better judgment, Georgie leaned in and touched her lips to his. "I need you to believe me." She ran her tongue along his bottom lip.

He inhaled a sharp deep breath. "Georgie."

Her lips hovered just above his. "I need to tell you something, but I don't want you to think it means, you know, that anything has changed."

His hands found her hips, held her still. "What?"

"I appreciate you being here tonight and listening to me, but I still don't have room—"

He captured her lips in a hot, searing kiss that sucked the oxygen right out of her lungs and all rational thought out of her head. His hand cruised up her back and into her hair to anchor her in place.

Georgie fought him. She had things she needed to say to him. "Wait," she gasped. "Nathan. I need to tell you . . ."

"I'm listening," he said as he kissed her again.

Her heart pounded, and it took tremendous effort not to give in to the desire that simmered between them whenever she was with him. She managed to free her lips and knew she must have seemed dazed as she looked down at him. Clearing her throat, she forced herself to concentrate. "Remember when you said you'd wanted me for weeks?"

"Uh-huh." He kept his hand firmly planted in her hair, his fingertips massaging her scalp, his lips cruising over her jaw. "It's true. I did."

Georgie trembled. "Well, I um . . ." She took a deep breath. "I did, too."

His eyebrows knitted with confusion. "Did what?"

A flush of embarrassment and desire started at her breasts and heated her face. "I wanted you, too. For weeks I watched you run by, and I . . . I wanted you like

I've never wanted another man. Ever. So what happened between us had nothing to do with rebounds. I just . . . I needed you to know that."

He studied her for a long moment during which Georgie had no idea what he was thinking. "How can you say that and in the same breath tell me you have no room in your life for me?"

"Because—"

"Make room, Georgie. I'm not going anywhere. I like the way I feel when I'm with you. It's been a really long time since I've felt this way, and I can't just walk away because you don't have room." He kissed her. Hard. "Make room."

Taken aback by his intensity, she said, "I'm going home to Atlanta. Soon." *And I might have to have a double mastectomy like my sister.*

"I don't know if you've noticed, but while you were busy trying to get things wrapped up so you could get back to your life in Atlanta, you went and got yourself a pretty nice life here. You've got an army of people at that center who'd lay down on hot coals for you, you've got two good friends living right here in your house, and last but not least, whether you want me or not, you've got me. Now I don't know what you had going for you in Atlanta, but since your boyfriend saw fit to dump you over the phone, I can't imagine it was much better than what's right in front of you. Here."

She fell back against the pillow and thought about what he had said. If she allowed herself to acknowledge that he might have a point, it would mean her whole world had once again turned upside down. She wasn't sure she was ready to let that happen—and it certainly didn't seem fair to him in light of what could be ahead for her.

"I'm right," he said. "You know I am." Propping himself up on his good arm, he looked down at her and leaned in to kiss her lightly. "When he kissed you, did your breath get caught in your throat the way it does when I kiss you?" His hand slid under her skirt to rest on her leg. "Did your skin heat under his hand the way it does under mine?" He caressed her leg. "When he made love to you, did you come over and over again the way you did with me?"

"No," she whispered. "No." As she gave herself over to him, Georgie's eyes fluttered shut. He made love to her with only his words, and yet he was able to penetrate the wall she had put up around herself. He knew the effect he was having on her, so she didn't try to deny it. Instead she reached for him, molded her lips to his, and sure enough, her breath got stuck in her throat, just the way he said it would.

His kiss was soft, his tongue gentle as he let her set the pace.

Georgie was drowning in him—his scent, the wet, hungry meeting of lips and tongues, his hand on her back holding her close to him, the warm, humid evening, the cadence of crickets drifting in through the open window. She had made love to him many times during that one unforgettable night, but here, in this moment, with just his lips sliding over hers, he touched her more deeply than anyone ever had.

He pulled back, and with one hand still resting on her face, he looked at her for a long time.

"Can I ask you something?" she said.

"Anything you want."

"Why me? I'm not even nice to you."

Laughter rippled through him. "Oh, you kill me," he said, still laughing as he wiped tears from his eyes.

"I'm serious!"

"So am I. You crack me up."

She pushed him away. "Fine, if you want to be like that."

"Come on," he cajoled, reaching for her. "I'm only playing with you."

"I know why you won't answer me."

"Is that so?"

"It's because you have no idea what you like about me."

"That's not true—"

"Oh, wait! I know what it is."

"I can't wait to hear this."

"It's because I was easy."

"*Easy?*" He roared with laughter, which only made Georgie madder. "Sweetheart, you're a lot of things, but easy ain't one of 'em."

"I was that one night."

"So was I."

She gave him a withering look. "Men aren't judged by the same standards."

"No one's judging you, Georgie, least of all me." He brushed a hand over her hair. "No matter what happens between us, I'll never forget the first night I spent with you. Ever."

"I've never done that before," she confessed.

"Done what?"

Her face grew hot with embarrassment. "On the first date . . . And some of the other stuff, too."

"It was a special night, for both of us. I hope it was the first of many."

"Which brings me back to my original question—why me?"

With a devilish grin, he said, "If I had to pick one thing, I'd have to say it was the dimples."

Her eyes narrowed. "Those are fighting words, Nathan. You have to know that."

"Luckily, I'm not afraid of you."

"Maybe you should be."

"Maybe."

"I still don't want to be involved with you."

His eyes drifted closed. "Okay."

"Are you going to sleep?"

"I think so."

"Nathan . . ."

"Might be the pill," he mumbled as he lifted his arm. "Is it bleeding?"

She raised the sleeve of his T-shirt and gasped. "It is! What should I do?"

"Do you have any Band-Aids?" He never opened his eyes as his breathing settled into a sleepy cadence.

Georgie vaulted off the bed and ran for the bathroom. She returned a minute later with a wet washcloth, gauze, and tape to find him snoring softly. With a deep sigh, she rolled up his sleeve, removed the blood-soaked bandage and gasped at the ugly, oozing wound. She pressed the warm cloth against his arm, all the while enjoying the view. He was so incredibly handsome, even asleep.

When the bleeding had slowed, she wrapped the new gauze around his arm. He never stirred, even when she pulled the tape tight over the bandage. Running her hand over his forehead, she was surprised to realize he had a fever.

The poor guy. He'd had a horrible day, and somehow he'd still had it in him to take care of her. Tess and Cat were right about one thing—men like him didn't come along every day. She was going to have to be really careful, because it would be far too easy to fall in love with him.

With all she had going on at the moment, the timing couldn't have been worse. She had always imagined what it would be like when she fell in love. Nowhere in those fantasies had there been breast cancer genes or senior citizens or probate court or a big house to take care of or a life in flux in another city hundreds of miles away.

Even though the time wasn't right for a serious relationship, maybe she could spend some time with him, have some fun and keep it light. As long as they both understood the score going into it, no one would get hurt, right? She untied his sneakers and pulled them off before she tugged the sheet up and over him. On an impulse, she leaned over and kissed his lips.

He murmured something in his sleep but didn't wake up.

The house phone rang and Georgie went into her mother's room to answer it.

"Georgie?" Bill Bradley said.

"Hi, Bill. How's Gus?" She braced herself for the answer.

"Seems to be the same. The doctors aren't saying much."

"I just can't believe this has happened. Have you heard any more from the police?"

"Roxy said they think his son Roger might've gotten into trouble with drug dealers. Apparently, they were looking for money he owes them at his father's house. The theory is he hid it there when he came to take him to the doctor earlier this week."

When her legs would have buckled under her, Georgie sat on her mother's bed. "Has Roger been to the hospital?"

"No one's heard from him. Gus's daughter, Dawn, is flying up from Florida tonight."

"Oh, well, at least he'll have some family with him."

"He has us," Bill said firmly.

"Yes, of course he does. Will you let me know if you hear anything else? Even if it's the middle of the night?"

"I will."

"I should've gone over there myself when you guys told me you were worried."

"Your mother talked about you and your sister all the time, did you know that?"

Surprised by the shift in conversation, Georgie said, "No, I didn't."

"It was always Ali this, Georgie that, Ali's coming home, Georgie's got a new apartment. The center was her job, but you and your sister were her life, honey. You two were her pride and joy."

Georgie's throat tightened with emotion. "Thank you for telling me that, Bill."

"I think you already knew. She'd be so proud of the way you've stepped up at the center."

"I hope so," she said, blinking back tears. "I'll see you tomorrow?"

"Yes, you will. Are you all right, Georgie?"

She glanced across the hall to where Nathan was sprawled out asleep in her bed. "Yeah, I'm okay."

Chapter 13

Georgie woke up just after two the next morning awash in sweat to find Nathan wrapped around her, moaning softly in his sleep. As she disentangled herself from his embrace, she was startled to find his skin blazing. Resting her hand on his sweaty forehead, she gasped.

"Nathan." She turned on the bedside light as she shook his shoulder. "Wake up."

"Mmm, hot, Georgie, hot . . ." His mumbling descended into incoherence.

Georgie tugged the covers off him and went into the bathroom to run a washcloth under cold water. She brought it back and bathed his face.

His eyes opened, and he blinked until he had adjusted to the light. "What's wrong?"

"You've got a fever. I'll see if we have anything you can take for it. Will you be okay?"

"As long as you come back."

She smiled as she ran the cloth over his face again. "You never miss an opportunity, do you?"

His eyes fluttered closed. "Can't afford to."

Georgie checked the medicine cabinets in all the bathrooms but couldn't find what she needed. She remembered a cabinet in the kitchen where her mother had kept some medicines, so she went downstairs to find Tess leaning against the counter drinking a glass of water.

"What are you doing up?" Georgie asked.

"Haven't been to bed yet."

"Oh, no?"

"I went to have a drink with Ben that turned into two, and now I'm up way too late. I'll pay for it tomorrow."

"You and Ben?" Georgie asked as she searched for the medicine. "That's an interesting pairing."

"No pairing, just a drink. He's okay once you get past all the BS. I brought your car home, by the way. The keys are on the counter."

"Thanks."

"I'm sorry about Gus."

"Me, too." Georgie sighed. "He's one of the good guys."

"What're you looking for?"

"Something for a fever."

"Are you sick?"

She glanced over at Tess. "Um, now don't get all, you know, *nutso* about it, but Nathan's upstairs, and he has a fever."

With obvious restraint, Tess asked, "Did he take the meds they gave him today?"

Georgie nodded. "It knocked him out. That's why he's here."

"That's the *only* reason?"

"*Tess!*"

She laughed. "I have what you need upstairs. I'll get it for you."

"Great. Thank you." Georgie took a fresh glass of ice water with her when she went upstairs.

Nathan had gone back to sleep.

Tess came down from the third floor with the pills and an ear thermometer. "May I?"

Georgie gestured for her to have at it.

Nathan didn't stir as Tess took his temperature.

"Wow, 103. He was fine before. What brought that on?"

"Well, he ah . . . kind of carried me upstairs when I was upset earlier."

"Georgie! He shouldn't have done that!"

"I know. I said the same thing."

"Let's get his clothes off."

"Do we have to?" Georgie asked, alarmed.

In full nurse mode, Tess lifted him and removed his shirt. As she reached for the button to his jeans, she turned to Georgie. "Are you going to just stand there?"

"Yeah, that was the plan."

"Georgie! Come on!"

Reluctantly, Georgie helped to work the denim over his legs.

"Please tell me I'm not hallucinating," he mumbled as the jeans cleared his feet, leaving him only in form-fitting boxers. "*Both of you?*"

Georgie rolled her eyes. "Clearly, he's fine."

Tess giggled. "Not tonight, big boy." She shook two pills from the bottle and helped him sit up to take them.

Georgie watched the whole scene with an odd feeling of detachment. Tess knew what to do, so it was best if she just stayed out of the way.

He winced when he tried to move his arm.

"Who did this hack job?" Tess asked as she surveyed the bandage Georgie had applied earlier.

"That'd be me," Georgie said. "What's wrong with it?"

"Other than everything? Was it bleeding?"

"A little," Georgie said.

Tess took off the bandage and inspected the wound. "It needs to be irrigated. I'll get some stuff."

When they were alone, Nathan held out his good hand to Georgie.

She laced her fingers through his.

"Why do you look so pale?" he asked.

"Do I?"

"Uh-huh."

"I was worried when I woke up and you were on fire."

"Don't look now, but I think you're starting to care about me."

"Nah. I was worried about disposing of your carcass if you spontaneously combusted in my bed."

Keeping his eyes closed and his fingers curled around hers, he laughed softly. "I'd love to spontaneously combust in your bed. Just say the word."

Georgie laughed. "You're too much." As she studied him, so handsome even in pain, she wished she had met him before her life spun into chaos and uncertainty.

Tess returned with a bundle of towels and a large syringe.

"What are you going to do with that?" Nathan asked, suddenly on full alert.

"It's just hydrogen peroxide, a little bit of alcohol, and water. It might sting but only for a second."

Nathan tugged on Georgie's hand. "Lay with me."

Tess nodded at Georgie to go ahead.

Feeling tremendous pressure to do what she was told, she positioned herself on the bed behind him so he could rest his head against her chest.

"What's going on?" Cat asked from the door.

"Nathan's burning up," Tess replied.

"If Nathan's burning up in Georgie's bed, what the heck are you doing in there?" Cat asked with an amused expression.

"I wish burning up in Georgie's bed meant what you think it does," he said.

"Relax your arm," Tess said, her eyes meeting Georgie's over his head. "Keep him still," she mouthed to Georgie.

Georgie nodded, her stomach clenching with anxiety. She tightened her arms around him.

"Just a small sting," Tess said in a cheerful tone.

"*Son of a bitch!*" he hissed. His face drained of color as he bit down hard on his bottom lip. "Come on! Enough!"

Tess kept an iron grip on his arm. "One more minute."

He moaned.

Moved by his distress, Georgie cradled his head against her chest and ran her fingers through his hair.

Tess dried the wound and applied a new bandage. "I'll take a look at it again in the morning. Try to get some sleep."

"Thanks," he said, his voice weak and hoarse with pain.

"Come get me if you need me," she said to Georgie.

"I will. Thanks, Tess."

"Night, guys," Cat said.

Tess went into the hallway, and Georgie heard her ask Cat about her date with Ian and Rosie.

Their voices faded as they made their way upstairs.

"*Cat and Ian?*" Nathan whispered.

"Apparently, Tess and Ben, too."

"Damn! I'm out of the loop for one night and the world goes mad!"

"Are you okay?" His lips were white with pain. "Can I get you anything?"

"Just one thing."

"What?"

"You. I want to hold you."

"You can't. Your arm needs to stay still, and you need to rest."

"Then you hold me. I can't sleep with you and not touch you."

She scooted from behind him to lie next to him. "I don't want to hurt you."

He turned onto his good side and reached for her with his injured arm.

Georgie moved an inch closer to him.

His hand landed on her hip. "That's what I need," he said with a contented sigh. "One more thing?"

"I'm afraid to ask."

"Do you think maybe you could kiss me?"

"Nathan—"

"Just one kiss." His lip curled into a pout. "Please? I'm injured."

"How long are you going to play that card?"

"For as long as it works?"

She kissed his cheek. "There. Now go to sleep."

"That stunk. You can do better. In fact, I *know* you can."

"If I kiss you, will you go to sleep?"

"I promise."

She propped herself up on one elbow and leaned in to press her lips to his and was about to pull back when his hand sank into her hair to hold her still.

His tongue traced the outline of her lips.

As she gasped with surprise, Georgie felt the now-familiar charge of desire he stirred in her.

He took advantage of her parted lips to slide his tongue into her mouth.

Her hand landed on his shoulder, and he flinched but didn't let her go. Instead, he moved the hand he'd had in her hair down her back and pulled her even closer to him.

"Nathan!" she said, tearing her lips free of his. "Your arm."

"Kiss me, Georgie."

"I did."

"Wasn't enough." He hooked his leg over her hips to draw her to him.

His body was warm and aroused, his eyes glassy with fever and desire. "Do you always wear boxers to bed?" he asked.

"Most of the time."

"Very sexy. And this little number. I like that, too."

Georgie glanced down to find her breasts spilling out of the thin camisole. When she tried to adjust her top, he stopped her.

"Don't."

Their eyes met, held.

Georgie knew he was going to kiss her again, and her breath got caught in her throat as anticipation did battle with her better judgment. Once again, this was on the verge of getting out of control, and she had to put a stop to it. She tried to pull away from him, but he resisted.

"Georgie," he whispered as he brought his lips down on hers.

She wanted to fight him. Really, she did. But as his mouth fused with hers, every ounce of reason seemed to desert her.

He moved to get a better angle, his erection pressing against her leg.

Georgie knew she shouldn't be sliding her hands over his back or sending her tongue to meet his. And she certainly shouldn't have been stroking him through the soft cotton of his underwear. All bad moves, for sure, but that last one, well, she just couldn't resist.

He groaned and pushed hard against her hand as he cupped her breast. When he ran a thumb over her nipple, the shock of the aching need that rocketed through her took her breath away.

He freed her breast from the cami. "Mmm," he said, his lips vibrating against her fevered skin. "So pretty. So perfect."

Georgie went rigid as she suddenly remembered blood tests and mastectomies. "Stop," she whispered. "Please stop."

Breathing hard, he let his head fall to her shoulder. "I'm sorry."

She was at once furious with herself, frustrated at the unfulfilled desire that still pulsated through her body and sad—so painfully sad.

The soft pressure of his lips against her shoulder made her go limp in his arms.

"You must think I'm a terrible tease—"

He stopped her with a gentle kiss. "I think you're the sexiest, most desirable, fascinating, *frustrating,* adorable, caring woman I've ever known, and it's been a really long time since I've wanted anyone the way I want you—and not just in bed."

Georgie had to fight to keep her mouth from falling open. *Oh! How could he say that? How am I supposed to resist him when he says stuff like that?*

His grin was small but satisfied. "Nothing to say?"

"You're not playing fair," she said softly.

He gathered her in close to him and reached over to shut off the light. "Nope."

Throbbing pain in his arm woke Nathan early the next morning at the time he usually got up to run. That wasn't happening today, though. He was furious to realize he felt weak and depleted from the fever that still gripped him. Being helpless, injured or sick never sat well with him. His mother had often called him her worst patient, which was saying something in his family.

To detract his attention from the pain in his arm, he watched Georgie sleep and wondered if she would retreat again when she woke up to find him in her bed. He smiled when he remembered her accusing him of not playing fair. Damn right he wasn't playing fair. Where would that get him? He was playing it straight, and clearly she was unused to that strategy.

Old Doug what's-his-name in Atlanta was probably the type to play games. She'd said he was a sports agent. *Imagine the ego on that guy. Probably thought he was God's gift to women.* Nathan hated guys like him who gave the rest of them a bad rap. Georgie deserved better.

Maybe it was time for some good old-fashioned romance. He smiled as he imagined her thrown off balance and unnerved. He liked her that way. The idea got better the longer he thought about it. He'd have to get some pointers from his brother Kevin, the king of romance.

"What are you all smiles about?" Georgie grumbled.

"Uh-oh," he said, curling himself around her. "Is someone not a morning person?"

She grunted and turned away from him, presumably to go back to sleep.

He kissed her neck and was pleased by the tremble that rippled through her.

"I see you're feeling better," she mumbled.

"Better but not perfect. I'll need some more nursing today."

"I'll see if Tess is available."

Despite the pain it caused him, he tightened the arm he had around her. "It's not Tess I want." He couldn't believe it was possible that the sound of her voice was enough to turn him on.

"Beggars can't be choosers," she said dryly.

"I'd like to hire you to take care of me today."

Georgie grunted. "You can't afford me."

"Don't be so sure," he said against her ear.

She squealed. "Stop!"

But instead of stopping, he nibbled on her earlobe. "I'll stop when you agree to nurse me back to health."

"I hope you've got lots of time."

He could tell he surprised her when he caressed her breast. "I've got all day. In fact, I'm on convalescence leave for the next few days, and I need a nurse."

Georgie squirmed out of his embrace and turned so she could see him. "I'm a terrible nurse. Didn't you hear what Tess said about that bandage I put on you last night?"

He shrugged. "Like you said, beggars can't be choosers."

"So you're begging?" she asked with a smile that brought out the dimples.

Nathan's heart literally skipped a beat as he traced a finger over one of them. He *really* loved those dimples. "Are you opening the center today?"

Her smile faded. "I guess not, since they'll be at the hospital. I'll need to get over there at some point, too."

"Spend the day with me?"

"I'm leaving Newport. Soon."

"So you've mentioned."

"I don't want you to forget that."

"What I'm suggesting is strictly a business proposition."

Her eyebrows knitted with skepticism.

"Business with benefits?" he asked with what he hoped was a cajoling smile.

When she reached out to caress his face, he almost stopped breathing. She studied him for a long time. "You're very difficult not to like. You know that?"

He laughed and kissed the palm of her hand. "I do so love your backhanded compliments, Georgie Quinn. Does that mean you'll take care of me today?"

Reluctantly, she said, "I'll do my best."

CHAPTER 14

As she brushed her teeth, Georgie could see Nathan stretched out in her bed and had to admit that she had liked waking up with him. Ugh! Despite her best efforts to stay aloof and uninvolved, he had an annoying way of ingratiating himself. If only he wasn't so nice and funny. And hot. *So* hot! Why couldn't he have been just a little bit ugly? Or self-absorbed? Humorless would have helped, too. *Anything* to give her a reason to resist him, to stay away from him, to *dislike* him!

All at once he was with her in the bathroom, reaching out to shut off the water she had left running while she brushed her teeth. Startled, she stared at him.

"Gallons of wasted water," he said with a sheepish grin.

Georgie turned the water back on and spit out the toothpaste. "Do you mind?"

"What?" He scratched his chest and stretched. "The door was open."

"You might want to put some clothes on. I don't live alone."

"They saw the goods last night when you and Tess stripped me. Speaking of which, I'd like to request a do-over when I'm not delirious with a fever. I didn't get to adequately enjoy it."

"In your dreams."

He wiggled his eyebrows at her.

Rattled by his close presence, Georgie pushed past him and crossed the hall to her room.

"I need my nurse to give me a sponge bath."

She spun around to discover he had followed her. "Not in your *wildest* dreams."

"A shower, then?"

"Feel free. Towels are in the closet."

"My nurse should accompany me. In my weakened state, I could fall or reopen my wound. You wouldn't want that to happen on your watch, would you?"

"You're seriously pushing your luck, and it's only eight thirty. Your nurse is going to quit if you keep up this sexual harassment."

"Can't blame a guy for trying," he said with a cheerful smile. "I'll be in the shower if you need me." He grabbed his jeans and T-shirt and headed across the hall. "Are you sure you won't join me?"

"Positive."

"Your bedside manner could use some work," he said as he closed the door to the bathroom.

Georgie couldn't resist a giggle. *Why does he have to be so funny? And cute? And all but irresistible? Why couldn't he be a typical guy and turn into a jerk as soon as he got what he wanted? He'd already had it all and was still hanging in there just the same. What was wrong with him? Was he some sort of masochist or something?*

She headed downstairs hoping Cat or Tess had made coffee. Her head buzzed from the lack of sleep, her worries about Gus, and her turmoil over Nathan. In the kitchen, she discovered a party going on.

Tess and Cat, still in pajamas, as well as Ben, Ian, and Rosie, were sitting around the kitchen table drinking coffee and orange juice. When Georgie walked in, Ian had the good grace to look away from her skimpy attire, but Ben took a full, measuring look. As she crossed her arms over her breasts, she wished she had taken the time to get dressed. "What's going on?"

"We were worried when Nate didn't come home last night," Ben said. "That's not like him, so we were hoping he was here."

"We filled them in," Tess said.

"How is he today?" Ian asked.

"Full of beans," Georgie said as she reached behind the pantry door for a zip-up sweatshirt her mother had kept there. She put it on and brought a cup of coffee with her when she joined the others at the table.

"That's a good sign," Tess said, wiping up a splash of Rosie's juice.

"He's in the shower," Georgie added.

Rosie worked her way onto Tess's lap.

"Rosie," Ian admonished. "Tess is trying to drink her coffee."

"She's fine," Tess said, wrapping an arm around the child. As she nuzzled Rosie's golden curls, a wave of pure longing crossed Tess's face. If Georgie hadn't been looking right at her when it happened, she might have missed it.

Georgie noticed that Ben, who was monitoring Tess's every move, hadn't missed it, either. On the other hand, Cat and Ian seemed to be having trouble looking at each other. *Very interesting.*

Rosie snuggled with Tess for a few minutes before she got up and went over to Cat.

"Can I sit with you now?"

Cat, who always seemed so composed, looked nothing short of panicked. "Um, well, I guess so."

Rosie climbed up onto Cat's lap, oblivious to the fact that Cat didn't want her there. While Tess had wrapped her arms around the child, Cat let hers hang at her sides almost as if she were hoping Rosie would take the hint and choose another lap.

Cat was saved when Nathan walked into the room, his hair wet from the shower.

Rosie bolted off Cat's lap and ran to her uncle.

He scooped her up with his good arm and kissed her noisily on her pretty lips. "What's up, buttercup?"

"After a while, crocodile."

As the other adults laughed, Nathan said, "We'll get it straight one of these days."

"What's the matter with your eyes?" Rosie asked.

"I don't know. Why?"

"They look funny. Are you sick?"

"I have a fever from the boo-boo on my arm."

Rosie rested her hand on his forehead. "You should go back to bed. My daddy makes me stay in bed when I have a fever."

"Don't worry, Georgie is going to take care of me today."

Rosie turned to Georgie. "Do you know what you're doing?"

Tess snorted under her breath.

Georgie shot her a glare before she looked up at Rosie. "I'll do my very best."

Rosie wrapped her chubby arms around Nathan's neck and squeezed. "I hope you feel better."

"Thanks, baby."

"*Uncle Nate!*"

"Oh! Sorry. Can't call you that anymore. I forgot."

"That's okay. I forgive you."

Georgie's throat tightened with emotion as she watched him interact with the child.

Cat got up from the table, and with a muttered "excuse me," she went out to the front porch.

"Do you have her for a minute?" Ian asked Nathan.

Nathan bounced the girl up and down, and she squealed with laughter. "Sure do."

Ian followed Cat to the porch.

Nathan's face was stiff with pain he was working hard to hide from Rosie, so Georgie directed him to a chair and got him a cup of coffee.

"Thanks," he said with a warm smile.

"What's up with those two?" Ben asked, nodding toward the door.

"She likes my daddy but not me," Rosie said with a frown.

The others stared at her in disbelief.

Ian found Cat sitting on the wicker sofa, vibrating with tension.

"Nice day," he said. *Great opening, Caldwell. Brilliant, in fact.*

She glanced over at him. "Uh-huh."

Ian sat down next to her. "Something wrong?"

"No," she said quickly. "Why?"

He shrugged. "You can't seem to look at me today."

"That's not true!" She turned to meet his steady gaze. "There. Are you happy?"

"It was just a kiss, Cat."

"Except that it wasn't. If it had been 'just a kiss,' I wouldn't be having such a hard time looking at you."

Struck by her honesty, he reached for her hand. "It *was* quite a kiss, huh?"

She shook off his hand. "This isn't going to happen, Ian."

"Why not? We're both single, at least I hope you are—"

"I am."

"So then what's the problem?"

"You're a nice guy—"

"Thanks. Have dinner with me tonight."

"If you'd let me finish—"

"Only if you're going to say yes."

She uttered an exasperated growl. "I have to work."

"You also have to eat."

"What about . . . what about Rosie?"

"I have people who help me out since I work a lot of nights."

"Where's her mother?"

"Out of the picture."

"So you're a . . ."

"Single dad? Yes."

"Oh."

"Is that a problem?"

Cat gnawed on her bottom lip for a moment.

As he watched her, he had an overwhelming urge to loop her brow ring around his tongue.

She looked up at him with vulnerable brown eyes that belied her tough exterior. "I'm not much of a kid person."

"I'm not asking you to be."

"But she's, you know, a factor."

"I'm asking you to have dinner with me, not marry me and raise my child."

She blanched, which made him laugh.

He leaned in closer to her and was amused by her sharp inhale. She was *not* as tough as she looked, not by a long shot. "I haven't done much dating since she came along. Since we're talking dinner, not marriage, it shouldn't be an issue."

"As long as it's just dinner, and as long as you know I'm not interested in an insta-family, then I'll go."

"Fair enough."

"What should I wear?"

"What do you *want* to wear?"

"Something like what I had on last night."

"Do you have another one of those tank tops?"

"Lots of them."

"That ought to do it."

"Just dinner," she said warily. "And it has to be early. I need to be at the club by eight."

"I'll pick you up at six."

"Why do you think Cat doesn't like you, honey?" Nathan asked Rosie.

She shrugged. "I don't know. Cuz."

"Well, it's not true," Tess said. "So you shouldn't give it another thought."

Rosie's eyes shifted toward the door. "He likes her."

"Maybe," Nathan said, "but he wouldn't be friends with someone who doesn't love you as much as he does, as much as we *all* do."

"That's right," Ben said. "We won't let him."

Rosie smiled at her uncle.

"Did you have breakfast, Rosie?" Tess asked.

She nodded. "I had cereal with my daddy at six thirty."

Ben winced. "Give the guy a break, will ya, kid?"

"Daddy says I get up with the chickens."

Nathan laughed and smoothed a hand over her hair. "It's a wonder he doesn't fall asleep on the microphone on the nights he has to work."

Smiling at the visual, Georgie stood up. "I'm going to take a shower. I want to get to the hospital."

"Who's going to take care of me while you're gone?" Nathan asked with a petulant pout.

Georgie rolled her eyes. "Rosie, will you keep an eye on Uncle Nate for a few minutes? Make sure he doesn't get into any trouble?"

"Okay, Georgie," Rosie said, her expression solemn.

"Rosie's in charge," Georgie said to Nathan on her way out of the room.

"Let's go check out the garden," Nathan said, holding out his hand to his niece.

When they were alone, Ben turned to Tess, and before he could lose his nerve, he said, "You're very beautiful in the morning."

She stared at him.

"I've been sitting here all this time hoping I'd get the chance to tell you that."

"Thank you," she said, flustered, as she stood up and got busy clearing the cups and mugs from the table. When she reached for his mug, he took her hand.

"Do I make you nervous, Tess?"

Looking down at him, she contemplated him for a long moment. "Yes."

"Why?"

"I'm not sure."

"Is it me? Or all men?"

"A little of both."

Pleased that she trusted him enough to make that confession, he closed his hand tighter around hers. "You have nothing to fear from me."

"That's good to know."

"I enjoyed being with you last night."

"I did, too. With you, that is."

Charmed by the color that flooded her cheeks, Ben said, "You know, this was the first morning since everything happened that I've woken up thinking about something other than my own litany of complaints."

"Is that so?"

He nodded.

Without releasing his hand, she sat down next to him. "I was thinking about something you said last night, about your friend Greg." She paused. "But if you'd rather not talk about it . . ."

"Tell me."

She glanced down at their joined hands and then raised her lovely gray-blue eyes to meet his. The muscles in his belly quivered, and for the first time in longer than he could remember, he felt a surge of desire. He wanted her. The realization would have knocked him off his feet if he had been standing on them.

"What you said about the guilt you feel because he died and you didn't?"

A muscle in his cheek tightened with tension. He didn't talk about this. Ever. But there'd been something about her that had compelled him to share it with her the night before. "Yes."

"Well, I wondered if maybe you found a way to tell his parents and girlfriend about what he said to you before . . . the accident—"

"You mean before he was murdered," Ben murmured.

"I'm sorry. I don't know the right way to say it."

"You're doing fine. Don't mind me or the huge chip on my shoulder."

Tess smiled. "Do you think it's possible that if you told them his last thoughts were of them, if you could somehow tell them that, then maybe it might help you, too?" Her words poured out in a rush, as if she were afraid she would lose her courage if she didn't get it out fast.

With his free hand, Ben rubbed at the stubble on his cheek and fought to swallow the huge lump in his throat.

She tilted her head as she studied him. "Ben? Are you all right?"

"Do you think they'd want to see me? Wouldn't I be a reminder that their son died and I lived?"

"If I had a son who died the way theirs did, I'd want to know that in his last moments he was thinking of me and the life we'd shared." She took his other hand and held on tight. "I'd want to know, Ben. Any mother would."

Without taking even a second to debate the implications, he released one of her hands and caressed her cheek as he leaned in to kiss her. When she didn't protest or push him away, he let his hand slide around her neck. Though he brought her closer, he kept the kiss chaste, despite the grinding need that pulsed through him.

"Does that mean you like my idea?" she asked with a small, private smile that warmed his heart. Her eyes, he noticed, were still focused on his lips—better there than on his lap, where she would find proof of just how badly he wanted her.

He nodded. "I like your idea. I like you."

"I have to get ready for work now."

"Can I see you later?" he asked, keeping his firm hold on her hand.

"I'm usually pretty tired after my shift, and I was up really late last night."

"We don't have to do anything special. Takeout and a movie?"

She hesitated but only for a moment. "All right."

"There's just one thing," he said, looking away from her when embarrassment threatened to derail him. He brought his eyes back to meet hers. "I can't pick you up, because I can't drive yet. In fact, I might never be able to drive again."

"Well, in that case, you're in luck. See, I have a car, and since I drove you home last night, I know where you live."

He smiled. "I like the way you say that."

"So I'll come by around eight?"

"I'll be waiting."

CHAPTER 15

Georgie emerged from the bathroom and heard Cat and Tess talking upstairs. With her hair in a towel, her mother's robe tied tight around her, and hoping to get the scoop on Ian and Ben, she went up to see what they were talking about.

"What do you think, Georgie?" Tess asked.

"About what?"

"Show her, Cat."

Cat came out of her room wearing a long, red print Gypsy skirt with one of her signature formfitting tank tops.

Georgie stared at her. She had never seen Cat in such a feminine outfit and was startled by the transformation.

"Don't you dare laugh," Cat warned her.

"Me? Laugh?"

"Just tell me what you think," Cat said with irritation. "Does it look okay?"

"You look great," Georgie said. "What's the occasion?"

"She's having dinner with Ian," Tess said. "I said I'd rather see her in something shorter that shows off her fabulous legs."

"I agree," Georgie said.

"But I don't *have* anything like that," Cat whined. "And I *refuse* to go shopping for dinner with a guy I met yesterday."

"I've got a few things that might work," Georgie said.

"Really?" Cat said, brightening. "You don't mind?"

"Of course not. What's mine is yours." Georgie smiled and added, "Are we *really* hanging out with three *brothers?*"

Tess winced. "I know. We're like a bad cliché."

"So what's the deal? You first, Tess."

She shrugged. "I don't know. I like him. He's gentle. He doesn't let many people see that side of him, but I've seen it."

"Nathan mentioned that he's had a lot of problems since he got back from Iraq," Georgie said. "I'd hate to see you hurt after everything you've already been through."

"I would, too," Cat said.

"I told her everything," Tess said to Georgie.

"Good. I'm glad she knows."

"It's nothing serious with Ben," Tess assured them. "Don't worry."

"Same with me," Cat said. "We're just having dinner."

Tess turned to Cat. "Can I ask you something?" she said tentatively.

"Sure."

"What's your problem with Rosie? She can tell you don't like her."

"No way," Cat drawled, rolling her eyes. "She's what? Three?"

"Almost four and very intuitive," Tess said. "She can sense it."

"Oh, please! Just because I don't go all soft and misty over her the way you do doesn't mean I don't like her."

"I didn't go soft *or* misty," Tess sniffed.

Cat looked to Georgie for confirmation. "Um, yeah, you did."

"We're not talking about me," Tess said hotly. "And she may be only three, but she's no dummy. If you're going to hang out with him, you have to be nice to her."

"I'm not hanging out with him. I'm having dinner with him, and you're making me regret that."

"All right, ladies, simmer down." Georgie stepped between them. "I know you might not mean to, Cat, but you do put out the vibe that you don't like her."

"Exactly," Tess said.

"I *don't* dislike her," Cat mumbled, clearly annoyed at being double-teamed.

"He's done an impressive job with her all on his own," Tess said.

"For sure," Georgie agreed. "Let me get those skirts so we can see if one will work." She went downstairs and returned a minute later with the clothes. A pair of high-heeled sandals dangled from her fingers.

Cat eyed the shoes with trepidation.

Georgie nudged her into her room. "Try them on."

While they waited for Cat, Tess went into her room to slip on bright green scrubs and Reeboks.

Cat emerged wearing a black tank with spaghetti straps that showcased her fragile collarbones, Georgie's denim miniskirt, the shoes and an expression of abject misery on her face. "I can't wear this."

Georgie and Tess stared at her.

"Holy smokes." Georgie rubbed her fingers against her robe. "You're a babe, Cat."

"No kidding," Tess said with envy. "Can I hire you to be my body double?"

"Shut up and get serious, will you? I'll fall on my ass if I try to wear these girly shoes."

"No, you won't," Georgie assured her. "You've got all day to break them in."

"I don't feel comfortable, though. He's going to know that."

Tess rested her hands on Cat's shoulders. "Georgie's right—you're a babe—and Ian's going to be so busy trying to keep his hands off you that he won't notice you're uncomfortable, believe me."

"You really think so?"

"I *know* so," Tess said. "Have a great time."

Tess hugged Cat, and Georgie was relieved when Cat reciprocated. Apparently, no hard feelings lingered from their conversation about Rosie.

"Thank you," Cat said. "Both of you."

"No problem," Tess said. "I've got to get to work, but I want to check Nathan's arm first, so I'll see you later."

After Tess went downstairs, Cat turned to Georgie. "What do you think of her and Ben?"

"Just that Nathan has some concerns. He doesn't know what we know about her, but he senses something's up."

"His cop radar's getting a hit?"

"Uh-huh."

"Well, we'll have to keep an eye on her," Cat said.

"Yes. What about you? Are you going to be okay?"

"Of course," Cat snorted. "I hate all this chick shit." In a high, squeaky, voice, she said, "Dating and guys and what should I wear. *Ugh.*"

Georgie laughed.

"You know what's really bugging me? Ian reminds me of an actor or someone famous, but I can't think of who."

"Dennis Quaid," Georgie said without hesitation.

"*Yes!* That's it!" Cat laughed. "God, that was driving me crazy."

"Happy to help." Georgie moved toward the stairs. "Tomorrow I'll need a full report on your night with Dennis."

"Georgie?"

She turned back.

"You and Nathan."

"What about us?"

"You know I'm on your side, right?"

"Of course."

"It's just that I can see how into you he is just by the way he looks at you. He's a good guy, and I'd hate to see him get hurt if you aren't as into him."

Startled by Cat's candor, Georgie had no idea what to say.

"I know it's none of my business."

"No, you're right," Georgie stammered. "I'm trying to keep some perspective, but he doesn't make it easy. He's so . . ."

"Adorable?" Cat asked, raising an eyebrow in amusement.

"*Yes!* And persistent. How am I supposed to defend myself against that? I've told him I don't want to get involved, but it's like he doesn't even hear me. And the more time I spend with him, the messier it gets. What am I supposed to *do?*"

Cat chuckled. "He's practicing selective hearing—it's a gift most men are born with. Let me ask you this: have you considered the possibility that he's 'the one'?"

"No," Georgie said firmly. "I haven't. I don't want that right now."

"Love doesn't work on a schedule, Georgie."

Georgie's eyes almost popped out of her head. "*Love?* What does this have to do with *love?*"

"Maybe everything?"

"I can't talk about it anymore. Have fun with Ian. You look amazing." Georgie ducked down the stairs before Cat could reply and stomped into her room where Nathan sat on the bed.

"Uh-oh," he said. "What's the matter?"

"Nothing." She retrieved underwear and shorts from her dresser and slammed the drawers shut.

"Something happened."

"Nothing happened! Will you please just—" She spun around to discover his face was once again ghostly pale. "What? What's wrong? Is it your arm?" She dropped the clothes on the floor, crossed the room to him, and cradled his face in her hands.

With a sigh, he closed his eyes and hooked his good arm around her waist. "Tess did that thing with the syringe again. Hurts."

Georgie felt all the starch leave her spine as she gathered him close to her.

They were quiet for a long time before he whispered, "You smell good."

"So do you."

Tilting his head, he gazed up at her.

"I'm sorry you're hurting." She shifted a hand to his forehead. "You're warm again, too."

"I just took some more pills."

"Why don't you go back to sleep while I'm at the hospital?"

He shook his head. "I want to be with you."

Exasperated, she said, "I'd come back for you."

"No need."

"You should take it easy today, Nathan."

"I will," he insisted as he stood up without removing the arm he had around her. Leaning in, he touched his lips to hers. "I'll let you get dressed."

As the door closed behind him, Georgie flopped backward onto the bed, her hands fisted tight against her eyes. She wasn't going to cry, she wasn't going to let him get to her, and no matter what Cat said, she was *not* going to fall in love with him. No way.

After breakfast at a diner on Thames Street, they took his car to the hospital, but Georgie insisted on driving.

"I didn't know it was possible for one person to eat that much in the morning."

He patted his full belly. "I'm a growing boy."

"No wonder why you run every day." After a long period of silence, she glanced over at him. "Can I ask you something that's probably none of my business?"

"Sure."

"Why are you still single?"

"Don't you mean—how is it possible that someone with my stellar good looks, charm, sense of humor, and overall sex appeal could still be on the market?"

He had nailed it perfectly, but she wasn't about to let him know that, so she rolled her eyes. "Give me a break, will you, please?"

Laughing, he shrugged. "Just worked out that way."

"You've never wanted to get married?"

"I didn't say that."

"Fine," she said, more annoyed with herself than with him. Why did it matter so much? If she allowed herself to contemplate the answer to that question . . . "Forget I asked."

"There was someone once. I probably would've married her."

"Except?"

"She died."

Georgie gasped and took her eyes off the road to look over at him. "Oh *God*, Nathan. I'm so sorry."

"It was a long time ago."

But something in his tone told her the pain was still a big part of him.

Her head spun with questions, but she couldn't seem to find the words.

"You can ask, Georgie," he said quietly.

"No, I can't. It's not my place."

He reached for her hand. "I met her during my freshman year of college, and we dated for a couple of years."

Riveted by his softly spoken words, she pulled into the hospital parking lot, turned off the car and shifted in her seat to face him. "What was her name?"

"Ellen."

Georgie bit back the litany of questions she wanted to ask and waited for him to comport himself.

"We were on Christmas break during our junior year, and we went to a party on Dixon Street. To get to the place, you had to go up a flight of outdoor stairs. When we were leaving, I ran back in to go to the bathroom and left her talking to some people on the landing."

Georgie held on tight to his hand, her stomach knotting with anxiety.

"I was only gone for like two minutes, but when I came back she was crumpled at the bottom of the stairs, and the other people were gone."

Georgie gasped.

"She was on life support for a month before her parents made the decision to let her go. I took that semester off from school and became totally obsessed with finding out what happened to her. Was she pushed? Or did she slip on some ice after the others went back inside?"

"Did you ever find out?"

He shook his head. "I was only gone for two minutes—the only *two minutes* of my life I'd give anything to have back. It just felt so random, you know? If I hadn't gone back in, she would still be alive. We'd probably be married, with kids. That life can just *do* that to you." After a long pause, he said, "I still find it hard to believe sometimes."

"I'm sorry," Georgie said as it became clear to her that he was the last guy in the world she should be dating. He had already lost one woman he loved. How could she ask him to risk losing another? "It sounds so inadequate, but I'm truly sorry."

He raised their joined hands to his lips.

"This is why you became a police officer, isn't it?"

Nodding, he said, "The not knowing how it happened was the worst part for me, her parents and all the people who loved her. I figured if I could keep that from happening to even one other family, then maybe Ellen wouldn't have died in vain."

Georgie clutched his hand.

"I worked really hard and became the youngest detective in the department's history. I've refused to sit for promotion tests that would move me off the streets and into a desk job. I'm right where I want to be, and I know I'm making a difference."

"You still think about what happened to Ellen, though."

"All the time." His face shifted into a wry grin, but his eyes were sad. "By now that particular failure is hard-wired into my DNA. I learned a lot from it, though. Life is short, love is sweet, regrets can either make you or break you, nothing lasts forever."

Life could be so unfair, so exquisitely unfair. "Awfully big lessons for a twenty-year-old."

"Yes, they were. I had a lot of issues after it happened. I was mad at the world for years."

"I can understand why."

"I let the anger really eat away at me. Took a long time to get past that." He glanced out the window and then back at her. "That day at the Dumpster?"

Georgie nodded.

"I haven't lost it like that in a really long time."

"Now that I know you better, I can see why you got so mad."

"Still… I was out of line."

"And you apologized rather nicely with lovely flowers." She leaned over to kiss him. "Thanks for telling me about Ellen."

"Thanks for listening." He held her gaze for a long moment. "There hasn't been anyone since then who's really mattered to me. Until now."

"Nathan—"

"I know what you're going to say, but I can't help how I feel." Reaching out to caress her face, he added, "There's just something about you, Georgie Quinn."

Georgie's stomach ached as Cat's warning echoed through her mind. If only he would stop doing and saying things to make loving him so damned easy!

They found the group from the senior center gathered in the waiting room of the intensive care unit. Georgie and Nathan were introduced to Gus's daughter.

"My father thought the world of your mother and has nothing but good things to say about you," Dawn said as she shook hands with Georgie.

"That's nice to hear," Georgie said. "Is there any change?"

Dawn shook her head. "He's still in critical condition, but he's holding his own."

"You know anything more about the investigation?" Bad Gus asked Nathan.

"I haven't spoken to anyone yet today, but I'll make a few calls and see what I can find out."

"We'd appreciate that," Walter said. "Roxy's working a detail, so she hasn't heard, either."

Nathan leaned in to speak privately with Georgie. "I'm going out to the hallway where I can use my phone. Will you be all right?"

"I hope so."

"If you want to wait, I'll go in with you."

"I'll be okay."

He kissed her forehead and left the room.

"You two seem *awfully* cozy," Annette said with a sly smile. "He's just as cute as a button."

"We're *friends*," Georgie said.

"Friends with benefits," Bad Gus muttered, and the others snickered.

Georgie's face heated with embarrassment. While she was glad to see them laughing again, she wished it wasn't at her expense.

"Do you want me to walk you in, honey?" Bill asked.

"I'd appreciate that."

He looped an arm around her shoulders. "Let's go, then."

Steeling herself for what she would see, she let Bill lead her around the nurse's station to one of the glass-walled rooms where the beeping of monitors and Gus's labored breathing were the only sounds. Georgie had to fight the immediate urge to turn and run. She had done that last night. Today she would stay and deal, no matter what it cost her, because that's what her mother would have done.

"Oh," she gasped when she finally glanced at Gus's face. What had been black and blue the night before was now angry purple and hugely swollen.

Bill squeezed her shoulder. "Looks awful, doesn't it?" he asked in a hushed voice.

Georgie couldn't speak over the lump in her throat, so she nodded.

"They say there're no broken bones, which is a miracle."

"So then why doesn't he wake up?" Georgie asked.

"There was some bleeding in his brain. They're hoping they can operate if he stabilizes a little more, but by then . . ."

"It might be too late."

"Yes, but they said we should talk to him, that familiar voices might stimulate him."

Georgie took a step toward the bed.

"I'll leave you alone," Bill said. "Talk to him. I know he'll hear you."

She heard the door swish shut behind him and tried to find a place on Gus's battered body where she could touch him without hurting him. Reaching for the hand that was attached to a finger monitor, she tried to think of something to say.

"Hi, Gus, it's me, Georgie, and I'm so sorry you got hurt. How could anyone do this to you?" A sob lodged in her throat, and she fought it back. He didn't need to hear that. Clearing her throat, she forced a cheerful tone. "I know you'd be teasing me if you could because I showed up here today with Nathan Caldwell, and I danced with him at the social last night. You remember how he made me cry at the Dumpster, right? Well, he came over that same night with flowers to apologize. He took me out to dinner, and well, some other stuff happened that you certainly don't want to hear about.

"Anyway, the thing is, I like him even though I don't *want* to like him. That's messed up, isn't it? Cat, my roommate, thinks he could be my 'one.' How funny is that? I mean, we just met a few days ago. Granted, a lot's happened since then, but still, the *one?* Crazy, huh?"

She watched Gus's chest rise and fall in a steady rhythm.

"But you know, if I was looking for 'the one,'" Georgie continued, "he'd make for a very attractive candidate. He's so cute, isn't he? Well, you probably don't think so, but I do. Cat and Tess say so, too. Oh, and get this, they're dating his brothers! We're turning the house into a regular bordello. I wonder what my mother would have to say about that!

"I miss her," she said with a sigh. "In all the chaos of dealing with the house and the center and her estate, sometimes it's easy to forget she's really gone. I find myself reaching for the phone because I want to tell her something. I used to tell her everything. We talked on the phone every day. Did you know that? I don't tell too many people that because, you know, it's kind of weird to still talk to your mom every day when you're almost thirty. But that's just how it was between us. We were always close. My friends used to fight like she-cats with their mothers, but I never did. The other day I even dialed her cell number . . ."

CHAPTER 16

Nathan stood riveted in the doorway, the desire to offer comfort warring with the overwhelming need to hear more of Georgie unfiltered and uncut. How he wished she would talk as freely to him. So, Cat thought he could be "the one" for Georgie. Interesting. *And she thinks I'm cute.* Very *interesting. . .*

". . . and it wasn't until her voicemail picked up that I remembered she was gone. I'm ashamed to admit I called back three times, just to listen to her voice on the message. Pretty sad, huh? And Ali and I can't get in touch with our dad. We tried to call him to tell him Mom died, but we never heard back from him. It's not like we've been close to him since he left Mom, but we thought he'd want to know what's going on." Georgie reached out to smooth Gus's hair off his bruised forehead. "And now Ali's having the surgery, and she's after me to have that stupid blood test. Is it so wrong to not want to know something like that? Why can't I just wait and see what happens?"

Confused and curious as to what she was talking about, Nathan ached over the sadness he heard in her voice, and offering comfort suddenly became more important than satisfying his curiosity. He cleared his throat.

She spun around.

"Hey," he said. "How's Gus today?"

"About the same." She eyed him warily. "How long were you there?"

He joined her at Gus's bedside. "I just walked in the door."

"Oh."

Nathan could tell she didn't believe him.

"Did you find out anything about the case?"

He glanced at Gus. "I'll tell you outside."

Georgie leaned over, sought out a spot on Gus's face that wasn't bruised, and pressed a light kiss to his forehead. "Get well," she whispered. "Please. I miss you."

Nathan realized she was crying, so he rested his hands on her shoulders.

She surprised him when she turned into his embrace and clung to him.

"Come on," he said, keeping his good arm tight around her as he led her to the hallway.

Her tears soaked through his shirt and warmed his chest.

"I'm sorry." She sniffed. "I seem to be crying all over you a lot lately."

"You've had good reason."

"I can't stand seeing him like that." She glanced up, and the devastation on her face broke Nathan's heart. "Tell me they caught the guy who did this."

"They got a couple of good prints from the door frame, and they're following up on a few other promising leads. They'll get him, Georgie. If they don't, I will. I promise."

"Don't make promises you can't keep."

"I never do."

"Thank you."

"For?"

"This." She slid her hands up to his shoulders and rested her face against his chest. "For being here."

A surge of tenderness took Nathan by surprise. With any other woman, he would want to shake her for all the mixed signals she was sending. But rather than shake her, he held her closer and was grateful for the opportunity even as he burned with questions he wished he could ask her.

After spending half an hour with the others in the waiting room, Georgie and Nathan left with promises to check in later. As they emerged into the sunny summer day, he watched her perk up like a drooping flower that had just been watered. "What do you feel like doing?"

"I have no idea. I can't remember the last time I had nothing to do."

He hooked his index finger around hers on the way to the car. "How about taking a ride? There's something I've been wanting to check out in Portsmouth."

"Sure."

"I need to go home and get changed first."

"Okay."

"I like this agreeable version of Georgie Quinn. She's easy to get along with."

"She's making a limited appearance today only."

"Then I'd better take full advantage."

Feeling like she was returning to the scene of a crime, Georgie followed Nathan into his house.

"I'll be quick," he said on his way upstairs. "Grab a drink if you want. The fridge is right around the corner."

She helped herself to a Diet Coke and stepped onto the back porch, where Ben was reading the morning paper.

"Hey," he said.

"Oh, hi."

He gestured to the other chair. "Have a seat."

"We're only here for a minute."

"Suit yourself."

They coexisted in awkward silence for several minutes before Nathan reappeared, wearing shorts and a T-shirt from a 5K race.

"What're you up to today, Ben?"

"Just hanging out, waiting."

"For?"

"Tess to finish work."

"Ben, about this thing with Tess—"

"I can't imagine how it's any of your business," Ben snapped.

"You need to be careful with her—"

"Why wouldn't I be?"

"You haven't exactly been known for your sensitivity to others since you got home."

"You're wasting your breath, Nate."

"Go easy with her, or you'll answer to me."

"Save your man-of-the-family act, little brother. It's getting old."

Nathan took a step toward him, but Georgie stopped him by resting her hand on his forearm. With a parting glare for his brother, Nathan led her inside.

"Where should I put this?" Georgie asked, holding up the empty can.

Nathan took it from her and tossed it into the middle section of a three-part bin.

"What's that?"

"My recycling center. Paper, plastic and cans, and compost."

Georgie wrinkled up her nose. "Compost? Gross."

He sighed with pretend exasperation, but she could still see the tension in his eyes from the confrontation with Ben. "I have so much to teach you. I noticed you ladies don't have a recycling bin. I'll get you one."

"No need. I'm not going to be there for much longer."

"What about Tess and Cat? Are you going to kick them out when you leave?"

She followed him to his car. "Of course not. They're going to take care of the house when I go home to Atlanta."

"You're really digging in on that, aren't you?"

"On what?"

"Going back to Atlanta."

From the driver's seat, she turned to him. "Why wouldn't I? I *live* there, Nathan."

"Whatever you say."

"If I have *any* prayer of putting my career back together, it has to be there. That's where all my professional contacts are. If I don't get back there soon, word's going to get out that Davidson's fired me. Do you think anyone will care that it was because my mother got sick and I got stuck running her senior center in Newport, Rhode Island? All they'll hear is 'fired,' and I'll be right back where I started eight years ago."

"I'm sorry. I'm pissed at Ben, and I took it out on you."

"Do you understand what I just said to you? Did you *hear* me?"

"Everything after you going back to Atlanta was kind of fuzzy," he teased. Reaching for her hand, he brought it to his lips. "I heard you, sweetheart. And what you said makes sense. I just hate the idea of you being so far away from me."

"There you go again."

"Whoops," he said with a sheepish grin. "Sorry."

"No, you're not. Where are we going anyway?"

"Take West Main." After a long period of silence, Nathan said, "What's going on with Tess, Georgie? I know you know."

"I can't talk to you about that."

"Is she in trouble?"

"Not with the law or anything like that."

"Then hiding? From something or someone?"

Georgie hesitated, only for a second, but it was enough.

"That's it, isn't it?"

"I can't, Nathan. Don't ask me to betray my friend."

"Even if I could help her?"

"You can't fix everything."

"Especially if I don't know what the problem is."

"Don't pout," she teased. "It's not pretty on you."

"I'm not pouting."

Georgie snorted. "Whatever you say," she said, tossing his words back at him.

"I may as well put this out there, too."

"What?" she asked with a wary glance.

"I could probably find your father if you really want to know where he is."

"You *were* listening! I knew it!"

He continued to stare straight ahead as if she hadn't spoken.

"Aren't you even going to *try* to defend yourself?"

"Nope."

Georgie fumed as she drove, trying desperately to remember everything she had said to Gus. Ugh! She had told him the whole thing about Cat suggesting Nathan could be "the one." Had he heard that, as well? Her fingers tightened around the steering wheel. Oh God, the blood test. She had mentioned that, too.

"So do you want me to take a stab at finding him?"

Despite her irritation, she couldn't help being curious. "What would that entail?"

"I could run a check on his credit cards to start with. There's a good chance he's leaving a paper trail of some sort. With a little digging, I could find it."

Georgie pondered that for several quiet minutes. "We haven't had much contact with him since he took off when I was in high school. The last we knew, he was living in Phoenix, but the number we had for him is no longer in service."

"I could find him."

"Can I think about it?"

"Sure you can."

"Thank you for offering."

He shrugged. "It's no big deal."

"It is to me." They drove through Middletown into Portsmouth. "Where's this place you want to check out?"

"Portsmouth Abbey."

"I used to go ice skating there on Sundays when I was in high school."

"I did, too. I wonder if we were ever there at the same time."

She smiled at him. "We probably were."

"Georgie."

"Yeah?"

He looked down at their joined hands and toyed with her fingers. "What you said to Gus about a blood test you need to have. What did you mean by that?"

Her stomach clutched with nerves. "I thought you weren't listening."

"I believe we've already established that I lied."

"It's nothing. Really."

"Didn't sound like nothing to me."

"I don't want to talk about it. Can we just have some fun today? I can't tell you how much I could use a day off from everything."

"Sure," he said, but she could tell he was hurt by her refusal to level with him. "I hope you'll tell me eventually, because until you do, I'm going to worry about you."

"That's not necessary."

He shrugged. "Can't help it." He flashed a teasing grin. "But just for the record, you don't have STDs or anything like that, do you?"

Relieved that he was letting it go—for now—Georgie laughed. "Shut up." She took a left onto Cory Lane, navigated the winding road, and turned into the driveway of the prestigious private school, which was deserted for the summer. Right away she understood the purpose of this mission. "Oh, you've got to be *kidding me!* We drove all this way to look at a *windmill?*"

"Not just *any* windmill. It's a wind *turbine* and the first of its kind in the area."

Georgie groaned. "We could've gone to the beach or flown a kite on Ocean Drive or watched the boats in the harbor, but *no*. We get to visit a gigantic windmill. Lucky me."

Nathan chuckled and opened his door. "I hate to say it, but sarcasm doesn't look pretty on you, Georgie Quinn. Take a walk with me."

Dreaming of the beach, Georgie got out of the car and took his outstretched hand. "You're going to owe me big-time for this, Caldwell."

"That sounds promising."

Georgie cracked up. At least he could be counted on for consistency.

As they navigated the dirt path that led to the base of the windmill, he told her it was one hundred sixty-four feet tall and each of the three blades was seventy-seven feet long.

"You're a nerd, Nathan. Seriously."

"I'm insulted." But he seemed more amused than insulted.

"So what's the point?" she asked, tipping her head up for a better view.

"They expect it to cut the school's two hundred thousand dollar electric bill in half."

"That much?"

"Yep. It'll probably reduce their heating bills, too."

"How much did it cost?"

"One point two five million. So in ten years it'll more than pay for itself, and it has a life expectancy of twenty-five years. Pretty cool, huh?"

"Very," she said with a decided lack of enthusiasm.

"This is the *future*, Georgie. We can't sustain our reliance on foreign oil. These kinds of alternative energy sources are going to become commonplace. There's another turbine over at the high school if you want to see an even bigger one."

"Thanks, but I'll pass. How did you become such an enviro nerd?"

"My mother is a hippie environmentalist."

Georgie stared up at his clean-cut self and tried to imagine him with a hippie for a mother. "No way."

He rewarded her with the grin that occupied every square inch of his face. "You've decided I'm too much of a nerd to have a hippie for a mother, right?"

"Something like that."

"Well, it's true. If you don't believe me, ask Ben or Ian. She lived on a commune in Utah for two years after college. They were way out in front of the environmental movement and so was she, which is why we recycled at home years before it was in vogue. Since there was nowhere local to take it back then, she and I used to drive it to a place in Boston once a month. She got our whole neighborhood on board, and the car was usually full to the gills with cans and newspapers and beer bottles. What I remember most vividly from those trips is the stench of beer."

Georgie laughed.

"These days, one of my favorite sounds in the world is the crash of bottles into the recycling truck on garbage day."

"No doubt the highlight of your week."

"My favorite day."

"You really are a nerd, Caldwell."

Smiling, he rested his hands on her hips and tugged her to him. "But you want me anyway."

She gauged the almost dangerous glint in his eyes. "Don't flatter yourself."

Hooking his good arm around her neck, he brought his mouth down on hers and set out to prove her wrong. While his kisses the night before had been about gentle seduction, this one was about passionate persuasion. His tongue slid past her teeth in teasing thrusts that made her desperate for more.

Georgie fisted his shirt, trying to gain purchase as her head spun and her heart pounded. She loved the way he kissed, how his soft lips moved over hers as his stubble rubbed against her cheek—not to mention the way he tasted and the spicy male scent that permeated her senses every time she was close to him. It was okay to admit all that, right? Just because she loved kissing him didn't mean she loved *him*, did it?

The hand that had been resting on the small of her back slid down to palm her bottom. He pulled her tight against his erection.

"Nathan," she gasped. "Someone might see us."

Raising his head, he took a quick glance around. "Who?" He returned his attention to her lips.

"Wait," she said, pressing her hands to his chest. "I need to catch my breath."

He flashed her a cocky grin. "Took it away, did I?"

"Don't look so satisfied."

"I'm far from satisfied," he said in a low, sexy voice, his blue eyes heavy with desire. He took her hand and started back to the car.

Georgie's heart continued to thud as she walked with him down the dirt path.

When they reached the parking lot, he angled her back against the sun-warmed car and molded his body to hers. Cradling her face in his hand, he kissed her lightly this time, as if he intended to keep her off balance. "You're so beautiful, Georgie," he whispered against her lips, bringing her in closer and then wincing when his injured arm protested the movement.

"No, I'm not. I'm short and my eyes are too close together and—"

He silenced her with another passionate kiss. "If I say you're beautiful, you have to believe me." His fingers slid beneath the hem of her shirt and heated her skin. "Have you been thinking about the first night we spent together?" he whispered in her ear.

Georgie's eyes darted up to meet his. "No," she said in a shaky voice that gave her away.

"Liar," he chuckled.

She shuddered from the skim of his lips over her ear.

"I think about it all the time. I *dream* about it." Under her shirt, his hands coasted up over her ribs. His thumbs grazed her nipples.

"*Nathan*," she moaned as she arched into his embrace. "Stop."

"Okay."

As he kissed her forehead and removed his hands from under her top, Georgie could have cried from the loss. *Wait*, she wanted to say yet again. *I didn't mean it!*

"Ready to go?" he asked with maddening nonchalance.

Was he serious? Could he really turn it off that fast? He was making her crazy one kiss at a time, which, she suspected, was his plan. She could barely stand, let alone drive, but with the brush of her hand across her burning lips, she made an effort to pull herself together.

"How about I drive for a while?" he asked with a smug grin that told her he was well aware of the effect his rapid withdrawal had on her.

"Fine." Georgie threw the keys at his head, plopped into the passenger seat and slammed the door.

"What's got you so hot and bothered?" he asked as he got in the car with the keys in his hand rather than sticking out of his head as she had intended.

She shot him a look of pure disbelief. "I'm neither hot *nor* bothered."

"Sweetheart, you're both, and that just infuriates you, doesn't it?"

"God, you're so full of yourself! How can you stand it?"

"At least I know what I want. You, on the other hand. Who knows from one minute to the next what you want? Hot, cold, warm, icy, *smoldering*, and then just as fast we're right back to frigid. That one's a real turn off, I gotta tell you."

"Are you through?"

"I'm just getting started."

"I told you what I wanted—way back at the very beginning. Remember? Do you have any memory of me saying I. Don't. Want. To. Get. Involved? Ringing any bells?"

"Involved? Is that what we are? Well, at least it has a definition now. That's progress."

"*Ugh!*" she shrieked. "You are the most aggravating person I've ever met! You hear only what you want to hear, you keep showing up, making yourself necessary to me, kissing me senseless, and what am I supposed to do? How am I supposed to deal with that? Can you tell me?"

He smirked, and it took all her willpower not to smack it right off his face. "Why are you making that face?"

"I'm necessary to you, huh?"

"*See what I mean?* You hear *only* what you want to hear! I swear to God, if you weren't already injured, I'd beat the daylights out of you myself!"

"That I'd like to see. In fact, the minute my arm stops hurting like a bastard, you're on."

"Now you're making fun of me, aren't you?"

"Well, *yeah*." He flipped a lock of her hair between his fingers. "I guess I am."

Smacking his hand away, she glowered at him.

"Do you really want me to leave you alone, Georgie?" he asked softly. "Do you want me to go away and never come back? Because if that's what it'll take to make you happy, I'll do it, even though I'd miss you and all your many moods like crazy. Is that what you want?"

As she glanced over to gauge his sincerity, her stomach hurt at what she saw on his face. The cockiness was gone, the humor was gone, and in their place was sadness. That she had done that to him dissolved what remained of her anger. "No."

"Are you sure? You need to be sure, because I don't plan to make this offer again."

"I'm not sure of anything. That's the problem."

"Here's something you can be sure of—I'm falling for you, Georgie Quinn, and you've become quite necessary to me, too. Vital, in fact."

"You really have to stop saying that stuff."

Leaning in to kiss her, he said, "Okay."

CHAPTER 17

With butterflies storming around in his stomach and as confident as a teenaged boy about to take out the hottest babe in school, Ian Caldwell wiped his sweaty palms on his jeans and stood on the front porch for a long time before he could work up the nerve to ring the bell. *When was the last time I was this nervous before a date? Never.*

"Come on in," Cat called out the window from the third floor. "I'll be right down."

Ian stepped into the foyer and took the opportunity to check the place out. He had been so busy trying not to stare at Cat earlier that he hadn't noticed much of anything else. The house was decorated in dark woods and bright colors—reds, yellows, and bold splashes of pattern, on big, solid furniture. Before he could get past the living room, he heard footsteps on the stairs and let his eyes wander up.

Legs . . . endless, creamy white legs on . . . were those *heels?* Had she worn *heels* for him? Only when he saw spots dancing in front of his eyes did Ian realize he had stopped breathing. God almighty, she was, without a doubt, the hottest woman he had ever known, and she had worn heels for *him!*

She landed at the bottom of the stairs and didn't seem to know what to do with her hands. Right then, Ian got that she was nervous, too. At least they had that much in common.

"Hi," she said.

"You look . . ." His voice trailed off when words failed him.

"The shoes are a bit much. That's what you were going to say right?"

Slowly, he shook his head and took a step closer to her. "That's not what I was going to say. That's not at *all* what I was going to say."

She swallowed. "What then?"

"Gorgeous," he said, taking another step. "Drop-dead, bowl-me-over, knock-me-out *gorgeous.*"

Her big brown eyes widened as she stepped back and encountered wall.

Ian had no idea what he thought he was doing when he propped his hands against the wall on either side of her head. "Cat."

"Yes?" she said, her voice heavy with what he hoped was the same desire that pulsed through him.

"All I can think about since last night is kissing you again."

"Oh. Really?"

Fixated on her mouth, he said, "Uh-huh." As much as it pained him, he didn't move to take what he wanted more than the next breath. Instead, he waited, for just the slightest signal from her, anything that would tell him they were on the same page—

Her hand snaked up around his neck and pulled his head down to her.

Okay, that would do it. As her lips connected with his, a bolt of electricity surged through him, and all the blood in his head set out for parts south. The kiss was a tangle of teeth and tongues and hands—hers on his ass hauling him as close as he could get without pushing her through the wall, and his, oh God, did he dare cop a feel of those unbelievable breasts? Thinking about them had kept him awake half the night wondering if they would feel as amazing as they looked.

Oh hell, why not? He moved his hands up and landed in heaven. A groan rumbled through him and echoed into her as the kiss went on and on. Finally, when the need for oxygen became more important than sucking her tongue into his mouth, he pulled his lips free and buried his face in her neck, encountering her dark, sexy scent.

Her fingers twisted into his hair, his erection nestled into the V of her legs. "Cat," he whispered as he closed his teeth over the tendon that joined her neck to her shoulder. "Jesus."

And then her hand curled around his, and she dragged him up the stairs. They raced to the third floor. She pushed him into her room, shut the door behind her, and flipped the lock. Nothing in his wildest fantasies could compare to the sound of that lock clicking into place.

"You have to work," he somehow managed to say as she tore his shirt over his head and fastened her lips to his nipple.

"I've got two hours. Is it going to take that long?"

"We'll be really, *really* lucky if it takes two *minutes*."

Her sexy, husky laugh was almost enough to send him into orbit. He wanted to slow it down, to take his time, but somehow he couldn't quite seem to make it happen. Fumbling, he found the hem of her top and tugged it up and over her head, uncovering the most magnificent breasts he had ever seen. He filled his hands, bent his head, and ravished.

She cried out and sank her fingers into his hair. "*Ian.*"

"Tell me what you want."

Tugging at the waistband of his jeans, she *showed* him what she wanted.

He shed his jeans, lifted her, and came down on top of her on the unmade bed. Lips fused, hands clutched, bodies locked together, the storm of passion blazed like an out-of-control wildfire. In all his life, Ian had never wanted a woman like this. Not ever, and as he pushed her skirt down over slim hips, he had the wherewithal to wonder if this woman, this moment, might become the gold standard by which all others were measured.

"Condom," she panted. "In the drawer."

His body plastered to hers, he reached over her, opened the drawer, and weeded through nail polish, earrings, and other chick flotsam in search of condoms. "*Where?*"

She reversed their positions and stretched her arm toward the table, placing a nipple right above his face. What was a guy to do with that? He sucked it hard into his mouth, and she let out a squeal of surprise and knocked the wind out of him when her pelvis gyrated against his erection. "Cat, honey, *come on.*"

With a soft giggle, she said, "Got one." She sat up, straddled him, and ripped the wrapper off with her teeth.

He had never seen anything sexier—until she used her mouth to roll it on him. *Jesus Christ, mother of God, Hail Mary full of grace.*

"Mmm," she said, her lips vibrating against his shaft.

"Cat." He reached for her, brought her up to him, and satisfied another fantasy when he looped her brow ring around his tongue. "Yup."

"What?"

"It's every bit as sexy as I imagined it would be."

Her eyes met his in the fading daylight. "You imagined that?"

"Uh-huh, and this." Using his legs to spread hers, he entered her slowly, giving her time to adjust. "And a whole lot of other things." With his hand cupping the back of her head, he urged her into another deep, probing kiss that, coupled with the action below, had him on the verge far too soon.

She sat up and sank down farther on him, which did nothing to help his faltering control.

Ian groaned and reached for her as she began to ride him with abandon.

Her breasts swayed in rhythm with the frantic motion of her hips.

Desperate to buy himself some time, he sat up, wrapped an arm around her back to hold her still, and feasted first on one breast, then the other. Her breathy sighs and quick, sharp gasps fueled his desire.

With great reluctance, he abandoned her breasts when her hands landed on his face and tilted it up. As her lips came down on his, he kept his eyes open, not wanting to miss a single second of her ascent. Anchoring her hips with his hands, he pushed hard into her once, twice. Her thighs quivered, her inner walls clutched him like a velvet fist, her head fell back, her lips parted. She clung to him as he went deep once more and drove her into oblivion.

Her rapturous scream took him with her.

Cat rested on top of him, her heart racing, her body still thrumming from the best orgasm she'd had in, well, *ever*. His fingers traced a path up and down her spine as his penis twitched inside her.

"You can't tell Nathan about this," she said.

He laughed softly, which sent him deeper into her. "Why in the world would I tell him?"

She lifted a shoulder in a halfhearted shrug. "Guys talk."

Gathering her face into his hands, he urged her to look at him. "Not this guy."

Cat believed him. The aura of honor about him made him trustworthy.

"I can't help but wonder why you'd care if I told Nathan in particular."

"Because. He'd tell Georgie, and I'd never hear the end of it after the way I razzed her when she and Nathan . . ."

"She and Nathan what?"

Cornered, Cat tried to think of something she could say to change the subject. Her mind went totally blank, so she resorted to a trick as old as the book. She kissed him—a soul-stirring, mind-altering kiss that, if she said so herself, was one of the best kisses she had ever given anyone.

He rolled them over and poured himself into the kiss.

Triumphant, Cat wrapped her arms around his neck to hold him in place.

"Nice try," he whispered. "Now spill it."

"Damn it," she muttered.

Ian laughed as he finally withdrew from her and kissed his way to her breasts. Dragging his tongue in lazy circles around her nipple, he denied her what she really wanted. "Tell me."

She gripped his hair and tried—unsuccessfully—to direct his mouth. With a groan of frustration, she said, "Fine. They did it. Are you happy now?"

"Not quite." He rewarded her with a quick stroke of his tongue over a turgid peak. "Something tells me there's more to the story."

"*Ian!*" she cried, arching her back and pulling his hair.

"Just tell me." He shifted his attention to her belly. "I won't say anything."

Finding it hard to breathe, let alone speak, Cat said, "They did it a bunch of times—the night they met."

Raising his head to find her eyes, he lifted an eyebrow. "Get out. Really?"

"Uh-huh. Now can you shut up and get busy down there?"

His broad shoulders pushed her legs apart as he moved farther down. "Glad to." He teased her with his tongue and fingers until she was a squirming, needy disaster area. "What's Cat short for?"

"How can you talk right now?" she panted.

Trailing a finger through her dampness, he said, "Not as much of a problem for me."

"If I tell you, will you stop fooling around and get down to it?"

"There's only one way to find out."

"Catherine, but if you call me that, you won't live to your next birthday."

"Catherine," he said as he slid a finger into her. "I like that. Old-fashioned and proper."

"Yeah, just like me." She pushed hard against his hand, begging for more.

"How old are you?"

"Twenty-eight," she choked out. "You?"

"Thirty-six. This might seem like an odd time to ask, when I've got my face buried in your, you know, but what's your last name?"

Cat's laughter faded to a moan when he closed his lips over her most sensitive spot. As he added a second finger and insistent flicks of his tongue, she climbed toward another climax.

Suddenly, he stopped. "I'm waiting."

"Kelly," she said without hesitation.

He dipped his head and went back for more. "Very pleased to meet you, Catherine Kelly."

She came with a scream that would have awakened the dead. Apparently, that wasn't enough for him because he coaxed her up and over again.

"Catherine Kelly's a screamer," he whispered, his lips coasting over her thigh. "Very improper and *very* hot."

Bathed in sweat and more sated than she could ever recall being, Cat closed her eyes and took deep, cleansing breaths. Her eyes flew open when he buried himself in her. "Condom," she gasped.

"Got it," he said, bringing his head down for a sweet, simple kiss.

She gripped his muscular arms as he held himself up and pumped into her. "Ian. . . "

"What, babe?"

"I think"—she gasped as he went deep—"I'm going to come again."

"Okay." He brought his mouth down hard on hers to muffle her screams of ecstasy. As he thrust into her, his muted cry escaped from their joined lips. "Damn," he gasped when he could speak again. He shifted to his side so he wouldn't crush her and brought her with him.

Cat curled up to him, nuzzled his soft chest hair, and went to sleep.

Holding her close to him as she slept, Ian was hit with a pang of guilt. He hated spending time away from Rosie, and hiring a babysitter so he could roll around in bed with a woman he had just met went against everything he believed in as a parent. Since Rosie came along, there hadn't been many opportunities to roll around with anyone, so it wasn't like this was something he did often—never, in fact. He took care of Rosie every day and worked most nights. That was his life.

His widowed neighbor, Mrs. O'Connell, was happy to watch Rosie whenever he had to work. Since she had his cell phone number and could always reach him, he hadn't mentioned to Mrs. O that he wasn't going to work. It wasn't that he had lied to her. He had just failed to mention that his plans for the evening didn't include work. Nothing about this evening had gone according to plan—not that he was complaining.

What an amazing woman Catherine Kelly had turned out to be. As he ran his hand over the incredibly sexy mermaid tattoo on the back of her right shoulder, he wondered if this would be a one-time thing or the start of something more substantial. He hoped it was the latter, because he hadn't had nearly enough of her.

With her asleep, he finally had the chance to process what she told him about Nathan and Georgie. No wonder why Nate had been so upset that Georgie didn't want to pursue a relationship with him. Nate wasn't a one-night stand kind of guy. In fact, since his girlfriend died in college, he hadn't dated much at all. He was due for some happiness, and Ian hoped his brother wasn't going to get his heart broken again.

Checking his watch, he couldn't believe it was already seven thirty. Ninety minutes had never gone by so fast. He hated to do it, but she had to be at work in half an hour. "Cat," he whispered. "*Catherine.*"

Her eyes flipped open, and for a moment she seemed surprised to find him in her bed.

He was aware of the exact moment that she remembered what had happened between them.

Her smile was sleepy and sexy. "Hey."

"Hey, yourself. You've got to go to work."

She groaned.

He turned them so she was on top of him. "Call in sick."

"I *can't.*"

"Aren't you the boss?"

"Yeah, but . . ."

"What?" He filled his hands with her soft buttocks and nibbled her neck.

"I'm drawing a total blank."

"When was the last time you called in sick?"

"Never."

"First time for everything."

"I'm not big on first-date sex, either."

Touched by her confession, he kissed her.

She surprised him with her passionate response.

"I can't believe I already want you again," he whispered.

"Aren't you hungry?"

"Don't worry about me. I can subsist on sex alone."

She propped her chin on his chest and smiled. "I just had the best idea."

"What's that?"

"How about I call in sick and we stay here all night?"

"Now why didn't I think of that?"

Cat squealed with laughter as he tickled her.

When he heard someone moving around in the hallway, Ian covered her mouth with his hand.

A knock on the door startled them.

"Cat?" Tess said. "Are you home?"

Cat and Ian stayed perfectly still until they heard Tess's retreating footsteps. And then they dissolved into laughter.

CHAPTER 18

Tess descended the stairs with an odd sense of having interrupted something. But what? Georgie, as far as she knew, was somewhere with Nathan. Cat was out with Ian.

Unless . . .

What if they hadn't gone *out? Well, wouldn't that be something?* Tess giggled. And after the way Cat had teased Georgie! Tess left the house and headed for her car. Normally she would walk the short distance to Ben's house, but if they decided to go out, she knew he wouldn't be able to walk far.

She had thought of him often during the long day at the hospital and was looking forward to seeing him. After she parked on Extension Street, she flipped down the mirror to touch up her lip-gloss. With a deep breath to calm nerves of excitement, she set off down the hill.

Ben stood in the doorway waiting for her.

"Hi," she said as she dashed up the stairs, thrilled to see him.

"I thought you'd never get here."

Because he looked so cute and happy to see her, she went up on tiptoes to kiss his cheek. "Sorry I'm late. We had a two-car accident come in right at shift change. How was your day?"

"Long and boring. Until now."

Tess felt his eyes on her as she stretched out the kinks of the day. "What do you feel like doing?"

"Anything you want."

"How about we get some food, rent a movie, and take it back to my house where there's actual furniture and even a TV?"

"Sounds like a plan," he said, gesturing to the door.

As she watched him struggle down the short flight of stairs to the street, Tess ached for him.

"Sorry," he said, his mouth tight with pain. "The simplest things take forever."

"Please don't apologize, Ben."

"I hate being a crip."

They walked slowly up the hill to her car.

"Can I ask you something?" she said.

"Uh-huh."

"Why didn't they amputate?"

"I wouldn't let them."

"You might've been better off."

"Maybe." He paused before he added, "I've never said that out loud before."

Tess stayed quiet, hoping he would say more.

"I was out of it for days. When I came to, I heard them talking about taking my leg, how every bone was shattered, my knee was a mess. I went nuts. They ended up sedating me, and when I woke up again, I still had a leg."

She opened the passenger door for him but didn't hover, sensing he wouldn't want her to.

"When they weaned me off the morphine, the pain was unlike anything I've ever experienced," he said when they were in the car. "I knew almost right away that I'd made a big mistake by not letting them take it."

"It's not too late."

"I've actually been thinking about it lately," he confessed.

"Really?"

He nodded. "The physical therapists say my mobility is as good as it's probably going to get, and the pain has been horrible, almost as bad as it was when it first happened. It makes me sick."

"Are you on anything?"

"It screws me up. I can't do another damned thing all day if I take it."

"Ben," she sighed, reaching for his hand. "You don't have to live in constant pain. That's no quality of life."

He raised her hand to his lips. "The quality of my life has taken a huge upswing in the last twenty-four hours."

Charmed by him, she smiled and squeezed his hand. Being with him made it easy to forget she had sworn off men forever. "What do you think of Thai food?"

He never took his eyes off her. "Love it."

"Ben?"

"Hmm?"

"I need my hand to drive."

"Oh, right," he said, releasing her.

"Just to get going. Then you can have it back."

Nathan parked in front of Georgie's house and went around to open the door for her.

She smothered a yawn as she took the hand he offered.

"Did I keep you out too late?" he asked with a smile.

"No. It was fun—more fun than I've had in a long time."

"For me, too." He stopped her on the first step. "What did you like best?"

She turned, and her eyes were level with his. "I'd have to say it's between the windmill and flying the kite at Brenton Point."

He smiled. "I liked the nap on the beach."

"It was all good."

"It *is* all good, Georgie. It's good between us. Do you feel it, too? Even just a little?"

Raising her hands to his face, she answered him with a kiss that made his legs weak. If only she knew that his heart was firmly in her hands, to do with whatever she wanted. No matter how many times he told himself that getting involved with a woman who wanted to be somewhere else and who was clearly keeping things from him wasn't in his best interest, he couldn't seem to stay away.

Her lips moved from his mouth to his jaw.

Nathan was frozen with surprise and desire and so many other emotions he couldn't begin to identify.

"Does that answer your question?" she asked in a sexy whisper.

"Yeah. That ought to do it. Does this mean we're involved, Georgie?"

With a resigned sigh, she said, "I guess it does."

"But you still don't want to be?"

"I want to go home to Atlanta, and your whole life is here. We're going to have a fairly significant geography problem before much longer."

"How about we see each other as much as we can until you have to go, and then we'll see."

Her face twisted into a grin that brought out the dimples. "What will we see?"

"What happens?"

"Can we keep it light and fun and not get too serious?"

"I can only promise to try," he said, even though he knew it was far too late—at least for him—to be promising light.

"You look much better than you did this morning." Running her hands over his face, she added, "The fever seems to be gone."

"It's because my nurse took such good care of me today."

Her arms encircled his neck, and she kissed him again, this time with seduction on her mind. Her tongue traced the outline of his mouth as her fingers combed through his hair.

He trembled and slipped an arm around her waist to bring her closer.

"Mmm," she sighed. "Now that's what I call fun."

"For whom?" he asked, his voice tight with restraint.

When she tossed her head back to laugh, he sank his teeth into the soft skin of her neck. Her laughter faded into a moan. "Nathan?"

"Yes?"

"Do you want to spend the night?"

More than life itself. "I can't, sweetheart."

She looked at him with a combination of hurt and surprise on her face. "Why?"

"You want to keep it light. Isn't that what you said?"

She nodded.

"I can't do that if I make love with you again. I just can't, and I suspect you might not be able to, either." He forced a smile. "But that doesn't mean we can't make out until our lips are numb." Tightening his good arm around her, he lifted her to him and walked them up the stairs. As they came down on the wicker sofa, he molded his lips to hers.

The kiss was hot and deep and endless. Georgie's fingertips dug into his shoulders, pulling him tighter against her.

What the hell is wrong with you, man? You could've had her naked and willing! Sure, but what happens when she leaves? Then what? Isn't some better than none? No, because with Georgie, some will never be enough.

The ringing of Georgie's cell phone interrupted their passionate embrace.

Nathan shifted so she could retrieve it from the pocket of her shorts and then helped her sit up.

"Joe? What's wrong? Is it Ali?"

Nathan felt her go tense.

"I talked to her earlier in the week. She seemed so certain that it was what she wanted. Has she changed her mind?"

Reaching for her free hand, Nathan held it between both of his.

"What can I do? Should I come there?" She listened for a minute. "All right. If you're sure. Are you okay?" She paused, listening. "I'm so sorry, Joe. I know this is hard on both of you—on all of us. Will you have her call me in the morning?

Okay. Thanks. Tell Ali I love her." She ended the call and stared off into the darkness, a sad expression on her face.

"What's wrong?" Nathan asked.

"My sister is having some problems right now. No one really knows about it, so my brother-in-law was just looking for someone to talk to."

"Do you want to talk about it?"

"She's…having surgery this week, and it's sort of a difficult situation."

"Nothing serious, I hope."

Georgie looked down at their joined hands and then raised shattered eyes to meet his. "It's a double mastectomy."

The pain he saw on her face hit him like a fist to the gut. "I'm so sorry, Georgie. Isn't that what your mother had, too?"

She nodded. "Maybe me, too," she said in a voice so small he almost didn't hear her.

Almost.

"What do you mean?" he forced himself to ask.

"That blood test you heard me talking about with Gus?"

He nodded, not at all sure he wanted to hear this now that she had decided to tell him.

"It's to find out if, like my mother and sister, I'm as much as seven times more likely to get breast cancer than the general population."

Nathan fought to keep the dismay off his face, sensing that was the last thing she needed from him just then. "And you don't want to have the test?"

"No! I want to go back in time three months to before I knew it was even possible that I could have the altered gene that my mother and sister have—and probably my aunt and grandmother, too. Three women in my mother's family have died of breast cancer in the last four years. So far only our cousin Bonnie has tested negative."

Reeling, Nathan tried desperately to process it all. "So your sister doesn't actually have cancer?"

Georgie shook her head. "Not yet anyway. But she has kids who are three and five, so she didn't want to wait around for it to find her."

"And you do?"

"It's not the same for me! She's happily married, has been for years, and her husband doesn't care if she has breasts or not. He just wants her alive."

"I would feel exactly the same way if it was the woman I loved," Nathan said, trying to keep his voice calm. For the first time since the Dumpster, he felt his control slipping.

"That's good of you to say," she said, sounding utterly defeated. "But it's the last thing you need to be dealing with, especially after what happened with Ellen."

"You're going to piss me off if you push me away because of this."

"I don't want to involve you."

"Too late," he whispered as he gathered her into his arms. "You're stuck with me. And you're going to have that test so you can get past this and get on with your life."

"Don't pressure me. Please?" She looked up at him with an expression on her face that broke his heart. "My mother was on me about it before she died, and then my mother's doctor, my sister and Tess. It's overwhelming enough without all that pressure on top of it."

"Will you talk to me about it, Georgie?"

"I want to, but it's not fair—"

He stopped her with a finger to her lips. "Shh. Don't decide that for me. I'm exactly where I want to be, with the person I want to be with."

She sagged into his embrace, seeming relieved to have finally shared her greatest worry with him.

Nathan's heart staggered as he realized that he loved her, and the thought of her getting sick and possibly dying from something that might be prevented . . . He stopped himself from going down that road. She had asked him not to pressure her, and he would do his best not to, but he wasn't going to let this happen to her. Not if he had anything to say about it.

In the meantime, he wanted to celebrate being in love again, despite all the obstacles that stood in their way. It had been a long time, far too long, since he had felt this way.

Through the open window, Nathan was startled by what sounded like Ben. Laughing. Nathan sat up straighter to listen more closely.

"What?" Georgie asked.

He glanced down at her. "I can't tell you when I last heard him laugh."

Another roar of laughter came from inside.

A lump of emotion settled in his throat.

Georgie wrapped her arm around his waist and rested her head on his chest.

"Sorry," he said, holding her close to him. "It just . . . it's nice to hear."

"I'm sure it is. Do you want to go in and see what they're up to?"

"In a minute." He tipped her chin up for a soft kiss. "My brother Kevin is having a cookout tomorrow afternoon. Come with me?"

"Is meeting the family within the boundaries of light and fun?"

He decided not to remind her that they had just stepped way outside the boundaries of light and fun. "You already know Ben, Ian, and Rosie."

"True."

"There're only three more brothers, a couple of sisters-in-law, two nieces, and a nephew. Plus my parents, of course, but they're in Florida, so you're safe on that front."

"Since there's no parental involvement, I'll go."

He caressed her face. "Are you going to be okay tonight?"

She nodded. "Thanks for listening."

"Any time, sweetheart." He took her hand to help her up. "Let's go see what's so funny."

Inside, they found Ben and Tess in the living room.

"Oh my God, you guys, check this out," Ben said, his eyes dancing with mirth. "We're playing dirty-word Scrabble. You won't believe how filthy innocent Nurse Tess is!"

As Tess blushed, Nathan took a peek at the board. His eyes almost popped out of his head. "Whose is *that?*"

"Hers!" Ben said, laughing. "She's downright smutty! I love it."

"He challenged me," Tess said as she added e-d to fuck. "What was I supposed to do? Twelve more points, please."

"How do you figure?"

"Double letter."

Ben shook his head. "I surrender. You win. Your mind is much dirtier than mine."

"Not possible," Nathan murmured and was surprised when Ben laughed rather than lashing out. "I'm heading home. Do you want a lift?"

Ben glanced at Tess, who was putting away the game. "Can you give me a minute?"

"Sure." Nathan hooked an arm around Georgie to lead her into the kitchen, where he maneuvered her back against the counter. "Ben wants to kiss her. So while he's doing that, why don't we figure out a way to waste a few minutes?"

She caressed his chest. "I feel like we're back in high school."

"Fun, isn't it?" he asked as he kissed her neck.

"Uh-huh. I wonder how Cat's date with Ian went."

"I'm sure you'll hear all about it in the morning, and then you can tell me. Now kiss me, will ya?"

On the third floor, Ian pressed his ear to the door. "Sounds like they're having a freaking party down there," he grumbled.

Amused, Cat watched him pace. "Come back to bed."

"Does this room have a fire escape? I might need it."

"You can't spend the night?"

"I've got to get home to Rosie."

Her smile faded.

"Come on, Cat." He sat on the edge of the bed and laced his fingers through hers. "You know I have a daughter. I have to get home to her, even though I'd love to spend the night with you."

"I suppose that's something. At least you want to."

"You could always sneak over to my house after the sitter leaves," he cajoled as he skimmed his lips over her collarbone.

"And have to be out by when?"

"Six?" he said with a sheepish grin.

"As appealing as that sounds, I have to say no thanks."

"So where do we go from here? I want to see you again."

"You want to see me *naked* again."

"That, too."

"What if that was all I wanted?"

"Sex only?"

"I just got out of a big, hairy deal. That's why I'm living here right now. I'm regrouping."

"So let me get this straight—the hottest babe I've ever met, with whom I've already had three rounds of what was easily the best sex of my life—wants a sex-only relationship?"

Laughing, she nodded.

"Let me think about it."

"*Seriously?*"

"I'm done. Yes. Deal."

"Shouldn't we shake on it or something?"

"Something." He brought his lips down on hers. "Definitely something."

After she put the game away, Tess returned to the sofa to sit next to Ben. "This was fun," she said.

"Yes."

"Are you going to think less of me now that you know about my dirty mind?"

"No."

"What's wrong, Ben?"

"I used to be smooth . . . with women. But I'm sitting here dying to kiss you, and I seem to have forgotten all my moves."

He looked so lost and so forlorn that Tess's heart went out to him—a dangerous thing for a woman who had sworn off men. Shifting to her knees, she moved carefully to straddle him without putting any weight on his injured leg. "Does anything hurt?"

"Not my leg, if that's what you mean."

Smiling, she guided his arms around her and let her lips hover close to his. "Is it coming back to you yet?" she whispered.

"Starting to."

She brushed her lips over his.

His hand slid up her back to cup her head. "Tess." He kept the kiss gentle and undemanding, almost as if he was afraid to ask for too much.

When she let her tongue wander into his mouth, he went still for an instant before he responded in kind.

He pulled her tighter against him, bringing her into direct contact with his erection.

"Ben," she gasped.

"Hmm?"

"I think you've got your moves back."

His lips were soft against her neck. "Thank God."

"Nathan's waiting for you," she said as she clung to him.

"How much you want to bet he's found a way to kill some time?"

Tess smiled and shifted her face in search of his lips.

He held nothing back this time, and when they finally resurfaced, Tess was light-headed and breathless.

"Are you working tomorrow?"

She shook her head.

"There's a cookout at my brother's. Want to go with me?"

"Yes," she said without hesitation, relieved to know she would see him again soon. "I'd like that."

"I like *you*, Nurse Tess. A whole lot."

"I like you, too, Bennett Caldwell. A whole lot."

They stared at each other for a long moment before he kissed her again.

"Are there other moves?" she asked in a saucy whisper. "Besides these?"

He growled against her ear. "This is nothing."

A bolt of heat and anticipation traveled straight to her core, making her tremble in his arms. "Maybe sometime you could show me some of the others?" His smile faded, only slightly, but she noticed it.

Sliding his hands up and down her back, he said, "I'd better go. Nate's waiting."

Stung by his sudden withdrawal, she moved off his lap.

He reached for his cane and pushed himself to his feet with a grimace. Once he had gotten his balance, he extended his hand and helped her up. Keeping his firm grip on her hand, he touched a light kiss to her lips. Their eyes met, and in his she saw longing and desire and fear—of what she couldn't be sure.

"See you tomorrow?" he asked.

"Okay." Whatever he was worried about, she'd find a way to get it out of him.

CHAPTER 19

After Nathan and Ben left, Georgie joined Tess in the living room. "You seemed to be having fun."

"I was." Tess's face softened into a dreamy expression. "He's lovely."

"*Tess has a boyfriend,*" Georgie sang.

"*So does Georgie,*" Tess retorted.

"It's starting to seem that way, isn't it?"

"You know, it wouldn't break my heart if you decided to stay here."

Georgie fiddled with the fringe on one of the sofa pillows. "My mother wanted me to move back here. For years she's been after me to come home where I belong. How can I do that now that she's not here anymore?"

"She wanted you to be happy."

"I guess," Georgie said with a shrug. "But I haven't even known him a week. I can't reorder my whole life for a man I just met—even if I like him more than I've ever liked any guy. That goes against everything I believe in."

"How do you feel when you're with him?"

"Safe," Georgie said without hesitation. "Amused, off balance, frustrated."

Tess chuckled. "Anything else?"

"Adored," Georgie said softly. "He makes me feel adored. I've never had that before."

"Georgie," Tess sighed. "How can you walk away from that without seeing it through?"

"This is exactly why I didn't want to get involved with him in the first place! I don't feel capable of any other big decisions right now." She glanced over at Tess. "I told him. About the test."

"And what did he say?"

"All the right things," Georgie conceded.

"See?"

"What's going on?" Cat asked from the doorway. She was dressed in only a bathrobe.

"What're you doing here?" Georgie asked. "I thought you were working."

"I had a headache after dinner, so I called in sick."

"I thought I heard you up there earlier," Tess said.

"How was dinner?" Georgie asked.

"Fine," Cat replied.

Georgie eyed her suspiciously. "Just 'fine'?"

"Uh-huh," Cat said, diverting her eyes.

"*Oh my God,*" Georgie said in a scandalized whisper.

"What?" Tess asked, alarmed.

Georgie never took her eyes off Cat. "You did the deed."

"I did not!"

Georgie sucked in a sharp breath. "You are *so totally lying!*" She couldn't believe it was possible, but right before her eyes, Cat Kelly blushed. "Oh, you dirty, *dirty* girl," she said, tossing Cat's words back at her.

Tess had apparently been rendered speechless until she said, "How was it?"

Cat dissolved into one of the big easy chairs. "So, *so* good."

Georgie cracked up. "You're *such* a hypocrite."

"I know! Just shut up about it, will you?"

"Where is he now?" Tess asked.

"Probably on the fire escape. He needs to go home, but he didn't want you guys to know he was here."

Georgie glanced at Tess. "Perhaps he fears we might be tempted to tell his brothers?"

"Something like that," Cat grumbled.

Tess giggled. "Your dirty secret is safe with us."

"Can I tell him the coast is clear? You guys won't say anything to him, will you?"

Georgie wanted to make her suffer—oh, how she wanted some suffering. "We'll do our best to refrain from comment."

"I hope you're enjoying this," Cat said with a scowl.

"I'm having a blast. You, Tess?"

"Totally."

Flipping them the bird, Cat left the room.

Georgie and Tess collapsed into hysterics.

"You're next," Georgie said.

"No way," Tess said. "Unlike you two, I have some self-control."

"It seems no one's safe from the potent Caldwell charm."

Georgie was stunned when Tess's eyes flooded with real tears. "What?"

Tess shook her head.

Georgie got up and moved next to her friend on the sofa. "Talk to me."

"It's just . . . I'm so happy here," she said softly. "I love it all—you and Cat, and as silly as it is, I love that we're dating brothers—adorable, charming, *sexy* brothers. I love my job and this house. I love that I feel safe here and that tomorrow I'm going to a cookout with Ben. Nothing special, but it's something I haven't done in so long, and I'm looking forward to it. I can't tell you the last time I looked forward to anything."

Deeply moved, Georgie said, "Why didn't you leave him sooner, Tess?"

"I couldn't. He controlled everything, and I was terrified of him."

"What about your family? Surely, they would've helped you."

Her smile was sad and ironic. "He was a partner in my father's law firm. My family didn't believe me."

Georgie saw Ian sneak out the front door but didn't take her eyes off Tess. "So how did you finally get away?"

"I ended up in the hospital with broken ribs that he told the doctors I'd gotten in a surfing accident." She snorted bitterly. "I've never been on a surfboard in my life."

Cat slipped into the room and took a seat without interrupting Tess.

"That was the first time he broke something. I knew if I went home with him that eventually he'd kill me. So I walked away from the hospital in the middle of the night, took a taxi across town to the hospital where I worked and got the thousand dollars I'd managed to stash in my locker along with a few photos and personal items. I took Amtrak to Rhode Island and shook like a leaf the whole way. I did private-duty work while I went through the process to legally—and privately—change my name and apply for a license."

"You walked away with the shirt on your back," Cat said, incredulous.

"I certainly didn't want any reminders of the seven years I'd spent as his punching bag."

"You were so brave, honey," Georgie said, reaching out to hug her.

"I'm still so ashamed, though," Tess whispered, "that I let him treat me that way for so long. What kind of self-respecting woman puts up with that?"

"You were terrorized, Tess." Cat moved to Tess's other side. "Nothing about it was your fault."

"I kept thinking if I was different somehow—if I kept a cleaner house, or made him fancy meals, or dressed the way he wanted me to or did what he wanted . . . in bed. I thought if I did those things, then maybe I wouldn't make him so mad."

"He ought to be in jail," Cat growled.

"Cat's right," Georgie said. "Let me tell Nathan about this. He'll know how to help."

"I don't need help. Not now. I was very careful. There's nothing to lead him here."

"But still, if Nathan knew, maybe—"

Tess stopped her with a hand to Georgie's arm. "I'm finally free, Georgie. I want to be free to enjoy what's happening with Ben. I just want to be normal for once. If you tell Nathan, he'll get the police involved, and I'll lose my happy new life. I'll have reason to be afraid again."

"He'd take care of you. You know he would."

"Yes, he would, but I still don't want you to tell him. Promise me you won't."

Georgie glanced at Cat, who tilted her head toward Tess as if to say they had to respect her wishes.

"I won't tell him," Georgie said. "Unless something changes and I get the sense you're in danger. If that happens, I won't hesitate to tell him."

"I guess I can live with that." Tess reached out a hand to each of her roommates. "We haven't known each other long, but I love you guys. I really, really do."

"Right back atcha," Cat said gruffly.

Georgie nodded in agreement.

A call from Ali woke Georgie early the next morning.

"I can't believe Joe called you!" Ali said. "I told him not to."

"Good morning to you, too." Georgie choked back a yawn and stretched. "I take it you're feeling better."

"I'm fine. I told him that, but Joe got all crazy because I couldn't stop crying. It's the only meltdown I've had since I made the decision. I think I should be allowed one major freak out over this whole thing."

"Of course you are. He was upset, Al. Don't be mad with him for calling me. He needed to talk to someone who knows what's going on."

"I'm not mad. I'm just ready for the whole thing to be done with."

"It will be. Soon enough."

"Yeah. Can we please talk about something else? How are you?"

"Hanging in there," she said with another big yawn. "You'll never guess who I've been seeing."

"What about Doug?"

"Over. The day after you left, the same day I met Jogger Guy."

"No way. No *freaking* way!"

"Yes way." Georgie told her sister the PG version of the story, and when she finished, Ali was silent. "Hello? Still there?"

"He's the one, Georgie," she said softly.

Georgie laughed. "You and Cat. Have you been talking to her?"

"Does he know? About the test and the gene and everything?"

"I told him last night."

"And?"

"He said it doesn't matter. That my life is more important than my breasts."

"Marry him."

"Okay, I'll get right on that."

"Are you going to have the test?"

"I'm thinking about it."

"Well, that's progress anyway. How's the sex?"

"Alison!"

"What? Don't tell me you haven't slept with him after the way you lusted over him for weeks."

Thinking of that first night with Nathan, Georgie felt her cheeks burn. "It's great."

"Marry him!"

"I'm glad you're feeling better, Ali. Give me a call before you go in the hospital this week?"

"Only if you promise me you're going to marry this sexy detective who cares more about you than your breasts."

"*Bye,* Ali." Georgie closed her cell phone and dragged herself out of bed to go do an errand she couldn't put off any longer.

She brought a stack of boxes back to the house and went straight upstairs before she could talk herself out of the task she had planned for the morning. Georgie knew her practical, organized mother would object to her clothes collecting dust when someone could be using them.

As she emptied the dresser, Georgie found a crocheted handkerchief that reminded her of the elderly widow who had lived next door to them when Georgie and Ali were little. Mrs. Marchant had complained about the lack of activities for seniors—not to mention the dearth of opportunities to meet single men "of a certain age." Nancy Quinn had seen a need and had done something about it by founding the center.

Georgie admired that quality in her mother and had struggled to live up to it. At first she had felt guilty about pursuing a career that combined her love of fashion with the aptitude for marketing she had honed through a variety of summer jobs at the boutiques in Newport. When held up against her mother's many accomplishments—accomplishments that had real meaning to real people—Georgie had worried that her choices were shallow in comparison. Her mother, however, had encouraged Georgie to follow her passion. "You've got a lot of years to work," Nancy had said. "You've got to love what you do."

And Georgie did love it. She loved the challenge and the process involved in presenting clothing, jewelry, shoes, and accessories in a way that enticed and seduced. She loved the brainstorming sessions with her high-spirited, creative team, the drawings, colors, fabrics, textures, and smells. Somehow she had to figure out a way to get her career back on track.

Working quickly and trying hard not to think about what she was doing, Georgie plowed through her mother's clothes. She divided them into piles of what she wanted to keep for herself and Ali, things to be donated and others to be thrown away. Georgie contemplated a dress that had gone out of style twenty years ago. Curling up her lip with distaste, she mumbled, "What was she thinking holding on to this?"

In the back of the closet, she found a pile of clothes she had sent her mother from Davidson's, many of them still with the tags attached. Not surprised by the discovery, she laughed. Try as she might, Georgie had never had much luck in upgrading her mother's fashion sense. Jeans and T-shirts had been the mainstays of Nancy's wardrobe.

When Georgie finished going through the clothes, she turned to the desk and sorted paperwork, some bills she hadn't noticed on an earlier mission, correspondence involving the center and a pile of old pictures. The clothes, the hats, the white gloves, and the cat-eye glasses made her smile. In the bottom right-hand drawer, she found a packet of papers tied with a pink ribbon. Curious, Georgie untied the ribbon and gasped at what she found—every letter she had written to her mother during her freshman year of college.

As she flipped through the pages and relived those first few scary months away from home—away from her mother—the wound of her loss tore open once again. Warm tears flowed unchecked down her cheeks as she realized no one would ever again love her quite that much.

Georgie had no idea how long she sat there clutching the letters when her ringing cell phone snapped her out of it. Reaching into the back pocket of her shorts, she retrieved the phone, wiped her face, and flipped it open.

"Georgie? It's Tara. Did I catch you at a bad time?"

"No," she said to her assistant at Davidson's. "How are you?"

"I'm sorry to bother you on a Sunday and all," Tara drawled in her deep Southern accent, "but you've got to get back here, girl!"

"Why? What's wrong?"

"Half the department's threatening to walk if they bring that witch Nina Taft in as director. They're planning to tell Lorraine they're going to quit if she doesn't hire you back."

"That's crazy," Georgie said, even though she was touched by her employees' loyalty. "You can't let them do that. Lorraine is under pressure from above. It wasn't her fault I got fired."

"Well, it wasn't yours either," Tara said indignantly. "It certainly wasn't your fault that your mama got sick, Georgie, and it's not like we're falling apart without you. We're holding things together just fine. You'd be proud of us."

Georgie smiled. "I have no doubt."

"We were totally *shocked* when Lorraine sent an e-mail around on Friday night telling us you'd been 'let go.' We all got together at Melinda's last night, and that's when I heard what they're planning to do about it."

"I was shocked, too," Georgie confessed. "Believe me. But I understand that Lorraine can't hold my job forever."

"That's bull crap." Tara snorted, too much a lady to curse. "You work your fanny off for her. Your job should've been safe indefinitely."

"I appreciate that, Tara, and I'm sorry I've put you all in such a bind."

"Is there *any* chance you can get back here? Soon? Before there's nothing left of our department? We *need* you, Georgie."

Feeling torn in a thousand different directions, Georgie thought it over. "I need some more time to get things settled here."

"If I know for sure you're going to be back in the next couple of weeks, I think I can convince the others not to quit."

"Just because I come back doesn't mean they won't still bring Nina in."

"If we tell Lorraine we're all going to quit if they do, that might get their attention."

"I don't want anyone making threats they aren't prepared to follow through with. You never know. She could call your bluff. Don't do anything crazy, do you hear me?" Blocking all thoughts of Nathan, Georgie said, "I'll be back in two weeks, if not sooner."

Tara released a heavy sigh of relief. "Thank you, Georgie."

"Hopefully, I can convince Lorraine to hire me back."

"We'll get you back. Don't worry."

"I appreciate that, Tara. I really do."

"How're you holding up?"

Georgie glanced at the letters in her lap. "I have good moments and bad moments, but I'm doing okay. Thanks for asking."

"We sure do miss you."

"I miss you all, too."

"Keep me posted on your ETA?"

"I will. You keep the troops from rebelling."

"I'll do my best. Take care, Georgie."

"Thanks for calling."

Georgie took the pack of letters with her when she left her mother's room and crossed the hall to stash them in her suitcase. In the bathroom, she splashed some cold water on her splotchy face and brushed her hair. She was anxious to get to the hospital to see Gus and needed to save enough time to shower and change before Nathan picked her up at two.

Her stomach twisted with nerves when she thought of him and the promise she had just made to her coworker. She had made it clear to him from the beginning that she intended to go home to Atlanta eventually, so it wasn't like he could be mad at her for doing just that. Right?

As she made the decision to keep the phone call from Tara to herself, Georgie realized it was time to get serious about wrapping things up in Newport. In all the madness of the last few months, it had been easy to forget that she had people relying on her in Atlanta, too. They had worked tirelessly for years to make her look good to her superiors. She couldn't let them down. She *wouldn't* let them down.

CHAPTER 20

At the hospital Georgie found out that Gus had stabilized and his doctors had him scheduled for surgery the next morning.

"He's not out of the woods yet," Bad Gus said. "But at least he has a fighting chance."

"Thank God," Georgie said, weak with relief.

"Roxy called to say they've got Gus's son Roger in for questioning," Bill added. "He's not talking, but they're working to crack him. They know he had something to do with this."

"I'll ask Nathan to see what he can find out," Georgie said.

Gus raised an eyebrow. "What's going on with you and that Caldwell boy?"

"We're *friends*," Georgie said for what felt like the hundredth time.

"My heart is broken," Walter lamented. "I really thought we had something special, Georgie. But how can I compete with tall, blond, built like a brick shithouse—"

"Don't forget *young*," Bill said with a guffaw.

"Well, there's that, too," Walter conceded.

Georgie smiled. "If I was sixty-something, Walter, I'd be *all* about you."

Encouraged, Walter said, "What's thirty years between friends?"

"A lifetime?" Bill said.

"Whose side are you on?" Walter huffed.

"I've got to run, you guys," Georgie said with an affectionate squeeze for Walter's arm. "Let me know if anything changes with Gus?"

"We will, honey," Walter said.

As she drove home, Georgie was surprised to realize how much she would miss the old men when she left. Despite her initial reluctance to get involved with them, they had managed to work their way under her skin. Just like Nathan. She would miss him, too. To claim otherwise would be a lie. How was it possible that he had wormed his way so thoroughly into her life in just a few days' time?

She thought about him as she showered and changed into black capri pants, a floral silk tank top and wedge sandals—an outfit much more in keeping with her usual look than the shorts and T-shirts she had worn lately.

Winding her shoulder-length hair into a twist, she secured it with a clip and applied eye shadow and liner using a technique she had learned at a Bobbi Brown demonstration at the store. She wondered if Nathan would notice.

Tess came down the stairs in a knee-length yellow sundress and sandals Georgie instantly envied. "Does this look okay?"

"I love it. The shoes are fabulous."

"Wow. Look at you."

"What? Is it too much?"

"You look amazing." Tess stepped closer. "What'd you do to your eyes? They're positively popping!"

"Want me to do it to yours?"

"Would you?"

"Step into my office."

A few minutes later, Tess studied the result in the mirror. "You're a wizard! Show me what you did."

Georgie walked her through the steps.

"That's it?"

"That's all there is to it."

Tess checked her watch. "I've got to go get Ben."

"Are you nervous at all? About meeting his family?"

"Why would I be? Are you?"

"No," Georgie said quickly. "Is Cat going?"

"Ian asked her, but she said no."

"I wonder why," Georgie asked as she smoothed on lipstick.

"From what I hear, she plans to have a somewhat unconventional relationship with him."

"How do you mean?"

In a scandalized whisper, Tess said, "S-e-x only."

"No way."

"Way."

Georgie shook her head in disbelief. "Damn, she's something, isn't she?"

"I give her credit. She knows what she wants and knows how to get it. I wish I was more like that."

"But a sex-only thing. That can't really work, can it?"

Tess shrugged. "If anyone can make it work, she can."

"I guess we'll see."

"All right." Tess checked herself in the mirror and ran a hand over her long dark hair, which she had left down for the occasion. "I'm going. See you in a few."

As Georgie made her way downstairs a few minutes later, Cat came in from a morning at the beach wearing a black bikini top with cargo shorts, her skin bronzed from the sun. "How was it?" Georgie asked.

"Fantastic. Just what I needed." She glanced up at Georgie. "Va va voom—look at you."

"Is it too much for a cookout?"

"Not at all. But somehow you manage to make capris look muy glamoroso."

"That's not a word—glamoroso."

"Did it get the point across?" Cat asked dryly.

Georgie's chuckle died in her throat when she saw Nathan come up the front stairs carrying a bouquet of daisies. Her heart hammered and her mouth went dry. She noticed he had shed the sling that had driven him crazy the day before.

"Hey," he said when he saw the two women standing inside the door.

Since Georgie didn't move to let him in, Cat did the honors.

He wore khaki shorts and a white polo shirt that offset his deep tan. "For you," he said, handing the daisies to Georgie.

Flustered, she took them from him. "I hope they're organically grown," she said, relying on humor to hide her emotional response to the flowers.

"I picked them myself, so I *know* they were."

Cat sighed. "That's so sweet. Isn't it, Georgie?"

"Um, yes," Georgie stammered. "Very. Thank you."

"I'll find a vase for them," Cat offered, taking the flowers from Georgie.

"Not coming today, Cat?" Nathan asked.

She shook her head. "I've got a million things I need to do."

"I hope Ian remembered to ask you."

"He did," Cat said on her way out of the room. "Have fun."

"Did you hear anything about how their date went?" Nathan asked.

"She said it was fine."

"Interesting. He's not talking either."

Georgie started toward the porch, but Nathan stopped her.

"Let me see you," he whispered as he backed her up against the door. Tipping her chin, he studied her face. "You're gorgeous," he said, but then seemed to reconsider. "No, not gorgeous."

"He giveth and he taketh away."

"Gorgeous isn't adequate." He took a closer look. "Stunning. Yeah, that's better. Stunning."

"Thank you." In search of balance to offset his overwhelming nearness, Georgie rested her hands on his hips. "Nathan?"

He hovered, teased, tempted. "Yeah?"

"You're invading my personal space."

His face lifted into a sexy half smile. "Am I?"

"Uh huh."

"As long as I'm invading, I may as well conquer," he said as he brought his lips down on hers.

Georgie curled her fingers through his belt loops and held on tight, expecting him to devour. Instead, he seduced with just the smooth glide of his lips over hers. His fingers caressed her neck, sending shivers darting through her.

When he finally ended the kiss, he gathered her into his arms and held her tight against him. "I couldn't sleep last night."

"Because of your arm?"

"No, because I was so mad at myself for not staying with you."

Georgie glanced up at him and wiped a smudge of lipstick off his bottom lip. "You look tired."

"It's your fault."

"How do you figure? You're the one who said no!"

"Big mistake. Who knows when I'll get another offer like that?"

"From me or will any girl do?"

"There's only one girl I'm interested in getting sleepover invitations from."

"What's her name?" Georgie teased.

"You don't know her."

She play punched him in the belly.

Laughing, he hooked his good arm around her. "Ready to meet the rest of the Caldwell brothers?"

"As ready as I'll ever be."

Kevin Caldwell's yard was a beehive of activity when Nathan and Georgie pulled up just as Ben and Tess were getting out of her car. While Georgie battled apprehension, Tess glowed with excitement. Ben kept a firm grip on her hand as he led her up the driveway.

"We grew up here," Nathan shared as they walked slowly to accommodate Ben. The sprawling three-story yellow Victorian had a wide, inviting front porch. "Kevin and his wife Linda bought the house from my parents when they moved to Florida."

"Ian and Rosie live in the Fonzie apartment," Ben added, nodding at the garage.

"That's nice for him to have support nearby," Tess said.

"He doesn't ask us for help very often," Nathan said.

"Where's her mother?" Tess asked.

"Don't ask," Ben murmured.

"Long story," Nathan said. "Put it this way—Rosie's a lot better off without her."

"I can't imagine she wants for much surrounded by so much family," Georgie said.

"She's very well loved," Ben concurred.

In the backyard, they were greeted by a mob. Georgie and Tess met Kevin, Linda, their kids John and Chloe, Hugh Caldwell and his wife Dani, who was hugely pregnant and holding hands with two-year-old Sarah, and Luke, their oldest brother. Ian waved from the swings where he was pushing Rosie.

The mob cleared, and Nathan gasped. "Uh-oh, I'm dead meat," he muttered. "Mom? What're you doing here?"

Georgie tightened her grip on his hand.

"We decided to surprise you all and come up for the party," she said as she embraced her sons. "I also wanted to check on Ben, who looks wonderful. And then you got shot, so I needed to see you, too. How's the arm?"

"Much better today."

"I'll be the judge of that."

"Um, Georgie," Nathan stuttered, "this is my mother, Bernie Caldwell. I would've warned you that you were going to meet her if I had *known*."

Amused by his distress, Georgie said, "Pleased to meet you, Mrs. Caldwell."

"And this is Tess," Ben interjected.

Bernie hugged both women. "Please, call me Bernie."

"But never Bernice!" her six sons said together.

"Brats," Bernie said as she linked arms with Tess and Georgie to lead them away from their dates. "Every one of them. A woman pours her heart and soul into raising six boys and ends up with six overgrown brats. How do you suppose that happens? Where did I go wrong?"

Tess giggled as they made their way to the bar.

Bernie's gray hair fell in soft curls down her back, and her hazel eyes, Georgie noticed, crinkled in the corners when she smiled the way Nathan's and Ian's did.

"Rosie told me all about you two and your other roommate. Cat is it? According to my informant, Nathan likes Georgie, Ben likes Tess and her daddy likes Cat, but Cat doesn't seem to like kids very much. How'd I do?"

Amazed, Georgie stared at her.

"What?" Bernie asked. "I know who to go to for information around here."

"Your source is well informed," Tess said, accepting a glass of white wine from Bernie.

"Is this Cat who doesn't like kids someone I should worry about?"

Tess shook her head. "Cat's a great person and a good friend. She just needs to get to know Rosie a little better, that's all."

"I hope so. What about you two? Anything I need to worry about?"

Georgie and Tess exchanged glances.

"Um," Georgie stumbled.

"Relax," Bernie said with a smile. "I'm teasing." She turned to Tess. "From what I hear, my Bennett has been a little more bearable the last few days. I suspect you've had something to do with that, so please accept my thanks."

"He's been through an awful lot," Tess said.

"We all have," Bernie said, shaking her head. "If I live forever, I'll never forget that phone call. But I know that as bad as it was, it could've been worse. So much worse."

Tess reached out and clasped her hand.

"Oh," Bernie said, rallying. "Here's my husband. Dan, honey, come meet Georgie and Tess."

Georgie had to suppress a gasp as she saw what Nathan would look like at sixty. Dan's hair was silver and tight with curls like his youngest son's, and his bright blue eyes were the same ones all his boys had inherited. But his resemblance to Nathan, in particular, was startling.

"Georgie's here with Nathan," Bernie told him, "and Tess came with Bennett."

"Nice to meet you both," Dan said as he shook their hands. "But surely pretty girls like you can do better than those two scalawags."

"Who're you calling a scalawag, old man?" Nathan asked as he wrestled his father into a headlock.

When Ian and Hugh jumped into the fray, Bernie deftly steered Georgie and Tess to safety while Ben egged on his brothers from the sidelines.

"Too much testosterone when they're all together," Bernie said, rolling her eyes.

"What's the secret to growing them so handsome?" Tess asked.

"I have no idea," Bernie said, her pride in her sons obvious as she watched the scrum on the lawn. "Quite a sight, aren't they?"

"Indeed," Tess agreed with a smile. "Especially right now."

Georgie and Bernie laughed with her.

Nathan's white shirt was stained with green by the time he resurfaced from the bottom of the pile, red-faced and sweating.

"Nathan!" Tess cried. "Your arm!"

"It's fine." He waved it around his head. "See? Good as new."

"You still need to baby it, or you'll tear your stitches," Tess reminded him.

"She's a nurse," Ben told his mother. "In the ER."

"This family could certainly use a nurse," Bernie said.

"Mom!" Ben cried. "Stop!"

"I'm only saying."

"*Mother.*"

Bernie made a face at him. "Don't *mother* me."

Georgie wondered if Tess was dying of embarrassment, but she seemed to be lapping it up like a hungry cat that had just found a bowl of milk.

Nathan surprised Georgie when he slipped his arm around her shoulders and kissed her cheek.

As she looked up at him with a forced smile, her stomach ached with nerves and anxiety and sadness. The sadness resurfaced so suddenly she had no time to prepare herself to absorb the blow. "Excuse me," she said softly.

CHAPTER 21

Nathan watched Georgie walk away, her hands jammed into her pockets, her shoulders hunched. He turned to Tess. "What was that all about?"

"I'm not sure, but I noticed that she started cleaning out her mother's stuff earlier. She's probably having a rough day."

Nathan swore under his breath.

"How long ago did she lose her mother?" Bernie asked.

"A couple of weeks ago," Tess said. "She was diagnosed with late-stage breast cancer three months ago."

"Oh my," Bernie said.

Nathan started to go after Georgie, but his mother stopped him.

"Let me."

"Mom . . ."

"The child needs some mothering, Nathan, and if there's one thing I know how to do, it's that."

"She's not in a good place right now—"

"Of course she isn't. Her mother just died. Let me talk to her. I promise to take extra special care of her."

Ben put his arm around Nathan's shoulders and nudged him toward the bar. "Let's get a beer, bro. Mom's on it."

Tess looped her arm through Nathan's and helped Ben lead him away.

Nathan looked back over his shoulder and made eye contact with his mother. She sent him a warm smile and a nod of encouragement.

He allowed Ben to force a beer on him, but the only place he wanted to be was with Georgie. For now, though, he would trust his mother to give her what she needed. Maybe she would do a better job than he seemed to be doing. In the meantime, he would take advantage of the opportunity to pump Kevin for some of those romance ideas he needed. He had a bad feeling he was running out of time.

Georgie sat on the front stairs to watch a group of kids play kickball in the street and was struck by a memory of the kids she had grown up with. They had terrorized Dean Avenue and the nearby streets from sunup to sundown all summer long. Most of the parents had retired and moved south. She wondered where the kids had ended up.

Twelve years had wrought so many changes that Newport had long ago stopped feeling like home to her. Except for an occasional weekend visit with her mother, she hadn't spent any serious time here in years—long enough to forget things like playing in the street without a care in the world.

Bernie held out a Diet Coke to Georgie. "Mind if I join you?"

She accepted the drink and scooted over to make room on the step for the older woman. "I'm sorry to run out like that."

"Do you think you're the first woman to run for her life from the Caldwell boys?"

Georgie smiled. "You have a lovely family. You're very lucky."

"And I know it. Took hard work, a lot of sweat, tons of worry, and a bit of heartache, but we survived—just barely. In fact, I haven't told Dan yet, but we're moving home to be with them in the next year or so. We've been gone long enough to prove they can stand on their own twelve feet without us."

"I can't imagine having six boys."

"I never did, either. I pictured myself with girls."

"*That* didn't work out."

"Nope, but I wouldn't trade my boys for anything. I've learned that life has a mind of its own, and we're just along for the ride."

"That's certainly how *my* life has seemed lately."

"I was sorry to hear about your mother."

"Thank you," Georgie said softly.

Bernie slipped an arm around her.

"You remind me of her," Georgie said.

"Do I?"

"She had a way of sorting through the BS and telling it like it is."

"I think I would've liked her."

"You might've known her. Nancy Quinn? She ran the senior center."

"Oh!" Bernie said, stricken. "I knew her well! My father-in-law was a regular at the center for years."

"So I've heard."

"I used to drive him there and always enjoyed chatting with your mom. I hadn't heard she passed away. I'm so very sorry, honey."

"Thank you. I've been working at the center until they can find someone to take her place."

"That's very good of you."

"The place means too much to too many people—it meant too much to my mother—to let it be closed down. I never expected it to take them this long to find someone, though. I need to get back to my real life."

"Which is where?"

"Atlanta."

"Ah, I see."

"And now you're wondering how badly I'm going to crush your son when I leave."

"Crossed my mind. Since he can't seem to take his eyes off you, I'd say it'll be fairly ugly."

With a moan, Georgie dropped her head into her hand.

"I made Dan wait two years for me," Bernie said with a chuckle.

Georgie looked over at her. "And he did?"

"Sure he did. He was warm for my form."

Georgie laughed.

"He was my college roommate's very sexy older brother. I was desperately in love with him from the first instant I ever laid eyes on him the summer between my freshman and sophomore years."

"Did he know?"

"No! Forty-five years later, he still doesn't know about most of the tricks I played on him. Sometimes men need to be led to what's best for them."

"That's very sneaky," Georgie said with admiration.

Bernie shrugged. "Does he appear to be suffering?"

"Not one bit."

"I'll tell you what, though, he suffered when I told him I planned to spend two years living and working on a commune in Utah. In fact, he was so furious he said it was over between us if I went."

"So what did you do?"

"The only thing I could do—I went. Took him a couple of months to figure out he couldn't live without me." She leaned in closer to Georgie. "I'll deny it to my dying day, but he had me sweating by then. I didn't expect it to take him so long to realize his life was worthless without me."

"He came to Utah?" Georgie asked, hanging on Bernie's every word.

She nodded. "He said he loved me and would wait for the rest of his life if that's how long it took for me to come to my senses. I liked that last part. Come to my senses! He was the one with the problem, not me. By then he'd made me mad enough that I informed him I planned to honor my two-year commitment to the commune, and if he was still around when I was done, then we'd see what happened."

"That's what Nathan said we'd do—see what happens."

"Might not be a bad idea. Worked out pretty well for me. Dan was exactly where I expected him to be when I 'came to my senses,' and we've been together ever since. He loved me. He waited. Not that complicated when it comes right down to it."

"Nathan doesn't love me. He likes me. A lot."

"Has he told you about Ellen?"

Georgie nodded.

"For so long, I wondered if he would ever get over what happened to her." Bernie glanced at Georgie. "I've never again seen that particular light in his eyes. Until today."

Georgie took a sudden interest in her feet.

"He's not going to let you go, Georgie. You may leave, but that doesn't mean he'll let go."

"What if I want him to?"

"Do you?"

"I've known him a week. How do I know what I want him to do?"

"I took one look at Dan Caldwell and saw my destiny. Don't tell me it can't happen. It happened to me. The road to happily ever after was bumpy and full of potholes, but I never had any doubt I was on the right road."

"I can't even locate the on ramp, let alone the road."

Bernie laughed. "What are you most afraid of?"

"At this moment? That my indecision will hurt Nathan."

"If I were being smug, I'd say that proves you care about him."

"Of course I do. How could I not? He's so . . . He's special."

"Always has been," Bernie mused. "He was the baby of the family, but rather than being useless and spoiled the way some babies can be, he was the practical one. The only one with a scrap of common sense when they were younger."

"According to him, nothing's changed on that front."

Bernie rolled her eyes. "He would say that."

"I'm attracted to him, maybe even wildly attracted—not that his mother needs to hear that."

"His mother is thrilled to know that. Don't worry."

"I don't want to hurt him, but I also don't want to feel pressured."

"You aren't responsible for his happiness, honey. Do what you need to do, and if it's meant to be, then it'll be."

"It can't be that simple."

"Why not?"

"I'm going back to Atlanta. Next week probably."

"I was in Utah and Dan was here. Utah's a lot farther than Georgia. And there're all sorts of ways to keep it going these days that we would've loved to have back then. I talk to my grandchildren on the computer every week."

Georgie leaned into Bernie's one-armed hug. "It's nice to know you'd come with the package."

Bernie laughed. "It wouldn't break my heart to have you around, either. Now, tell me, what do we think of this Tess who has my Bennett's tongue hanging out of his mouth?"

"She's as lovely as she looks."

"No baggage?"

Georgie hesitated. "Some."

"I guess that's to be expected. What about Cat?"

"She's been a good friend to me."

"That's something."

"Motherhood never really ends, does it?"

"Not for me it won't."

"Thank you," Georgie said, clutching the other woman's hand.

"Thank *you*—for putting that light back in my Nathan's eyes. It's been a long time coming."

Ian gripped his guitar and strummed the opening bars to "Saved by a Woman," a song he had spent the morning messing around with.

The Caldwell family gathered around the stone fireplace in the backyard Ian shared with Kevin's family. Rosie cuddled into her grandmother's lap; Bernie's hand was curled around her husband's. Georgie reclined against Nate's chest, and Tess snuggled with Ben on a double lounge chair. Kevin and Linda sat on another lounge, while Luke—perpetually single and happy that way—tended to the fire. Hugh and Dani had taken Sarah home to bed.

As he sang about the trouble and worry that came with loving a woman, Ian's fingers flew over the neck of the guitar. He liked this song by Ray LaMontagne, he decided, as he played it for an audience for the first time. He'd have to work it into his set.

Venturing a glance at the others, he noticed Georgie smiling up at Nate. Ben's lips were fused to Tess's, a sight that filled Ian with an unfamiliar sense of longing. While he was relieved to see Ben happy for a change, Ian wished the woman who had taken up residence in his mind had come today.

Since his parents were visiting and would be happy to stay with Rosie, he could go see Cat at the club later. He wondered what she had been up to all day. Would she share that with him or was sharing outside the bounds of their agreement? Had she thought about him the way he had thought of her? Had she relived every detail, over and over again, like he had?

Out of the corner of his eye, he saw Georgie hook her arm around Nate's neck to bring him down for a kiss. It was a simple thing, really, watching his brother kiss a woman he was clearly crazy about, but it only served to bring home to Ian what was lacking in his own life.

For the first time in years, he was tired of being alone. He wanted someone who would think nothing of kissing him in front of his family. He wanted someone who wanted him—and his daughter. Was that too much to ask? But the woman he wanted, the one he craved more of, wasn't interested in him or his little girl. She had made that perfectly clear.

Rosie's laughter echoed through the yard.

Ian's eyes were riveted to her, the firelight burnishing her golden curls. She was everything to him. He had sacrificed everything *for* her and would do it again in a heartbeat. It mattered to him that he be a man she could be proud of and look up to, which was why he had been plagued all day by doubts about the deal he'd made with Cat.

As his brothers settled into relationships with women who had the potential to change their lives for the better, he was headed for trouble. He knew it and hated it but was just as certain he would go to her the first chance he got.

CHAPTER 22

Tess and Ben didn't leave Kevin's house until almost eleven because she insisted on helping Linda clean up. Ben liked how Tess put others first. The kindness that radiated from her touched everyone around her and had been the first of many things that attracted him to her. Hell, he liked just about everything he knew about her, which wasn't much, he had realized as they sat by the fire.

"Are you tired?" she asked.

He noticed she had adjusted her pace to his, as if walking this slow was natural to her. "Not particularly. You?"

"Not really."

"Do you have to work tomorrow?"

"Not until three. I traded shifts with someone who needed tomorrow night off."

Ben was already sad to realize he wouldn't see her tomorrow night. A sure-to-be endless day had just gotten longer. "Can we go somewhere? To talk?"

"Where do you want to go?"

"How about the beach?"

"I have a blanket in my car."

"Perfect. Let's go to King Park."

"Where?"

"I'll show you."

When they were in the car, he directed her. "So you're not from here? Newport?"

She shook her head. "I've lived with Georgie for the last few months, but I moved to Rhode Island almost a year ago."

"From where?" When she didn't answer right away, he glanced over to find her jaw set with tension. "Is that a trick question?"

"No," she said softly.

"You don't want to tell me?"

"It's not that."

Ben let it rest until they had pulled into the angled parking spaces at King Park, which overlooked Newport Harbor.

Tess retrieved the blanket from the trunk of the car.

He appreciated her patience as he hobbled across the lawn, through the playground to the beach. God! How he missed being able to get around effortlessly—something he, like most people, had taken for granted until it was gone.

Tess spread the blanket on the beach and took his cane for him.

As if she knew he wouldn't want her to witness his struggle as he lowered himself to the blanket, she looked out at the boats at anchor.

"We might need a crane to get me out of here," he said when he had landed.

"I can get you up." She blushed when she realized what she had said.

Finding her adorable, Ben laughed. "Please, feel free."

She shot him a withering look. "You know what I meant."

"I know what I *heard*." He reached for her hand and laced his fingers through hers. "Are you going to tell me why you don't want me to know anything about you?"

"It's not that I don't want you to know."

"Then what?"

She ventured a glance at him. "I . . . my last relationship was difficult, and I don't ever want to think or talk about it again. I'd like to pretend my life began the day I moved here."

Ben stretched out on the blanket and brought her with him. "It breaks my heart to think of you being unhappy."

"Ben," she sighed, resting her head on his chest. "That's the sweetest thing anyone has ever said to me." She ran a hand over his chest. "I took a solemn vow to never get involved with a man again."

While he was desperate to know what had caused such a beautiful young woman to make that kind of vow, he couldn't bring himself to ask. "You're going to have to break it."

"I think I already have." She shifted onto her belly and propped her chin on her fist so she could see him. "How'd you manage that so quickly?"

Threading his fingers through her long, silky hair, he urged her closer. "How did you manage to make me forget I'm supposed to be moody and sullen?"

She laughed at the grumpy face he made.

"Kiss me," he whispered. "Before I die from wanting you to."

As their lips met in the dark, her sweet fragrance wafted through his senses and surrounded him. Ignoring the pain in his hip, he shifted onto his side and brought her up tight against him. He smoothed his hand down her back until he encountered the soft skin of her leg.

Her tongue tangled with his in teasing thrusts that made him crazy with desire.

Encouraged by her passionate response, he changed the direction of his hand on her leg.

With a shudder, Tess let her head fall back in a gesture of helpless surrender.

His leg screamed in protest, but Ben ignored it as he shifted her under him. He wasn't interested in being an injured man right then. He was interested in being just a man with a woman who made his blood run hotter than any woman ever had.

Her fingers were gentle as they combed through his hair.

With the pale light of the moon beaming down on them, their eyes met.

"You've got your moves back," she whispered.

"You think so?"

"Uh-huh. What else have you got?" she asked with a saucy smile.

Laughing, he captured her bottom lip between his teeth as his hand moved up to cup her breast. He was gratified by her sharp inhale. "Lovely, lovely, Tess," he said, skimming his lips over her neck to her ear.

Her hands slid down his back, and it was his turn to be surprised when she grabbed his ass, pulling his erection into snug contact with the V of her legs.

"Tess," he choked.

"We can't," she moaned.

Confused, he raised his head to look at her. "Can't what?"

Pushing against his erection, she said, "This. It's too soon."

"Since we're on a public beach, I think I can control myself."

"Good. We can't be like everyone else."

"Who everyone else?" he asked, puzzled.

"Your brothers, my roommates."

Ben's eyes widened with surprise. "I knew about Nate and Georgie, but Ian and Cat, too?"

With a guilty expression, Tess nodded. "You can't say anything."

"Damn! That didn't take long."

With the light touch her of her fingers, she brushed the hair off his forehead. "It's been a long time," she said softly. "Since I've felt this way."

His lips moved over her face, her forehead, the tip of her nose. "What way?"

"Excited, giddy, safe."

The last word was slow to register. Once it did, Ben struggled to process it. "Were you unsafe? Before?"

It seemed to cost her something to reply with the slightest of nods.

Rage ripped through him. That someone could hurt her. He held her tighter, flooded with tenderness and protectiveness and so many other things he had given up on ever hoping to feel. Here it all was. Right here in his arms was the answer to his every question. "You're safe now," he said fiercely. "With me."

This time when he kissed her, he kept it gentle and waited for her to tell him what she wanted. She didn't disappoint. In an almost dainty movement, her tongue traced the outline of his mouth.

Ben's heart slowed to a crawl. A sudden, blinding light scared the crap out of him. "What the—"

"Newport Police, folks."

"*Great*," Ben grumbled.

Tess giggled.

"Shh," Ben hissed. Squinting, he looked up at the cop. "I'm Nate Caldwell's brother."

"Oh, for Christ's sake." The cop killed the offending light. "Why didn't you say so?"

"Um, because I was too busy being blind?"

The cop laughed. "Which brother are you?"

"Ben."

"The one who was in Iraq?"

"That's me." Ben wondered if the word Iraq would be forever attached to his name.

"How you getting along?"

Ben glanced down at Tess under him and then back up at the cop. "Pretty well until you showed up."

She shook with silent laughter.

"Oh, jeez, sorry, man. You don't have any alcohol with you, do you?"

"Not a drop."

"Then you enjoy your evening."

"I plan to."

"Ma'am," the young patrolman said to Tess before he walked away.

She laughed so hard she cried. "I feel like I'm seventeen again."

"And getting caught making out on the beach?"

"I never got caught," she said haughtily.

"First time for everything." His lips flew over her face, purposely avoiding her efforts to recapture his mouth. "What do you say we take this somewhere more comfortable?"

"What'd you have in mind?" she asked, breathless.

"Your place or mine?"

Her fingertips dug into his back. "Too many people at mine."

"Mine it is, then."

A long line stretched from the front door of Club Underground all the way around the block.

"Shit," Ian mumbled. He had waited until midnight, an hour before last call, hoping to avoid the mob scene. "Now what?" Wandering around to the back of the building, he found the evening's band taking a smoke break. He recognized one of them. "Hey, Scotty."

The other man blinked in the darkness. "Ian Caldwell? Hey, dude, what's up?"

Ian clasped his outstretched hand. "Long time, no see."

"What're you up to?"

"I need to see the manager, and the line out front is insane."

"Dude, have you met her? The manager? H-o-t."

The desire to punch the lusty look off his friend's face took Ian by surprise. "Yeah, I know her. Can you get me in the back?"

"Sure." Scotty nodded to one of his band mates, who opened the back door for Ian.

"Thanks, guys."

"See you around," Scotty said.

Inside, Ian waded through a sea of barely dressed bodies in the back hallway to get to the large main room, which pulsed with retro dance music that Ian hated. A headache started in his right temple as he pushed through a crowd of kids so young he wondered how it was possible they were legal.

He arrived at the bar as a group was leaving and grabbed one of the abandoned stools. Five minutes passed before he was able to get a bartender's attention to order a beer. Scanning the crowd, he looked for Cat's trademark red spikes but all he saw was one glassy-eyed, sweaty kid after another. When had they gotten so young? He would ground Rosie for life if she ever hung out in a place like this.

He was well into his second beer and the band had started up again when he finally spotted Cat across the bar talking to a guy. Ian bit back a pang of jealousy when he saw that she had her hand on the guy's shoulder as she leaned in to hear him over the music. Throwing her head back, she howled with laughter. When she came back down, her eyes connected with Ian's. He watched as her laughter died, and her head tilted as if she was asking a question.

Ian smiled and tilted his own head in invitation.

She leaned in to say something to the friend she had been talking to, patted him on the shoulder, and started around the bar. On the way, she stopped to issue a warning to a group of men who, judging by the ball and chain around the neck of one of them, were apparently part of a bachelor party, signed something thrust in front of her by one of the employees, and consulted with a towering man who had to be one of the bouncers. Standing next to him, Cat seemed almost fragile. She appeared to be giving the big man some instructions. After he had walked away, she continued on toward Ian.

He never took his eyes off her as she made her way around the bar. When she was finally standing right in front of him, he had to contain the urge to haul her into his arms and greet her properly.

She leaned in close so he could hear her when she spoke, and the dark, sexy scent he would recognize anywhere as hers engulfed him, making him instantly hard. "What're you doing here? Not exactly your scene."

He feigned offense. "I love this place."

Her lips curled into a skeptical smile. "Then why haven't I ever seen you here before?"

"You weren't looking?"

"You're full of it."

He loved the way her warm breath felt against his skin as she spoke into his ear. "How was the family thing?"

"Fun." He hesitated for a second. "I missed you." What the hell? Why not?

The comment seemed to rattle her.

"My parents surprised us by showing up."

"All the more reason to stay away."

He let his gaze wander down the front of her, coming to rest on breasts that were on prominent display under a snug T-shirt. "They liked Georgie and Tess."

"They're the kind of girls you bring home to Mom."

"And you're not?"

"The moms tend to be put off by the brow ring and tattoo."

Wondering if that's why she had them, he shrugged. "My mother has six sons. Not much fazes her."

Her eyes widened. "*Six?*"

Ian smiled as he nodded and continued to fight the overwhelming desire to touch her.

She directed his attention to the fat wad of cash she had rolled into her fist. "I was heading up to the office. Want to come?"

So badly he ached. "Yeah," he said, reaching for his wallet to pay for the beers.

She stopped him. "It's on me," she said with a signal to the bartender. Pointing to Ian, she made a writing gesture.

The bartender responded with a thumbs-up.

"Thanks," Ian said. He followed her back the way he'd come in. Halfway down the long, dark hallway, she ducked through a door that led to a stairwell.

Using a key at the top of the stairs, she pushed open a heavy door and stepped into a large, cluttered space. One whole wall was a window that looked down over the club.

"My home away from home," she said as she stashed the money in a safe behind her desk.

Cases of beer were stacked against one of the other walls, her desk was piled high with paper, and a screen saver on her computer provided the only light in the room.

When she reached for a switch on the wall, Ian took her hand before she could turn on a light, brought her into his arms, and captured her mouth for a deep, searing kiss. Tongues met in a fierce battle, and when her teeth clamped down on his, Ian almost passed out from the surge of pure lust that streaked through him.

He scooped her up.

She wrapped her legs around his waist and tightened her arms around his neck.

Pressing her back against the window that overlooked the club, he broke the kiss. "One-way glass?"

"Uh-huh," she said, pulling him in for another torrid kiss.

Long, passionate minutes passed before Ian came up for air. Planting his lips on her neck, he whispered, "I've needed this all day."

"Mmm," she sighed, tilting her head to encourage the attention he was paying to her neck.

"You, too?" he asked, hating his needy, hopeful tone.

"I liked finding you at my bar."

The confession made him ridiculously happy. "There's no chance of this window letting go, is there?"

"That would suck," she joked, rotating her pelvis against his straining hard-on. "*Cat.*"

"*Ian,*" she teased in the same tone as she bit down on his earlobe.

He was so painfully hard, he was afraid it would break right off if she kept pushing on it. "Does that door have a lock?"

He saw a moment of hesitation in her eyes that disappeared as fast as it had come. "Sure does."

He let her slide down the front of him and, for the second night in a row, watched her slide a lock into place.

She turned back to him, and with a sexy, confident smile, she reached for the hem of her T-shirt and lifted it up and over her head. Her eyes locked on his, she unbuttoned her camouflage pants and let them slide into a puddle at her feet.

Ian's hands rolled into fists at his side as he bit down on his lower lip to keep his tongue from hanging out of his face. Watching her strip for him was like having every fantasy he'd ever had come true all at once.

Her smile shifted from confident to tantalizing as she reached back to unhook her bra. She took it off and threw it at him.

Surprised, he caught it, felt the heat of her body in the soft cloth, and was certain he was going to explode any second.

As she sashayed toward him, Ian was paralyzed and terrified that she'd only have to touch him and he'd be done.

"You're kind of overdressed for this party," she whispered, inching his shirt up and over his head, her lips exploring each new bit of skin as she uncovered it. "Condom?"

"Wallet," he managed to say.

Reaching into both back pockets and squeezing his ass, she removed his wallet and flipped it open.

He watched her smile fade when she encountered a photo of Rosie. That would be something he could think about later, after he had slaked the burning desire. Taking it from her, he found the condom and tossed the wallet on the floor with his shirt. There was something highly erotic about getting naked in front of a window where hundreds of people who couldn't see them gyrated to music they could feel but not hear.

Unbuttoning his shorts, she pushed them down and kneeled in front of him. "Cat," he gasped as she took him into her mouth. No way would he survive this—not after the striptease. "Babe, wait." He wove his fingers through her short hair. "I can't . . ."

She sucked hard and skimmed her tongue over the tip.

His legs failing him, Ian leaned back against the window. This was going to be quick. "Cat."

"Let go," she whispered before she took him deep again. "Let it go."

He closed his eyes tight against the pain and the pleasure of her hot, wet mouth sliding over him. Cupping the back of her head, he held on as the climax slammed into him hard and fast. When it was over, he slid down the glass to the floor and gathered her into his arms. Her breasts were soft against his chest as her lips toyed with his nipple. He was amazed to feel his dick stir to life again.

"Good?" she asked.

"So good I think I died for a minute there."

"Do I need to give you CPR?"

"No, but some mouth-to-mouth might be in order."

Smiling at his joke, she crawled up his chest to lock lips with him, and then suddenly they were rolling across the carpeted floor. He cupped her breasts and bent to suck hard on her nipples. As she squirmed under him, begging him with the rise and fall of her hips to hurry, he stopped long enough to locate the condom and roll it on.

Perched over her, he wanted to take it slow, to savor the sweet satisfaction of having her spread open beneath him. But she wanted fast. She wanted frantic. And she wanted it now. After what she had given him, he happily obliged. Since she had taken the edge off, he had plenty to give.

Long, deep strokes, the wet slap of his flesh against hers, the press of his body tight into hers. He couldn't believe it was possible to top the night before, but here on the floor of her office, with the flash of strobe lights from the club giving her skin a variety of rapidly changing hues, it was even better.

Dipping his head, he caught her nipple between his teeth and reached down to where they were joined to coax her. He felt her tighten around him and sucked hard on her nipple. Her legs fell open wider as the orgasm rolled through her in wave after wave of sensation.

She shrieked with pleasure, and rather than muffle it the way he had the night before, Ian let her scream, the soundproof room keeping the noise in as much as out.

He watched her face as she came back down to realize he wasn't done yet. Not even close.

CHAPTER 23

Nathan walked Georgie to the front door. Cat had left the porch light on when she left, but otherwise the house was dark.

"Looks like I'm the first one home."

"Seems like it."

An awkward pause hung in the air between them.

"Georgie—"

"I had fun today." She smiled up at him. "Sorry. What were you going to say?"

His face grew serious.

Her heart raced.

"I want you so much," he said in a soft, sexy voice. He rested his hands on her shoulders and looked into her eyes. "I want to feel your silky skin against mine. I want to kiss you and taste you and smell you. I want to be inside you, so deep I can't tell where you end and I begin. I want you. Desperately."

No one had ever said such things to her. "Nathan," she sighed. "I want you, too. I want to spend another night with you the way we did before. I want that so much."

He hooked an arm around her neck and kissed her with a ravenous appetite that took her breath away. That this strong, decent, kind, beautiful man wanted her this much . . .

"Nathan." She pushed gently but insistently on his chest. "What you said last night, the reason you couldn't stay. Nothing's changed. And if we do this, it'll only make it harder—"

"Not possible," he joked.

"Stop," she said, laughing. "Don't make jokes. I'm serious."

"I know." His mouth twisted into a grudging expression. "And I know you're right, as much as it pains me."

She looped her arms around his waist and pushed hard against his arousal. "Does it help to know I want you just as much?"

"Ah, yeah," he said through gritted teeth. "Sure."

"I do. And if I wasn't certain it would make things worse rather than better, I'd be dragging you upstairs right now."

He groaned. "I could do without that visual if you're saying no."

"I'm saying I wish. I wish so many things were different."

He leaned his forehead against hers and stayed there for a long time before he pressed kisses to both her cheeks. "Are you opening the center tomorrow?"

She nodded. "And then I'll be at the hospital waiting to hear about Gus's surgery."

"I have court first thing, and then I'll try to come by the hospital."

"You're going back to work? Already?"

"Light duty this week. I have to appear at a hearing on that pedophile case." His face clouded. "I was the first one in, so I'm the only one who saw . . ."

Georgie swallowed. "Saw what?"

"What he was doing to her before he pulled a gun from under the pillow and started shooting." His tone was matter-of-fact, but she saw the truth in his eyes.

"Do you want to talk about it?"

"Once in court will be plenty. Besides, I'd never want you to have that picture in your mind. Never."

She reached up to cradle his face in her hands. "You take care of everyone, Nathan Caldwell. Who takes care of you?"

"I'm advertising to fill the position right now. Interested in applying?"

"You make a joke whenever something strikes too close to home."

"I do?" he asked, seeming genuinely surprised.

"Uh-huh."

He shrugged. "I don't need a lot."

"Everyone needs some."

Turning his face into her hand, he kissed the palm. "Are you offering?"

"For what it's worth, I wish I could."

"It's worth a lot. What about you? Who takes care of you when you're in Atlanta?"

Georgie had to think about that.

"Doug the agent?" he asked with a sneer.

She laughed. "Hardly."

"Then what were you doing with him?"

"He was a distraction."

"Is that what I am?"

"No, Nathan, you're a delight." She shifted her hands from his face to the back of his head, pulling him down to her. Pouring herself into the kiss, she tried to show him, to tell him.

He raised his head to stare at her.

Georgie's heart thumped in her chest.

"I have to go," he whispered. "Before I can't." Hugging her tight, he touched another light kiss to her lips. "I'll see you tomorrow."

"Thank you for sharing your family with me. It was a wonderful day."

"My pleasure, sweetheart." He squeezed her hand and released it. "I'll wait until you get in."

Georgie unlocked the door and turned back to him. "Sleep well."

"Not likely," he said with that irresistible smile.

From inside, she watched him amble down the stairs to his car. He waved on his way by.

Georgie stood there for a long time wondering why she had let the best thing that had ever happened to her leave.

She trudged up the stairs with a heavy heart. While she had succeeded in putting most of her worries aside during the day with Nathan, they all came back down on her the minute she was alone in the big, quiet house.

After being surrounded all afternoon and evening by Nathan's big, loving family, she was more acutely aware of what was gone from her own life.

She wondered if Tess had given in to temptation and slept with Ben. They had been awfully cozy by the fire, and Georgie wouldn't be surprised if Tess didn't make it home that night. Cat was at work, but Ian had put Rosie to bed in Kevin's house and left a short time later. Georgie had suspected he was going to find Cat.

Wound up and frustrated after sending Nathan home, Georgie decided to do some more work in her mother's room. She changed into the boxers and cami she slept in and put her hair up in a high ponytail. She taped together another box and took it in with her.

The room was so quiet, almost eerily quiet, that she flipped on her mother's bedside radio and brought the jewelry box over to the bed. She sat to go through the mostly costume pieces, again making a small pile of things to keep for herself and Ali and a larger pile to get rid of. A few of the pins brought back memories of Christmases and Halloweens past. Long after Georgie and Ali had given up trick-or-treating, their mother had still dressed up to hand out candy to the neighborhood kids.

Inside a velvet box, she found her grandmother's engagement ring and realized she needed to add it to the list of valuables she had to bring to probate court on Tuesday. At some point, she and Ali would have to decide what to do about all the valuables, including the house.

At the bottom of the jewelry box, she found a false bottom that she lifted to make sure she hadn't missed anything. Two pieces of paper were folded into the small space. One was addressed to Ali, the other to her.

Georgie opened hers to find a key taped to the bottom and her mother's familiar handwriting.

My darling Georgie,

If you've found this, then you've reached the point where you feel strong enough to go through my things. I'm so sorry for all I put you and your sister through the last few months, but having you both here with me brought me such joy in my final days.

By now you've probably discovered there's not much of any value among my things. As you well know, I was never one for fancy clothes or jewelry. The things I valued most in my life couldn't be paid for with money or worn on a finger. You, my darling child, you and your sister were the ones I cherished above all others. You were the loves of my life.

Georgie held the letter aside when she was so blinded by tears she could no longer see through them to read. A few minutes passed before she could work up the courage to continue.

When I look back over my life, I have few regrets. But the ones I do have are not insignificant. I regret that I smothered you, that when you went far away to college you never came home again because you knew if you did you'd never truly be independent from me. I'm sorry it took me so long to let go, and I'm sorry you felt you had to go so far away—and stay there so long—to make your own way.

I'm proud of you, Georgie. Truly proud of the caring, compassionate, independent, successful woman you grew up to be. Since I'm not around for you to kill, I suppose it's time to confess that I've been planning your wedding in my mind for years. Upstairs in the attic you'll find my wedding dress hanging in one of the garment bags. I have little hope that it'll suit your finely tuned sense of style (how you came by that with me as your mother is anyone's guess!), but it's yours if you'd like to wear it or alter it to suit you. My feelings won't be hurt (even in heaven) if you wear something of your own choosing. Whatever makes you happy makes me happy.

I've been squirreling away the money to pay for this big day I dreamed of for you from every paycheck I've ever received at the center. The key below is for a safety deposit box at the credit union. Inside you'll find a passbook for an account in your name. When you're ready to get married, I hope you'll use this money to pay for a day that makes all your dreams come true. Or, if you'd rather, use it as a down payment on a house. Either way, I hope you'll think of me and remember always how very much I love you.

Be kind to yourself, follow your heart, put love before everything else, and be happy, Georgie. Be very, very happy, my love. You made my life.

Mom

Georgie's sobs echoed through the quiet room. Without taking the time to think about the implications, she crossed the hall to her room and rifled through her purse in search of the note Nathan had written to her after the first night they spent together. When she found it, she wiped her eyes and used her cell phone to call the number he had given her.

His voice was heavy and sleepy sounding.

"Nathan."

"Georgie? Sweetheart, what's wrong?"

"I . . ." She couldn't seem to form a coherent thought, let alone a sentence.

"I'm coming. I'll be right there."

Before she could protest or remind him he had court in the morning, the phone went dead.

Downstairs, Georgie unlocked the front door and sat on the bottom step, her face buried in her crossed arms. She hadn't known this kind of pain was possible. The numbness that followed her mother's death had lifted, leaving her raw and unprotected from this latest blow.

When she heard the pounding of Nathan's footsteps on the porch stairs, she raised her head.

Before she could get up, he was through the door wearing only gym shorts and running shoes.

He came to a halt at the sight of her tearstained face and dropped to his knees in front of her. She could tell by the sheen of sweat on his forehead that he had run to her. Right in that moment, the door to her heart swung open and let him in.

Reaching out to brush a tear off her cheek, he said, "What, baby? What happened?"

"I found . . ." She shook her head when she couldn't continue.

He pulled her onto his lap and sat on the floor with his arms around her. "Georgie," he whispered, curling his hand around her neck under her ponytail. "Shh."

"I'm sorry," she said. "You were sleeping."

"I wasn't. I was thinking of you and wishing I was with you."

His hair was damp and his jaw smooth.

"You smell good," she said, burying her runny nose in the crook of his neck.

"I took a long *cold* shower when I got home."

Despite her tears, despite her heartbreak, he made her laugh. "You forgot your shirt."

"Be glad I remembered the shorts. I was moving pretty fast."

"I just wanted to talk to you, but thank you for moving fast, for coming."

"What did you find, sweetheart?"

"A letter from my mother."

"Georgie." He tightened his hold on her.

"Do you want to read it?"

"Only if you want me to."

"I do. I want to show it to you." When she started to get up, he stopped her. "Wait until you're ready."

He held her for a long time before she said she felt better. She got up and extended a hand to him.

Keeping his hand wrapped around hers, he followed her upstairs. At the door to her mother's room, he took a long look at the boxes. "Don't you have anyone who can help you with this?"

She shook her head, picked up the letter and handed it to him. "Let's go in my room. I've had enough in here for today." On her way out, she turned off the radio and the light and closed the door behind her.

Nathan stretched out on Georgie's bed and held out his arm to invite her to lie with him.

She curled up next to him and listened to the steady cadence of his breathing as he read the letter.

"Wow," he said when he finished. "That's amazing."

"You know, it's funny. She used to say all the time that she couldn't picture herself as an elderly woman. What's ironic is that she knew everything there was to know about old people except how to become one."

Nathan fingered the key taped to the bottom of the letter. "Are you going to get the passbook?"

"At some point. I still can't believe she did that."

"It's an incredible gift, Georgie, the letter, the money, all of it. I don't know if you can see it that way right now, but maybe someday . . ."

"I know it is. It was just so shocking to find it. I could *hear* her talking in that letter. It brought her back, however briefly, and then when it was over, it was like she had died again. I think that's what got me so upset."

"I can't imagine life without my mother," he confessed. "Even at thirty-three and even from afar, she plays such a huge role in my life."

"I can see how she would be more like a wonderful friend now that you're all grown."

"She is. Yours was, too."

"Yes. In some ways, my very best friend, and yet I had no idea she dreamed of my wedding. She opened the center when I was six and worked without a paycheck the first year. So for twenty-three years she's been saving for a wedding she didn't live to see. That makes me so sad. It kind of makes sense, now, though."

"What does?"

"The night before she died, we talked about some of the things she was going to miss—my wedding, any kids I might have. She was very concerned about her death ruining those things for me and wanted me to know that she'd be with me, for all of it."

"I'm sure this is part of what she meant. I'll bet it's a lot of money."

"No doubt."

"You don't have to do anything about it now, Georgie. Not until you're ready. And when you are, I'll go with you to get it if you want me to."

She looked up at him. "You will?"

"Sure I will."

Pressing a kiss to his chest, she said, "Thank you. For coming when I needed you, for being such a good guy."

"It's not everyone I'd run half naked through the streets of Newport for."

"I should hope not," she said with a laugh.

"Guess who's over at my house."

"Who?"

"Tess—in Ben's room, giggling up a storm while trying to be quiet so I wouldn't know they're in there."

"No way! She said she wasn't going to be fast and easy like the rest of us."

"The rest of who?"

Uh-oh, Georgie thought, remembering she hadn't told him about Ian and Cat. "Me and you. They know what happened."

"Me and you and who else?"

"I hate that you're a detective," she grumbled.

"It would do you well to remember that and not try to put stuff past me." He poked her ribs, which made her squeal. "Who else?"

"Who else is there?"

"Ian and *Cat?*"

"Down and dirty," Georgie confirmed.

"After they went out to dinner?"

"Apparently, there was no dinner."

"No way."

"You can't let on that I told you. I promised her I wouldn't."

"This is good. He needs a *girlfriend*. It's been too long."

"I wouldn't exactly call her his girlfriend. I don't think that's how it's going to be."

"What do you mean?"

"Picture more of a friends-with-benefits arrangement."

"Sex buddies?"

"Something like that."

"Huh." Nathan ran a hand over his chin as he considered it. "That's not his style. I'm surprised he agreed to it."

Georgie shrugged. "Whatever floats their boat."

"I wouldn't go for that, personally."

"No, you wouldn't."

Their eyes met, and Georgie couldn't look away. "I'm tired," she whispered.

"Go to sleep. I'll go in a minute."

"No."

"No?"

Her hand traveled from his chest to his taut belly and back up again. "I'm tired of fighting whatever this is that's happening between us. Fighting it is so exhausting."

"Georgie." He released an unsteady breath. "You've had a long day, an emotional day. This isn't the time—"

She stopped him with a finger to his lips. "Make love to me, Nathan. Make love to me the way you said you wanted to before."

He swallowed hard. "No condoms."

"I know where there're some. I'll go get them."

His hand closed around her arm, stopping her from getting up. "Are you sure, Georgie? Really sure?"

"Yes. I'm sure."

CHAPTER 24

Tess scooted over against the wall to give Ben plenty of room to get into the full-sized bed. The T-shirt he had given her to sleep in rode up over her underwear, so she tugged it back down with a hand that had grown damp with nerves. Jumping into bed with a man she had met two days ago—not to mention sharing his toothbrush—went against everything she believed in. However, jumping into bed with *Ben* just felt right. Why? She had no idea, and she wasn't in the mood to question it.

He hobbled across the hall from the bathroom wearing only a pair of sweats with socks.

As she took in her first view of his bare chest, her mouth went dry with longing. As he came closer, she noticed the scars that dotted his right side and remembered what he had told her about his shrapnel wounds.

"Kind of hot for sweats, isn't it?"

"It's more comfortable when it's covered up," he said, gesturing to his leg.

Tess held out a hand to help him into bed. "Okay?"

"Yeah." He grimaced as he adjusted his leg. "Give me a second."

As she watched him breathe through the pain, she reached out to lay a hand on his chest and felt his heart beating fast.

He covered her hand with his but kept his eyes closed tight against the agony.

"You can't live like this. We have to do something."

"We?"

"Yes. You and me."

"You make me believe anything's possible."

"It is."

He finally opened his eyes and turned so he could see her. "You aren't going to tell me you're an alien or a felon on the run or married or anything else that's going to ruin my life forever, are you?"

Since she no longer considered herself married in any way that mattered and had no desire to ever be married again, she shook her head.

"That's good, because some time during this weekend, it might've even been when you were being so testy with me on the way to the hospital the other night—"

She poked him in the ribs, making him grunt with laughter.

"—or maybe it was when I saw you holding Rosie and I could tell you want a child of your own more than you want just about anything. It could've been when I found out what a dirty mind you have buried under that innocent façade when we played Scrabble. Of course, it was probably the first time I kissed you. Was that *only* yesterday?"

Barely breathing as she waited for him to get to the point, Tess nodded. "Ben?"

"Hmm?"

"What are you talking about?"

"I'm trying to decide exactly when I fell in love with you, Tess."

"You . . . Oh."

He twirled a lock of her long hair around his finger. "Is that a good 'oh' or a bad 'oh'?"

"That's a really good 'oh.'" She reached out to caress his face. "Because I love you, too."

"You don't have to say—"

"Unlike you, though, I know exactly when I realized it."

"Is that so?"

"Uh-huh," she said, with a teasing smile.

"Are you going to tell me?"

"How bad do you want to know?"

"Bad." He drew her into his arms and worked his good leg between hers. "Very, very bad."

"In that case, it was when you stared up into that cop's flashlight on the beach. The expression on your face was priceless. I just knew."

"A really romantic moment," he said dryly. "I'm touched."

She arched an eyebrow. "Do you want me to take it back?"

"Please don't," he whispered, burying his face in her hair. "Please don't ever take it back."

"Ben?"

"Yeah?"

"If we, you know, love each other, I'd really like to . . ."

"Make love?"

Stroking his hard length through the soft fabric of his sweats, she nodded. Never once, in all the time she'd been married, had she ever done anything quite so brazen. It wouldn't have occurred to her then to reach out and take what she wanted.

"I want to," he said. "You can't imagine how badly I want to."

"To the contrary. I have my hand on the evidence."

"I don't know if I can," he said with a small, sad smile.

"Between the two of us, we can figure something out, no?"

"I don't know if I'm ready," he clarified. The conversation alone seemed to embarrass and diminish him. Perhaps there was more to his injuries than he had let on. Either way, this wasn't how she wanted it to go, not after having just declared her love for him.

Tess removed her hand, regretting she had pushed him.

He returned it to where she'd had it. "That doesn't mean we can't mess around a little."

"I don't want to hurt you."

"You won't."

As she gently stroked him through his clothes, he slid a hand under her shirt and groaned when he encountered the warm skin of her back.

"You feel so good," he said.

"Tell me about your life before you got hurt. Before the war."

"I'm not sure I can talk when you're doing that."

She moved her hand up to his belly. "Then we'll get back to it."

Whimpering in protest, he bemoaned the loss.

"You'll live," she said, giggling. "The faster you talk, the faster you'll get what you want."

As if he was on speed, he said, "Before I got called up to active duty in the Guard, I was an architect. I worked for a local firm, had a nice apartment downtown, a girlfriend who said she loved me, and a lot of good friends who seemed to scatter—along with my so-called girlfriend—when I came home in pieces." He pushed her hand down and groaned when she resisted.

"You're an architect," she said with amazement.

"Was."

"Are."

"It's been a couple of years."

"But you could go back to it. You don't need your leg to sit at a drafting table."

"I need my leg to stop hurting so much it crushes every ounce of creativity I might've had. It's all I can do to take a shower every day. I'd be no good to them in this condition."

"Surely they held your job for you."

"They said the door's always open. They're good guys to work for. I loved that job."

"You have to have your leg removed, Ben. Prosthetics have come so far in the last few years. You could regain your mobility and get your life back on track."

"The question is whether they can give me enough of a stump to make a prosthesis feasible."

"So you've asked about it."

"In broad terms. No specifics."

"Even if you had to be on crutches, you'd be better off than you are now living in agonizing pain."

"Would you love me less if I had only one leg?"

"Don't you *ever* ask me that question again, Bennett Caldwell. Not ever, ever again."

"I love when you get all bossy with me like that," he said, mimicking her tone.

"You want to see bossy, mister?"

"Oh yeah. I want to see that."

She leaned in to kiss him, reveling in the soft feel of his lips gliding in time with hers and the knowledge that he loved her. Filled with a sense of safety and contentment she had forgotten existed, she ran her tongue over his bottom lip.

He cupped her cheek and kept his lips close to hers. "I've been thinking about what you said, about going to see Greg's family. Before I make any definite decisions about my leg, I think I'd like to see them, but only if you come with me."

"Of course I'd go with you. Where are they?"

"Pittsburgh. I was going to call his folks tomorrow and see if they're up for it. What's your work schedule like next weekend?"

"That soon?"

"I want to get it over with so I can stop thinking about it."

"You make the plans, and I'll get the time off."

"Thank you." He kissed her and pushed her hand back down to where he wanted it most. "You've let a perfectly good hard-on get away with all this talking."

"Let me see what I can do about that."

Cat was stretched out on top of Ian as his hands moved in a tantalizingly slow pattern up and down her back. She wanted to purr like a kitten, but this Cat didn't purr—at least she never had before.

Ian Caldwell. *Mmmm.* The man sure knew how to please a woman. Just thinking about it made her wonder if he was up for another round. Glancing out the window to the club, she saw the bouncers clearing the room and the band breaking down their equipment. She choked back a yawn and was surprised to realize it was already one o'clock. *Time flies when you're having fun,* she thought with a smile.

Her employees knew the drill for closing. She would have to lock up the money and account for it in the morning, but the only thing that required her immediate attention was the splendid male chest under her lips.

Flicking her tongue over his nipple, she watched with fascination as it sprang to life. Another part of him weighed in against her belly.

"Don't start anything," he mumbled. "That was our only condom."

"That's so disappointing. I expected better from you."

"Oh? And why's that?"

"You've got that whole Boy Scout 'be prepared' thing going on."

In her ear, he whispered, "Do I fuck like a Boy Scout?"

She hooted with laughter. "Your attention to detail is admirable. Do they give a badge for that?"

"I can't remember. I'll check my eagle sash and get back to you."

"I knew it! I'm sleeping with a freaking eagle scout! This'll wreck my reputation as a bad ass."

"Me and Nate both," he said proudly. "And I hate to point out that there hasn't been much sleeping involved, but we can fix that." He held her face in a gesture so tender, her heart staggered. "Come home with me tonight. Sleep with me."

"Is that allowed under the terms of our deal?"

"The hell with the deal. I want you in my bed."

He was so good—a good, kind, honest, caring man who definitely did *not* fuck like Boy Scout. Cat knew she didn't deserve him, but she couldn't seem to resist him, either. "Where's Rosie?"

"Staying with my parents at my brother's house. Coast is clear."

"Are you sure? Maybe we'd be better off at my house."

"I'd rather not run into my brothers when I'm sneaking out in the morning."

She contemplated that. "All right. Your place it is."

Since Ian had walked into town, they took Cat's Jeep to his house.

"My place is in the back," he said, pointing to the long driveway.

"Who lives there?"

"My brother Kevin."

"Your parents are staying *there?* Right next door?"

"They're sleeping on the other side of the house." Flashing a teasing smile, he added, "We'll close the bedroom window so you can make as much noise as you want."

"I don't know about this, Ian. What will they say when they see my car here?"

"They won't say anything. We stay out of each other's crap. Otherwise, I wouldn't live here."

"Why do you? Live here?"

"It helps to keep my expenses down so I can work less and spend most of my time with Rosie."

Admirable, she thought but didn't say it.

"If it makes you more comfortable, I'll move your car out to the street, okay?"

"That would be better. Thank you."

"Go on up." He pointed to a flight of stairs. "Door's unlocked."

"Take it easy on my clutch. She's sensitive."

"Like her mama." He kissed her cheek and nudged her out of the car.

With a mixture of trepidation and curiosity—and another glance at the big dark house, the *close* big dark house—Cat went up the stairs. Inside, her first impression was one of neatness. Yes, there were toys, and yes, a guitar was propped in the corner, but everything was neatly stowed.

She had expected a bachelor pad, but instead she found a home where Rosie was front and center. Her pictures from infancy to the present hung in frames on the wall along with her artwork. Cat studied the progression of photos. She really was a cute kid, if you were into kids, that is.

Ian came bounding up the stairs.

Cat spun around to shush him. "You'll wake up the dead making all that racket!"

"They aren't going to wake up, babe. Don't sweat it."

She shouldn't have liked him calling her that quite as much as she did, but the sexy, proprietary way he said it appealed to her even though she knew it wasn't wise.

"Beer?"

"Sure."

He opened two bottles and brought them with him to the sofa. "Hungry?"

"No, thanks. I'm good."

Reaching for her feet, he surprised her when he knocked off her flip-flops, swung her feet into his lap, and began rubbing them.

Cat had no choice but to let her head fall back against one of the oversized pillows.

He pushed his thumbs into her tense arches. "Feel good?"

"Mmm," she said. That urge to purr again!

"You must get tired being on your feet all night."

"You don't have to do that," she said, frantic to remind him—and herself—that they weren't about this caring and sharing thing. They were about one thing and one thing only. She would remind him of that. Really she would, just as soon as she got enough of the *divine* foot massage. The man had amazing hands, and as he had proven a few times already, he knew how to use them.

"I like doing it," he said, surprising her again by pressing his lips to the sole of her foot.

In danger of losing her equilibrium, Cat took a long sip of her beer, closed her eyes, and gave herself over to the pleasure. She hadn't even known she *liked* having her feet rubbed until Ian Caldwell rubbed them. "Nice place," she said a few minutes later.

"Miss Priss is the queen of this roost, as you can see."

"She's lucky to have you."

He seemed taken aback by the unexpected compliment. "I'm the lucky one. She's by far the best thing in my life."

"How'd you end up raising her alone?"

"I'm not doing it alone. I've got a huge village around me."

"I'll rephrase the question. Where's her mother?"

"I don't know. Last I heard she was moving to North Carolina."

"She has nothing to do with her? With Rosie?"

He shook his head, but his jaw pulsed with tension she might have missed if she hadn't been looking so closely. "She hasn't seen her since the day she was born."

Cat watched, waited, and wondered if he'd say more.

"You really want to hear this?" he asked warily.

"Yeah, I guess I do." Why she wanted to know was something she'd think about later.

He rolled his head as if to relieve tension in his neck. "She was a waitress at one of the clubs where I worked in the summer. She was young—too young for me."

Intrigued, Cat realized he was ashamed that he had dallied with a younger woman.

"We started hanging out, one thing led to another. She told me she was on the pill, so I was sketchy with the condoms—stupid on a number of levels, I know. I discovered later she was on the pill, but more often than not, she forgot to take it."

"How'd you find out she was pregnant?"

"When she asked me to pay for an abortion." He took a drink of his beer. "I went nuts. Don't get me wrong—I'm not a holy roller or anything, and I'm all for a woman's right to choose. But not when it's my kid and not when I was willing and able to give the child a loving home."

"So she agreed to have the baby?"

"Hell no. I had to beg and plead and cajole and give her all kinds of money. It got really ugly really quickly, which made for a *long* nine months. She was so pissed at me, we were hardly speaking by the time Rosie was born."

"Were you there for the birth?"

For the first time since the conversation began, he brightened. "Yeah," he said softly. "It was the most amazing moment of my whole life. When Rosie came out, her mother refused to even acknowledge her, so the doctor handed her to me. I took one look at my daughter and knew that all the fighting had been worth it. Rosie's mother told me to fuck off. I said, 'Gladly,' and I walked out with my little girl. We've never seen or heard from her again."

So much to admire, so much to respect. *Be careful, Cat. Be very careful.* "What does Rosie know?"

"That her mother wasn't ready to be a mom and her whole family loves her."

"Will you tell her the rest someday?"

"I don't want to, but I suppose I'll have to at some point."

"It's an amazing story."

"It seems like a bad dream now. I never think about it anymore."

"Thank you for telling me." What she thought but didn't say was here's a man who doesn't take the easy way out. Here's a man who stands up, who does the right thing. He was honorable, just as she had suspected. The realizations, one on top of the other, sent her reeling. If he touched her now, if he took her to bed and made love to her, she'd be lost.

Clearing her throat, she said, "Ian?"

"What, babe?"

"Will you play for me?"

CHAPTER 25

Georgie returned from the third floor to find Nathan sitting on the bed untying his sneakers. He looked up at her, smiled, and she melted from deep inside straight out to the goose bumps that appeared all of a sudden on her arms. Her skin burned with awareness—of him, of what they were about to do, of what it meant.

Nathan must have sensed her sudden bout of shyness, because he got up and crossed the room to her. "Whose stash did you raid?"

"Cat's. I left her a few in case they need some, too."

"Ian would never be unprepared in that regard. Once burned and all that." Nathan reached for the hand with the condoms and took them from her. "Only three, huh? Won't be a complete do-over of our first night."

"I don't know if I'd survive that again."

"Me either." He laughed softly as he led her to the bed. He sat and looped his arms around her, drawing her in close to press his face to her belly.

Georgie ran her fingers through his tight curls. "Why does this feel like the first time?"

"Because it is."

"I guess you don't remember another time or five."

He tipped his face up so he could see her. "How could I forget? But everything's different now, so it *is* like the first time again."

Raising an eyebrow in amusement, she said, "Everything?"

"Everything," he said emphatically.

"Nathan—"

"Shh." He guided her into bed.

They lay facing each other, holding hands.

"I was someone different that night, Nathan, someone I didn't even recognize. I don't want you to be disappointed."

"Georgie Quinn," he said as he brushed the hair back from her face, "the only person I want to be in bed with is *you*. The *real* you."

"The real me isn't a temptress or a sex goddess."

He laughed. Hard. "Want to bet?"

"I'm being serious," she said, annoyed that he would laugh right then.

"You're perfect just as you are. Anything with you will be enough."

"You were supposed to stop saying those things."

"I'll try harder." He brought her in tight against his aroused body, raised her chin, and kissed her as if he had all the time in the world to give her.

The result devastated her and stripped away her remaining defenses. He kissed her for what seemed like forever before she felt the first tentative brush of his tongue over her lips. His patience was in sharp contrast to the urgency he'd shown her earlier when he had spelled out just how desperately he wanted her.

Georgie's hands traveled over his warm, smooth back as one sweet, undemanding kiss faded into another. Since he kept his hands on her face, she had only the press of his throbbing erection against her leg to tell her that this slow seduction was affecting him every bit as much.

By the time he finally sent his tongue deep into her mouth, she was ready to beg him for it. His hands fell from her face to her shoulders and then her breasts. Through her thin cami, he teased her nipples into pebbled points. Dipping his head, he suckled her until the fabric was damp and clinging. A sharp, hot wave of desire grew into a painful throb at her center.

He pushed at her top, and when she raised her arms to help him take it off, he anchored them to the pillow. "Leave them there," he whispered as he moved down to explore what he had uncovered.

Georgie closed her eyes and floated on a cloud of sensation. She felt her boxers travel over her legs, and then his lips skim from her feet to her knees to her thighs, pushing them apart as he moved up. Fighting the burning need to touch him, she rolled her hands into fists as he stroked his tongue over her, into her, once, twice before she exploded. The blast was so strong, so intense, two hot tears fell from her tightly closed eyes.

He left her only long enough to sheath himself. When he returned, he kissed the tears from her cheeks as he entered her slowly. "Georgie," he whispered. "Look at me."

Her eyes fluttered open to meet his in the soft light of the bedside lamp.

"I was so afraid we were only going to get that one night together," he said as he thrust into her. "As much as it was, it wasn't enough. Not nearly enough."

Georgie arched her back and reached down to hold him still.

Keeping his eyes open and fixed on her, he molded his lips to hers.

After a long, breathless moment, she lightened her grip on him so he could move.

His lips hovered close to hers, their breath mingling. Suddenly, he hooked his arm under her leg and pushed it up to her chest, sending him deeper than he'd ever been, deeper than anyone had ever been.

Georgie came with a low moan as she gave herself over to him so completely, so thoroughly that it never occurred to her to remember that she'd had no plans to give that much. In that moment, there was only him, joined with her, one with her.

"Georgie," he gasped as his orgasm gripped him. He released her leg and let his forehead land on her shoulder, his breath coming in short pants. When he finally looked up at her, he wore his heart in his eyes. "Georgie, I lo—"

"No," she said, pressing her fingers to his lips. "Don't. Please."

He withdrew from her and shifted onto his back, propping an arm over his eyes.

"Nathan." She turned into him, touched her lips to his chest, and rested her hand on his belly. "Stay with me."

"I'm here," he said, but he kept his arm over his eyes. "We should get some sleep. We both have early mornings."

Georgie got up, found her clothes, and crossed the hall to the bathroom. Closing the door, she slid down to the floor and rested her head on her folded arms.

Cat woke up facedown and naked in Ian's bed and tried to figure out how she had gotten there. She remembered being stretched out on the sofa in a dreamy half sleep, listening to him sing to her in that deep, sexy voice of his. She must have dozed off, because she had woken up as he carried her to bed. They had shed their clothes into a pile on the floor, fallen into bed, and gone straight to sleep. During the night they had spent wrapped around each other, he had never once tried to make love with her.

Until now.

She sighed with contentment and the first stirrings of desire as his tongue moved over the ridges of her spine, down to the twin globes of her bottom. As he paid homage to each cheek, Cat squirmed under him, which raised her up just enough for him to slide his hands under her to cup her breasts.

His teeth clamped down on the tendon at the base of her neck.

Pushing back against his erection, she begged him to fill her, to take her, to possess her. At this moment, he could have anything he wanted.

He guided her onto her hands and knees and entered her from behind.

Cat cried out from both the thrill and the impact.

He ran his thumbs over her nipples and squeezed her breasts as he pushed into her again.

Oh, God, this was good—*so, so good*. Maybe the best she'd ever had. No, definitely the best. He was so hard, and she was so wet and oh, oh, *oh*, he knew what he was doing. Didn't it make all the difference in the world to be with a man who knew what he was doing? Who knew just where she needed him to touch her? She didn't have to draw him a map or give him directions. He just knew. Somehow, he knew.

Her orgasm built like a wave rolling toward the beach. She needed just one more—

"Daddy?" a little voice called from the living room. "Daddy? Why's your door closed?"

Ian pulled out of her so abruptly that Cat fell to the mattress with an ungraceful thud. "*Shit!*" he muttered as he slipped on a pair of shorts and quickly zipped them. "Sorry, babe." With that he left the room and closed the door behind him.

"Hey, punkin' head," Cat heard him say as she tried to catch her breath while mourning the loss of the orgasm that had gotten away. It would've been a beauty. As she throbbed from head to toe with unfulfilled desire, she lay still to listen, trying to figure out how in the world she was going to get out of this without a close encounter of the kid kind.

"I trowed up," Rosie reported.

"Oh no!" Ian sounded remarkably composed for a man who had experienced sexus interruptus a mere forty seconds earlier. And how, exactly, was he managing to hide the evidence of what he had been up to? "Really?"

"Yep. Gram says I ate too many marshmallows last night."

"That's what I thought until she woke up with a fever this morning," another voice chimed in. A woman. An older woman. Fucking A! His mother! *Great.*

Cat sat up, found her clothes mixed in with his on the floor, and got dressed as fast as she could. Thankfully, he had a bathroom attached to his room, so she could at least attempt to repair some of the damage before making her debut.

As she washed her face, used his toothbrush, and did what she could with her hair, she got progressively more pissed. This was *exactly* why she had no business being involved with him. If she had any prayer of making a quick getaway, she was going to have to face his kid *and* his mother, neither of which should play *any* part in a sex-only relationship. Damn it, damn it, *damn it!* Why hadn't she listened to her gut and stayed the hell away from him? Why had she come here knowing it was possible something like this could happen?

When she was as put together as she could hope to be under the circumstances, she went to the door to his room and rested her forehead against it for a long time. They seemed to be settling in for a nice, long visit, she realized with a groan. And he wasn't doing a goddamned thing to try to get rid of them. In fact, if her nose served her correctly, he was making coffee! Ugh! *Get them out of here, Ian! Get them out of here, so I can get out of here!*

Resigned to the fact that it wasn't going to happen, Cat took one last deep breath—more to calm her fury than her nerves—and opened the door.

Rosie zeroed in on her right away. "What's *she* doing here?"

"Rosie, be nice and say hello to Cat," Ian said, his voice tight with tension.

"Hi," Rosie said without looking at her, which was fine with Cat.

"Hi, Rosie."

"Cat, this is my mother, Bernie."

Cat ventured a brief glance at the attractive older woman who had the same smile as Ian and Nathan. As she accepted the outstretched hand of the mother of the man who had been doing her doggie style ten short minutes ago, all she could think about was how *wrong* this was, on every possible level. "Nice to meet you," she mumbled.

"Likewise," Bernie said, her eyes skirting over Cat in a visual inspection that Cat was certain she would fail.

"Um, I have to go." She grabbed her purse off the coffee table where she had left it the night before and bent to scoop up her flip-flops. To no one in particular, she added, "I'll see you later." Seeing her chance, Cat made for the door.

"Stay and have some breakfast," Ian said.

Was he *serious?* "I can't," she said without turning back to look at him. If she looked at him right now, if she made contact with those blue eyes . . . No, it was better this way. "I have . . . stuff. I've got to go." She darted out the door so fast it was a wonder her head didn't spin.

Ian chased after her. "Cat!" He caught up to her, grabbed her shoulder, and turned her around. "Wait. I'm sorry," he said as he tried to embrace her. "I'm so sorry."

Cat pulled free of him. "You have nothing to apologize for. It's your home. She lives there."

"And that's the problem, isn't it?" he asked, running a frustrated hand through his rumpled hair.

She was going to cry. If she didn't get out of there immediately, there were going to be tears, and Cat Kelly didn't do tears. "I'm the one who's sorry, Ian. I really am, but this is so not my scene."

"Don't go," he pleaded. "Don't walk away because of one fucked-up morning."

"It's always going to be like this, and it *should* be like this. She comes first. I get it."

"That doesn't mean—"

"I can't." She took a last glance at that face, that one-in-a-million face. Damn him. "I'm sorry."

She left him standing in the driveway and went out to the street to find her car.

CHAPTER 26

Georgie knew the exact moment that Nathan slid out of bed because she had been awake next to him for hours.

He found his shorts on the floor, slipped them on, and left the room without a sound.

As she pulled the sheet up tight around her, she wondered if he was coming back or if he would leave without talking to her. *Wait.* She peered down to the floor where two size-twelve sneakers lay sprawled.

When she heard the toilet flush, she sat up straighter in bed, her heart pounding with anticipation and dread and fear. She wouldn't be surprised if he came back to say enough was enough. Who could blame him?

"Oh, hey," he said. "I hope I didn't wake you."

"No, I was up."

He sat on the bed to put on his shoes.

"Are you nervous?" she asked, desperate to break the awkward silence that hung between them. "About court?"

"Not really. I just want to get it over with."

She couldn't think of a single other thing to say. How could she put into words what she felt when she wasn't even sure, exactly, what she was feeling?

He finished tying his shoes and turned to her.

Her stomach twisted with fright. Here it comes. She didn't want him to profess his love, but neither did she want him to say good-bye. *Not yet,* she cried silently. *Please not yet.* She braced herself.

"I have some work I need to get done on my house this week." He reached for her hand. "So I'll be pretty tied up at night."

"Okay." If he was going to end it, she wished he would just do it fast and get it over with.

"But will you save Friday night for me?"

Flustered and surprised, she stared at him. "I'd understand if you didn't want to see me—"

Bringing her hand to his lips, he sent goose bumps scurrying over her skin. "Why wouldn't I want to see you?"

"Because I'm driving you crazy?"

He smiled, but it didn't reach his eyes the way it usually did. "Yeah, you are, but I guess I'm a sucker for punishment, because I keep coming back for more."

"Are you going to stop coming back one of these days?"

"I'm not planning on it." He paused before he added, "So, Friday? Yes?"

Relieved to know there would be more, she nodded.

He leaned over to kiss her. "I'll try to come by the hospital later to check on Gus."

"Good luck in court."

"Thanks." With one last kiss, he got up and headed for the door.

"Nathan?"

He turned back to her.

"Thank you for being here last night when I needed you."

"There's nowhere else I'd rather be, Georgie. I'm hoping one of these days you'll realize that."

She listened to his footsteps on the stairs, heard him talking to Cat downstairs, and through the open window, she listened to him jog down the hill toward home. How far they'd traveled since she had lusted after him on his morning runs, and yet they were no closer to figuring out what they were going to do about all the feelings flying between them. Reaching for the bedside table, she flipped the two remaining condoms between her fingers and regretted that they hadn't gotten used.

Cat appeared at her door. "What's up?"

"Not much." Georgie studied her roommate. "Have you been crying?"

"No," Cat said quickly—too quickly.

"What's wrong, Cat?"

"Nothing."

Georgie patted the bed.

Seeming relieved by the invitation, Cat came in and stretched out next to her. "Are you naked under there?"

"No," Georgie snorted.

"Were you?"

"At one point. I raided your stash," she said, pointing to the condoms on the table.

"Finally got around to doing it again, huh?"

"We were talking about you, not me."

"I'd rather talk about you, since I won't be needing condoms for a while after this morning."

"What happened?"

Cat shrugged, but there was something so defeated in the gesture that Georgie reached for her friend's hand.

"The thing with Ian . . . it's not going to fly."

"Why not?"

"Timing, complications, the usual stuff." She told Georgie what had happened earlier.

"*Ugh,*" Georgie groaned.

"No kidding. Easily the single most embarrassing moment of my life."

"I'm sure it was no treat for him, either."

"Probably not," Cat conceded. "I just wish he hadn't managed to ruin me for sex with all other men."

"That good, huh?"

"There are no words."

"Same here," Georgie said with a sigh.

"Must be something in the genes," Cat said, and they shared a laugh. "Get this—I found out last night that the two of them were eagle scouts." She stuck her tongue out.

"Doesn't surprise me one bit about Nathan," Georgie said. "Ian, on the other hand, I'm not sure I see it."

"Oh, I can." Cat shared the story of Rosie's birth.

"Wow," Georgie said in a subdued tone. "If that doesn't tell you everything you'd ever need to know about who he is…"

"Yeah." A deep sob seemed to take Cat by surprise.

"Oh, honey," Georgie said, slipping her arm around Cat.

"It was fun," Cat said between sobs. "I know it was only a couple of days, but I don't want it to be over."

"Why does it have to be?"

"It'll never work, so why put myself through it? Look at me. I'm a total disaster after three days. I can't tell you when I last cried over a guy. This isn't me. I don't want this crap in my life."

"But if you really like him . . ."

"I *do* really like him. A lot. Maybe more than I've ever liked any guy. I wanted to keep it casual, but . . ."

"Nathan said he was surprised Ian agreed to that. Apparently, it's not his style."

"I knew you'd rat me out to Nathan." Cat laughed through her tears. "I *knew* it."

"Sorry," Georgie said, trying and failing to show some chagrin.

"No, you're not!"

The front door squeaked open and then closed.

"Guess who never came home last night?" Georgie whispered.

"No way!" Cat hissed. "Little Miss I'm Going to Be Better Than You Two?"

"One and the same."

"She's as weak as we are! Let her think we're sleeping in."

As they listened to Tess futz around downstairs before heading up, they muffled their giggles in Georgie's comforter. When the sound of Tess's footsteps grew closer, Cat whispered, "Ready?"

Georgie gave her a thumbs-up.

In the hallway, Tess tiptoed past Georgie's open door.

"AHEM!"

Tess almost jumped out of her skin. "What are you guys *doing?* Are you in *bed* together? What the heck?"

"We've been worried sick," Cat said. "We've been lying here all night wondering if we should call the police or the hospitals. We had no idea what to do."

"Shut *up*," Tess said, rolling eyes that sparkled with delight and satisfaction.

"And where have you been, young lady?" Georgie asked in her best stern voice. Apparently, Cat approved, because she poked her under the blanket.

"You know exactly where I was. The big question is where did *Nathan* sleep last night, because his bed was very, very empty this morning."

"Who cares about that?" Cat said. "We already know about them. What about *you?* How was it?"

Tess flopped down across the foot of the bed. "We didn't, you know, go all the way." Her cheeks turned bright red. "We did a lot of other stuff—a lot of really *good* stuff—but not the main event."

"Why not?" Cat asked.

"He said he wasn't ready."

"Really?" Georgie asked. "Aren't they, as a gender, *always* ready?"

"So you think it's weird, too?" Tess said. "Let me tell you, it wasn't because of me. Despite what I said to you guys, I really wanted to."

"And he knew that?" Cat asked.

"Oh, yeah. I was hardly subtle. But I'm wondering if it's something to do with his injuries."

"Could be," Georgie said.

"He told me he loves me," Tess shared with a giddy smile.

"*Already?*" Cat said.

"We both just *know*. It's so fast, but I love him, too."

"Good for you," Georgie said as a knot of emotion settled in her chest. Why couldn't it be as simple for her and Nathan? "No one deserves it more."

"It's the best thing ever."

Cat sniffled.

"Are you *crying?*" Tess asked, shocked.

"Don't be ridiculous," Cat snapped.

"Ian," Georgie said to Tess. "No go."

"*Why?*" Tess cried. "He told Ben he's totally into you."

"He did?" Cat brightened for an instant before she seemed to remember the situation was hopeless.

"It's because of Rosie, isn't it?" Tess asked.

"You guys think I'm a monster, but you don't know why I feel the way I do," Cat said.

"Then why don't you tell us," Tess said. "Tell us why you'd sacrifice the chance to be with a really great guy just because he has an adorable daughter. I've got to be honest with you, Cat. I don't get it."

"Because you're a kid person. Is it so hard for you to believe that I'm not?"

"I think there's more to the story than you've let on."

"There is," Cat said grudgingly. "I don't want to get into all the details, but for a number of reasons, I've spent the last ten years raising my younger brother and sister. My brother is *finally* going to college next week. I just got my life back. I can't start all over again with someone else's kid—no matter how great a someone he is. Can you understand that at all, Tess?"

"Of course I can. It makes much more sense to me than you deciding not to like Rosie simply because she's under five feet tall."

"Rosie's adorable," Cat conceded. "I'm not blind to that. But I *know* what he's got ahead of him. I know about years of lunches and homework and school buses and curfews and sports and sleepovers and birthday parties and dances and friends. *I've already done it!* I just want to be *me* now. I want to be Cat. Not Cat with someone else's kid in tow. It's not fair to me—or to Ian—to get further involved with him when I *know* I don't have it in me."

"Would it matter at all," Georgie ventured, "that if you were to end up with him—with them—you wouldn't be doing it alone this time?"

"I don't know," Cat said, dejected. "What if I tried it and a year or two later I realized I couldn't do it? Then you've got a child rejected by her own mother and me, too. I don't have that in me, either."

"I hate that it seems so hopeless," Tess said. "I liked you with him."

"*I* liked me with him, too," Cat said. "But we can't all end up with happily ever after here. Two out of three ain't bad."

"Don't lump me in there quite yet," Georgie said.

"Oh, I don't know," Tess said with a smug smile. "I like the odds where you two are concerned."

"I wish I shared your confidence," Georgie said. "I really wish I did."

Georgie stopped for donuts and coffee and opened the center right at ten. She set up the Monday morning ladies' craft group and got them started before letting the kitchen staff know she was going to the hospital.

On the short drive, she said several prayers for Gus. Bringing the extra donuts and coffee she had bought for her friends, Georgie entered the ICU waiting room, where Walter, Henry, Alice, Bill and Annette were sitting with Good Gus's daughter, Dawn, while Bad Gus paced, nervous energy coursing through him. His wife Donna nibbled on her thumbnail as she watched him move back and forth.

"Hi," Georgie said when they greeted her. She set the treats on a table. "What's the latest?"

"Been two hours already," Gus said. "They said ninety minutes. What the hell's taking so long?"

"Take it easy, Gus," Donna said.

He scowled at her and resumed his pacing.

"No news is good news," Walter said.

Georgie took a seat between Annette and Walter, her stomach aching with nerves. Like everyone else in the room, she just wanted to hear that Gus was going to be okay.

The others helped themselves to coffee, but they didn't talk. The quiet among the usually boisterous group only fueled Georgie's anxiety.

They waited for what felt like forever before a doctor came into the room and signaled to Dawn.

"It's okay," she said. "You can tell them, too."

"He did very well," the doctor said. "We took care of the bleed, and he's stable."

"What happens now?" Dawn asked.

"We wait and we hope. He'll be in recovery for the next few hours, but I'm optimistic that he'll regain consciousness."

"And if he doesn't?" Gus asked.

"Let's cross that bridge when we come to it." To Dawn, the doctor added, "I'll check in with you when we get him back to his room."

"Thank you," Dawn said.

"Well," Walter said when the doctor was gone, "I guess that's the best we could've hoped for."

"Damned doctors," Gus grumbled. "Never want to give guarantees. So busy covering their asses so they won't get sued. Quacks. Every one of 'em."

Sensing he was upsetting the others, Georgie looped her arm through Gus's. "Let's take a walk."

Donna sent her a grateful smile.

"You need to settle down," Georgie said to Gus as they strolled arm in arm down the long hallway. "It's not good for you to be so wound up. Think of your heart."

"My ticker's in great shape since I had the bypass," he protested. "It's just this whole thing infuriates me. That someone like Gus could be attacked in his own home. He's never harmed a flea, for God's sake."

"I know," Georgie agreed. "It's terrible."

"And that his son might've had something to do with it. If the head injury doesn't kill Gus, hearing that might. Makes me mad, Georgie. Really mad."

His face was red, his breathing choppy.

"Gus is lucky to have a friend like you."

"We go way back," he said, softening a bit. "I've always thought of him as my better half—and *not* in the queer sense."

Georgie winced at the politically incorrect statement. "I know what you mean, don't worry."

"Let's face it," he said sadly. "There's no Bad Gus without the Good Gus."

He was breaking her heart, but she refused to give in to the urge to weep. "He's going to be okay."

"And how do you know this?"

"I have a good feeling about it. He's made it this far, right?"

"That's true." He stopped walking and turned to her. "Thanks, Georgie." He ran a hand through his thick shock of white hair. "I appreciate you calming me down. I get so mad sometimes, even though I know it won't help anything."

"You're entitled." They started back toward the waiting room. "So what do you think of the Sox's chances to clinch the division?"

He brightened. "Damn good. With a seven-game lead going into August? There's no way the Yanks can catch us."

She didn't think he needed to be reminded of how many times the Yankees had caught the Red Sox before. They walked along arguing baseball, and Gus scoffed at her assertion that the Braves had a real shot at going all the way this year.

"There's your young feller," Gus said. "Cleans up real nice, don't he?"

Georgie looked up to find Nathan standing at the end of the hall wearing a dark suit. Since his hands were tucked into his pockets, she saw the badge clipped to his belt before she noticed his eyes were locked on her.

Georgie could only return his stare.

"Oh boy," Gus chuckled. "You've got it bad, don't you?" He kissed her cheek. "Go see him. I promise to behave." Gus shook hands with Nathan on his way by.

As Georgie approached Nathan, she had to remind herself to keep breathing. "You look good." She resisted the immediate urge to run her hands all over his crisp white shirt. "Really good."

He smiled, but in his eyes, she saw exhaustion.

"How was court?"

"Grueling."

Without hesitation, she slid her arms into his suit coat and around his waist, resting her face against his red silk tie.

He propped his chin on the top of her head and held her close to him. "Have you noticed," he asked, "how you fit perfectly right here?"

Georgie closed her eyes against the rush of emotion and tightened her hold on him. She felt his lips on her forehead.

"How's Gus?"

"The surgery went well. We just have to hope he comes out of it."

"That's good news. I heard this morning they've made some arrests in his case."

Georgie drew back to look up at him.

"A couple of dealers Roger was in deep with. He picked the wrong people to screw over."

"What about him? Will he be charged?"

"It's not looking that way. We know he's been dealing but can't prove it. He may get lucky and get a second chance. Apparently, he's been bawling his head off over what happened to his father since the minute they brought him in."

"Maybe it'll scare him straight."

"We can only hope so. If it doesn't, he'll either be dead or in jail before much longer. After this incident, you can bet he's on our radar."

"How does someone like Gus end up with a kid like that?"

"Who knows? My brother Hugh was big-time into drugs for years. It was a total nightmare for my parents, for all of us."

"I never would've guessed that about him. He seems so together now."

"His wife Dani saved his life by giving him a reason to get it together. She got him into rehab, and he's been clean more than eight years now."

Georgie shuddered. "Just the thought of that makes me want to stay childless."

"Do you *want* kids?"

"You are *not* getting me to have that conversation. No way."

Flashing that irresistible Caldwell grin, he said, "I guess it wouldn't be good for my cause to tell you I want six."

Her mouth fell open. "You've got to be kidding me."

"I figure it might take two or three wives to get the job done, but hey, you gotta have a goal."

She would have laughed at how ludicrous he was being if she hadn't been trying so hard to decide if he was serious. "Well, um, on that note, I'd better get back in with them." She gestured toward the waiting room. "Will you come tell them what you told me about the case?"

"Sure."

She started toward the door.

"Georgie." His hand on her shoulder stopped her. When she looked up at him, he said, "We'll have as many or as few as you want."

Staring at him, she opened her mouth to speak, but nothing came out.

"I know," he said with a smile. "I have to stop saying that stuff."

"Yes," she said hoarsely. "Please."

"I'm trying. Really I am."

"Try harder." She took his hand to lead him into the waiting room, where they spent a half hour with the seniors before Nathan walked Georgie to her car.

"You've got probate court in the morning, right?"

Touched that he had remembered, she said, "Yes."

"Do you want me to go with you?"

"No, you have work—"

"Georgie, if you need me, I'll be there."

"I appreciate that, but I'll have the attorney with me. He says it should be perfectly routine."

"Call me when you're done."

"Okay."

"I'll miss you tonight. I wish I didn't have so much work to get done this week before the kitchen guy starts next Monday."

"You'll have to sleep at some point, won't you?" she asked with a coy smile.

His expression was puzzled. "Yes."

Sliding her hands over his chest, she looked up at him. "Maybe you could come sleep with me? When you're done working?" She loved the flash of surprise that crossed his face but was saddened to realize he had no expectations where she was concerned. Knowing that, she decided to take him from surprised straight to floored. "We never got around to using those other two condoms last night."

If eyes could sizzle, his did as they bored into hers. "And I'm supposed to function for the rest of the day after hearing that?"

Giggling at the expression on his face, she backed him up to her car, took a quick look around the deserted parking lot, and brought him down for a kiss intended to make his head spin. As he gave as good as he got, she wormed her way closer to him so she was almost inside his suit coat and slipped a hand between them to stroke him.

He gasped and broke the kiss. "Georgie! What're you *doing?*"

"The suit is hot, Nathan." She squeezed him and was rewarded with a throb in response. "Really, really hot."

He let his head drop back, his eyes fluttered shut and his fingers gripped her shoulders. "You're killing me," he whispered.

"I'm sorry," she said without an ounce of contrition. "I'll stop." But rather than stop, she squeezed him again.

He cupped the back of her head and brought his lips down hard on hers, his possession so thorough that Georgie wondered how she had managed to lose control of the situation so quickly.

"Got time for a nooner?" he asked as his lips cruised up her neck to her ear.

She laughed. "No and neither do you."

"I could make time. I'll tell them my arm's hurting again."

"You wouldn't do that, because that would be lying, and you don't lie. Hurry up and get your work done. I'll be waiting."

He kissed her again, more softly this time. "I'll be there."

CHAPTER 27

As Georgie stood with her attorney in front of the judge the next morning—the day after her sister's successful surgery—listening to the two men discuss her mother's assets and possessions, she finally understood what people meant by an "out of body experience." She felt like she was floating above the room, looking down at the proceedings, because surely these strangers couldn't be talking about her mother like she was just another commodity. They didn't know her. They didn't have the right to talk about her things like she was any old dead person.

Georgie was on the verge of saying so when the judge addressed her directly.

"To the best of your ability, Ms. Quinn, have you identified all your mother's possessions?"

She cleared her throat. "Yes, your honor."

To the attorney he said, "You've advertised for creditors?"

"We have, your honor."

"Very well, in that case, we'll reconvene forty-five days from today to finalize the estate."

"Excuse me," Georgie said. "Will I need to be here for that?"

"Yes, is that a problem?"

Georgie exchanged glances with her attorney. "I'll be back in Atlanta by then."

"You can grant power of attorney to someone to appear for you, but it's less complicated if you're here yourself," the judge replied.

"We'll work something out," the attorney assured the judge as he led Georgie away. He consulted with her briefly and then dashed off to meet with another client.

Georgie emerged into the bright sunshine to find Nathan leaning against her car. Shaking her head with amusement and amazement, she walked toward him. "What're you doing here?"

He shrugged. "You seemed quiet this morning, and I was worried it wouldn't be as routine as you hoped."

"I thought you were going to try harder to stop saying and doing exactly the right thing all the time." She stepped into his outstretched arms and absorbed the sweet comfort of his embrace. "How's a girl supposed to remember she's trying to resist you when you keep doing these things?"

"Maybe if I do them often enough, she'll stop resisting?"

"She doesn't seem to be fighting too hard at the moment."

"She didn't put up much of a fight last night, either," he reminded her.

Georgie's cheeks heated when memories of the passionate night they had spent together came flooding back to her.

"How was court?"

"As you would say, grueling. It's all so impersonal, to be talking about her money and her things like who she was doesn't matter at all."

"Unfortunately, in this arena, it doesn't. I'm sorry it upset you."

"It's over. For now."

"How's your sister today?"

"About the same. Sore and tired. Joe said she had a good night, though."

"I'm glad to hear it." He caressed her face and trailed a finger over her bottom lip. "So, I've been thinking…"

"About?"

"The blood test."

"Nathan, I told you—"

Resting his finger over her lips, he said, "Wait. Just hear me out. Please?"

Looking up at his amazing blue eyes, she found the courage to put aside her fear—but only because he was asking her to. With the slightest of nods, she gave him permission to continue.

He let his hands fall to her shoulders. "What if it's negative?"

She shook her head. "It won't be."

"You don't know that, honey," he said, his tone urgent.

"My mother and sister tested positive. How do you figure I've managed to dodge the bullet?"

"What if you *have* dodged it? What if you're the lucky one? Maybe you're stressing for no reason."

Georgie had to admit that the possibility hadn't occurred to her. She'd been so sure.

"It's a fifty-fifty shot, sweetheart, and I'm betting on you."

She looked up at him, so handsome and so sincere. His strong, steady presence made her believe anything was possible—even the impossible. Ali was right and so was Nathan. The fear was debilitating, and in Georgie's case, paralyzing. Since wishing it away hadn't worked, it was time to take action. Taking a deep breath, she said, "Okay."

His face lit up with surprise. "Yeah? Really?"

She nodded.

He swept her right off her feet and into his arms. "No matter what, Georgie, *no matter what,* I'll be right there with you. I promise."

Closing her eyes tight against the rush of emotion, she held him for a long time until he finally put her back down.

"How do you feel?" he asked as he caressed her face.

"Relieved to have made a decision. Don't let me back out, okay?"

"No way." He leaned in to kiss her.

Georgie held on to him for a long time, absorbing the comfort he offered so willingly.

"Hey, did you happen to talk to Tess this morning?" he asked.

"No, I didn't see her. Why?"

"I guess she and Ben are going to Pittsburgh on Thursday so he can visit the family of the guy he was with when he got hurt. Greg died, and Ben's had a lot of trouble accepting that. Apparently, Tess encouraged him to see Greg's family, thinking it might help him."

"She's such a good person," Georgie said. "After everything she went through—" She stopped herself, horrified by what she had almost said.

"What did she go through, Georgie? It drives me crazy that you won't tell me, especially now that my fragile brother is all wrapped up in her."

"I can't. I promised her."

"All this secrecy makes me want to go into detective mode in the worst way."

"Don't," Georgie said. "Please just leave it alone. Please."

"I'm getting a bad vibe on this, and my vibes are almost never wrong. But I'll let it go—for now." He tucked a strand of hair behind her ear. "How about a cup of coffee?"

"Do you have time for that?"

"I took a couple of hours off so I could come check on you."

She reached up to caress his face. "I'm glad you did."

After an emotional two-hour visit with Greg's family and his longtime girlfriend, Tess backed the rental car out of their driveway. She had so much she wanted to say to Ben, so many feelings ricocheting through her. She could only imagine what he must be going through after reliving the worst day of his life.

Glancing over at him, she saw that he was gripping his cane and staring out the window. "Are you okay, Ben?"

"You were right to encourage me to do that. They were so grateful to know he'd been talking about them just before it happened."

"I know it wasn't easy for you, but you did a wonderful thing for them."

"As sorry as I am for his parents and his sisters, I feel worse for Kristy. I mean, we've been together a week, and I already know I couldn't live without you. They were together for years, planning a wedding. How do you go forward without that person?"

"I can't imagine." Tess reached for his hand. As his fingers curled around hers, she was flooded with gratitude that he hadn't been killed that day in Iraq. Just the thought of how close he had come was enough to reduce her to tears.

"What's wrong?"

She shook her head.

He reached out to brush the tears off her cheek. "Pull over, hon."

"I'm okay."

"Pull over," he insisted.

Bringing the car to a stop on the residential road, she wiped her face. "I'm sorry."

"What is it?"

"I was just thinking how close I came to never having the chance to know you at all. You could've died that day, too, Ben. And if that had happened, I would've had to live my whole life without ever knowing you were out there somewhere, without knowing it was possible to love someone this much."

He leaned over to embrace her. "I was so pissed at Nate for dragging me to a dance at a senior center. Who knew I was going to meet the girl of my dreams there?"

She laughed through her tears. "Just when you least expect it."

"There you were, surrounded by old men drooling over you, and nothing will ever be the same again." He held her as tight as he could in the cramped car.

"I was proud of you today," she said. "You were so good with them."

"That's nice to know. I was really nervous."

"I couldn't tell." She kissed his cheek and brushed the dark hair off his forehead. He looked tired and drawn, signs his leg was bothering him. "Are you still mad at me about the wheelchairs?"

"Yes."

She laughed at his quick answer. "It was like a mile to the gate. You would've used up a whole day's worth of energy just getting through the airports."

"It's humiliating to be pushed through airports in wheelchairs. I spent months working my ass off to get free of those damned things."

"Well, I'm not going to apologize for doing what was best for you, so you have to get over it."

"There you go being bossy with me again," he teased. "You're going to have to work on that when we're married. I can't be nagged nonstop this way."

His use of the word "married" stopped her heart. The shock must have shown on her face.

"Too much too soon?" he asked.

"No."

"Then what?"

"Nothing. Do you have the directions to the hotel?"

Their hotel room overlooked the Monongahela River.

"This is beautiful, Ben."

He hobbled over to the window to check out a barge sliding through the glassy water. "Greg's mother told me this was one of the nicest hotels in Pittsburgh."

"I hope you didn't go to all this expense for me."

"Who else would I do it for?" he asked, amused.

"I don't need fancy hotels. That's not me."

"Which is why it was fun to do it."

She wrapped her arms around his neck and went up on tiptoes to kiss him. "You should rest for a bit. I can tell you're in pain."

"How do you know?"

"You wear it on your face."

"Should I be worried that you can read me so easily?"

"Very."

"Will you come with me?"

"Twist my arm." She reached for the hem of his navy blue polo shirt and lifted it over his head. When she started on the button to his khakis, he stopped her.

She looked up to find his face tight with tension. "What?"

"I'm okay with them on."

"All right." She pulled down the comforter and blanket. "Which side do you want?"

"I don't care."

As they stretched out on the bed together, Tess wondered how to eventually broach the subject of making love with him. Just being around him made her burn with a kind of desire she had never felt before. But if he didn't feel the same way, that was going to be a problem, not to mention a terrible disappointment. After what she had been through with her ex-husband, she wasn't going to settle for anything less than everything ever again.

Ben laced his fingers through hers, brought their joined hands to his chest, and was asleep within minutes.

Over the next hour, Tess wondered how he could possibly sleep when they were alone together in an elegant hotel room. Somehow she had to move this whole thing forward. But how? What if there was a medical reason he couldn't have sex, and he was afraid to share that with her? He knew she was a nurse, so why would he think she wouldn't understand? She hated the idea of embarrassing him, but she wanted him, and after her disastrous marriage, she was desperate to know what it was like to really make love.

Her heart ached when she remembered the last time she'd had sex. Kurt had forced himself on her, and when she resisted, he punched her in the ribs, breaking two of them. She shuddered at the horrible memory. But this wasn't the time for such thoughts, not when the man she loved was right here next to her. This was the time for action.

Raising herself up on one elbow, she watched him sleep for several more minutes before she leaned over to press soft kisses to his belly.

He tensed, squeezed her hand, and then settled back into sleep.

No way, mister! She added her tongue to the mix, dragging it in lazy circles through the thatch of hair that trailed off into his pants. Even though his breathing stayed steady, she was fascinated to watch him become aroused. *Do I dare?* She bit her lip as she studied his adorable face. *Yes, I do.* Moving very carefully, she unbuttoned his pants, slid the zipper down, and reached in to wrap her hand around him.

While Tess held her breath and hoped her heart wouldn't leap right out of her throat, he only sighed in his sleep. *Was he for real?* This was clearly going to require radical action. She moved closer and took him into her mouth.

He awoke with a start. "Tess. Jesus Christ, what're you doing?"

That he sounded mad didn't deter her. She moved her tongue over the sensitive head, and he sucked in a sharp deep breath. It was all she could do not to smile when she realized she had him. Pushing at his clothes to gain better access, she moved her hand in time with her mouth, drawing him in and then backing off slowly.

She ventured a glance up at him and found him watching her intently, his eyes narrowed with desire and something else. What was that? *Later,* she thought. *I'll worry about that later.* Keeping up the steady pressure of her mouth and hand, she put everything else out of her mind and focused only on bringing him as much pleasure as she could.

"Tess," he said through gritted teeth.

She felt the change in his breathing, knew he was close, and redoubled her efforts.

With his fingers in her hair, he tried to warn her, but she didn't back off. He came with a restrained groan that was more reluctant than rapturous. When she tried to move up to kiss his belly, he turned away from her.

Stunned and frightened, she stared at his back.

"You shouldn't have done that," he finally said.

"*Why not?*" she cried. "I love you! I want to *make* love with you."

"I can't."

"Of course you can. You just did."

"It's not that."

"Then *what*, Ben? Is it me? Do you not want me?"

"No, honey," he said with an ironic chuckle. "That's *not* it. I want you more than I've ever wanted anything." He shifted onto his back and reached for her.

Resting her head on his chest, she studied him. "Then tell me what's wrong. I want to understand. Is it your leg?"

"Yes."

"Does it hurt?"

"Always."

"We can work around it. I'm not going to hurt you, Ben."

"I know." His cheek pulsed with tension. "It's just that it's . . ."

And right in that moment she finally got it. "You don't want me to see it, do you?" She realized she had never seen him in anything other than long pants, even on the hottest of days.

"It's horrible, Tess." His eyes filled. "Totally disgusting."

"And you think that *matters* to me?"

"It matters to *me.*"

She sat up.

"Where're you going?"

"Right here." She raised her skirt, turned her leg, and showed him her scars. "Do you think I'm proud of these?"

He lifted himself up for a closer look. "How the hell did that happen?"

"I got burned."

"By what?"

"A cigar."

His head whipped up, his eyes met hers, and what she saw there told her everything she would ever need to know about him.

"Someone did this to you."

"Yes."

He shook his head, and when tears filled his eyes, he covered his face with his hand. "I can't hear this. The thought of someone hurting you on purpose . . ."

"I didn't tell you to upset you, and it's the last thing in the world I want to talk about right now." She took him by the shoulders, pressed him down on the bed, and straddled him while being careful to steer clear of his injured leg. "I have scars, too, Ben. Yours won't make me love you any less. Nothing could. Do mine make you love me less?"

"No," he said emphatically. "They make me want to kill someone."

She smiled. "How about you use that energy more productively?"

His hands found her hips and then moved up her back to bring her down for a kiss. "I love you," he whispered against her lips. "I never dreamed in a million years that I would find you."

"Well, now that you have, whatever will you do with me?" she asked with a teasing smile.

"Everything—as long as you promise not to look."

"I won't look. We'll need condoms. A lot of them."

"Am I going to survive this?" he joked.

She laughed and kissed him with all the joy and love she felt in that moment.

"Nate stuck a box in my bag as I was leaving."

"I knew I loved him."

"He's such a dad. I swear to God. He drives me nuts."

"Except that he saved us the trouble of having to go buy them right now."

"That's true. Maybe he's not so bad after all."

"Mmm," Tess agreed as she kissed her way down the front of him. Keeping her promise not to look, she removed his pants and quickly covered his injured leg with the sheet.

The relief on his face was palpable, as she had known it would be when she eliminated his worries from the equation. As she lifted her dress up and over her head, she didn't want him thinking of anything but her.

"Come here," he said, his voice heavy with emotion and desire.

She stretched out on top of him.

He hooked an arm around her neck to bring her in for a sizzling kiss while using his other hand to unhook her bra.

"Very impressive," she whispered as he moved her up so he could reach her breasts. "And you thought you'd lost your moves."

"It took finding you to get them back," he said, drawing her nipple into his mouth while brushing his thumb over her other breast.

Tess looked down to find him gazing up at her. "Where'd you say those condoms are?"

He directed her to a zipped pocket in his bag. When she returned to the bed, she shimmied out of her panties and rolled a condom on him.

Being careful not to go anywhere near his injured leg, she straddled him and took him in slowly.

He sighed as his fingers caressed her thighs and came to rest on the series of circular scars.

Tess rolled her hips to take him deeper and looked down to find him watching her with eyes full of love. "Good?" she asked.

"*So* good. You?"

"*Mmm,*" she said with a smile. "Anything hurt?"

He shook his head, reached for her hands, and held on tight as she began to move faster. "Tess, honey, what do you need?"

"Only this."

Using his good leg for leverage, he moved with her and drove her up so fast, she had no time to prepare for the powerful orgasm that crashed through her. With his hands on her hips, he anchored her, surged into her one last time, and went with her.

CHAPTER 28

Cat scrubbed at the dingy brass rail that ran the length of the bar and tried to remember the last time she'd had someone clean the damned thing. With sweat rolling down her face, she used all the elbow grease she could muster to attack the black patches on the once-shiny railing. Music pounded through the club's sound system, which along with the hard work, was supposed to be keeping her from further obsessing about Ian. Her plan was failing miserably.

She hadn't seen or talked to him in three days—three *long* days. From Nathan she had heard that Rosie was still sick with some sort of bug that seemed to be lingering. *He must be so worried about her. Otherwise, he would've at least* called *by now, right? Guys like him fight for what they want, don't they? He said he wanted me. I guess not enough to fight for me. You're so pathetic, Cat. Since when do you care if a guy likes you enough? Since I met Ian Caldwell.*

With a moan of frustration, she rested her head on the bar, hating herself for the moan, the frustration, all of it. Cat Kelly was *not* a woman who cried over men. Cat Kelly was a woman who scorned *other* women who cried over men. Just the fact that she was about to weep—*again*—over him should have been enough to make her hate him. But she didn't.

No, she didn't hate him. She missed him and his big broad shoulders, those blue eyes and that smile. And she missed feeling, well, like a *girl* when she was around him—not that she would ever admit that to anyone, even under the threat of torture. She missed him so much she was sick from it. *You haven't known him long enough to miss him that much.* Yes, I have, the other side of her brain answered defiantly. *I've known him long enough. Just long enough to know he's worth missing like crazy.*

Trying and failing for the hundredth time to forget about the sign she had seen in front of The Landing, advertising his appearance there that afternoon, she wondered if he had managed to keep the gig or if he'd had to cancel to stay home with Rosie. *There's one way to find out. No. You are* not *going there to stalk him. That goes beyond pathetic straight to downright desperate. You're the one who walked away. He still has a kid. You still don't want to be shackled with a kid. But if I could talk to him, if we reworked the boundaries of the sex-only relationship, then maybe we could still see each other once in a while without it getting all messy.*

Rubbing the soft cloth over the brass with much less enthusiasm than she'd had a few minutes earlier, she let that idea run around in her mind for about ten seconds. "The hell with this." She chucked the rag across the bar, grabbed her purse, and left without shutting off the music.

She set off on foot toward the waterfront—just to see if he was working and to maybe catch a glimpse of him. Even as she told herself it would be enough, she knew it was a lie.

On the way, she tried to keep her mind clear of distractions and clutter. It was best that she not think too much about what she was about to do. Skulking around the side of the building, she leaned toward the bar to see who was performing and nearly fell into the water.

"Damn it," she muttered as she recovered her footing and stalked through the front door. "I'm allowed to be here just like anyone else. So what if he sees me?"

"Talking to yourself, Cat?" asked Ernie, the bartender, with a bark of laughter. They had worked together at another club years ago. Guitar music wafted in from the outdoor bar, but because whoever was out there wasn't singing at the moment, she couldn't tell if it was Ian.

"Shut up, Ernie, and get me a beer."

"Still grumpy as ever, I see."

"Who's playing?" she asked before she could chicken out.

"Ian Caldwell." Ernie turned up his nose. "Too mellow for you and me."

"Yeah," Cat agreed, her heart racing as she reached for the money she had stashed in her pocket.

"It's on me."

"Thanks, Ernie." Taking the beer with her, she drew in a deep breath for courage and stepped onto the deck. Feigning surprise at seeing Ian there, she turned in what she considered to be an award-winning performance. However, judging by the smug smile that appeared on his too-handsome-for-words face, he knew right away that she was full of shit.

Feeling rebellious, she took a seat on one of the barstools, propped her feet on a second stool, and got busy flirting with the bartender—another guy she knew from around town.

While Cat did her best to ignore him, Ian played Neil Young's "Heart of Gold." She didn't want to be impressed that he handled the harmonica part, too, with one of those around-the-neck contraptions. As he sang about searching for a heart of gold, he stared at her with a blank expression on his face. Not that she was looking, per se. More like she was monitoring him out of a tiny corner of her eye.

Something that felt an awful lot like shame settled in her gut as she received his message, loud and clear.

He played another song she hadn't heard before, about a man who loved a woman who kept disappearing on him. He wasn't even *trying* to be subtle! If he thought he was going to rattle her, it wasn't going to work.

Yeah, right.

Who was she kidding? She would be squirming in her seat if she had to withstand this campaign of his for another minute. Finishing her beer, she said good-bye to her friend at the bar and headed inside without so much as a glance at the small stage in the corner.

Ian called to her, but she didn't stop. He caught up to her, grabbed her arm, and spun her around.

"What do you want?" she snapped.

"I could ask you the same thing. What're you doing here, Cat? Trying to rub some salt in the wound?"

She tugged her arm free and realized Ernie was watching them with interest. "This is not the place," she growled. "And FYI, you suck at subtlety."

"Okay to use the office?" Ian asked Ernie over his shoulder.

"Fine by me, man," Ernie replied with amusement.

Ian half walked, half dragged Cat into the office and slammed the door behind him.

"Stop acting like a Neanderthal," she huffed as she shook him off.

"Why are you here?"

"It's a public place. I didn't realize you'd gotten custody of The Landing in our divorce."

"Save your crap for someone who can't see right through it and tell me what the hell you're doing here!"

"I have absolutely no idea." She reached for the door.

"Don't you dare leave," he said in a low angry growl she wouldn't have thought him capable of. "Don't come here and do this to me and then walk away again. Don't you dare."

"Do what to you?"

He stepped toward her.

She backed up against the door and was reminded of him pressing her against another wall and kissing her senseless. A rush of raw desire stole the breath from her lungs. Maybe if they did that again now, they could forget they were so pissed with each other. Reaching up to him, she brought him down and kissed him.

When he pressed his body tight against hers and thrust his tongue into her mouth, her heart sang from the simple joy of being close again to him and all the emotions that came with him.

"Is this what you want, Cat? A quick fuck to relieve the tension? That's all I'm good for, right?"

She pushed hard against his chest, but he didn't budge. "Get *away* from me, you big stupid jerk!"

He tightened his arm around her waist. "Yeah, I must be stupid to still want you."

"Well, I don't want *you*, so you can let go, and I'll just be on my way."

"If you don't want me and you're not after a cheap fuck, why *are* you here?"

"Stop throwing that word around. It's beneath you."

"You didn't think so when *you* were beneath me."

"That's really funny, Ian. Hysterical." She punched his shoulder. Hard.

He released her abruptly. "Ow! *What the hell was that for?*"

"For making me want you when I don't *want* to want you!"

"I think my head just exploded."

"Good, then you'll be dead, and I won't have to think about you anymore."

A satisfied smile worked its way across his face. "You've been thinking about me, huh?"

"Lose the smile before I smack it off your face."

He did as he was told but his eyes continued to dance with amusement. "How's Rosie?"

The amusement faded. "Don't go there, Cat. You don't care about her."

"*I don't want her to be sick!*"

"She's fine. Thanks for asking. Next?"

"I was wrong to come here." Filled with regret, she shook her head. "I wanted to see you. I won't deny that. But I was right the other day when I said there's no point."

"Because I have a daughter. I know. My bad luck."

"You don't think that, so don't say it."

"Leave her out of it. She's off limits."

"She may as well be standing right here between us, and we both know it! Why pretend otherwise?"

His normally genial blue eyes turned icy. "This conversation is over. I have to get back to work. I have a daughter to support."

"*I know you do!* Stop throwing her in my face!"

"You're about to cross a line with me, Cat. A great big line that no one gets to cross."

"You're not being fair."

"*I'm* not," he drawled, rolling his eyes. "Right. I have a daughter who, by her very existence, automatically disqualifies me from your life, and *I'm* the one not being fair? You haven't even bothered to get to know her, and you've already decided she's not worth your time."

"I already know everything I *fucking need* to know about her!"

Blanching, he took a step back from her. "Don't use that word when you're talking about my child."

"I'm sorry," she said, mortified, running her fingers through her short hair. "That came out all wrong."

He continued as if she hadn't spoken. "You don't know her because you don't *want* to know her. You've made that crystal clear from day one."

"But you don't know why," she said in a small voice.

After a pregnant pause, he said, "I'm not going to pull it out of you, Cat. If you want to tell me, fine, but make it quick. I'm working here."

Cat looked at him, trying to decide if he was worth tearing off the Band-Aid she'd worn on her soul for so long she almost didn't remember life without it. Again, who did she think she was kidding? He was *so* worth it. If they couldn't be together, he needed to know why. She owed him that much.

"I've got to go."

"No. Wait." She bit down hard on her lip, took a deep breath, and vowed to get through this without tears. "I never knew my father. For most of my life, it was just me and my mother. She was always a little nutty, but in a fun way, you know?"

His sullen shrug told her he was still pissed. "I guess."

"I was eight when she married my stepfather. Chuck was an okay guy, not about to set the world on fire with ambition or anything, but he was nice enough. My mother wasn't getting any younger, so they had two kids in two years, Marina and Dylan. Two babies right on top of each other put a lot of strain on them and their marriage. They had these loud screaming fights, and then he would take off, sometimes for days on end, leaving us to deal with the kids. A lot of times she left me alone with them, even when I was as young as ten."

"That's a lot of responsibility for a kid," he said, his posture losing some of its rigidity as he listened to her.

"It was, but I loved them. I'd waited forever for siblings. They were never a burden to me. Anyway, my mother and Chuck finally got divorced when I was in eighth grade. She started dating again right away, and I did a lot of babysitting. I spent far more time with them than either of their parents did. I got them off the bus, made sure they did their homework, made their dinner, gave them baths, read them stories."

"Cat," he said, his eyes soft with sympathy she didn't want from him.

"Wait." She held up a hand to stop him from coming toward her. If she didn't get this out now, she'd never work up the courage again. "As I got closer to finishing high school, I noticed my mother was spending even less time at home. In the meantime, I was plotting my escape despite how worried I was about what would happen to Marina and Dylan after I was gone. I knew they were worried, too, but we never talked about it until I got accepted to the Berklee College of Music in Boston."

Ian released a low whistle. "What do you play?"

"Used to play," she clarified. "The piano. I taught myself on an electric keyboard I worked a year to pay for, and I got really good."

"You must've been amazing to get into that school. No one gets in there."

"In the end, it didn't matter. The night before my graduation, I came home to find my mother packing. I asked her where she was going, and she said she couldn't be a single mother again. She'd already done it with me and wasn't going to do it again. 'What are we supposed to do?' I asked her. 'What you've always done, Cat,' she said. 'You're more their mother than I ever was.'

"She walked out the door that night, and I've never spoken to her again even though she still lives here in Newport. She saw the kids a couple of times early on, but after a while I decided it was more upsetting for them to see her than not to, so I put a stop to it. She never uttered a word of protest and just disappeared from our lives."

"What about their father?"

"He helped out some financially, but I raised those kids all by myself. I gave up the chance to go to Berklee, but it was worth it, Ian. I'm so proud of them. Marina's a sophomore at Providence College, and Dylan's leaving next week for Syracuse—both of them on academic scholarships. Somehow, between the three of us, we managed to pull it off."

"I'm awestruck, Cat. I'm struggling through it at thirty-six with more help than I know what to do with, and you raised two kids, *alone*, when you were *half* my age."

She shrugged off his praise. "I just wanted you to know it's not personal, my thing with Rosie."

"I understand that now."

"Remember when I told you I'd just gotten out of a relationship?"

"The big hairy deal?"

"That's the one. We dated for four years and broke up because he wanted to get married and have kids. He moved in with Dylan and me last year. When Dyl got his own place this summer, I snapped up the chance to move in with Georgie. I couldn't very well stay where I was after saying no to his proposal."

Ian looked down at the floor, his shoulders stooped with dejection.

Cat went to him and reached up to caress his face. "I'm sorry if I hurt you. I never meant to. I knew if I stuck my hand in this fire, we were both going to get burned, but I couldn't seem to resist. I still can't."

"Cat," he whispered as he crushed his lips down on hers.

She clung to him, meeting each ardent stroke of his tongue with her own and gasping in surprise when he lifted her off her feet and into his strong arms. The kiss was long and deep and desperate. It went on until Cat couldn't take another minute of being that close to him while knowing she couldn't have him. "We can't keep doing this, Ian," she said. "It just gets worse every time."

He let her slide down the aroused front of him. "I know."

They held each other a long time until a knock on the door startled them.

"Are you guys doing it in there?" Ernie called in a joking tone.

"No," Ian replied without releasing her. "Come on in."

The door opened. "The boss is looking for you, dude. I told him you had a situation." His eyes darted from Cat to Ian and back to Ian again. "Everything all right?"

"Yeah," Cat said, stepping out of Ian's embrace. "I was just leaving."

"See you around, Cat," Ernie said as he walked away.

With a small smile for Ian, she said, "Don't be a stranger."

"Cat."

Looking up at him, she took a moment to memorize every precious detail.

In a soft voice packed with emotion and regret, he said, "Did it ever occur to you that you might have a lot in common with a little girl whose mother abandoned her?" He caressed her cheek with his index finger and kissed her forehead. "Take care, babe."

She watched him go, feeling as if he'd ripped her heart right out of her chest and taken it with him.

CHAPTER 29

The lab technician removed the needle from the vein in Georgie's arm and pressed a gauze pad into the crook of her elbow.

Georgie looked up at Nathan.

He offered an encouraging smile.

"Four to six weeks," the tech said, reading from the orders her mother's doctor had faxed over. "It says here he'll call you if any further treatment is warranted. And you checked the box for mail notification of negative results. Is that correct?"

"Yes."

"Do you have any questions?"

She had so many questions, her head spun with them. She wanted to ask the tech, what would you do? If the result is positive, would you have your breasts removed? "No. Thank you."

With a curt nod, the tech took the vials of blood and left the small room.

Nathan helped Georgie up. "That wasn't so bad, huh?"

"I guess not." She glanced down at the bandage holding the gauze in place. "Four to six weeks. That's a long time to wait."

"It'll go by faster than you think."

"What do we do now?"

Slipping an arm around her shoulder, he led her to the clinic's main door. "We put it out of our minds and live our lives."

It sounded like a good plan. Georgie just hoped she could do it.

Georgie woke up alone early on Friday morning and was sad to realize Nathan had never made it there the night before. Realizing she had grown accustomed to waking up with him, she sat for a long time on the edge of her bed trying to decide when she'd started encouraging what was happening between them. *Right around the time you accosted him in the hospital parking lot and invited him to come sleep with you.*

Suddenly, the idea of going back to Atlanta held zero appeal. *What if I stayed here?* It was the first time she allowed herself to seriously consider the possibility. *I could think of something to do here for work, couldn't I? I mean, it wouldn't be Davidson's, but maybe at one of the department stores in Providence. How about what I owe my employees in Atlanta? They're counting on me. I have to go back long enough to clean up the mess there. After that, I can do whatever I want.*

Still pondering her options, she showered and headed to the center early. By nine thirty, she had done six months' worth of filing that cleared the huge pile of paper she had inherited from her mother, paid the bills, balanced the checkbook, and sorted through a stack of correspondence. At the very bottom of the pile, she found a copy of the application for the recycling Dumpster and was reminded of the day she met Nathan. So much had happened since then.

She picked up the phone and called the city's public works director.

"This is Georgie Quinn over at the senior center," she said when Charlie Foster answered his extension.

"Nancy's daughter?"

"That's me."

"I'm sorry about your mom. She was a character."

"Thank you. The reason for my call is a copy of an application I have here that shows my mother requested a recycling Dumpster almost a year ago, and we still don't have it."

"Well, now, Georgie, these things take time—"

"Do you know about Styrofoam, Charlie? Do you know that when your grandkids have grandkids, the stuff we use today will *still* be sitting in the landfill?" *Nathan would be so proud.* "It doesn't break down. Ever. We *need* that Dumpster. I don't have the staff to clean more than a hundred trays a day. If I'm going to provide a hot lunch for the city's seniors, I need my Styrofoam trays. Can you see the pickle I'm in?"

"Yes, but—"

"No buts, Charlie. I've been trucking smelly recycling trash over to the Rec Center for weeks now. I could charge the city to get the stench of liver and onions out of my car. So what do you say? Get a Dumpster over here?"

"I'll see what I can do."

"I'd appreciate that."

"You are *so* your mother's daughter," he said with a chuckle.

The statement stopped her heart. "Thank you, Charlie," she said softly. How could he know there was no higher compliment he could pay her?

She finished cleaning up the small office and even straightened the pictures on the wall, most of which were of her mother with her constituency throughout the years. Georgie smiled as she righted the one of her mom with the dirty old men from last year's Christmas party.

At ten o'clock, she unlocked the front door. Walter came bounding in, lifted her right off her feet, and swung her around. She wouldn't have thought he had it in him! "What's gotten into you?" she asked when he set her down.

"Gus is *awake!*"

"Oh!" She hugged Walter. "Oh, thank God."

"He still has a long road ahead of him, but he's going to make it, Georgie. He's already talking to everyone like nothing ever happened."

"Does he know about Roger yet?"

Walter shook his head. "Dawn decided to keep that from him until he's stronger."

"Probably not a bad idea."

"I've got to get back over there, but we wanted to make sure you heard the news. Will you tell everyone here?"

"Of course. I'll come by after lunch."

He kissed her cheek and bounced out the door.

Georgie stood there for a long time, her hand over her heart, thanking God for what surely had to be a miracle. Her cell phone rang, and she tugged it out of her pocket.

"Georgie, it's Tara," her assistant from Atlanta whispered. "Something's going on here today. I can't really talk, but all the muckety-mucks' doors are closed, and that bitch Nina is screaming at Lorraine!"

"Wow," Georgie said, sucked right into the drama. "Nobody screams at Lorraine and lives to tell."

"I know! Someone's coming. I've got to go, but I'll call you later if I can. Hurry up and get back here."

The line went dead just as the center's phone rang. Her head began to spin from what was shaping up to be a crazy day. Georgie ran to answer the phone.

"Georgie, Richard Andrews here," the city's recreation director said. "Have I caught you at a bad time?"

"Not at all. What's up?"

"We've found her!" he said, his voice ebullient.

"Found who?"

"The perfect replacement for your mother—not that your mother can ever be replaced, but someone who can pick up the torch and carry it forward. She's got a degree in gerontology and just moved here with her husband, a naval officer who'll be teaching at the War College for the next few years. She's ideal, Georgie, and she really wants the job."

"Oh," was all that Georgie seemed able to say. She looked around at the center, the place she had once seen as a prison, and her heart began to ache.

"I'm going to send her over after lunch. Around one thirty? I'll just need your okay after you see her with the folks, and it's a done deal. Georgie? Are you still there?"

"Yes," she said. "I'm here."

"Her name is Barbara Samuels. I'll fax over her résumé. Give me a call after you meet her?"

"I'll do that."

"Fingers crossed, Georgie. This is what you've been waiting for. I can't thank you enough for pitching in over there the way you have. I don't know what we would've done without you."

"No problem," Georgie said, in what had to be the understatement of the decade.

After lunch, Georgie ran home to shower off the stench of beef stroganoff before her interview with Barbara, all the while telling herself it was *good* that they had found this woman. It was what Georgie had been waiting weeks for. Except, for some reason, it didn't feel good. It felt like everything was coming to an end, and as much as she had once yearned to get home to Atlanta, now she wanted to stay here. If only she could have the same type of career here that she'd had in Atlanta.

As she was leaving the house to go back to the center, the mailman came down the hill.

"Afternoon," he said, handing her the day's mail.

"Thank you."

"Lovely day," he said before continuing on with a whistle.

"Yes," Georgie agreed. She flipped absently through the stack of catalogs and bills and stopped short at the sight of her father's familiar handwriting. "Oh my God! Oh God. *Finally.*"

Throwing the rest of the mail onto the wicker table, Georgie sat on the porch sofa and tore open the envelope.

Dear Ali and Georgie,

I received a shocking phone call from Georgie's friend Nathan Caldwell yesterday. Girls, I had no idea your mother was even sick, and the news of her death has left me speechless. Nancy was always such a life force. I can't believe she's gone, and I'm so very sorry for your loss.

I want to apologize for being out of touch the last few months. I've been through a rough patch lately, including the end of my marriage and some significant financial problems. I hate to think that my failure to meet my obligations to your mother might have caused her any dismay during her final days. We closed recently on the sale of our house, and I've enclosed a check to cover the outstanding alimony I owed your mother. Please keep the money and use it for anything you need.

I'm sorry I wasn't there for you girls when you needed me, but I want you to know I'm here anytime you need me in the future. I've enclosed my card with my contact information. I hope to hear from you both. I love you very much.

Dad

P.S. Despite the dressing down I received from him, Nathan seems like a nice young man who cares a great deal about you, Georgie.

Georgie wasn't sure if she wanted to strangle Nathan or hug him for getting involved without her knowledge. She would have to think about that later, once she'd had time to process her father's letter and share it with Ali.

Relieved to know her father was still alive, she glanced at the check for thirty thousand dollars before folding up the whole thing and returning it to the torn envelope. Taking the mail into the house, she ran the letter from her father upstairs to stick it under her pillow and then left to go back to the center. She was reaching for her phone to call Ali when it rang. A check of the caller ID showed the 404 area code. Atlanta.

"Georgie," a voice whispered. "It's Lorraine."

"Why are you whispering?"

"I'm in the supply closet."

"What the heck is going on down there today? Tara already called me."

"It's a world gone mad. They *fired* Terry Paulson," Lorraine said, referring to the regional manager who insisted Georgie be replaced. "Nina is going to be out on her ass, too, but they told me I can't tell her yet. God, I can't *wait* to tell her. That smug bitch has made my life a living hell this week. Everyone hates her."

"So I've heard."

"Listen to me, Georgie. Have your butt in your seat at nine a.m. on Monday, and we'll act like nothing ever happened. The person they bring in to replace Terry won't figure it out until you've been back for weeks. I've even heard rumblings that they've got their eye on yours truly for his job. If that happens, I'd move you up to my office. I'd insist on it as a condition of my promotion."

The big time, Georgie thought, as all the pieces slid into place for a promotion she had dreamed of for years. She would have full control over ten stores, more than a hundred employees working for her, and a boss she already knew she could work with successfully.

"Don't breathe a word of this to anyone," Lorraine added.

"I won't."

"Can I count on you to be here on Monday, Georgie?"

Georgie's heart ached when she thought of Nathan, but how could she pass up this chance to erase the firing and get her career back on track? Surely he would understand that she *needed* to do this, wouldn't he?

"Georgie?"

"Yes," she said. "I'll be there."

Barbara Samuels arrived in a white summer suit that Georgie instantly recognized as Dior. In her late forties, Barbara had thick blonde hair cut into a bob that suited her to perfection, make up that was subtle but artfully applied, and an accent Georgie would know anywhere.

"Are you from Georgia?"

"Savannah," Barbara confirmed. "How'd you guess?"

"Twelve years in Atlanta. I know Georgia when I hear it."

"I lived in Buckhead for five years before I was married."

"That's where I live now!"

Barbara smiled at the coincidence. "What do you do there?"

"I'm in the marketing department at Davidson's."

"Oh," Barbara said. "I *love* Davidson's."

"So do I. I'm looking forward to getting back there to make sure they haven't ruined the place in my absence."

"How long have you been here?"

"Three months. Since my mother got sick."

"I was so sorry to hear of your mother's death. They speak very highly of her at City Hall."

"Thank you," Georgie said. "How about I give you the tour, such as it is, and we'll go from there?"

"Sounds good."

By the time they returned to the office half an hour later, Georgie knew they had a winner. Barbara had stopped to speak to each of the seniors Georgie introduced her to, listened to them when they talked to her, and treated them with the respect and dignity they deserved.

"You have a way with them," Georgie said.

Barbara sat in the chair on the other side of the desk and crossed her legs. "I've learned that all they want is someone to listen to their stories. I've gleaned an awful lot of wisdom over the years from those stories."

"I wish you could meet the core group, but they're over at the hospital." Georgie explained about Gus and then checked her watch. "In fact I need to get over there, too."

"Would you mind terribly if I tagged along?"

"Of course not. That'd be great."

On the way to the hospital, Georgie outlined the routine at the center. "If you take the job, you might want to leave the Dior at home or you'll end up with flounder stains on your jacket."

"You have a good eye for fashion."

"I aspire to wear Dior exclusively," Georgie said with a smile, adding, "In my dreams, that is."

"I was forty when my husband shocked me with my first Dior suit for Christmas."

"Even with my store discount, it's out of my reach." Georgie realized it wouldn't be if the promotion came through. "I should warn you: the men you're going to meet are sort of territorial when it comes to me. In fact, they ran off the last candidate we had because they wanted me to stay. They loved my mother, and her death was a huge blow to them."

"Say no more. I understand."

They rode the elevator to the ICU, and Georgie introduced Barbara to the group. "Don't even *try* to scare her away," she said as they grudgingly shook Barbara's hand. "I'm going in to see Gus. You guys be nice to her, you hear me?"

Her request was met with a chorus of mutters.

Barbara sat down between Walter and Bill, who did their best to ignore her.

Filled with trepidation that Barbara might be gone when she returned, Georgie left them and went around the nurse's station to Gus's room. He was asleep when she walked in, so she was careful not to disturb him. His color was better than it had been the last time she saw him, and there seemed to be fewer tubes and machines.

She was getting ready to leave when his eyes opened. "Hey, gal."

Her eyes filled as she reached for his hand. "It's about time you got back. The dirty old men have been out of control without their voice of reason."

He chuckled softly.

"How are you feeling?"

"Like I had a hot poker stuck in my head. Oh wait, I did."

Georgie smiled. "I heard they cleaned things up while they were in there. Got rid of the clutter."

"Bought me twenty more years."

She squeezed his hand. "I've missed you."

"What's wrong, Georgie?" he asked, his sharp blue eyes trained on her.

"Nothing."

"Are you sure?"

"You don't want to hear about my problems."

"Trust me, I'd rather hear about your problems than worry about what I'm going to do about that son of mine."

"Gus…"

"It's okay, Georgie. I know he had something to do with it."

"Nathan said Roger has been a mess since it happened."

"Good," Gus said with uncharacteristic sharpness. "Maybe it's the wakeup call he's been needing for years now."

"Let's hope so."

"Talk to Gus. I'll close my eyes and listen. You talk."

With only a second's hesitation, she unloaded on him. And when she was done, she was fairly certain she had put him to sleep. "Gus?"

"I'm here, honey. Just processing. I'm so sorry you're going through such a worrisome thing with the gene test. That's tough."

"It's all I think about," she confessed. "I just keep running the scenarios over and over, and they all suck."

"Yes, they do, but Nathan's right—until you know for sure, you can't let it hold you hostage."

"I'm trying, but so far I haven't been very successful."

"What about Nathan? Do you love him?"

"I don't *know*," she moaned, flopping down into a chair. "How can I love him? I only met him a couple of weeks ago. And it's all been so intense and immediate, because we knew I was leaving soon. There's nothing *real* about that."

"You're suffering from a lack of perspective, so let me tell you what I'd do if I were you. Go to Atlanta, get this big promotion, and be without him for a while. If you love him, it won't take you long to figure it out."

"What do I tell him? 'Hey, it was nice, I might be back, I might not'?"

"That would work."

"I can't ask him to sit on his hands and wait for me."

"So don't. Let it be his choice."

"That's an awfully big gamble, Gus. What if I lose him?"

"Then you weren't meant to have him."

"I'm going back to Atlanta tomorrow. They've found someone to replace my mom and me at the center. She's perfect—and she has *outstanding* fashion sense."

"Which is very important to our gang," he said with a smile. "And PS, no one can replace the Quinns."

Leaning over to kiss his forehead, Georgie was caught off guard by a rush of emotion. "I never wanted this job, but I'm so glad I met you. Thank you for being my friend through all of this. And thank you *so much* for not dying."

"You're welcome," he said, laughing. "It was a pleasure seeing you every day, Georgie. I'll miss you. Drop us a line once in a while from the big city?"

"I promise."

"Take care of yourself, honey. Play it out in Atlanta so if you decide to leave, it'll be with no regrets."

She nodded, grateful for his insight and wisdom. "Feel better," she said from the door as she blew him a kiss.

Wandering back to the waiting room lost in thought, she stopped short when she discovered Barbara with her suit jacket off, playing poker with the guys. Georgie took a moment to study each of the old men who had once driven her crazy and tried to determine when exactly she had come to love them.

"Full house!" Barbara laid her cards on the table. "Read 'em and weep, boys!"

Groaning, the men folded.

Barbara's victorious smile told Georgie it wasn't the first hand she had taken. She looked up to find Georgie watching and gave her a thumbs-up.

Georgie's face lifted into a small, sad smile as she watched the new executive director of the Newport Senior Center bond with her friends. Before she and Barbara left to go back to the center, Georgie hugged each of the men and promised to see them soon. Her heart broke when Bad Gus dabbed at tears before wrapping her in a fierce hug.

"Give me a call if you ever decide to lower your standards," Walter teased as he hugged her.

Laughing, Georgie said, "You'll be the first to know."

"Are you going to tell us what's going on with you and that Caldwell feller?" Bill asked.

"We're just *friends*," Georgie said.

Bill rolled his eyes. "That's the biggest crock of crap I've ever heard."

As the others nodded in agreement, Bad Gus said, "Thank you, Georgie, for sticking it out with us. I know we didn't always make it easy."

"It was my pleasure," she said sincerely. "I'll be dropping by to check on you when I come back for probate court. I want a good report from Barbara, you hear me?"

They laughed and guffawed at her bossiness but agreed to do their best to behave.

The two women drove back to the center in silence. For what would probably be the last time, Georgie parked in the executive director's spot, turned off the car, and took a second to collect her thoughts before she turned to Barbara. "Let me ask you something."

"Anything."

"If one of them failed to show up one day and no one had heard from him, what would you do?"

"I'd go to his house to find him."

"And if, say, his car was in the driveway but he didn't answer the door?"

"I'd knock it down."

Georgie nodded in approval and extended her hand to the other woman. "As far as I'm concerned, the job's yours. When can you start?"

"Monday?"

"Great. I'll let Richard know it's a go."

"I'm sure you're thrilled to be getting back to Atlanta."

"Yes," Georgie said softly. "Thrilled."

They went inside to discuss keys, security systems, and Dumpsters on order. Georgie explained her mother's filing system, wrote down the password for the computer, and showed Barbara where to find the checkbook, the purchase orders, and the inventory schedule—most of which Georgie had been forced to figure out on her own after her mother fell ill.

"I guess that's about it." Georgie handed the other woman her Davidson's business card. "Here're my cell and work numbers in case you have questions. Feel free to call me anytime."

Barbara took the card and shook Georgie's hand. "Thank you. Good luck to you, Georgie."

"You, too. Take good care of the place. It means a lot to us." Georgie spoke for herself and her mother.

"I'll give it all I have."

"Don't give it everything. My mother made that mistake."

Seeming to sense she needed it, Barbara gave Georgie a quick hug before she left.

Georgie took one final trip through the center to make sure everything was where it belonged and to shut off lights. In the office, she gathered the last of her mother's personal effects into a box, and on an impulse, took the Christmas photo of her mom and the gang off the wall and added it to the box. That one she would keep.

She stood for a long time at the main door, remembering snippets of people and conversations and jokes and smells—some good, others not so much. Never in her wildest dreams had she imagined that leaving for the last time would be hard, but she also hadn't expected to find a family here.

"You done good, Mom," she whispered as a lone tear rolled down her cheek. "I'm so proud of you."

Since Nathan would be coming to pick her up at the house soon, she reached for the last of the lights, flipped them off, and closed the door behind her.

CHAPTER 30

Georgie arrived home to find Ben and Tess making dinner—or rather Tess was making dinner while Ben hugged her from behind and kissed her neck until she dissolved into giggles. Watching them together filled Georgie with delight. It occurred to her that they had found each other because her mother got sick, because they advertised for roommates, and because she had met Nathan.

"Hey, you guys."

"Hi." Tess gave Ben a nudge so she could turn around to talk to Georgie. She was positively glowing, and Georgie could tell she had succeeded in getting Ben right where she wanted him on their trip.

"How was Pittsburgh?"

As they exchanged heated glances, Ben seemed more relaxed and healthy-looking than Georgie had ever seen him.

"Great," he said.

"Yeah," Tess said, tearing her gaze off him to look at Georgie. "Great."

Georgie rolled her eyes and laughed.

"How was your day?" Tess asked, clearly trying to change the subject.

"You would not *believe* the day I've had. All I want is a bath and my bed."

"But you're going out with Nate, right?" Ben asked, his eyebrows knitted with concern.

"Yes, why?"

Tess and Ben exchanged glances again.

"No reason," he said.

"What's going on?" Georgie asked.

"Nothing," they said together.

"What do you guys know that I don't?"

"Not a thing," Tess replied. "Are you hungry?"

"No, I'm suspicious." Georgie stood with her hands on her hips and stared them down. Tess wilted first under the pressure.

"Georgie, *come on.* He'll kill us if we say anything, and he has a gun. Just let it go."

"What am I letting go?"

Ben limped over to rest a hand on Georgie's shoulder. "He's planned a special surprise for you, so please do all the people he's driven crazy this week a favor and try to shake off whatever happened today and get into the right frame of mind. Can you do that? For Nathan?"

Intrigued by this new sensitive side of Ben, Georgie nodded. "I can do that."

The doorbell rang.

"He's early!" Georgie cried. "I'm not ready!"

"I'll get it," Tess said. "We'll entertain him while you change."

As Tess headed for the door, Georgie made for the stairs but stopped halfway up when she heard Tess cry out with distress.

"*No! You* cannot *come in here!*"

Georgie turned to find Tess battling frantically to keep someone from getting in the door.

"Ben!" Georgie bolted down the stairs to help Tess. "Call 911!"

Cell phone in hand, Ben hobbled from the kitchen as he dialed.

The two women were no match for the determined man on the other side. He pushed through their barricade and grabbed Tess's arm.

"Let go of me!" she shrieked, clawing and punching at the handsome man in the dark navy suit.

He slapped her hard across the face.

"*What the fuck?*" Ben screamed.

He and Georgie hurled themselves at the battling duo, and the four of them landed in a pile on the floor.

Ben howled with pain, which distracted Tess long enough to put her at a disadvantage with their attacker.

"You fucking bitch," the big blond man said as he grabbed a handful of Tess's hair and hauled her to her feet, his face purple with rage. "You thought you were so smart, but you're nothing but an ignorant whore. You thought I wouldn't find you, didn't you? Well, you thought wrong. You're coming home with me."

"I'm not going anywhere with you, you son of a bitch." Tess fought like a wild animal.

Georgie crawled to Ben and cradled his pasty, sweating face in her hands. "Did you make the call?" she whispered.

He grimaced as he nodded and reached out to pull one of the attacker's legs right out from underneath him.

The man fell hard, knocking over a table and vase, which shattered on the tile floor.

"Tess," Ben said, reaching for her.

"Her name is *not* Tess. It's Elise." The other man rose to his knees. "She's my wife, so get your fucking hands off her!"

The shock registered on Ben's face at the same instant the door swung open.

His gun drawn, Nathan quickly assessed the scene. "Get on your feet, hands on your head," he ordered the blond man. "*Now!*"

Glowering at Tess the whole time, the man took his time following Nathan's orders.

Nathan reached for a radio on his hip to call for backup and an ambulance before he cuffed the bigger man. "What's his name?"

Her face awash with tears, Tess looked down at the floor and mumbled, "Kurt Margolis." A bright red handprint marked her cheek.

"Mr. Margolis, you have the right to remain silent," Nathan began, reading Kurt his Miranda rights.

"You can't arrest me!" Kurt bucked at Nathan's tight hold on him. "She's my wife!"

"Tess, did you let him in here?"

"No."

"Breaking and entering is a felony in Rhode Island, Mr. Margolis. I'd also like to know how my brother, an injured veteran, ended up on the floor surrounded by glass? Did you have anything to do with that?"

"Ben was trying to get him off Tess," Georgie said, her voice shaking as badly as the hands that cradled Ben's head in her lap.

"Assault," Nathan said. "Another felony."

"He beat me," Tess said in a small, defeated voice. "For years. I have the scars and medical records to prove it."

"And the felonies just keep on coming," Nathan said, no doubt effecting the lighter tone for Tess's sake. "Do you get why you're being arrested yet, Mr. Margolis?"

"Fuck you."

"Hmm," Nathan said, "does that sound like resisting arrest to you guys?"

"It did to me," Ben managed to say. He held out his hand to Tess, but rather than take it, she fled to the kitchen.

"Go with her," Nathan said to Georgie.

"But Ben . . ."

"I'm okay, Georgie." Ben raised his head to let Georgie up. "Take care of Tess."

As Georgie hurried into the kitchen, she heard the scream of sirens in the distance. She found Tess bent in half, sobbing.

Georgie wrapped her arms around Tess and clung to her.

"I'm so sorry, Georgie. I brought this into your home, into your mother's home."

"Shh." Georgie ran her hand over Tess's silky dark hair. "It's your home, too, and none of this is your fault."

"I was so sure he wouldn't find me here. I put us all in danger."

"It's over now. Nathan has him, and he'll make sure he goes to jail for a long, long time."

"And Ben," Tess sobbed. "Did you see his face when Kurt called me his wife? I lied to him about being married. He'll never forgive me for that."

"He loves you, Tess. He'll understand why you kept it from him. How could he not after witnessing that?"

"I should've known. Everything was perfect. Of course that's when Kurt's going to show up."

Georgie eased her friend into a chair and went to the fridge to grab an ice pack. She took the chair next to Tess's and held the ice against her face.

"Does it look awful?" Tess asked in a broken voice.

"No, honey," Georgie said, bringing Tess's head to rest on her shoulder. "It looks like it hurts."

Nathan came into the kitchen. "They're taking him in."

"What about Ben?" Tess asked.

"The paramedics are with him. Are you all right, Tess?"

"He hit her pretty hard in the face," Georgie said, raising the ice pack to show him.

Nathan winced. "Bastard."

"I should've told you," Tess said, weeping again. "Georgie wanted me to. She begged me to. That she could've been hurt, and Ben. I'm so sorry, Nathan. This is all my fault."

He knelt down in front of her and took her hand. "How in the world is it your fault?"

One of the patrolmen came to the door. "Detective? They're taking your brother in. They think his leg is fractured."

"Oh *God*," Tess moaned.

"He's asking for Tess." To Georgie, the cop added, "If you have a broom, I'll take care of that glass for you."

Georgie got one for him. "Thank you."

"Tess?" Nathan said. "Ben's waiting for you."

"I can't."

"Yes, you can," Georgie said. "You have to. He needs you."

"I'm sorry." Tess got up. "You all are the best friends I've ever had, and I love you. But I can't stay here. Not after this."

"If you run away from the people you love, Tess, doesn't he win?" Nathan asked.

Her shoulders stooped and shook with sobs.

Nathan went to her and took her into his arms. "It's going to be okay now. We've got him, and we're going to throw the book at him. It's over. Don't let him ruin the rest of your life."

A harried-looking paramedic appeared in the doorway. "Which one of you is Tess?"

Tess lifted her head off Nathan's chest. "Me."

"The patient refuses to allow us to transport him until he sees you. We need to get him in, so do you think you could come out here?"

Tess nodded and wiped her face, gasping when she brushed against her bruised cheek.

Georgie and Nathan each kept an arm around her as they walked her out to where Ben waited on a stretcher.

He extended his hand to her.

She bent over him, rested her forehead on his chest and wept. "I'm sorry."

Ben brushed his hand over her hair. "We're going to figure this out. Come with me. I need you."

Wrapping her fingers around his, she kissed his forehead. "Okay."

"Nate?" Ben said.

"I'm here."

"Go do your thing with Georgie."

"No way," Nathan protested. "We can do it anytime."

"I want you to do it tonight. Tess will be with me, so there's no need for you to come to the hospital."

Georgie watched Nathan struggle with the choice. "If that's what you want."

"I do."

"I'll come by in the morning, then. Do you want me to call Mom and Dad?"

"Hell no," Ben said. "I've got Tess." He looked up at her. "That's all I need."

The paramedics rolled Ben out to the porch. Tess followed them.

"Detective?" the patrolman said. "The lieutenant said to take care of your family tonight. You can file your report in the morning. Do you need anything else?"

"I can take it from here. Thanks."

The moment they were alone, Nathan wrapped his arms around Georgie and rested his cheek on the top of her head. "When I heard your address come over the air, I swear to God, I lost five years off my life."

A shudder rippled through Georgie as she relived the horror of it. "I thought he was going to kill her. Right in front of us."

"I sure do wish I'd known what she was dealing with."

"I wanted to tell you, so badly, but I had to respect her wishes. She was very determined to have a new life here with no reminders of the past."

As if he needed to touch her to confirm she was all right, he framed her face with his hands.

"You were so good with her, Nathan. You said exactly what she needed to hear."

"I've never been so happy to see you." His kiss was soft but laced with relief and desire and something different, something more. "If you're not up to going out tonight, I'd understand."

"Are you kidding? I'm dying to know what you're up to."

He seemed taken aback. "How do you know I'm up to something?"

"A clue here, a clue there."

"Did someone tell you? I swear I'll kill whoever—"

She silenced him by pinching his lips together. "They were afraid you'd shoot them if they told me."

"Good," he said through squished lips.

"A lot happened today. I have stuff I need to tell you."

"We'll get to that. We've got all night."

"You found my dad."

He shrugged. "Took all of ten minutes."

"Thank you."

"I wanted to give you one less thing to worry about."

She went up on tiptoes to kiss him. "What should I wear?"

"Something shamefully sexy."

"I don't have anything like that."

"Yes, you do. You've got that little black T-shirt and those jeans. The ones with the flowers on the butt."

"You like those, huh?"

"Oh, yeah."

"I'll be right back."

"I'll be right here. And Georgie? Bring your toothbrush."

She smiled at him on her way upstairs and was reminded of him waiting for her to get changed for their first date. And that this could be their last. Refusing to think that way, she rushed around getting ready. On her way out of the bathroom, she grabbed her toothbrush and skipped down the stairs. She couldn't wait to see where they were going and to get her mind off the horror she'd just witnessed. Tess had been so shaky when she left. Georgie hoped her friend would be okay.

He took her toothbrush and tucked it into his shirt pocket. "Ready?" he asked, offering her a hand.

As his gaze roamed over her with obvious approval, Georgie felt a bolt of heat and anticipation travel through her. She took his hand and followed him out the door.

"Nathan?"

"Yeah?"

"I don't feel right about sending Ben and Tess to the hospital alone. Would it be okay if we went by there first? Just to make sure they're okay."

"Absolutely. I didn't feel right about it, either."

"Oh good, thanks."

He leaned in to kiss her cheek. "Our plans will keep for a bit."

Chapter 31

Ben and Tess waited a long time for the orthopedic surgeon to arrive. The nurses had given him an IV for the pain, but there wasn't much else they could do for him until the specialist got there.

"I know what he's going to say," Ben said. "They can't set it again."

Tess pressed hard on her lips, hoping the distraction would keep the tears at bay. He didn't need her blubbering right now. He needed her to keep it together.

"Come here," he said.

She moved from the chair in the corner to his bedside.

He patted the bed next to his good leg. "All the way."

Tess perched on the edge.

Holding out his arms to her, he said, "That's not all the way."

She fell into his embrace and let the tears come, knowing she was powerless to stop them. "I'm so sorry, Ben. You're here because of me."

"Tess, honey—"

"That's not my name. You know that now."

"I'm never, ever going to call you anything else. For the rest of our lives, you're my Tess. In fact, Tess Caldwell has a nice ring to it, doesn't it?"

"You can't still want to marry me," she sputtered. "I lied to you, about everything. Your leg is broken because of me, because of that monster I'm married to."

He tipped her chin to find her eyes and gently placed his hand over the purpling bruise on her face. "We both know my leg has to go. This'll just speed things up and save me from having to actually make a decision. So, in a way, you kind of helped me out."

She laughed. "That's insane logic."

"Baby, I can live without my leg. What I can't live without is you. On Monday, I'm going to find you the best divorce attorney in town. We're going to get you free of him, and the minute you are, you're going to marry me. You got me?"

"Yes, Ben," she said, pressing her lips to his. "I've got you, and I'm never letting you go."

Nathan put his arm around Georgie and stepped back from the doorway to Ben's room.

Georgie smiled up at him, thrilled for Ben and Tess.

"Looks like everything is just fine here," Nathan said.

"Yes, it does. I'm so happy for them."

Nathan kept his arm around her as they exited the ER. "She's just what he needs. That's for sure."

"I'd say that works both ways."

Nathan helped her into the car and drove them to his house. "I need you to wait here for a minute, okay?" he said as he pulled up to the curb and cut the engine.

She wanted to tease him, to make him suffer a little, but found she couldn't do it. Something about this felt serious. "Okay."

He left her with a kiss. "No peeking."

She watched him go up the stairs, use his key in the door, and disappear inside. Lights went on and then off when dimmer lights replaced them. Then the light in his bedroom went on and off. In all, she figured three minutes had passed when the front door opened and he came out to get her.

"What's going on?" she asked as she took his hand. "Where are we going?"

"Are you always this difficult about surprises?"

"Yes. I operate on a need-to-know-everything basis."

"I'll keep that in mind." He led her to the top of the brick stairs. "Stay here for a sec." He brushed a hand over her eyes. "Keep them closed."

"Hurry up!" she said, dancing from one foot to the other.

He went inside but was back less than a minute later. "Okay." Taking her hands, he guided her in.

Georgie heard Petula Clark singing "Downtown." Confused and painfully curious, she fought to keep her eyes closed.

With his hands on her face, he kissed her. "I know how much you've missed Atlanta, so I thought if I brought Atlanta to you, then maybe you wouldn't be in such a rush to get back there. You can look now."

Georgie opened her eyes slowly. At first she didn't understand. There were white lights and an ivy-covered trellis over a table set for two. And then she saw the murals, one on each of the four walls, of the Atlanta skyline, the Olympic rings, CNN, Coca-Cola, and the aquarium. One wall was devoted to the Braves and Falcons.

Nathan put on a Braves hat and held another out to her.

Numb with shock and surprise and a growing sense of panic over what she hadn't yet told him, she took it from him. "I . . . I'm . . ."

"Georgie Quinn is speechless. I never thought I'd see the day."

She moved in for a closer look at the skyline. Running her hand over the paint, she asked, "Did you do this?"

"Kevin and Hugh did. They're both artists. I have to give Kevin credit for the idea. Ben and I built the trellis because in every picture I saw of Buckhead, there was ivy."

"I'm overwhelmed, Nathan. Truly."

"I was hoping it would make you a little less homesick."

"It does," she said, her heart heavy with the knowledge that by this time tomorrow, she would be back in Atlanta.

The music shifted to Ray Charles singing "Georgia on My Mind."

Nathan turned his hat around. "Dance with me, Georgie."

When he brought her into his arms, Georgie couldn't deny the fit was utter perfection. It would be so easy to decide right here, right in this moment he had orchestrated just for her, that no one would ever fit her better.

"This is my favorite version of this song," she said.

"I've had Georgia on *my* mind from first time I ever saw you sitting on the porch when I ran by."

Looking up at him, her heart in her throat, she said, "Thank you. No one has ever done anything like this for me."

"I was only sorry that finishing it kept me from coming over last night." He touched his lips to hers. "Hopefully, we can make up for it tonight."

Georgie planted soft kisses along his jaw. "I take it there's no kitchen guy coming on Monday?"

"You're looking at him."

"So you *are* capable of lying when it suits your purposes. Good to know."

He chuckled. "I have dinner for us. Are you hungry?"

"Not for food."

He studied her for a long, breathless moment before he leaned down to scoop her up and over his shoulder.

Georgie squealed with surprise as he carried her upstairs. "I didn't get to look at all the murals!"

"They're not going anywhere."

No, but I am, and oh, God, I'm so confused!

As they landed on his bed, she realized she hadn't been there since the first night they spent together.

"Don't move," he said as he got up to light candles on his bedside table. Standing by the side of the bed, he never took his eyes off her as he unbuttoned his shirt and let it fall to the floor.

As she watched him in the amber light, Georgie's heart contracted.

He hovered over her, using his arms to prop himself up.

Georgie reached for him and let her fingers slide through his hair. Over his head, she noticed something on the ceiling and nudged him aside so she could see the huge poster of Martin Luther King Jr. On it Nathan had written, "I have a dream." Laughter that began as a low gurgle soon escalated to hysterics. She wrapped her arms around him and brought him down to her as she continued to laugh.

His lips found her neck, her jaw, her ear. "Want to know my dream?"

Still recovering from the laughing fit, she nodded.

"I have a dream that one day Georgie Quinn will sleep next to me every night."

"Nathan—"

Before she could say anything else, he kissed her as if his life depended on it.

Georgie hovered between sleep and wakefulness, aware of Nathan's lips cruising over her fevered skin. She refused to open her eyes, to acknowledge the morning, to accept that today was the day she had waited and hoped for. Despair was her predominant emotion as he nudged her legs apart and sank into her yet again.

Her arms encircled his neck, her hips met his questing thrusts, and she had yet to open her eyes. As long as she kept them closed, she could believe it was still nighttime.

"Georgie," he whispered, cupping her breast and laving her nipple. His hips moved at a desperate pace, almost as if he knew it could be the last time.

The climax was quick and powerful and draining all at the same time.

His body tensed, slowed, and then surged. With a gasp of release, he rested on top of her for a long moment before he rolled to his side and brought her with him.

She buried her face in the chest hair she had admired long before she'd known how much more there was to admire. Biting her lip hard against the rush of emotion, she steeled herself and opened her eyes to bright sunshine streaming into the room. "We need to talk."

After she told him everything, she escaped to the bathroom, needing some distance from the emotional firestorm brewing between them.

He stormed into the bathroom behind her, his face set with anger and dismay. "When were you going to tell me? The second before you stepped on the plane?"

Georgie brushed her teeth and tried to find the words, hating that she had hurt and surprised him, especially after he had brought Atlanta to her, and especially after what they had shared throughout the long night.

Reaching out, he shut off the water.

She turned it on again.

He shut it off.

"Damn it!" Georgie said through the suds in her mouth. "Leave it alone! I *like* the water running when I brush my teeth."

"It's wasteful!"

"I don't care!"

Staring at her like he had never seen her before, he shook his head. "You've made that painfully clear."

She spit into the sink, rinsed off the toothpaste, and shut off the water. "Don't turn water into a metaphor, Nathan. I do care about you. You know I do."

"No, I don't. I know you've *enjoyed* me. There's a big difference."

"Now you're going to tell me how I feel?"

He hooked an arm around her waist and brought her up tight against his bare skin. "Stay. Stay with me."

"I need some time to figure things out."

"How much time?"

"I don't know."

"You could have everything you want right here, Georgie. You have your mother's house, so turn it into a bed and breakfast. Start a consulting business. There're hundreds of stores and shops right here in Newport that could benefit from your marketing expertise. My sister-in-law Linda has a jewelry store on Bowen's Wharf. I asked her if she'd be interested, and she said she'd snap up that kind of help in a heartbeat. She knows everyone in the business community. Word of mouth alone would get you started. Use the money your mother left you to build something of your own."

Amazed at how much thought he had put into it, she stared at him. "You've got it all figured out, don't you?"

"All I'm saying is you could have a meaningful career right here. Stay, Georgie. Be with me." He dropped soft kisses on her face. "Stay with me."

Remembering Gus's advice to play it out in Atlanta so there would be no regrets later, she wiggled free of Nathan's embrace. "I have people counting on me at work."

"They fired you! Right after your mother died! What do you *owe* them?"

He was wearing her down and chipping away at her defenses.

Desperate to regain her equilibrium, she said, "I'd like to take a shower, please."

His face sagging with defeat, he took two towels from the closet, handed them to her and walked out, slamming the door behind him.

Georgie washed her hair with shampoo that smelled like him. She heard the bathroom door open and then close again a minute later. The steam rose around her, engulfing her in a cloud of misery and confusion. She turned off the water before she could earn a lecture on the wastefulness of long showers.

Tugging aside the shower curtain, she bent in half to roll her hair into a towel and straightened to see that he had written, "I love you, Georgie Quinn" on the steam-covered mirror. "Oh," she gasped. "Oh, you *cannot* do this to me! That's not fair!" Somehow she managed to get the other towel wrapped around her before she yanked open the door to find him dressed and leaning against the wall in the hallway.

She stared at him.

He shrugged. "All's fair . . ."

Shaking her head, she pushed past him, went into his room, and willed her trembling hands through the motions of getting dressed. Tugging her wet hair into a tight ponytail, she pushed her feet into her flip-flops and hung the towels on the closet door to dry. With a last glance at the bed where two of the most important nights of her life had taken place, she rushed past him down the stairs. For a moment, she stood in the room he had transformed into scenes from Atlanta, and wished with all her heart that she could chuck her life there as easily as he thought she could.

She heard him come down the stairs and turned to him. "I need to take care of some things—things that are important to me."

"All right."

"That doesn't mean I never want to see you again. Far from it."

"Okay."

"Will you call me?"

"No."

"Why not?"

"If you want me, Georgie, you know where to find me. I'm not going to chase you anymore. I'm all done banging my head against a hard wall. It's starting to hurt. And it's starting to make me mad, which worries me."

His words resonated through her like painful arrows, knowing the battle he'd fought against anger in the past. "It's okay for you to get mad with me. God knows I've given you enough reason. It doesn't scare me when you get loud or angry. *You* don't scare me, Nathan."

She could see that he was relieved to hear that. "I prefer happy over angry any day."

"Thank you for this," she said, gesturing to the skyline mural. "Tell your brothers, too. It was a lovely thing to do."

"You're welcome." He stood with his hands in his pockets, the way he had that night in the street when he had brought her flowers to apologize for upsetting her, the way he had in the hospital when he'd come right from court to be with her after Gus's surgery.

But this time the stance wasn't welcoming. It was defensive. She had finally succeeded in pushing him away. At the door, she let her hand rest on the doorknob. Keeping her back to him, she said, "I enjoyed every minute I spent with you, Nathan, and despite what you think, I *do* care about you. More than you'll ever know. I'm just not ready for all the things you want from me."

Without giving him the chance to reply, she went out the door and down the stairs.

Cat lasted a month. Thirty long, draining days spent running from the simple fact that she was in love with Ian—desperately and completely in love. Over and over, his parting line ran through her mind, torturing her with its exquisite truth. *Did it ever occur to you that you might have a lot in common with a little girl whose mother abandoned her?*

Standing at the bathroom sink, she stared at her reflection in the mirror. She'd gone to a lot of trouble to cultivate a reputation as a badass. It had served her well as the manager of one of the hottest clubs in town, but as she reached up to remove the ring from her brow, she knew her badass reputation had no place in the life of a soon-to-be four-year-old girl.

Wetting her hair, she combed it out until the spikes collapsed into soft waves around her face. In her room, she bypassed her trademark tank top for a black T-shirt that covered the mermaid tattoo. Buttoning the only pair of jeans she owned that didn't hug her hips, she checked herself in the full-length mirror one last time, grabbed her purse and keys, and went downstairs before she could lose her nerve.

As she parked in front of the big yellow house, it occurred to her that she had no idea what their schedule was like during the day. What if they weren't home? Would she ever again work up the courage to do this?

Probably not.

Tucking her purse under the seat, she took only her keys with her when she got out of the Jeep and started down the long driveway. Behind Kevin's house, Ian pushed Rosie on the swing. Relief coursed through Cat at the sight of them, making her want to laugh and cry at the same time. When he saw her watching them, shock and surprise registered on his face.

Rosie's lips curled with distaste. "What does *she* want?"

"Actually," Cat said, crossing the yard to them, "I came to see you."

"Why? You don't like me."

"That's not true. I don't know you well enough not to like you. So I was thinking, maybe we could take a walk to the park and get to know each other.

After that, maybe I won't like you, but at least I'll have given you a chance. What do you say?"

Rosie glanced up at her father and then back at Cat. "You're teasing me, aren't you?"

Smiling, Cat said, "Why don't you come with me and find out?"

"Can I, Daddy?"

"Only if you want to."

Rosie studied her for a long, *long* moment, during which Cat tried to decide what she would do if the child said no. In planning for this mission, she hadn't considered that possibility.

"Okay." Rosie jumped off the swing and took Cat's outstretched hand. "We'll be back in a little while, Dad."

"Take your time," he said softly.

Cat didn't dare look at him as she led his daughter to the driveway. One thing at a time.

They walked to Morton Park in silence until Rosie looked up at her. "Why is your name Cat? That's kind of a weird name."

Cat laughed at her bluntness—a woman after her own heart. "It's short for Catherine."

"That's an old lady name."

"Why do you think I go by Cat?"

"My real name is Roseanne, which was my daddy's grandmother's name, so I guess that's an old lady name, too."

"It's a beautiful name."

"Do you love my daddy?"

Resisting the urge to suck in a sharp deep breath of surprise, Cat glanced down to find Rosie's cherubic face turned up, watching her intently. "I do. I love him a lot."

"That's good, because he's been really sad since you broke up with him."

"Has he?" Cat's heart thumped with excitement and hope. For the first time in a month, she had reason to hope.

"Uh-huh. *Really* sad."

Cat cleared the emotion from her throat. "What's your favorite thing to do at the park?"

"Swing."

"Then swing it is." Facing the child, Cat lifted her onto the swing, but before she gave her a push, she clutched the chain with both hands. "I love your dad very much, and I want to be with him more than anything, but I'm afraid I'd make a lousy mom to you, Rosie. How do you feel about that?"

"My real mom was kinda lousy. She didn't want me."

Cat gasped. "That's not true! Of course she did."

"No, she didn't. My daddy made her have me."

"Rosie . . ."

"It's okay. I don't care. Why would I want a mom who doesn't want me?"

Cat wondered how she ever could have thought this child wasn't worth her time.

"Could we maybe make a deal? If I'm lousy, will you tell me? Will you come right out and say, 'That was lousy, Cat'? Whatever I did, I'll never do it again."

"Okay."

"You promise?"

"I promise," Rosie said solemnly.

"Do you know what I could really use right now?"

"Nope."

"A hug. Would it be okay, if, you know . . ."

Rosie held out her arms.

Cat scooped her up and clung to her. "I'm so sorry you thought I didn't like you." The sweet smell of baby shampoo and little girl filled her senses and her heart. "You deserve so much better than that."

Pulling back, Rosie placed her pudgy hands on Cat's face. "My very *favoritest* thing to do at the park is play cloud art, but Daddy hates it because he never sees *anything*."

"Oh, I love that game! I used to play with my brother and sister all the time."

Rosie looked up at the puffy clouds. "Want to play?"

"I'd love to." Cat carried Rosie to the grassy field where they stretched out next to each other and gazed up at the sky. They studied the clouds for several quiet minutes before Cat pointed to one.

"Elephant!" Rosie cried.

They exchanged a high five.

"Daddy would say—"

"There's no elephant up there." Ian's shadow covered them both. "I don't care what you guys say."

Rosie rolled her eyes at Cat. "See what I mean?"

"We'll have to work on him."

Ian lowered himself to the ground next to Rosie.

"Cat loves you, Daddy. She told me."

"Is that so?"

"Yep. You should tell her you love her, too, so you can stop being sad all the time."

With amusement and love and relief and joy dancing around inside of her, Cat watched him struggle to decide how he felt about his daughter managing his love life.

"Not until she tells me herself," Ian said, his fierce blue eyes issuing a dare.

Cat met his steady gaze. "I love you, Ian."

"I love you, too, Catherine."

"That's an old lady name," Rosie informed him. "You can't call her that."

"Yes, ma'am."

"Can we go back to our game now?"

Ian reached over Rosie for Cat's hand. "Absolutely."

CHAPTER 32

On the same day Cat sealed her fate, Georgie sat alone in the apartment she had worked hard to turn into a stylish, comfortable home. After she had fallen in love with the apartment's high ceilings, big windows, and elaborate crown molding, she had obsessed over every piece of furniture, accessory, and detail. But as she let her gaze travel from one corner of her living room to the other, she realized she had felt more at home in Nathan's empty house than she ever had here.

Not a day had passed in the long month since she last saw him that she hadn't thought of him. Well, if she were being truthful, she would admit to thinking about him all day *every* day.

During the lonely weeks in Atlanta, she had waited on pins and needles for the results of her blood test and had driven Tess and Cat crazy calling to ask if anything had come from the lab. She finally broke down a week ago and called the doctor's office only to learn they hadn't heard yet. They promised to notify her as soon as they could. Since then, her heart had raced and her stomach lurched every time the phone rang. The good news from the calls home had been how happy her friends were with Nathan's brothers.

It had occurred to Georgie earlier, during an endless, boring meeting at work, that she had failed to properly appreciate the lessons of her mother's life and death. She was putting work ahead of what really mattered, and if she had learned anything from the last few months, it was that life is too short to waste on something your heart is no longer in. Her priorities needed a serious reordering, and they needed it now.

Yes, the promotion had been nice. Yes, the extra money came in handy. Yes, it was gratifying to hold a prestigious position with more authority than she'd ever expected to have. But none of it satisfied her half as much as a day at the senior center had.

That realization had made her laugh out loud in the meeting as she came to a decision she would put into motion tomorrow. Her time in Atlanta had come and gone. It was time to go home. She had followed Gus's advice, played it out, and figured out where she belonged. Now she could only hope that she would still be welcome there.

When the doorbell rang, she pulled on her mother's robe and got up to answer the door.

A delivery boy held a huge bouquet of pink roses.

Georgie's heart raced with excitement as she signed for them. She put them on the kitchen counter and dug out the card, expecting to read about organic farming. However, there was no mention of organics. "Heard you were back in town. Give me a call. I've missed you. Love, Doug."

Georgie laughed so hard she cried. *So predictable!*

"Oh, Nathan," she whispered. "I hope you waited for me. I really hope you did."

Drained after an emotional good-bye with her coworkers, Georgie took a cab home the following afternoon, since she had never gotten around to shipping her car back from Rhode Island. Carrying a box of personal items from her office, she trudged up the stairs to her second-floor apartment and came to a halt on the landing.

Nathan.

Sitting outside her door eating . . . *a peach?* Nathan was sitting outside her door eating a peach and letting the juice run down his chin like a six-year-old boy.

"You are *not* here," she said as she stepped in front of him. "You can't really be here on the same day I quit my job and told my boss I'm moving home to Rhode Island. That only happens in really bad movies."

Letting his gaze wander from her stiletto heels to her pencil skirt to the tailored blouse she had left unbuttoned as low as she dared for work, he swallowed—hard—and took another bite of his peach.

"I thought you weren't going to come after me."

"I didn't think it would take you this long to come to your senses."

"Your mother said the same thing about your father when he took months to chase her to Utah."

"Clearly, I'm much smarter than him, because it only took me one month—a month too long, I might add." He took another juicy bite of peach. "I don't know if I've ever told you this, because it's kind of my secret shame, but chicks dig me."

Resisting the urge to howl with laughter and weep with joy, she kicked off her shoes and slid down the wall to sit next to him. "Is that so?"

He offered her a peach from the bag on his lap. "It's my burden in life."

She picked a fat, ripe peach and took a bite. "You carry it well."

"I try," he said gravely. "Anyway, as I was saying, chicks tend to dig me. So I thought if I came down here, took a look at the place, and tried the peaches they're so famous for in these parts, then maybe I could figure out why the only chick I dig would rather be here than with me."

"You did hear me say I quit my job and I'm moving home to Rhode Island, didn't you?"

Wiping the juice off his chin with the back of his hand, he said, "What I didn't hear is why."

"You know why."

"No way," he said with a chuckle. "You're not getting off that easily, Georgie Quinn."

"I love you, Nathan." Suddenly, it wasn't hard at all to tell him what she'd always known, from the first time she saw him run by her house. "I love you so much that if I have to spend another second without you, I'm going to lose my mind."

"That's good, because I love you, too, and if you don't come home with me right now, today, I'm going to have to quit *my* job to move down here and start all over again as a lowly patrolman in the Atlanta Police Department. You wouldn't do that to me, would you? You know I was *born* to be a detective."

Exasperated, she said, "Have you heard *anything* I've said?"

"Only the parts I like, which, for once, was all of it." He flashed that grin she loved so much. "But I had the other thing, about moving here and being a lowly patrolman, all rehearsed, so I couldn't let it go to waste." He reached out to caress her cheek.

She turned her face into his palm and pressed her lips to his warm, peach-flavored skin.

"I also wanted you to know how far I was willing to go, what I was willing to give up, to be with you, Georgie."

"You were supposed to stop saying those things," she reminded him with a teasing smile.

"Never." He ran a finger through the groove in her cheek. "Since I'm on a roll, I may as well tell you I fell in love with your dimples first."

She stuck her tongue out at him.

"Well, if you're offering. . ." He shifted his hand from her face to the back of her neck and brought her in for a deep, soulful kiss that made her heart sing and her blood boil. *God, how she had missed him!*

He tugged a piece of paper from his shirt pocket. "Tess asked me to give you this. It came to the house yesterday."

"What is it?" Georgie glanced down at the postcard and gasped when she saw the return address for the medical laboratory. "Oh! Oh God." She turned the card over. The only word that registered was "negative."

He kissed her forehead. "I knew what I was doing when I bet on you."

Overcome with relief unlike anything she had ever experienced, she swiped at tears that flowed unchecked down her face. "Nathan?"

"What, sweetheart?"

"What'd you think of the peaches?"

"They're sweeter at home," he whispered as if he was afraid he'd get run out of town if he got caught dissing Georgia's peaches.

"Isn't everything?"

EPILOGUE

Georgie handed the key to Nathan. "You do it."

"Are you sure?"

She nodded and twisted her damp hands in her lap. As he inserted the key into the safety deposit box, she fixed her eyes on the wall of the nondescript room the bank had given them to use.

Nathan retrieved the green passbook and closed the box.

"How much?" Georgie asked.

He whistled. "Thirty-seven thousand, six hundred."

Georgie released a deep breath she hadn't realized she'd been holding. "Wow."

"That'll pay for one hell of a wedding."

"Yeah." She took the book from him and flipped through more than twenty years of deposits. "All I need now is the guy," she joked, hoping to elevate the mood in the small, airless room.

"That's not funny," he said in all seriousness.

"Oh come on! I was kidding. You were supposed to laugh."

"Say something funny and I'll laugh."

"I laugh at your bad jokes."

"Usually after you hit me."

"So then hit me so you can laugh."

"I'd rather kiss you."

"That's fine, too," she said, delighted by him. The three weeks they'd been back together had been the happiest of her life. That she had once resisted the overwhelming love she felt for him seemed so foolish now that her priorities were finally in proper order. And since she had tested negative for the altered gene and Ali was recovering well from her surgery, Georgie felt as if she could finally give herself permission to be happy.

Leaning over to kiss the pout off his lips, she returned her attention to the passbook. "I don't have the big white wedding dream some girls have."

"Apparently, your mother didn't know that."

"We never talked about it, which is why the money was such a surprise to me."

"We can have whatever kind of wedding you want."

"You wouldn't care if it was small?"

"Whatever you want, sweetheart."

She flipped through the pages of the book again, noticing the earlier deposits had been five, ten, or twenty dollars, while the more recent ones had been several hundred dollars. "Sometimes I feel kind of guilty, you know?"

"Why's that?"

"That my mother and sister had to go through such an ordeal and I was spared."

"You got lucky, Georgie. They'd never begrudge you that."

"I know, but what would you think if I donated half the money to breast cancer research and the other half to fund a scholarship in my mother's name?"

"That's a great idea."

"The scholarship could go to a student who plans to study gerontology."

"Even better."

"Are you sure? It's going to take me a while to show a profit with my consulting business. This would come in handy in the meantime."

"We don't need it. I've got us covered."

"I'm not going to leech off you, Nathan."

"If you're my wife, it's not leeching."

Raising an eyebrow, she said, "Am I going to be your wife?"

"Didn't we just talk about our small wedding?"

"That's not the question I need to hear."

"Right here? Now?"

"Why not?"

"The atmosphere leaves something to be desired."

"I don't need atmosphere. Do you?"

He slid off his chair and dropped to his knees in front of her.

Georgie was surprised by the gesture, even though she knew she shouldn't have been.

He took her hands and brought them to his lips. "Georgia Quinn, I've loved you since before I even knew your name. Will you marry me?"

"Hmm."

His eyebrows knit with aggravation. "This is *not* the time for jokes."

"I need to consider the whole package. If I say yes, I not only get you, but Tess and Cat as my sisters-in-law, and Bernie as my mother-in-law. That's a *real* perk."

Annoyed, he started to get up, but she stopped him.

"Yes, Nathan," she said, laughing, "I'll marry you, but on one condition."

He brought her down for a passionate kiss.

"Wait!" she said, tearing her lips free of his. "You haven't heard my condition."

"I didn't hear anything after yes."

She smacked his shoulder.

"All right," he said with a long-suffering sigh. "What's the condition?"

"I *need* the water on when I brush my teeth."

He studied her as he considered it. "This could be a deal breaker."

"I *need* it, Nathan. I promise to recycle and conserve and reuse—I'll even include those exact words in my vows, if you want. All I'm asking for in return is a little extra water. Marriage is about compromise."

Moaning, he dropped his head to her lap. "Just don't do it in front of me."

Georgie celebrated her victory by clapping her hands. "Does this mean we're engaged?"

"No." He withdrew a sapphire-and-diamond ring from his pants pocket and slid it onto her left hand. "This does."

She gasped. "Where did *that* come from?"

"I've had it for a week, but I was afraid you'd think I was rushing you. I've been carrying it around just in case."

Resting her hands on his face, she kissed him. "It's a beautiful ring. I love it, and I love you, so stop worrying that I'm going to change my mind. It's not going to happen."

"Good," he said, his voice gruff with emotion. He kissed her again and then checked his watch. "We've got to get going."

"To where?" she asked, confused.

"You'll see."

They were almost to downtown Newport when Nathan pulled the car over. "I know you're going to jump all over me for this, but I need to blindfold you."

"*What?* No way!"

"No blindfold, no surprise. I'm under very strict orders."

"Whose orders?"

"I'm not at liberty to divulge that information."

"What's going on, Nathan?"

He held up a black bandanna. "If you want to find out, let's get this over with."

With a furious scowl, she let him tie the bandanna over her eyes.

"Now hush up."

"You're going to pay for this, Caldwell."

"I'm not afraid of you, Quinn."

Georgie fumed for another ten minutes, long enough to lose track of the number of twists and turns he took before bringing the car to a stop.

"Stay here." He got out and shut the door.

Georgie stewed in the hot car for several minutes until he came back for her.

"Right this way, madam."

"This is not funny, Nathan. I don't know what you think you're doing, but whatever it is—"

"Georgie," he whispered. "You need to shut up."

"You're really going to talk to me like that, not even thirty minutes after we got engaged?"

The sound of snickering got her attention.

"Are there other people here?"

"A few."

"I'm going to shoot you with your own gun."

The snickering escalated to rippling laughter. Georgie's heart beat fast as she realized there were a *lot* of people listening to them. *What the hell?*

"Sit," Nathan directed.

With a huff, she did as she was told.

He untied the bandanna, took it off, and sat down next to her.

Georgie squinted against the sudden blast of light and blinked the senior center parking lot into focus. A stage had been erected outside the front door, which was covered by a black cloth. The dirty old men stood to the side of the stage wearing ties and satisfied smiles. Good Gus winked at her from his wheelchair. Behind them, Barbara sat with all the regulars.

Georgie turned around from the front row to find at least fifty other people, which, of course, was why Nathan had told her to shut up. Her cheeks burned with embarrassment. Georgie gasped when she discovered her sister Ali and her family sitting in the next row. Tess, Ben on crutches, Cat, and Ian with Rosie on his shoulders were in the back with the rest of the Caldwell family. Bernie blew her a kiss.

"Congratulations," Ali whispered, her eyes bright with excitement. "I told you he was the one."

With a smile for her sister, she turned back to Nathan. "What's going on?"

He took her hand. "Listen."

"Good afternoon, ladies and gentlemen. I'm Mayor Sam Watson, and I'm pleased to welcome you to the Newport Senior Center. Before we get to the reason we're here, I'd like to congratulate Detective Caldwell and Georgie Quinn on their very recent engagement."

Nathan grinned at her as the crowd responded with enthusiastic applause.

"Just friends, my ass," Bad Gus said to laughter from the other seniors.

"Now, without further ado, I'll let Bill Bradley tell you what's going on, Georgie."

"I'd appreciate that," she said to more laughter.

Bill bounded up the stairs and shook hands with the mayor.

"Good afternoon and thank you all for being here today." Bill gestured to the rows of seniors. "On behalf of the many people who have benefited from the senior center, it's my pleasure to welcome you and to congratulate Georgie and Nathan on their engagement." He led a round of applause.

"When I retired ten years ago, my greatest worry—and my *wife's* greatest worry—was that I'd be hanging around the house all day with nothing to do. But thanks to Nancy Quinn and the program here, I've found plenty to do. I've also found some of the best friends I've ever had in my life, as well as a sense of community and purpose. In short, I've found a second family. We're here today to honor Nancy and her years of service to Newport's senior population."

"Oh," Georgie said softly as her eyes filled.

Nathan squeezed her hand.

"Nancy saw a need and did something about it. Every one of us, and many who came before us, has benefited from her devotion and her commitment. Her death was a tremendous blow to those of us who loved her and called her our friend. As we mourned Nancy, we also feared the loss of a program we had come to rely upon as a vital part of our daily lives. But thanks to Nancy's daughter Georgie, the program not only survived, it thrived. Georgie sacrificed her own career in Atlanta to give us a few critical months until Barbara arrived to rescue her. Georgie, we know we drove you to drink at times, but we're eternally grateful for everything you did for us."

Georgie was stunned and embarrassed when the entire crowd stood up to cheer.

After everyone returned to their seats, Bill called Walter and Bad Gus to the stage.

"By unanimous approval of the City Council, which declared today Nancy Bryant Quinn Day in the City of Newport, it is my honor and privilege to dedicate the Nancy Bryant Quinn Senior Center. Boys?"

Walter and Gus tugged the cloth off a new sign, which included a gold-leaf portrait of Nancy.

Staggered, Georgie stared at her mother's likeness.

Nathan slid his arm around her shoulders.

"Georgie, honey," Bill said, "I know we're putting you on the spot, but if there's anything you'd like to say . . ."

She glanced at Nathan.

He nodded with encouragement.

From behind her, Ali squeezed her shoulder.

Georgie stood and made her way to the stage. Each of her friends from the center hugged her as she went by.

On the stage, Bill greeted her with a hug and turned the microphone over to her.

As Georgie took a moment to compose herself, she looked out at the crowd, smiled at Ali, Tess, and Cat, and then glanced over at the Dumpster, remembering that first encounter with Nathan. A new, green recycling Dumpster sat next to it. Her eyes met his, and his smile told her he knew exactly what she was thinking.

"Well," she finally said, "hasn't this been quite a day?"

The crowd laughed and applauded in agreement.

She took a deep breath. "I want to thank everyone who had anything to do with this," she said, gesturing to the sign. "It's a wonderful and fitting tribute to my mother, and my sister and I are deeply grateful. I talked to my mom every day of my life, but I didn't know her, really *know* her, until I worked here. For that priceless gift, I'm also grateful."

After a pause to collect her thoughts, she continued. "I agreed to fill in until a new director was hired and made no secret of the fact that I was less than thrilled to be here. But like Bill, I, too, found a family here, and I love each and every one of you. I should also note that my roommates and I found our future husbands here—none of them seniors."

As laughter rippled through the audience, Georgie concluded by saying, "I'm reminded of something Nathan once said about what he learned from a loss in his life. He said it so eloquently, and I hope I'm remembering it correctly. It was something like this: Life is short, love is sweet, regrets either make you or break you, and nothing lasts forever. Thanks to the time I spent here, I'm able to move forward with no regrets. My mother's life was far too short, but today you've ensured that her legacy will live on forever. Thank you so much for that."

The audience once again surged to their feet in applause.

Georgie started down the stairs.

Nathan met her at the bottom and lifted her into a hug.

Finally, she had found her way home.

Join the Georgia On My Mind Reader Group at facebook.com/groups/GeorgiaOnMyMindBook/ *to chat about the book with other readers!*

ABOUT THE AUTHOR

Marie Force is the *New York Times* bestselling author of contemporary romance, including the Gansett Island Series, which has sold more than 2.2 million books, and the Fatal Series from Harlequin Books, which has sold more than 1 million books. In addition, she is the author of the Green Mountain Series from Berkley Publishing as well as the new erotic romance Quantum Series, written under the slightly modified name of M.S. Force.

Her goals in life are simple—to finish raising two happy, healthy, productive young adults, to keep writing books for as long as she possibly can and to never be on a flight that makes the news.

Join Marie's mailing list on her website at marieforce.com for news about new books and upcoming appearances in your area. Follow her on Facebook at www.Facebook.com/MarieForceAuthor, on Twitter @marieforce and on Instagram at www.instagram.com/marieforceauthor/. Contact Marie at marie@marieforce.com.

OTHER TITLES BY MARIE FORCE

Contemporary Romances Available from Marie Force

The Gansett Island Series

Romantic Suspense Novels Available from Marie Force

The Fatal Series

One Night With You, *A Fatal Series Prequel Novella*

Book 1: Fatal Affair

Book 2: Fatal Justice

Book 3: Fatal Consequences

Book 3.5: Fatal Destiny, *The Wedding Novella*

Book 4: Fatal Flaw

Book 5: Fatal Deception

Book 6: Fatal Mistake

Book 7: Fatal Jeopardy

Book 8: Fatal Scandal

Book 9: Fatal Frenzy

Book 10: Fatal Identity

Single Title

The Wreck